THEY BURN THE THISTLES

by the same author

MEMED, MY HAWK
THE WIND FROM THE PLAIN
ANATOLIAN TALES

THEY BURN
THE THISTLES

YASHAR KEMAL

Translated from the Turkish by
MARGARET E. PLATON

COLLINS AND HARVILL PRESS
London 1973

This book was first published
under the title of
INCE MEMED, Part II
by Ant Yayinlari,
Istanbul

ISBN 0 00 261507 X

Set in Monotype Imprint

Made and Printed in Great Britain by
William Collins Sons & Co. Ltd., Glasgow
for Collins, St James's Place, and Harvill Press,
30A Pavilion Road, London, SW1.

THE River Jeyhan flows through the southern part of the Anavarza plain. From Mount Hemite it descends in a straight course, without winding, to the rocky outcrop of Anavarza. In some places the water scoops out hollows, undermining the banks, and from time to time they cave in with a huge crash. In other places the river runs under precipitous banks, like a sword-cut across the plain, but as parts collapse they become jagged and form small, sandy inlets at the river's edge. Elsewhere, the river broadens out across the plain, spreading a layer of pebbles over it. The shallow, gleaming water teems with myriads of huge carp, which dive towards the brightness of the pebbly bed, or slither over one another with undulating movements. There are also small reed-beds by the edge of the river, the haunt of big green frogs and cloud-coloured, long-necked herons.

Here and there the riverbanks are fringed with tamarisks, chaste-trees, willows, alders and bramble-thickets. Bees, red hornets, wasps and blue gadflies build their nests in the heat. The buzz of insects fills the air. And the long-beaked sand martins, glinting blue and iridescent like a beetle's carapace, come each day and scoop long narrow holes in the sheer, sword-cut banks, and build their nests deep within the earth. Between Mount Hemite and Anavarza Castle on this bank, that is to say on the same side as the castle, stand the villages of Hemite, Orhaniye, Selimiye, Endel and Kesikkeli. Since the river changes course from time to time, it occasionally retreats from these villages, or moves to the other side of them, or sometimes even floods the houses. There have been times when the river in spate has swept away half the village.

Near Anavarza Castle the River Jeyhan forms a great whirlpool, like a huge lake where the water revolves without ceasing. The waters whirl round and round at a dizzy speed, forming little hollows and swellings like waterspouts, bubbling and frothing continually. A twig or a leaf that falls into the whirlpool is never carried away, but continues to float round and round on the surface of the water. And when a butterfly falls into the water, or as hosts of them flutter over it, sheat-fish, bigger than a man, leap to the surface, opening their wide whiskered mouths. Snapping up a mouthful of butterflies, they drop back into the water, which turns yellow with froth.

The rocky outcrop of Anavarza looks like a ship lying from north to south. It is crowned by ancient, crumbling walls, a heap of ruins. They propel the Anavarza ship slowly and steadily forward over a motionless sea.

If you climb the high, steep, red rocks of Anavarza and look in the direction of the rising sun, the first thing you see will be the misty peak of Hemite. If at dawn the air is warm and the mists thin out towards the peaks, you will also see a clump of trees and a shrine on the summit. From Mount Hemite onwards the mountain tops become more rounded. In the vicinity of Bozkuyu village the land is bare and lies fallow, looking dead-white in the distance. Round about Jiyjik the soil changes and becomes darker; there the green of the forest starts and flowers spring up everywhere. In one of the fields of Jiyjik there is a Byzantine mosaic. It blossoms like a big wild garden in the middle of the plain.

To the north lies Kadirli, and at Kadirli, Sülemish hill . . . On this hill stands a single clump of scented myrtles. Sülemish hill is bare but green. At its foot Savrun brook runs bubbling to the plain. Kozan Way runs through the northern sector of Anavarza plain, and Sumbas brook, cutting across Kozan Way, flows past the foot of the Anavarza crags. On the further side of the brook, to the west of the castle, lies the village of Hadjilar . . . and beyond that is the village of Aslanli, where live the last remnants of the Lek Kurds who of old were called 'birds of prey'. Further on is Dumlu Castle, with sails set, racing towards the Mediterranean Sea. Dumlu Castle is lost in mist, and its reddish rocks quiver in the heat.

This plain is the fertile plain of Anavarza. In the middle of it lie the Ahjasaz marshes: a dark, buzzing, vast, impenetrable tract of reed-beds. On the edges of the marshes stand some Turcoman villages, their houses made out of rushes and canes. The Ahjasaz

6

marches start to the south of the place where Savrun brook flows into the River Jeyhan. To the north, the village of Vayvay stands just on the edge.

The rich earth of Anavarza yields a crop three times a year. From this dark, greasy, crisp earth a different kind of plant springs every day of the year. Each plant is huge. It is twice, three times, five times larger than in other soils. Even the colours of the flowers, of the brilliant green grasses, of the trees are different. The greens are crystal-clear, the yellows pure yellow like amber. The reds blaze like flickering flames, and the blues are a thousand times bluer than elsewhere. The wings or shells or backs of beetles, ants, butterflies and birds shimmer with a myriad unexpected, bewitching colours. The beetles, butterflies, birds and grasshoppers hover like a storm-cloud over the plain. One day you may see a swarm of butterflies palpitating and tossing with a thousand different hues over Anavarza plain. Trees, plants, earth, ground, sky are all covered with butterflies. Yellow, red, green, blue, white, the butterflies in clusters, each as big as a bird, form up in a whirling cloud of thousands, millions; then they rise to the sky, dive to the earth, scatter over the plain, and again rise and hover like a cloud, creating an amazing, different, fascinating world. Another day, you may see the big, red, long-legged ants scuttling from one end of the plain to the other on their springy legs. Another day, the breezes bring only the bees.

The fireflies of the plain are big too. Ahjasaz is decked out at nights as if carpeted with stars. Plants, trees, flowers, leaves and branches flash on and off the whole night long, and there are many flying in clusters, darting about like a host of fiery constellations. The stars on the ground and in the sky seethe, join and coalesce.

Greenish flies, grasshoppers and maybugs with their hard engraved wingcases, fly in swarms.

Everything on the plain of Anavarza – plants, trees, flies, birds, animals – is continually coupling and breeding. The creatures of the Anavarza plain are different from other creatures. They belong to a fertile, healthy, shining, magic world.

The edges of the Ahjasaz marshes, and for some distance inside, are full of beds of narcissi. These grow waist-deep and their flowers are as big as roses. All round the margins of the marshes

7

are fields of yellow narcissi, and so the scents that come from Ahjasaz are not marshy smells. A scent of narcissus, wafted from the soft earth, permeates the hot air, stones, plants, trees, people, flies and birds. In summer the whole of Anavarza – flies, beetles, animals and birds – smells of narcissus. In the mornings, with the warmth of the sun, it is a strong, heady scent. In summertime it intoxicates the people of Ahjasaz. It intoxicates all the creatures of the plain.

In olden times thousands of gazelles, coming from the desert, filled the Anavarza plain, and three black-eyed gazelles that have survived from those days gallop like lightning over the plain. They pass through the narcissus-scented breezes and the swarms of butterflies, bees and birds, and roam day and night from Mount Hemite to Anavarza Castle, from Anavarza Castle to below Vayvay, from Vayvay to Hadjilar, to below Dumlu Castle, and from there to the banks of the River Jeyhan. In the whole of Anavarza there is no creature that would hurt these gazelles, whether it is a snake, a bird of prey, a man, a wolf, a jackal or a dog. Anavarza respects them as the last sacred creatures, and they roam at will over the plain.

The Ahjasaz marshes are so thick with reeds that no bullet can penetrate them, no snake can enter. The water bubbles up in places, boiling hot; you could scald your finger if you put it in. In some places the water looks different; that bubbling liquid does not seem to be water at all. The bottom is pebbly and bright, ice-cold. The light sparkles on the pebbles at quite a distance. In some places the water is dirty and smells of decay.

The soil in the marshes is not the same all over. There are great differences in it. In places there are reeds as tall as trees, in places there are short, squat bushes, and low, shiny rock-plants. In other places there is a smooth grassy patch, solid green. In others, huge trees in a thick, impenetrable wood. All kinds of trees and plants ... Climbing plants, too. At sunrise blue flowers as big as your hand open on these climbing plants. There are thick canes, wild roses, and water-lilies floating on the bright water, each one a cup. And the carp, sheat-fish, tortoises and big green frogs ... Mosquitoes in clouds. Black adders, water-snakes, red-tailed

8

foxes; frightened jackals, and thousands of water-fowl, grey-green, with long legs and neck.

When you descend to the plain from the Taurus Mountains, the plain is utterly silent. Not a bird, not a voice, not a sound of running water is heard. The flat plain swallows up all sounds. Indeed, if there is sun, if it is hot, no sound at all is heard from the plain. It continues thus until you approach Ahjasaz. Then suddenly a din breaks out, which startles and paralyses you. Strange, confused sounds rise from the marshes. A clamour of birds twittering, frogs croaking, the bubbling of the marsh-water, strange insect noises, the murmuring of the forest, the rustling of the reeds, cocks crowing, dogs barking, jackals howling; all these sounds combine together in the reed-beds, and burst upon one like a cannon at the edge of the marshes. Ahjasaz is a frightening place, and people are reluctant to enter it.

The earth of Anavarza, the thousand-year-old ruined city of Anavarza, the fortress on the steep crags, the foaming River Jeyhan, Savrun and Sumbas brooks, the birds, the eagles, the huge flowers, the monstrous flies, the crops multiplying a thousand-fold, the marshes, with their cold bright streams beneath the yellow heat, the dusty tracks, the leaping fish – all of them, in the fertile, teeming, breeding atmosphere of Chukurova, expanding in the warmth, stretch themselves with lust and longing.

As the sun sinks into the west behind Anavarza Castle, an orange butterfly, delicately patterned, and as big as a bird, remains motionless on a branch, its wings folded, stroking its head and eyes with its legs; its body quivers gently, steeped in the radiance of the setting sun. Just as the sun sets, the whole of the Anavarza plain – trees, water and sky – sinks into a uniform blue. The butterfly also turns blue.

The earth of Anavarza is not earth, but gold. A man like Ali Safa Bey knows this is so; a man like Ali Safa Bey feels the appetite for earth right to the bottom of his heart. Everyone has some desire, good or bad; everyone has some secret passion. Ali Safa Bey's dark unquenchable desire was the worst of all. Ali Safa Bey's passion was the fertile dark soil of Anavarza. Every day that dawned, Ali Safa Bey trod firmly on the dark earth, and as the world awoke his eyes would gleam with desire for the Anavarza plain. This awakening, the mating insects, the wholesome fat snakes, the gleaming green frogs, the swift tortoises, the hard-backed iridescent beetles, the bees, birds and gazelles, the burgeoning flowers, the sprouting crops, the brilliant green ricefields, the butterflies, the water, the marshes, the streams, the tracks, the sand-devils, the eddying silver-grey rain-clouds, all this world, bubbling, raging, blustering, tossing, ceaselessly coupling and breeding – this world, ever approaching a disastrous end and ever being born again, made him feel dizzy, intoxicated him. He would have liked to take Anavarza in his arms and embrace it. He would not be satisfied until there was not a foot of Anavarza farmland that he did not own. Why should he not own the whole plain? Why should he not extend his domain further and further? Ali Safa Bey used to say that life is a struggle. More land, more land. If life is not a struggle, it is not worth living. The fight for land is the most sacred, the most reliable struggle. If one does not fight in this world, what good is one? One would be little more than a vegetable.

But the struggle for land was gradually getting harder. The Turcomans, who had been reluctant to occupy land and to settle in one place, and who disliked Chukurova, Anavarza, the heat, the mosquitoes and the reed-huts, were realizing increasingly that there was nothing else worth having but land. The days when he could get fifty *dunums** of land for five kilos of salt, a goat, ten liras, a foal or a cow were long past. Fifteen or twenty years ago he could have bought up a whole village for three thousand lira, lock, stock and barrel, and could have settled the villagers elsewhere. But now the situation had changed radically. The people who lived in those reed-huts would even shed blood to keep their land. When Ali Safa Bey was consumed with passion for something, he went about his business even more secretly. He could not reveal his desires. But through his greed, through what he paid for the land, he himself had opened the villagers' eyes. To fight with already alerted villagers was more difficult, but it was more enjoyable. This resistance was in harmony with his need for self-respect. It must not be too easy to get hold of something so valuable as land.

* A *dunum* or *dönüm* is approximately a quarter of an acre.

One of the Anavarza villages was Vayvay, which was large compared with the others. The Vayvay villagers were an obstacle in Ali Safa Bey's path. Neither bandits, nor fear of the Government, nor good words nor bad, availed with them. They stuck to the land like goosegrass, they stood firm against intimidation and attempts to terrorize them. If Ali Safa Bey could cope with Vayvay, the rest would be easy. The whole of Anavarza would come into his possession like slipping on a sock.

Vayvay stands at the upper end of the Anavarza plain. It is half an hour's walk up from Topraktepe, on the left-hand side of Dedefakili swamp, at a place where Savrun brook widens into a pebbly bed. All the village houses are huts made of reeds, canes and brushwood. They look out from a height over the level plain of Anavarza.

From the River Jeyhan to Sülemish hill Anavarza is so smooth and flat that the marshes, villages, mounds, hills and even the clumps of trees look like a sea. Before daybreak, Anavarza plain is pure white, just like the sea. Not a sound is heard. This region, where many noises fuse into a single roar, is not yet awake.

While the plain is still white, the orange butterfly as big as a bird, is seen perching on a branch, its wings quivering; it strokes its head with its forelegs and stretches itself out towards the rising sun.

2

THORN-TREES grow in the richest and most fertile soil. Though they grow no taller than a man, a whole clump will spring from a single root. The young trees are honey-coloured; as they get older the colour deepens and turns from honey to black. In springtime the thorn-trees are the first to come into leaf. Early in the season the leaves are a soft green, and the flowers a misty yellow, but later on the leaves turn to a darker green, and with the coming of summer the flowers change from yellow to orange.

On the plains of Chukurova and Anavarza there are hundreds of acres of thorn forests, untouched by the axe, trackless and deserted. No other tree is so thorny as these. The whole trunk, right up to the smallest branches, bristles with short triangular thorns and, as the tree turns black, they become as hard as iron nails. It is a difficult task to dig up a thorn-tree, for its strange roots, long and twisted, cling tenaciously to the soil.

You will not find horses, donkeys, cattle, pigs or wolves wandering in the thorn forests. Nor can dogs penetrate the thickets. Anyone who mistakenly enters the forest emerges torn and bleeding. It is the home of hares, badgers and small jackals, and occasionally you will see red foxes whose tails are no longer bushy. In springtime the forest teems with insects. Clinging to the spiky branches are thousands of wasps' nests and hornets' nests, and honey-bees that have left their hives swarm there in thousands, millions . . . Spiders spin their webs in the thorn forest. Early in the morning, as the sun comes up, you see it wrapped in a thin white veil. Huge cobwebs, strung from tree to tree, sway in the breeze.

It was drizzling, half rain, half mist. There was no wind. The Anavarza plain was hidden, but as the sun rose a dim brightness could be seen now and then behind the mist. The man, huddled in his patterned cloak, was sleeping with his knees drawn up to his stomach. His rifle was resting on a tree-root and his head was pillowed on it. From the edge of the forest a flock of birds rose overhead, screeching noisily; the man opened his eyes, then closed them again. A moment or two later he sat up, rubbed his eyes and looked dazedly about him. His body was numb and his legs ached. He stretched, and rose to his feet; his mouth had a sour taste in it, and he spat. The spittle pierced a cobweb and fell on to a bud. He bent down, picked up his rifle and slung it over his shoulder. A long silver-mounted Circassian dagger hung from his left hip, almost to his knee, and beside it over his groin was a pistol. He was wearing three cartridge-belts over his thick, hand-woven, striped silk shirt. The large black field-glasses round his neck looked brand-new. The thick embroidered woollen sandals were also new. Embroidered stockings came up to his knees, and he was wearing brown woollen shalvar-trousers, like those that are hand woven and hand-dyed with walnut juice by the villagers of the Taurus Mountains.

From three different directions came the sound of cocks crowing and dogs yelping. The man turned to the south, but could not make out any landmark. A long cockcrow came from the south, and from the west a medley of sounds, with here and there some frogs still croaking from night-time. From the east too there came a strange humming sound which stopped and began again. From a long way off, beyond the thorn forest, came a long shrill whistle. The air was warm and close. The sun had risen to the height of a minaret, but was not visible; only a vague brightness could be discerned through the drizzle.

He walked eastwards, but he was worn out, and his legs would scarcely carry him. He had been on the move for four days. Although his rations had run out the day before at noon, he was not hungry – it simply did not occur to him to feel hungry. He had been surrounded by soldiers at Savrun Spring four days before – a whole crowd of soldiers who had kept up a hail of bullets. Fortunately, it was evening when they encircled him, and as the light faded rain began to fall. Towards midnight he slipped through the soldiers like a cat over a wall. But he could no longer live in the mountains. Soldiers, helped by villagers armed with sticks, stones and firearms, were hunting down the brigands, searching every hollow and thicket. A week ago Big Ali, who had retreated to a precipitous mountain peak, had been captured by a host of peasants who had scaled the mountain.

There was only one refuge, one ray of hope, one way of escape, and that was the village of Vayvay, where Old Osman lived. He was in a dilemma. There was a risk that as soon as he reached the village the people might hand him over to the authorities. On the other hand they might take him to their hearts like a brother or a son. Osman was very old, with one foot in the grave ... He had had no news of him for a long time. If Osman were dead, who at Vayvay would know him? On his way he had stayed a night with Yellow Ümmet but Ümmet was frightened. And what if Old Osman were frightened too? Old Osman had weathered many storms; he was a brave old man with the heart of a child, but he was only human, and you never knew ...

Thinking and brooding would not get him anywhere; however it turned out, he would go to Vayvay. Even if there had been another course open to him, another hiding place, he would still want to go to Vayvay. He longed to know what would happen. How would Osman and the villagers who had been so kind and friendly to him treat him now? He recalled the case of Unlucky Big Ali, who had never done them any harm, who had indeed been an enemy of the rich and a friend of the poor. After his capture on the peak, the peasants had brought him to the commandant, raining blows on him and spitting in his face. 'Commandant, let all your enemies live just so long,' they said, and celebrated the event for three days and nights.

He contemplated the possibility of being bound hand and foot by Osman as soon as he entered the village, and of being brought before Ali Safa Bey. What sort of man was he?

When he had hidden in the thorn forest the previous night, the thorns had torn his legs, and blood was oozing from the wounds. The rain continued without respite. The bees huddled one upon the other in their wet hives.

The thorn-trees grew so close together that he could not walk fast. He struggled on until noon, when he reached a gully which cut the thorn forest in two. On the slope of a mound where four gullies met stood three huge trees. The trunk of the middle one was hollow, and large enough for two people to shelter in. He stepped into the hollow tree and rested his back against it. The rain had not soaked through his cloak, and only his legs and feet were wet, for the closely-woven, ample, patterned cloak came down to his knees. He removed his rifle and laid it aside. Then the field-glasses, dagger and pistol joined the rifle. He shut his eyes. He was terribly hungry, but he paid no heed. When Yellow Ümmet had given him directions about getting to Vayvay, he had said, 'You'll cross from Narlikishla to Savrun and hide in the thorn forest. Walk straight up from the forest and you'll reach a mound. You'll see three trees on the slope of the mound. Vayvay is two hours' walk from there. Go into Vayvay at night. In the middle of the village there is a huge tree, and at its foot a marble stone with an inscription on it. It gleams white even at night, like a lamp. When you get to the tree turn with your back to it and walk south. Even if it is so dark that you can't see a thing, move south. You will get to a door. Ask for Old Osman, and the door will open straightaway.'

'What if the door doesn't open?' he said to himself. 'Or, if it opens and I find all the men of the village assembled there?'

Half dreaming, half imagining things, he waited till evening in the hollow tree, and then emerged. The air had got colder, and rain was still falling. The night was dim, and a misty darkness was descending over the thorn forest. The flowers gave out a sweet heady scent. He put his rifle, field-glasses, dagger and everything under his cloak, so that from outside nothing was visible. There was only one drawback: Chukurova people didn't wear cloaks. They were typical of the mountain people. But no-one would see if he entered the village after dark.

A glimmer of light appeared ahead of him. He was so tired that he was just dragging his feet along. The drizzling rain continued. He pulled himself together when he smelt manure; it meant that he had left the thorn forest behind and reached the outlying houses. A deep-throated barking came from a dog. It was very dark. He wasn't worrying about anything; why then was his heart beating so rapidly? As he entered the village a man came towards him; he did not hesitate, but walked on and called out a greeting. The man replied, and, not recognizing his voice, said,

'Hallo, traveller. Where have you come from, and where are you going to at this time of night?'

'From the mountains,' he answered, 'and I'm going to Narli-kishla.'

The man did not stop and said gently, 'Good night and good luck.'

'Good night,' and he shivered involuntarily.

The road went right through the middle of the village. To his right a big tree loomed up. He stopped at the foot of it, and could see the white marble stone shining in the darkness. It was pitch-black. There was no light in any of the houses, except one. And a deathly silence . . . He leaned against the tree, so worn out that he stayed there, unable to move. His heart was thumping, and he felt too dizzy to tell which was north, south, east or west. The rain continued to fall, and the boughs of the trees above him creaked. Then he straightened up; come what may, he must walk on. In a few moments he touched the brushwood wall of a house and groped for the door.

'Osman Agha, Osman Agha, Osman Aghaaa . . .'

A deep male voice said sleepily, 'Who's there?'

'God's guest.' The door opened at once.

'Come in, friend,' said a man dressed in underclothes. 'Come in, and I'll light the lamp.'

'I'm looking for Old Osman's house. Is this it?'

'Wait a minute, friend, let me get dressed and I'll take you there. Come in. Is it raining?'

'Drizzling.'

The man came out, and led him in silence to Old Osman's house.

'Osman Agha, a guest has come for you. I've brought him along.'

The door opened at once. A woman's voice said, 'Welcome. This is an honour. God's guest. You come in too, Veli; it's early yet. Osman is mending a saddle. Come in.'

'I'm sleepy,' said the man, and went away.

The woman said, 'Good night, Veli,' and called the guest in. 'Please come in, friend.'

Old Osman's deep voice came from the fireside: 'Who is it?'

'I don't know,' answered the woman. 'A stranger. In a cloak. He must be one of the hill-folk.'

'One of the hill-folk?' exclaimed Old Osman. 'So he's one of the hill-folk, eh? Welcome, this is an honour. Come over to the fireside, come and sit down. Is it raining?'

'Drizzling.'

Old Osman had left the saddle and sat looking the motionless traveller up and down.

'Why are you standing there? Sit down, friend,' he said. 'Good Lord, sit down! What's up with you?'

He could not sit down. If he did, they would see the rifle.

Old Osman got to his feet, and placed his hand on his guest's shoulder:

'Sit down, my boy.'

He did not sit down.

'Kamer, bring a cushion for our worthy guest.'

The woman answered from the other end of the room, 'I'll bring one.'

Old Osman said, 'My son, your cloak is very wet. Where have you come from, and where are you making for?'

He answered gaily, 'I've come from the mountains, and I'm going to Old Osman's.'

'So you're going to Old Osman's, that's strange.'

'It's strange,' agreed the guest.

Kamer brought the cushion, and placed it on the left-hand side of the fireplace, saying, 'Here you are, friend.'

'Sit down, my boy!' bellowed Old Osman. 'Take off that cloak and sit down. It's the first time in my life I've seen a guest who wouldn't sit down.'

He was in a dilemma, but he did not begin to take off his cloak. Kamer bent down and whispered to her husband, 'There's something wrong with the boy.'

'What's the matter?' asked Osman pityingly. 'What's wrong with you?'

The guest smiled. 'Don't you know me, Uncle Osman?' he asked in affectionate tones.

Old Osman came up close to him, grasped his shoulder and peered into his face. 'Slim Memed, my hawk, my little one! Guest, you look like my little one, my hawk!' he exclaimed, embracing Slim Memed. Trembling, shaking from head to foot, he went on, saying delightedly, 'Is it you, is it you, my hawk, my guest? The stranger. God's guest, it's you?'

Memed could not utter a word. He was speechless, floating in a pleasant dream. 'Damn you, Kamer, come here! Look who's here! Come, come quickly, Kamer.'

The woman called from the other end of the long room. 'What's that you're saying, Osman?'

'Come here,' said Osman, 'Quick, come and see who it is, come and see who's come.'

'Who is it?' asked Kamer.

'My hawk,' shouted Old Osman, 'my hawk, my hawk!'

'Don't shout, are you crazy? Don't shout. The boy's on the

run,' said Kamer. 'Slim Memed, is it you, child?'

'It's me, Mother Kamer,' said Memed.

'Welcome, child. If my crazy husband will let you go you'd better sit down. God knows from what faraway mountains you've come.'

'Be quiet, woman,' said Old Osman. 'I'm not letting go of him. I'm not letting go of my hawk before I've given him a proper embrace.' And hugging Memed he patted him on the shoulders and back.

Kamer said, 'The child's tired. The child's tired. He's worn out.'

She grasped him by the arm, and pulled him away from Memed. Old Osman stood looking admiringly at Memed while Kamer tried to take off his cloak. Then Slim Memed pulling himself together, stripped off his cloak, and removed his rifle, pistol, field-glasses and dagger and propped them against the wall; then he sat down on the cushion Kamer had brought a few minutes before.

Old Osman sat down opposite him. He did nothing but gaze at Memed. He could not take his eyes off him, lost in wonder. Memed was smiling. Mother Kamer was talking, but Old Osman stayed looking at Memed without moving a muscle.

'My eyes aren't deceiving me, are they? My ears aren't deceiving me, are they? So you're my hawk? I've seen you again in this world with my own eyes . . . I've seen you, I've seen you . . . Welcome back, my boy.'

Old Osman was gradually recovering himself. 'So you've come! So Osman has been fortunate enough to live to see Slim Memed once more! How lucky he is! So Osman can die happy . . . !'

He got up and stroked Memed's head, gazing at him. 'Good heavens, you're Slim Memed, my hawk,' he exclaimed.

Kamer intervened: 'Keep calm, you crazy fellow, don't say Slim Memed's name again. Don't shout.'

'For heaven's sake,' he shouted, 'for heaven's sake!'

Both Kamer and Memed were alarmed.

Then he said, 'The boy is starving. My hawk is starving. Quick, Kamer, quick.'

'You startled me out of my wits,' said Kamer. 'I'll put the pilaff on the fire this very moment.'

'Don't worry, Uncle Osman,' said Memed gaily, 'I'm not going to die of hunger.'

'Quick, he's starving. Bring the cheese first, bring the yoghurt, there's honey too, isn't there, and dripping, fresh dripping?'

'Mother Kamer,' said Memed, 'there's no need to cook pilaff at this hour of the night, let me have whatever is ready.'

'Didn't I tell you my hawk was starving? Quick, warm up the *tarhana**,' and he pointed to the pan by the fire.

Kamer at once put on the trivet and moved the pan over the fire. 'I don't know what I'm doing. He'll drive me to distraction that man of mine.'

Osman said, 'Just wait a little, my hawk. It's getting hot now. she's cooked it well, the tarhana soup.'

He poked the fire, and put on more wood. The flames shot up.

'Please, Osman,' begged Kamer, 'keep quiet, pull yourself together.'

She spread the mat used for meals in front of Memed. In a short time the soup was hot. Kamer poured it into a large soup-plate, which she placed before Memed. The soup was smooth, hot, and smelt delicious. Without stopping and without a word, Memed quickly drank the lot. Kamer also brought honey and yoghurt, and Memed quickly finished that too.

Kamer heaped on the table helpings of all the food there was in the house: butter, sugar, cheese, walnuts, apples, plums, dried mulberries . . .

At last Memed said, 'Thank you very much. May God's blessing be on this house.'

Kamer continued to press him, 'My child,' she said, 'you've come from faraway places, from high mountains . . .'

'Thank you, Mother, I should burst if I ate any more. I'm absolutely full up,' said Memed cheerfully.

A wave of happiness came over him. The warm welcome at Old Osman's house had made him forget all his sufferings, and he felt like a young boy again. 'I feel light as a bird now I'm in your house, Uncle Osman,' he said.

Kamer cleared away the remains of the meal, and then put on

* Wheat mixed with yoghurt and dried in the sun.

the fire an ancient Turcoman copper coffee-pot with a folding handle. 'How do you like your coffee, child?' she asked.

Memed was disconcerted. In the whole of his life he had scarcely had any coffee. He blushed, embarrassed. Then, making a gesture with his right hand, 'Any way at all,' he said.

Old Osman intervened: 'Let him have it like mine,' he said, 'and you can make the two cups together.'

They waited in silence for the coffee to be made. Memed went on smiling, opening his big eyes very wide. When Mother Kamer poured the coffee into the cups it smelt good, and he sniffed appreciatively. His hand shook as he picked up the cup by the handle and a little coffee was spilt into the saucer. Memed watched Old Osman to see how to hold the cup and how to drink the coffee. His hands shook too, much more than Memed's, but he did not spill the coffee. With his shaking hands he suddenly lifted the cup to his lips and sipped the coffee, sucking in air noisily at the same time to cool it. Memed imitated him, except that he did not suck in air, and burnt his mouth. The coffee had a strange bitter taste. As soon as it had cooled a little, he drank it in sips like Osman. He would never again taste such coffee. Wherever afterwards he drank coffee he would think of Mother Kamer's coffee, but he would never again come across that special taste and smell. He would remember that taste throughout his life, and would seek for it in every cup of coffee he drank.

Osman finished his coffee and put his cup down beside the chimney. 'It must be cold outside, I feel chilly,' he said.

'It's drizzling,' said Kamer.

'It's a good thing you came, my boy,' said Osman. 'Thank God you've come. You've put heart into me. We're helpless in the hands of that scoundrel Ali Safa. He obviously won't leave us in peace in this village. This hurts my pride, it offends my manhood, Memed, my boy. I have reared ten children, but they're just ten timorous rabbits! I am very old, and the villagers are cowed, they are terrified of Ali Safa. A frightened man is a bad man. God's curse upon frightened men.'

His long white beard trembled. His face, deeply furrowed, and copper-coloured in the firelight, showed his distress. His slanting green eyes, half hidden under his bushy white eyebrows, gleamed for a moment, then clouded over. There was something childlike in all Old Osman's expressions. In his broad smile, breaking out at the slightest thing, in his wondering look as he raised his brows, in his eager appreciation of people, animals and every living thing, in every gesture there was something childlike. When he was a youth and even in middle age the villagers had called him 'Boy Osman' on account of his temperament. How was it that they changed 'Boy' to 'Old'? Neither Old Osman nor anyone else knew when this happened. No one in the village remembered that he had been called 'Boy Osman'. Only one person did not forget, and that was his wife Kamer. When she was cross with him she always called him 'Boy Osman'.

She came across the room in haste. 'What in the world are you saying to the boy, before he's even taken off his sandals, before he's got his breath, or brushed the dust from his feet, Boy Osman? Boy Osman! You may live to be a hundred, a thousand even, and you'll never learn sense. The boy has just escaped from a fire, he's managed to get here, he's scarcely escaped with his life, and then you don't even let him get his breath . . . Look at the state the boy's, in can't you see? Worn out. He's come like a wounded bird to take shelter in a thicket. At this very minute there may be a whole army of soldiers after him, a whole crowd of aghas. Those aghas are still terrified of Slim Memed's very name. Won't they know that he's come down to Chukurova? Won't they find out that he's come to your house? And then you begin on our situation, our troubles, before the poor boy has even recovered his breath . . . Let me tell you, Boy Osman, with that reasoning you'll hand over Slim Memed to the aghas. Don't I know you? If the aghas get hold of him they'll hand him over to the authorities, and they'll hang our Memed. Then under the gallows you'll weep and pray, Boy Osman . . .'

As soon as he could get a word in Old Osman said, 'You're right, Kamer, you're quite right. Now be quiet, woman, be quiet!'

'You ought to be ashamed of yourself. Let the village go hang! Let Ali Safa Bey go to hell! It's inhuman – when he hasn't had a moment's rest . . . If Ali Safa is driving us out, let him drive us out. It's all because of your chicken-heartedness.'

'Be quiet, Kamer,' yelled Osman furiously. 'Shut up, you old hag.'

Memed listened, smilingly, to the argument going on between the couple, whom he dearly loved.

'Shut up, you old hag. Memed is our son and our hawk. Ah, Kamer, it would not be right, would it, for Memed not to know what a state our village is in?'

Kamer, slightly mollified, agreed. 'All right,' she said, 'then tell him about Zeynel. He's the one to blame. Bald Zeynel.'

Old Osman pursed his lips, worriedly: 'My hawk,' he said, 'we are in a very bad way. In these days you can't take refuge in the mountains. Those hill-folk were always rather wild and now they've become quite savage. They know neither Slim Memed nor Gizik Duran. They would hunt down their own fathers and hand them over to the police. If you go to Anavarza you'll be captured in a couple of days. Now you'd better stay here with us, and nobody but my old woman, not even our children, must know that you are here. Nobody saw you coming here but Veli, did they?'

'Nobody.'

'Good. Not even our children will know. Only my old woman, you, I and God himself . . .'

Kamer shook her head so that the gold coins on her brow beneath the white kerchief jingled.

'Ah, don't I know you, Boy Osman,' she said. 'You'll tell the whole village tomorrow. Oh, don't I know you!'

Osman jumped to his feet in a great rage. 'Woman, don't exasperate me!' he said. 'Am I mad, am I crazy? If I go and tell one, he'll tell another, and he'll tell a third. Until it gets to Zeynel's ears. Zeynel doesn't let a bird fly through the village. Zeynel would go to that scoundrel Ali Safa, and say that Slim Memed is in Osman's house, in Vayvay village. Then Memed would swing, wouldn't he? And when Memed was dead, the aghas would become Pashas, the villagers would be driven out, the villages destroyed.'

'That's how it would be, Boy Osman.'

'Memed, my hawk, tell that old woman something for me. Tell her not to madden me at this hour of the night, or to put me in a rage.'

Kamer realized that Osman was extremely angry, and she remained silent. Seeing this, Osman too was quiet.

Kamer said, 'Let's go and make a hiding-place for the boy.'

Osman said, 'Let's make a place where no one will find him. My hawk must eat, drink and sleep there. He must grow fatter and taller too. Don't smile, Kamer. He looks too much of a child to be Slim Memed.'

Kamer said, 'May God restore him . . .' and sighed. She was going to say 'to his mother and father', but remembered that he had no mother or father. 'May God restore him to his nation and people,' she said. But this did not satisfy her, either. The Government and the men in authority were his enemies. If they found him they would drown him in a spoonful of water. 'May God spare his life for the poor who suffer under tyranny,' she said in the end.

Old Osman took a torch from the fireplace and went to the other part of the house. 'Come along, Memed,' he said. 'We'll make you a place here, and then we'll talk till morning, my boy.'

Memed and Kamer came too, and stood in front of the closet. It stretched from one corner to the other. It was a huge painted cupboard, reaching to the ceiling, and black with soot. Old Osman opened the big door, and inside it could be seen rows and rows of bulging sacks. There was a wide shelf above the sacks and that part was full of silk-covered down quilts and mattresses.

'Look, Memed,' said Osman, 'here is your home. And talking about your other home . . . That old woman didn't give me a chance . . . talking about your land . . . Remember the land the villagers bought for you? Let's make this place ready for you, then we'll talk. The old woman will start nagging at me again. We'll take out these sacks, my boy. Hold the torch, my dear.' He held out the torch to Kamer, who was standing there watching them, and she took it from him.

They quickly took out five sacks of wheat and put them against the wall.

'Now wait,' said Kamer. 'It's my turn now. Memed, my boy, get down that mattress. I can't manage it.'

'She's an old woman now,' said Osman at once.

'I'm not getting any younger,' admitted Kamer. 'Get down the mattress, dear.'

Memed got it down. Kamer placed it in the cupboard.

'That pillow, too, and the quilt.'

The bed smelt of soap, almost like incense. Memed thought that if they let him he would sleep for three days and nights; he was worn out with lack of sleep.

'Now come over by the fire,' said Old Osman.

'Leave the boy alone, please, Osman,' said Kamer. 'Can't you see he's out on his feet?'

'Well, my hawk,' said Osman, 'If you're so sleepy, we'll talk tomorrow.'

3

OLD OSMAN could not sleep all night, and at cockcrow he got up and lit the fire, pushing the coffee-pot over the flame. He was so happy that he could not sit still; he was beside himself with joy. Twice he went and opened the closet and looked at Memed sleeping, though he could hardly make out his form in the darkness. After drinking his coffee he went to Memed again and again; his heart beat fast and there was a warm gentle emotion within him such as he had not felt for a long time.

He took from a carved walnut chest the clothes which he kept for weddings and festivals, which were old but in very good condition. In colour they were a dark blue verging on ultramarine. The pockets and sideseams of the shalvar-trousers were embroidered with silver thread. The coat fitted his old, thin, withered body perfectly. You could see that it had been made by a good tailor. He put them on. The coat and the shalvar, the striped tunic of pure silk, and the blue waistcoat. Over the waistcoat he hung his heavy engraved silver watch-chain. Instead of a sash he put over his stomach the gold and silver-chased holster belt left him by his grandfather and next to it he put a gold-chased leather powder-case, and then a handsome revolver inlaid with mother-of-pearl. After carefully polishing them, he put on black leather boots. On

24

his head he put a fine felt hat, wound round with a silk kerchief. He strode up and down the room several times. As the sun rose he opened the closet where Memed was sleeping. He was curled up in a ball, the rifle by his head.

Old Osman said to himself, smiling, 'This rascal is a smart chap. When did he fetch his gun and put it by his head? Even in my house he doesn't trust anyone. He's a brave young fellow, it's a shame to shut him up here. Well,' he went on, 'our boy is light in weight but heavy in worth. He's our hope, our son. He couldn't get enough to eat in the mountains to grow . . . but if he stays here for a bit, and we feed him up, perhaps he'll grow taller and broader, and turn into a stout fellow.' He looked at Memed's face again with admiration, love and compassion. 'It doesn't matter whether he grows taller and broader or not. It's not a fault . . . The hawk is small too, but it doesn't relinquish its prey.' This time he laughed aloud. 'Everyone thinks of Slim Memed, whether they saw him or not, as a huge fellow twice the height of an ordinary man. It is better so. No-one will even believe that this poor boy is Slim Memed. We could take our oath and we couldn't get anyone to believe us. So now he can hide and bide his time until he marches out again to kill the aghas and climb up Alidagh and, once more, on the summit of the mountain balls of light will burst out brightly. Perhaps he will even get to the peak of snow-capped Duldul. Right to the summit. It is a good thing that he is small, like a bird of prey.'

Feeling a warm affection within him, he bent down and kissed Memed on the forehead. Then he closed the closet door and again began to walk up and down the room. Just then Mother Kamer woke up. She picked up a water ewer and went outside. She too had taken her broad white kerchief with crocheted edges out of the chest and bound it round her head. When she saw Osman she stopped and smiled. But then, alarmed, she said, 'Osman, you don't dress like that every day. Won't the neighbours notice something different about you?'

'To hell with the neighbours,' said Old Osman angrily, some-what daunted. 'If the neighbours had been a bit cleverer they wouldn't have become the victims of two or three landowners. Look, just look, he's sleeping like a babe in the closet, his mouth open, snuffling a little. Curled up in a ball, a tiny handful of a man. But in that man there's a brave heart, a good brain, and great humanity. He's so big-hearted that both the aghas and the Government are frightened of him. Terrified of him. There were five hundred bandits in the mountains, but that didn't worry the Government, why not? Because they were not generous, big-hearted men. Now just on account of Slim Memed alone, the mountains are full of soldiers. They're thick with soldiers hunting out that poor fellow on behalf of the great landowners, the mighty Government. I'm telling you!'

He took a few hasty steps, his boots thumping the floor, and opened the door of the closet:

'Look, like a baby . . . If the Government saw him like this, it would be ashamed of itself.'

He closed the door, and becoming more serious, put his hand on Mother Kamer's shoulder. 'Kamer, dear,' he said affectionately, 'if the Government saw my little hawk like that, if the aghas saw Memed like that, maybe they would be even more afraid. Wouldn't they say it's the unexpected stone that wounds the head. Wouldn't they say, "If this boy raises his head thus, and if the others have a little courage, and humanity, what won't they do?" There you have it, Kamer darling. To be a man, to be humane, is a very different proposition.'

He again began to walk up and down. 'To be a man, to be a man,' he repeated, striding up and down. 'I have one foot in the grave. At the most I may last another ten years. Then my soul will be borne out of its cage and away . . . One must be a man, Kamer. That's everyone's duty. It's fear that makes one abase oneself, and lose one's humanity. I know it, I tell you.'

Mother Kamer brought a piece of flat bread and a bowl of milk and gave it to him. Old Osman chewed the bread in his toothless mouth, and raised the bowl of milk to his lips. Soon he had eaten the bread and drunk the milk.

'Kamer, I'm going out into the village. If our hawk awakes he mustn't go out; take some soup to the cupboard. Take him a petrol can so that he can relieve himself, and take it outside without anyone seeing. Tomorrow I'll make a door through into the stable.'

The drizzle had stopped. There was not a cloud in the sky. A gentle, warm, hardly perceptible breeze coming from the plain, from Ahjasaz, brought waves of scents: sun-warmed narcissus, grass, marsh, insects, butterflies, reeds and rotting marsh vegetation. Old Osman squatted down on the threshold of the street door, and filled his pipe with amber-coloured contraband tobacco, then lit it and drew on it. He coughed three times so loud that he could be heard at the other end of the village. Those who heard him said, 'This is one of Old Osman's good days.'

Old Osman rose to his feet, stuck his pipe into the right-hand side of his toothless mouth and clasped his hands behind his back. Trying hard to walk upright and only slightly bent, he moved forward, stooping a little. He put on the air of someone seated on a handsome, mettlesome Arab horse. Looking at the world from a height, as if he knew a great secret and wasn't going to tell it . . . From his house he went to Selver the Bride's house at the other end of the village in the same manner: arrogant, confident, taut, half-smiling, with a 'Look, villagers, here I come' attitude. Everyone thought that he was going to Selver the Bride's house to talk to her. But he turned round at Selver's door with the same arrogant air, and seeing him turn, Selver hurried out, calling,

'Osman Agha, why did you come right up to my door, and then turn away again?' Selver was the same age as Osman Agha. Her husband and sons had all gone into the army, and had never returned. She had no relatives, and lived all alone in a hut at the end of the village. A long way away in another village she had a grandson.

'Let's have a coffee together, Osman Agha.' Old Osman stopped and smiled. 'Selver,' he said in a complacent, secretive way, 'it is not the right moment for coffee-drinking, thank you.'

Drawing himself up still further he walked away, grinning from one ear to the other.

Everyone who saw Old Osman in this state, with his best clothes on and a cheerful face, realized that something was up. Women, children, invalids, old folk sitting at their doors watched Old Osman coming and going, all dressed up and smoking his pipe. What had come over him? There was no special event in the village.

Osman walked up and down, up and down, till noon, without

saying anything to anybody. He merely smiled sweetly at those who approached him questioningly, his eyes sparkling, with a condescending air. With his hands clasped behind his back he walked puffing endlessly at his pipe all the while.

His eldest son Hüsam hastened to his mother.

'Mother,' he said. 'What's come over Father, what's up?'

'I don't know,' said Kamer. 'How should I know what that crazy fellow is doing? It's how the fit takes him; he keeps on walking about. Something's got into him.'

Kamer too was different from usual, and this aroused Hüsam's suspicions still further.

'Something's up, Mother. You're even closer than Father, you'd die rather than say anything. But Father will talk. Otherwise he'll burst . . . In two days if he can't talk, he'll burst. So why don't you relieve our curiosity? In the last few years Father has never dressed up or thought of going into the village like that. The last time he did so was when Slim Memed went away.'

At the mention of Slim Memed Mother Kamer's face went ashen; her hands and lips trembled. This did not escape Hüsam.

Hüsam went towards the huge tree in the middle of the village, where the assembled villagers awaited his news with curiosity. Before he reached them he called out,

'I couldn't find out a thing. If Father won't speak, do you think she will? Don't worry, Father won't hold out more than two or three days. Only don't look at him now. If we pretend not to notice him, he will get angry and tell us sooner . . . Go back home, everybody . . .'

Old Osman entered his home at midday, went to the closet and said hello to Memed. After sitting down and quickly eating his meal, he hurried outside again. He lit his pipe and puffed out smoke, then started pacing up and down. As he walked, he darted glances out of the corner of his eye to see if the villagers were curious. Not seeing anybody around, he said to himself, smiling, 'I know you, you cunning devils. I know you. I know you are watching me secretly, so that I won't be able to contain myself. Don't bother, whatever happens, I'll die rather than reveal the secret.'

Osman went on like this from dawn to dusk for three days. On

28

the evening of the third day he went home, his face pale, and his hands trembling as he smoked his pipe.

'My! I'm tired, I'm exhausted,' he said. 'Three days of this! Three days from morn to night, how can anybody stand up to that, eh, Kamer? There's not a soul in sight, but I know them. They're dying, they're bursting with curiosity.'

He did not even look at Slim Memed, he did not even drink his coffee; as soon as he had sat down by the fire, he fell asleep and began to snore. His mouth was open, like a dark hole.

4

SHOTS rang out from the direction of Savrun brook. It was early, before cockcrow. Suddenly a noise, a clamour broke out in the village. All the dogs began to bark at once, asses brayed, cattle lowed, horses whinnied; shouts and cries and screams filled the air. Nothing could be seen in the dark, wet night. Everyone rushed outside in their underclothes. Old Osman kept calm.

'Kamer, dear,' he said quietly, 'there's something wrong in the village. That scoundrel has been up to more of his dirty work; he's got somebody into trouble.'

Memed seized his gun, and jumping out of the closet, came to the door. He was in two minds about whether to go out or not. Osman lighting a torch, saw him there, and looked at him wryly, mockingly.

'What's up, Slim Memed? What is it, my hawk?' he cried. 'Are you preparing for battle? Go and sit down, get back to bed! It's nothing to do with you. That devil has been up to some of his dirty work. He has destroyed some poor fellow's hearth. There's work like that every night in this village; go to bed. If anything unexpected happens I'll let you know.'

Osman was dressing and talking at the same time. Relaxing, Memed lowered his gun, and holding it by one end, went across to the fire. Among the ashes there were two embers still glowing from the evening before.

'What are you looking for, Osman for heaven's sake?' asked Kamer when she saw Osman, panting in agitation, search for something. 'What are you looking for?'

Osman flew into a temper. 'Damn and blast you, Kamer. What am I looking for? I'm looking for my watch. And I'm looking for trouble for you, Kamer. They're raising hell outside. Let them! They deserve it, these villagers, stupid asses! They deserve it five hundred times over! Do you understand?'

'What are you going to do in the middle of the night with your watch, with that hell of a row out there? Here's your watch! Take it!'

Old Osman took the watch, saying, 'Damn and blast you, woman.' There was a slight smile on his lips.

Their wrangling, affectionate and harmless, made Memed feel confident. The world that these two old people had created was a world of endless affection and tolerance. The noise outside got louder and louder. Memed pondered over the two childish old people. 'If only everyone were like that,' he said to himself, 'if only people were like that. How beautiful mankind would be!'

Putting on his watch, Old Osman stretched himself, looked at his boots and legs, and lit his pipe with an ember from the fire. The noise outside grew louder, and came nearer the house. He left the house almost at a run. As soon as he got outside, he stopped in the yard.

'He's set it on fire, the scoundrel!' he shouted. 'And why shouldn't he since we're not men enough to resist? We're a whistle that he plays on . . . He'll do the same to all of us in turn . . . He's done what he said he'd do, the filthy wretch. He's burnt down Yobazoghlu Hassan's house . . . Maybe he's killed Hassan! Killed him . . . Alas, Hassan, brave Hassan! My fine, independent Hassan! They've killed the poor fellow. A brave man's mother soon has reason to weep. There was only one brave man in the village, and that devil has killed him . . .'

He regretted saying that a brave man's mother soon has reason to weep. Would Memed have heard? If he had heard it would be a shame. He had come to take refuge there like a wounded bird. And then you arouse him by shouting about a weeping mother.

You are stupid, Osman! When the wolf grows old he's the laughing-stock of dogs, they say. But Osman, growing old, is getting like a dog! Let's hope he didn't hear.

He opened the closet in order to find out whether Memed had taken the remark to heart or not:

'Child, guest!' he called inside. 'Put out your head and look outside, the flames are rising high into the sky.'

Memed came out as far as the front door. 'There's no need to go out, my boy. Look at those flames lighting up the sky, look at the flames, then go to bed and sleep sound, my hawk. If you wish, go out to relieve yourself. Perhaps you feel like relieving yourself outside. But don't go any further than that corner, not a step further.'

He took a step forward towards the burning house.

'I was on the run once. I stopped in one house for six months. Do you know what I most longed for, my boy? To have a good piss under the stars. The first night I went out I had a good long piss under the stars. Now's the chance, you do the same. But don't go further than that corner.'

Memed quietly slipped out of the door.

Yobazoghlu's three buildings which stood side by side were all on fire. The main building was his house; the one below was the stable, and the next was the storehouse. The fire also caught Mad Durak's house and it began to blaze. There was a strong north-east wind blowing, and this made the flames leap to the height of a minaret. The leaping flames darted here and there in the darkness.

The whole village was outside, children, youths, ancients, invalids, some dressed, some dressing by the light of the fire, some in their underclothes . . .

Yobazoghlu Hassan, with his hands pressed to his head, was rocking himself from one side to another; he could not take his eyes off the burning hut. His wife and children at his side were intoning a lament, crying bitterly. The fire-raisers had set the third building on fire from the doors, and this was why Yobazoghlu and his family had only just been able to escape with their lives, without bringing out a scrap of furniture or clothing. If they had been inside a moment longer they would have been burnt to death.

From the stable came the piercing whinny of a terrified horse.

It was rushing from one end to the other of the long stable, whinnying again and again, shrilly, clamorously. Pieces of the burning roof were falling on the horse, sending it mad with pain. No one could do anything. The youths, the other men stood listening to the horse's desperate cries.

Old Sefché, the Warden, said, 'Isn't anyone going to open that door? Is there no hero, no man at all?' and he went from one to another, begging them to take action . . . 'If you open the door, he'll find the doorway and come out. I feel sorry for that horse, a thoroughbred animal like that. Thoroughbreds are like people. They can do everything but talk. They weep and laugh and think. They're a man's best friend. Isn't there a man among you? Oh, I'm too old, too old to open it . . .'

The horse's cries grew louder and more heart-rending.

Yobazoghlu Hassan suddenly moved, and he began to turn like a top where he stood, then he snatched from one of the youths a horse-cloth which they had wetted in order to spread it over the burning hut. He wrapped it around himself and plunged into the blazing stable. As quickly as he had gone, he reappeared, holding the horse by its halter. Immediately the horse emerged, it reared, snatching the halter out of Hassan's hand, and galloped to the village square: like Hassan a few minutes before it turned round and round, then headed towards the plain, and was swallowed up in the darkness.

The huts could now scarcely be seen for the flames; they were like a fiery threshing-floor on the edge of the village.

Yobazoghlu threw off the horse-cloth, and again putting his hands to his head gazed at the flames, as if unable to tear himself away.

Everybody was watching the fire without moving. A rending noise came from the buildings. The roofs, and the brushwood walls were collapsing, clattering down. The bellow of the last cow caught inside ceased.

Everyone stood frozen to the spot; their faces were yellow and drawn. Only Old Osman moved about, and went back and forth, talking, his pipe in his mouth, his hands behind his back, a smile on his lips, puffing smoke into the air. Every now and then he stepped up to Yobazoghlu's side, and said,

'You have my sympathy, friend. Experience is the best teacher.'
He did not notice whether Yobazoghlu had heard him or not, but
came back again, to say, 'Friend, what you did wasn't right. It was
a shame, what you did. You endangered the whole village. So this
is your punishment. Could there be a better one, my friend?
Anyway, you might all have been burnt to death inside, you and
your wife and children. Congratulations, friend, congratulations
on this valuable experience. Henceforth I am not afraid of what
you'll do. A man who has come face to face with death is a little
better, a little more courageous. You are a brave man at heart, but
you are a pig-headed animal, aren't you?'

Shadows moved in and out of the houses. Shadows moved in
and out of the flames. There was a smell of charred meat; a smell
of wool and hair. The burnt smell mingled with fresh spring
scents.

At last Old Osman got tired of walking to and fro, and stopped
in the light. His back was turned to the burning buildings, and he
felt the warmth on it. He raised his head, and, smiling, let his eyes
rove over the villagers, one by one. Over women, men, youths,
ancients and children.

As he turned to the right he came face to face with Sefché the
Warden who was coming towards him.

'Look,' he said, 'look, my friend: What beautiful flames they
are. How beautiful to see them in the darkness of a spring night.'
He cackled with laughter. The whole village heard his laugh, and
eyed him with amazement, muttering to one another. 'How well
the flames suit the night, as the bullet suits the heart; how well it
suits us to stay here, helpless, brooding over the fire; how well it
suits us to stand holding our heads in our hands, how well those
loud laments suit our hearts, how well we look wearing women's
clothes, how well humanity suits us! Look, friend Sefché, look!
How beautiful are those scarlet flames. As the wind blows, they
become longer, broader and more beautiful. As the fire grows my
heart too swells and broadens. My heart turns into a blacksmith's
anvil. How well the anvil suits the heart. How well Ali Safa Bey
suits our chicken-heartedness. How well humanity suits us. Look,
friend Sefché, look at the flames, how well they suit this night of
ours.'

Sefché the Warden could not understand him in this laughing mocking mood, or find any meaning to what seemed a madman's words; so, shaking his head, he went away from Osman. As he walked, he exclaimed: 'Allah, Allah, Allah, Allah. The man's going mad. He was never like that before. The village is on fire, and he stands there making a joke of it. My, my, Old Osman! You really have reached your dotage. You stoop nowadays, and your brain is addled. Alas, comrade, you were like an eagle. A curse on old age! When a man grows old, he becomes like a child, like a little baby. Oh, the poor chap! Allah, Allah!' Sefché the Warden was two years older than Osman. He stooped a lot; he was bent double with age. Old Osman and Sefché the Warden had strange habits, unusual manners and traditions, and ways of doing things which the villagers did not know about, had never seen and did not understand, but they were both perfectly suited to these ways and ceremonies. They wore the same kind of clothes, they both wore holsters. They were never without their old inlaid revolvers on their hips. Ever since they could remember they had shaved their heads with a razor, leaving a two-inch patch of long hair right on the top of their heads. Sefché had such long hair on the crown of his head that when he let it loose it came down to his waist like a woman's.

The darkness lightened gradually, and noises and cries and other sounds came from the other villages. From Ahjasaz came a burst of sound like a cannon. A hoarse sound like a shell exploding underground.

The burnt smell mingled with the smells of the marshes, the narcissi, the flowers and the spring . . . For a moment a deep silence filled the air. Every sound was suddenly stilled. Then a horse neighed shrilly in the distance, and fell silent. The crackling noises of the fire had stopped long before. The air was filled with the smell of charred meat. The villagers' noses were full of smoke and fat from the burnt meat, and they all began to cough.

The flames gradually died down, but glowing embers remained till morning. When dawn came the houses were a smoking heap of black charcoal. Inside them were only a few burnt utensils, some twisted ploughshares, a heap of calcined flints . . . Not even the bones of the burnt animals remained. A stream of black grease

34

had trickled into the trench behind the stable.

Children, sleepy women, tired old men, youths, middle-aged women – they were all sweaty and tired, and they squatted down on the damp earth towards the rising sun. Their heads were on the ground, their faces gloomy and hopeless. Their drooping heads did not move. They did not look at anything. There was a feeling of shame in the air. If they did raise their heads, it was as if they were afraid to look at one another. There was not a sound. All around nothing was heard but the buzz of insects flying from flower to flower or leaf to leaf.

Only Old Osman was up and about. Facing the rising sun, his shadow stretching out over the plain, he stood like a statue in the first light of day. There was a smile on his face. He stayed thus for a while, puffing smoke from his pipe towards the rising sun. A light wind from the north-east swept the smoke away. Then Osman moved, and it was as if a giant with a thousand sleeping heads had moved just one. He began to move in front of the seated crowd, and among the smoking ruins. His hands behind him, his pipe in his mouth, his head upright . . . The villagers slowly raised their heads and watched him. They could not understand why he was roaming about the site of the fire with a look of jubilation.

Until morning Osman walked around, smoking. Then he went up to Yobazoghlu Hassan who was worn out, his right hand swollen with burns, his left hand on his head, his face yellow; he had aged fifteen years in a single night, and his face was shrivelled. Osman said to him fondly, jubilantly, in a booming voice,

'Yobazoghlu Hassan, your late father was of the Kizilbash sect, but he was a Kurdish hero. A brave man. He was a solitary man, but no one had anything against him. I saw a child at dawn, at night, in the evening. The child was like the sun. He was a small man but with a pure heart. The mighty Government feared this boy, and so did the great eagle-eyed Mustafa Kemal who routed the Greeks and all their allies. And the aghas trembled before him. They could not keep their trousers up for trembling, Yobazoghlu. Do you understand, Yobazoghlu? I have only a few words to say to you: Why don't you burn down Ali Safa's house? He burnt yours. He did well, he did fine, more power to his elbow . . . let him kill us. We deserved it, my friend. We are men who deserved

35

contempt, my friend. Very right, very proper. Let that villain Ali Safa do his worst, why not? It would be a good thing. Don't be afraid, my friend. Don't be afraid. Let fear not enter your heart. A timid heart is not acceptable. It can soon be silenced. Don't be frightened. That infidel has done all this in order to frighten you. Don't be afraid! You're a brave man, a man of courage! Don't be afraid, I say! For a man who is afraid cannot be saved, at any time, anywhere, in the air, on the land, or in the sea. Don't be afraid. Your horse that escaped will return, and that villain Ali Safa will get his deserts. The horse you saved from the fire will come back; does your swollen hand, that you burnt in order to rescue him, pain you much, my son? How can it not pain you? Let it pain you, burnt hands will heal. Your horse will come back, back, back. Even if horses that escape a fire do not return, even if they can't be saved, yours will come back. Friend Hassan, Kurdish Hassan, I tell you, I tell you . . .'

His voice grew louder, it was an extraordinary voice, full, deep, like a giant's . . . 'Your horse will come back, friend Yobazoghlu, and a sun will rise from every peak!'

Smiling, surveying the crowd once again from under his bushy eyebrows, he said in a confident way, emphasizing each word:

'From every peak a sun will rise. A sun will rise. A sun, a sun, a sun . . .'

With his deformed forefinger, gnarled like the root of a thorn-tree, he pointed to the sun:

'A sun like that will rise. A sun as beautiful as that. Bright. And warm. Like that. From every peak a sun will rise. Your horse will return, will return home.'

He swung round, and made his way rapidly home. All heads turned to watch him. The crowd followed him with their eyes until he reached his house and banged the door shut.

36

5

DAY was breaking. Yobazoghlu's horse was standing motionless in the middle of the plain. His shadow stretched towards the crags of Anavarza. Facing the rising sun, thousands of birds were singing with one voice, and filling the air with flurry and tumult. The stallion's head was in the air, his neck outstretched as if he smelt fresh grass. The whites of his dark eyes were bloodshot. On his left flank there was a swelling caused by a burn. Then flies began to circle over the swollen place. At first the stallion swept them away with a switch of his tail, but then smaller black flies began to cluster round his eyes. Without moving from the spot he began to toss his head, for a while; then for a time he would take no notice of the flies settling round his eyes or on his burnt flank, and would stand motionless.

The air was filled with warm sun and the birds stopped singing, and the bees began to hover in the warmth. Then, as it grew hotter, the sweating bees hid themselves in the huge flowers. Of the bees that had been hovering in the air with shimmering wings, buzzing to and fro, not a single one was left in the heat. Only the big hornets and, larger than those, the long thin, blue and red enamelled dragon-flies, whirled and swept onwards in the heat. They flashed to and fro through the air, looking in the distance like a piece of sunlight. The heat thickened and became steamy. Plants, trees, flowers and birds were all enveloped in the vapours of the lush spring warmth. A cloud of butterflies whirled and went on its way. A swarm of bees went to settle in a nearby plane tree. Everything smelt of sun-warmed fresh earth. In the steamy heat the earth of Anavarza smelt fresh and crisp as if it had been newly created.

The eyes of the stallion, standing stiff and motionless, were ringed with flies. The burn on his flank could hardly be seen for flies. It was black with them. A butterfly had settled on the horse's long, clean mane, and was opening and closing its blue wings.

A reflection coming from the waters of the nearby marsh quivered on the left-hand side of the stallion's neck, and made it gleam.

For some reason or other the horse suddenly stirred, tossed his head, lashed out with his hindlegs once or twice, shook off the flies, and began to gallop over the plain from one end to the other. He went as far as the farm of Tarsuslu below Vayvay, and then stopped. He galloped so fast that his legs were just a blur.

When the horse came from Tarsuslu farm to the outskirts of Narlikishla it was afternoon. Near Narlikishla the marsh waters constantly bubble and foam. There was a long, fat black snake moving slowly through the grass to the edge of the marsh. It had just come out of its hole, and was gradually awaking, losing its numbness. Its black back had a green glint as it reached the light. The snake was almost under the horse's hooves, when it slipped away. A big beetle which had settled noisily on a barberry shrub circled noisily four times round the horse's head. He took no notice.

Suddenly, from far away, a flame flickered over Ahjasaz. The horse, as if given wings, leapt into the air, and again and again leapt into the air. He stretched his neck, he threw out his legs, and reared up. Then he began to gallop, and making a great circle came back to the starting-place. Here he stopped and sniffed the air. Then again he froze, motionless. There was not even a quiver of his flanks or a flick of his ears.

Far, far away, on the track leading from Kozan a man was walking. As soon as the stallion caught sight of him, he tossed his head, whinnied madly, and dashed off. He galloped so fast that his belly seemed to touch the ground. He galloped till sunset, until he was in a lather, but on he went. He passed the crags of Anavarza and made for Dumlu Castle. There, in the neighbourhood of Hadjilar, he saw another man coming from a great distance, and he galloped equally fast in the opposite direction. There were some flashes of lightning over Hadjilar. As soon as he saw the lightning, the darkness was rent by a whinny of mortal terror. Towards morning he reached the outskirts of Topraktepe, exhausted. He was black with sweat and lather, and panting like a bellows. He was too worn out to go any further. At daybreak the first rays of the sun showed him with his ears drooping, his head lowered towards the ground, his right hindleg drawn up to his belly, shrunken, shrivelled up, cowed.

Yobazoghlu Hassan's horse was a pure-blooded Arab stallion. He was a long, slim, loose-limbed, dark-brown stallion, almost black. Really dark-brown horses are rare, and they are the handsomest of the pure-blooded ones.

The brown horse had belonged to Ali Safa Bey until a year before. A close friend of his from Urfa had sent him the horse when it was a two-year-old colt, together with its pedigree. With the pedigree there also went a chronicle recounting the noteworthy features of the brown horse's stock. The arrival of the horse gave rise to general comment, and all the landowners of Chukurova from Kozan, Adana and Tarsus came to visit Ali Safa Bey in order to see it. For this reason Ali Safa Bey was devoted to the brown horse.

Ali Safa Bey had even brought an old groom for the horse from Urfa where he had looked after these thoroughbred horses. According to its owner, the horse was as clever as a human being, except that he could not talk. He understood everything, every movement, and reciprocated friendship, enmity, love, good or bad treatment. If Ali Safa Bey was distressed, he too was distressed, and his big dark eyes were clouded with grief. If Ali Safa was happy, the horse would snort with joy, and his eyes would sparkle with delight.

Ali Safa Bey said,

'I love him better than myself.'

Ali Safa Bey had become deeply involved in an impossible struggle, but he recovered himself when he mounted the brown stallion, and became master of the world. To hear people say, 'Safa Bey, the rider of the dark-brown stallion!' filled him with immense pride. The affection he felt for this horse surprised even him. He turned it all over in his mind. 'It means,' he would say, 'that the old, wild Turcoman blood is still running in my veins at the same speed. Arab horses are thoroughbreds, people are not; people have other characteristics. They are not like horses. People are not horses, so what is this attachment I feel for horses?'

A day came when his passion for the stallion came into conflict

39

with his passion for land. The primitive Turcoman blood in his veins, usually opposed to land, met with a check.

In the district of Vayvay, he needed to have a piece of land, however small, near the village. A good plot of land which was necessarily the key to the Vayvay farmlands. After a long search the notary of the county town found him the right plot, with a title-deed that would extend or reduce the boundaries to the utmost. Wherever you took them they would go. Moreover this deed was within the boundaries of Vayvay village. It was a property of seventeen dunums and it belonged to Yobazoghlu Hassan. Within that title-deed could have been included five thousand, ten thousand, fifteen thousand, up to fifty thousand dunums. Ali Safa Bey was beside himself with joy at having found such a title-deed. Before getting the deed transferred to his name, he immediately handed over five hundred liras as a gift. For three nights he could not sleep for sheer happiness. On the third day in the morning he called Yobazoghlu Hassan, and said to him,

'Give me those deeds, Hassan.'

Hassan at once replied, 'With pleasure, Bey.'

'I am a friend of your father's; your father and mine were close friends. We are brothers, relatives, and if you suffer I suffer with you. One doesn't leave one's close friends, Hassan . . .'

'At your service, Bey.'

'We are brothers, friends, relatives, but friendship is quite different from doing business with someone. How much do you want for the deeds to your seventeen dunums? What do you want in exchange for it?'

'As you wish Bey, it is only a little plot of land. Do just as you wish. We can go to the town tomorrow and I can turn it over to you at once. Since our fathers were friends, what can a little bit of land matter . . . It's of no importance at all. Don't you worry about it. May God keep you in health for us.'

Ali Safa was flattered – 'That's all very well,' he laughed, 'but I cannot agree. You must take something for it. I would not want the field under those conditions. You must accept something for it.' Hassan looked straight ahead of him, shamefacedly, without replying.

'No, Hassan,' Ali Safa went on. 'I do not want the field. Tell me what you want. You suggest something first, then I myself will give you exactly what you want whether it's a kurush, an ox, a goat or a sheep . . . Or a horse . . .'

Hassan did not lift his head or respond in one way or another.

It passed through Ali Safa Bey's mind that Hassan was behaving like a girl, just like a girl, he said to himself. He does not raise his head and look at me. Even at that age he blushes like a young girl. He dislikes the idea of taking money for the field. It is a Turcoman tradition not to speak in front of one's elders, and not to bargain with them. But I must make him accept.

There were a lot of things behind this question of the seventeen dunums. He could not accept the field without giving something in return.

'Tell me, Yobazoghlu,' said Ali Safa Bey in his unctuous voice, 'tell me, my dear friend. Tell me, my admired brother. I'll never forget this really handsome behaviour of yours. I'll even have it inscribed on my tombstone. Tell me now.'

Yobazoghlu raised his head; there was a gleam in his eye. His small face looked like the face of a naughty, roguish child, a child planning some mischief, ready for some prank . . .

Ali Safa Bey was glad when Yobazoghlu raised his head. The fellow has seen reason, he said to himself. His face looked like that of a boy of seventeen. Hassan's quite old. Anyway, we are the same age. Hassan was still smiling bashfully, and without taking his eyes from Safa Bey's face, he said,

'Bey, if you insist . . .'

'I do insist, Hassan. Unless you will take something in return, by God, I can't accept. Not only land: I couldn't even accept gold.'

'Well, my heroic Bey, if . . .'

The Bey took a deep breath, and as if shaking a heavy burden off his back, said,

'Tell me, Hassan, tell me, my friend. Ask me for whatever you want.'

'I would like your brown stallion, Bey. Either the stallion or nothing. Give me the stallion and you shall have the field. I'd like him together with the saddle and bridle you use.'

The Bey turned pale, but said nothing. If he had opened his

41

mouth, he could only have stammered something unintelligible. At last he said,

'Is that so, Hassan? You want my brown Arab stallion?'

'Please forgive me, Bey,' said Hassan, getting to his feet. 'Either the horse, or nothing.'

And without looking back he disappeared outside.

The Bey came to his senses some time after he had gone, and then he was mad with rage. He walked up and down the hall of his house, thinking and thinking about what he should do. If at that moment Yobazoghlu had been within reach, he could have torn him limb from limb, so outrageous did Yobazoghlu's request seem to him. 'How can he dare, how can he expect to have my horse, that ignorant peasant, that village bully?' shouted Ali Safa Bey. 'How does he dare to talk to me?'

His anger lasted a long time. For some days he could find no way out. He sent important people from the town to intercede with Hassan, aghas from the neighbouring villages, everyone he could think of. He offered him lots of money, and acres and acres elsewhere, but Hassan turned a deaf ear.

'Either the Bey's brown Arab, or nothing,' he said. 'Either the Arab stallion,' he insisted, 'or nothing!'

Ali Safa Bey could find no other way out. Putting on the embossed bridle and the embroidered saddle, he sent the stallion to Hassan's house one morning. His inner resentment against Yobazoghlu grew fiercer and fiercer.

The formalities of turning over the title-deeds were completed in a couple of days. When Ali Safa took them in his hands, he first smiled, then clenched his teeth, and looked at Hassan and the assembled Vayvay villagers with blazing eyes:

'Well, now I've got you where I want you,' he said. 'Did you intend to take from me my horse, the horse I love as much as myself? You would take him and let that gipsy mount him as if he were a man?'

Hassan and the villagers did not understand why he was so angry, but they were afraid.

They were afraid but there was nothing they could do. After Hassan had obtained the horse, he mounted it and rode from one town to another. And at those places he would say,

'This horse belongs to Yobazoghlu. I gave seventeen dunums of barren earth for this stallion. The stupid fool . . .'

Then gradually he would grow over-bold, and say,

'If I wished I could have had not only Ali Safa Bey's horse but his wife for seventeen dunums of barren land. I spared him his wife, but I asked for his horse. He gave me his horse; tell me, with your hand on your heart, wouldn't he have given me his wife?'

He made everybody laugh with his buffoonery.

Ali Safa Bey, hearing about these crazy jokes day after day, was mad with rage. He sent his men several times to warn Hassan: 'Let him shut his mouth. If he doesn't I shall bloody well do it for him.'

Hassan took no notice.

'I'm not going to shut my mouth,' he said. 'I'll not shut up,' he boasted. 'I'm not afraid of him or his henchmen. Let them do their worst! Let them come and try! Why, even if that bandit of his, Kalayji, were still alive in the mountains I wouldn't be afraid. Didn't he give me this handsome horse for just seventeen little dunums of land and a mere scrap of paper? Compared with me, he's not worth twopence. If he wishes, let him have me killed. Who cares? I'll say a dirty dog cut me up. I've still got a little plot of land, and the title-deeds to go with it. I'll give it to him, and next year I'll have Ali's wife. I'll take her pillion on the Arab stallion and wander from one village to another. Compared with me, he hasn't a ha'porth of self-respect. Let him kill me.'

One day when he was riding along a track near the thorn forest five shots were fired at him but he was not hit. That was because he was on the horse, and it was galloping like the wind. The bullets did not come near him. Hassan galloped like mad everywhere, over the whole plain. Several times they rained bullets on him, but again nothing happened to Hassan. He flew like the wind through the hail of bullets. He took no notice, grew even more insolent, and talked openly everywhere, at gatherings and weddings.

They took him to the police station and beat him until his nose and mouth were bleeding, and for a fortnight afterwards he passed blood. It had no effect.

'I'll take his wife,' he said. 'Sooner or later. I'll take her pillion on the Arab stallion and I'll parade her all over the summer

43

pastures in the hills. I still possess another plot of land and another title-deed.'

Three times the horse was stolen; Hassan went and found the horse and brought it back.

'If the horse dies what happens?' he asked. 'Since he once gave me the horse that is dearer to him than himself, when he gave me it didn't he lose his self-respect? If the horse dies, would he recover his self-respect?'

*

The sky was engulfed in deep blue darkness. There was a rain of shooting stars. The brown stallion breathed noisily, alternately distending and closing his nostrils. He galloped on and on, stopping now and then to sniff at the air lengthily, then plunging on again, rearing and whirling on himself as he ran, and tracing a circle as large as a threshing-floor of crushed grass and flowers and insects, all trampled flat.

The dark-brown stallion, after a long round, together with a shooting-star, entered the narcissus-beds of Ahjasaz. The narcissus flowers were tall enough to touch his belly; they gave off a heady scent in the warm spring air. The big, gliding, gleaming stars in the sky were reflected in the shimmer of the horse's bare rump. His rump quivered broadly, voluptuously, violently. He plunged into the limpid waters of Ahjasaz, where the big, broad leaves of the water-lilies floated on the surface.

6

WHEN someone knocked at the door Ali Safa Bey was upstairs in his mansion, waiting impatiently. Both the men who dismounted from their horses were covered with mud from head to foot. The horses too were splashed with mud.

Ali Safa Bey hurried downstairs at once. 'What news?' he asked. 'I saw the fire. It was a fine blaze. What news is there of Hassan and the stallion?'

Murtaza replied, 'When Adem knocked at the door Hassan opened it. That's right, isn't it, Adem?'

'That's right,' said Adem, raising his twisted little face.

'Hassan fell down, bellowing like an ox. The door was shut on him at once. That's right, isn't it, Adem?'

'That's right, the door shut.'

'Then,' said Murtaza, 'I set light to some rags soaked in paraffin, and put half of them on the threshold of the door, and the other half I pushed into the grass on the side of the cottage where the wind was coming from. It burst into flames at once. Then I went to the stable, and set fire to the stable door. It caught fire at once, and I heard the stallion whinny inside. There was a north-east wind blowing, and the flames soon spread, till they lit up the whole place. The villagers began to talk and shout out. So we made off, but three men followed us right into the reed-beds. The horse in the burning stable was mad with terror, and whinnied as if he were pleading, bitterly. The noise he made tore your heart. Three men came right to the edge of the reed-beds, but they didn't go in. We fired three shots at the three men from the reed-beds. That's right, isn't it, Adem?'

'That's right,' said Adem. 'I fired three shots at them. But it was night, quite dark, and I didn't hit them.'

'The stallion whinnied so that the sound rang out over the whole plain. He seemed to be weeping as he burnt, and the sound is still ringing in my ears . . .'

'He got burnt to death,' said Adem with a sigh. 'The poor wretch was burnt to death. He was weeping just like a human being, it tore at your heartstrings.'

'We got into the reed-beds, safe and sound. Then there was a long, long whinny from the stallion, an endless whinny. Then all at once it was cut off.'

Ali Safa Bey's expression became sombre, angry. 'Let him burn,' he said. 'Let the stallion burn. Burn to ashes.' He took a deep breath. 'Well, go and wash the horses down. And change your clothes. Where has Zeynel got to? He'll know exactly what's happened. Until Zeynel's here, we can't be certain of anything.'

'We can't be certain,' they echoed as they went off.

The sun had risen now and the mists were slowly dispersing.

The chorus of birds was over. A wheel track went over the green grass towards Anavarza. A man was heaping up manure outside a stable. Another one, wearing a brown serge cloak, was grooming a bay horse. A cloud of butterflies, in a riot of colour, alighted in front of them, then took flight again. From the red crags of Anavarza, shrouded in white mist, a violet, bright, shining, limpid cloud was rising into the sky.

Murtaza and Adem washed themselves and came back. They did not open their mouths. They stood before the Bey respectfully at attention. They made an effort to be on the alert in order not to be found wanting in the eyes of the Bey. They did not look him in the face, or raise their eyes from the ground. Ali Safa Bey rose from the divan, covered with a Turcoman blanket, on which he sometimes sat, and began to stride up and down the carpeted room angrily, impatiently, striking his whip against his corrugated yellow boots. 'Look, Bey,' said Murtaza, 'that's Zeynel coming up the road, isn't it?'

The Bey, shading his eyes with his hand, looked out. He saw Zeynel coming up through the bramble thickets, and his gloomy face brightened.

'It is Zeynel,' he replied. 'I wonder what happened to the stallion.'

'The stallion died,' said Murtaza triumphantly. 'That's right, isn't it, Adem?'

'He did indeed. Even his bones were burnt up, every bit. Not a bit of hair was left.'

Zeynel arrived, breathless, a few moments later. His face was pale, and his lips drooped. One could see that his legs were trembling.

Ali Safa Bey, somewhat disconcerted, said,

'Sit down there, sit down and rest a bit, my son, my dear brother Zeynel.' He looked anxiously into his face, hardly concealing his impatience. Zeynel's crooked chin looked more crooked and more bent to the right. 'Murtaza, bring Zeynel some water. If he drinks, he'll pull himself together.'

Zeynel sat down. Murtaza brought the water and held it out to Zeynel. Zeynel's hand shook as he took the cup, and some water was spilt on the floor.

46

'Tell us, Zeynel: What happened?'

'Nothing happened,' said Zeynel. 'Nothing at all. Hassan's house and a stable and a barn were burnt down ... Nothing happened.'

'What about him?'

'He wasn't touched.'

'And the stallion?'

'He was in the fire. The stable door itself was alight. But Hassan saved the horse. He nearly got burnt to death for the sake of the horse. He plunged right through the burning door into the flaming stable and dragged the horse out.'

'How did the villagers react, Zeynel? Were they cowed, frightened?'

'Cowed, yes, and how! Every single one was petrified, like a tree without leaves. Every living thing is so overcome with terror they can't even breathe.'

'Aaaah, the stallion was not burnt to death ... The fact that they are frightened is good, very good ...'

'There was only one, that was Old Osman, who didn't take any notice. He kept on puffing away at his pipe, and laughing as he watched the fire.'

'Is Old Osman up to something again? Won't he come? Do you mean he won't come and discuss things with me, Zeynel?'

'I know him, Bey. He had changed his garments, and put an old pistol in his belt. He's got something up his sleeve, but nobody knows what.'

'Perhaps he's in his second childhood,' said the Bey. 'He's well past eighty, Old Osman. Well, we'll see.'

'I can't understand it,' said Zeynel. 'He's certainly not in his second childhood. He goes on roaming round the village like a black cloud. He came and stood in front of me, and gazed at me from head to foot, puffing smoke into the air, and then stamped three times on the ground. Old Osman knows something. He is preparing for a struggle. He wasn't like that three days ago. Then he was dragging himself along, cowed, like a corpse.'

'These lands are our own property,' said Ali Safa Bey. 'We shall rise above our difficulties, whatever trickery Old Osman is up to. I am strong, and I have right on my side. Only the horse shouldn't

47

have escaped. That is a sore spot with me. That horse must be caught and shot.'

Then Adem said, 'I am an old hunter, Bey. Wherever that horse is, I'll shoot him within a day or two. Or else I'll catch him and bring him to you.'

'Don't bring him to me, kill him,' said the Bey. 'Don't come back to me unless you've shot that stallion. Be off with you now, and shoot the horse. Shoot him, I say. Let this affair of the horse finish once and for all.'

'I've got a good idea,' said Zeynel. 'It's sure to drive the villagers from their homes and make them run all the way to the Mediterranean Sea without once stopping to look behind. It's sure to frighten them out of their wits.'

'You always have good ideas, Zeynel,' said Ali Safa Bey. 'I know your talents. You shall have a beautiful fertile little farm on this plain all for you. Let's go and have dinner while you expound your new plan.'

'I'll tell you all about it,' said Zeynel. 'It's a fine one.'

7

THE dew fell on the silent crowd who were sitting, heads bowed, in front of the ruins of Yobazoghlu Hassan's burnt-out house. They were numb with cold. Nobody stirred. The crowd seemed to be frozen into a block.

Day dawned. It was a bright cheerful day. All the birds on the plain began to sing in unison. Bees began to buzz and fly here and there: their thin wings shimmering. From the far-off village houses came the sound of babies crying. Then some small children began to cry too. At this moment from behind the ruins of the house from which smoke was still rising straight into the sky the long shadows of two policemen were seen. They came up to the silent crowd and greeted them.

'Our Sergeant wants Yobazoghlu Hassan,' they said, 'and he wants him now.'

Seyfali, tearful, thin-faced, fragile, got up on his long legs.

'The poor chap's house was burnt down,' he said, 'look at the smoke coming out of it. It was burnt to ashes.' He bent his neck like a poppy on its stalk. 'Was it right or lawful? Look at that, friends, just look! His animals were burnt to death. They fired on the poor wretch too. His children, his wife, and his horse, that beautiful Arab stallion, were burnt too. Go and tell the Sergeant what trouble we're in. Perhaps the Sergeant can find some way to help him. His flour, wheat, and oil were also destroyed. His hens, his beds were also burnt. Look, it's still smoking. Tell the Sergeant to ask him who set fire to his house. Nobody knows who set fire to Yobazoghlu's house. Take Yobazoghlu with you. It's a good thing you came. The Arab stallion was also getting burnt alive, but Yobazoghlu rushed into the burning stable and rescued the animal. He tossed his head and went off.'

Yobazoghlu got up out of his numbed position. His back was steaming slightly. He walked towards the policemen. One of them straightway took a pair of handcuffs out of the satchel he had on his back. He handcuffed Yobazoghlu's hands together.

'Why is that?' asked Seyfali.

'Mind your own business, Headman,' said the policeman sharply.

'I'll come too, shall I?' said Seyfali.

'No,' shouted the policeman. 'We're not going on a spree.'

Pushing Yobazoghlu before them they walked off. They crossed the fields where the crops were newly sprouting, and came out on to the sandy track.

The morning sun was growing warm, and a stale-smelling steam rose from the crowd like the smell of sweat. They watched Yobazoghlu until he disappeared from sight. They were silent.

The Sergeant received Yobazoghlu in an ugly mood. Foaming at the mouth, he shouted at the top of his voice, 'You people have no regard for anyone, no consideration! You've no humanity, no comradeship! You've no thought for rank, for aghas or beys! You don't even obey God or the Prophet! You disregard the police and the Government . . . !'

He was shaking, overcome with frustrated rage, beside himself with fury.

He kicked Hassan in the belly. Yobazoghlu was doubled up with pain. Then he got hold of Yobazoghlu's neck with his huge hands, and dragged him into an empty cell. Then the policemen brought a cudgel made of cherry-wood and put it into his hands. He brought it down on to the writhing man wherever he could strike him, on his head, eyes, belly or back. And brought it down hard, and as he hit, he raved:

'So you burnt down your house, didn't you. You burnt down your own house with your own hands, didn't you? You expect me to put up with that? Whoever heard of a man setting fire to his house with his own hands? For God's sake, are you off your head? Have I got to send you off to the lunatic asylum now? From the police station ... What if your children and your wife had been burnt alive in the house? You'd have been strung up, wouldn't you? Well, what do you say? Why don't you say something? Why did you set fire to your house? If everybody in those villages behaved like you and set fire to his house, what would become of the Government of this country? Well, what would become of it? You're setting a bad example to the masses, burning down your house ...'

With red face and neck, streaming with sweat, the Sergeant went on beating Yobazoghlu until he was tired out, and then he handed the cudgel to the policeman who was standing to attention beside him, saying,

'Break his bones. These people set a bad example. One day they'll rise up against the Bey, Allah, the police and the Government. Hit him! Hit him, by God! Hit him, in the name of the Prophet! Hit him hard! You must teach them properly not to set fire to their houses, with children inside them, not to set a bad example to the peasants. Hit him hard!'

The policeman began to strike him exactly like the Sergeant. And as he hit him, he too said aloud,

'You dog,' and he clenched his teeth, tensed his jaw, screwed up his eyes, and went on talking in a Black Sea accent, 'You dog, whoever set fire to his house with his own hands! And your stable, too, and the Arab horse in it like a gentle deer, and your lovely children? My God, you beast, you good-for-nothing ...'

Yobazoghlu did not say a word. It was like beating a corpse.

50

The Black Sea policeman got tired too. A third policeman took the cudgel. Yobazoghlu fainted. Every part of him was numb, and there was blood trickling from his mouth. His back, his hands, his legs were also bleeding. He was covered with blood all over.

The Sergeant gave his orders: 'Take that dog and throw him on to the path. If he dies, you will say you shot him when trying to escape. He was killed during an exchange of fire. The Bey will look after us. If he recovers his senses, tell him that he is to leave Vayvay and go away. Ali Safa Bey has given him a house and a field in another village, in another place. If he stays at Vayvay and opposes the Bey again, he'll only leave this police-station as a corpse. Tell him not to do anything else so crazy as to burn down his own house.'

The Sergeant was sipping his coffee noisily.

'Yobazoghlu's come round,' they said. 'Shall we hit him again?'

'No, don't hit him. Bring him here.'

There was a table made of thick, unplaned boards covered with a torn, green cloth, with holes burnt in it here and there. Behind it on the wall there were six brass arrows stuck on a red cloth. The tips of the arrows were blackened, and fly-dirts all over the still bright arrows had made a curious decoration on them. Against the arrows hung a picture of Mustafa Kemal standing in his colourful Field-Marshal's uniform, gazing sadly out of his blue eyes, a whip in his hand. In the picture you could see the head of a bay horse, and behind the horse's head there was a vague glimpse of a lake.

'Come here! Stand to attention. Yes, like that. Now, be off to your village, take your wife and kids, and go and settle in Narlikishla. The Bey has granted you a house in that village, and a field too. It seems the Bey's father and yours were friends. That is why he has given you a house. If you stay in Vayvay, the next time you won't leave this police-station alive. The Bey said so. And if you set fire to your house again, you know what'll happen. According to my law to burn your house down is a capital offence. This time I'm letting you go at the request of Ali Safa Bey. The next time you'll be executed. Yes, this time I've overlooked your crime, but next time I'll have you killed. Be off with you, and a pleasant journey, Hassan Pasha!'

51

Blood was trickling from Hassan's face and hands, and he could hardly open his eyes. His clothes hung in rags about him. Hassan looked like a heap of blood-stained rags. He staggered off, able to think of nothing but the pain. Only shame kept him from wailing aloud like a woman. He traversed the village of Yalnizdut and descended into the ravine. There two horsemen were awaiting him, and they seized him.

'Ali Safa Bey sends you greetings,' said a voice he knew. But Hassan could not make out whose voice it was. He opened his eyes, and looked at the speaker appealingly.

'Don't hit me any more,' he said. 'I'll do whatever the Bey says.'

'Ali Safa Bey said that you are to go and live in the village of Narlikishla. There is a house there ready for you. Only you are warned, said the Bey, not to mount the Arab stallion again. And not to burn your house down again. According to the laws of the Republic you can be executed for burning your house down. You know that the Republican Government has never permitted houses to be burnt down. You would have burnt your children alive inside the house. The Bey said, well, he must have gone out of his mind. The Bey said, he also tried to burn the horse I'd given him as a present, he must have gone off his head. As soon as you get back to the village you're to take your family and go to Narlikishla. Since the Bey has given you a house, you're to say prayers for him night and morning. Do you agree?'

'Very well,' groaned Hassan. 'Very well, friend, you didn't hit me, very well. I won't ride the Arab horse, and I won't burn my house down again.'

'Otherwise the Bey will have you killed.'

'Tell him not to have me killed.'

When he reached his village, midnight cocks were crowing, and the villagers, unable to sleep, had assembled at the Headman's house, and were awaiting him anxiously. Yobazoghlu, seeing a light in Seyfali's cottage, went in that direction. Unable to speak, he tottered towards two young men who had got up to receive him and collapsed in a heap at their feet. When he recovered consciousness it was morning and he was lying in bed. The villagers did not sleep a wink that night, but stayed watching by his bed. Mother

52

Kamer put poultices on to his wounds, and said prayers for him. Old Osman, shuttling between Seyfali's house and his own, reported what had occurred to Slim Memed, who was still concealed in his house.

Yobazoghlu was not able to get up for a week. He was glad to have escaped with his life.

One morning he made the rounds of the village, calling at every house, and took leave of everyone. To everyone he saw, young or old, he said,

'I am leaving, friends. The Government has exiled me. Who's to measure himself against the Government. The Government has ordered me to go and settle in Narlikishla. The Government has crushed me, killed me. Tell me, can you stand up against the Government? No, you can't. We emerged honourably from a ten-year struggle. But can you stand up against the Government? I shall not ride the Arab stallion again. Never again shall I mount him. And I shall not burn down my house again. I am leaving, please forgive me, friends.'

Yobazoghlu withdrew from his village like a sad, broken melody. Behind him trailed his wife and children, until they were lost to sight in the distance.

It was daybreak.

8

━━━━━━━━━━━━━━━━━━━━━━━━━━━━━━━━━

'You are not to open the door to anyone today,' said Old Osman to his wife Kamer, like a soldier giving strict orders. 'We're not at home today. I'm going to make a door into the stable so that our hawk can relieve himself in comfort. I know from experience that when you are on the run the most difficult thing is to open your bowels. If you can't do that comfortably, you get very depressed, you come to the end of your tether. I'll open up a door into the stable, Mother Kamer, so that our little hawk can relieve himself really comfortably.'

Mother Kamer locked and bolted the door fast. 'Come, Memed,' said Osman, 'come and help me. Help me to make a door there, so that you can relieve yourself in comfort. You don't want to keep on grunting and groaning over petrol cans, in closets, in the house.'

From between the shutters and the boards of the door came sunlight that pierced the half-darkness of the house like arrows. Thousands of particles of dust were dancing and whirling in the sunbeams.

'We'll open the door there,' said Old Osman as Memed came up to him. He was pointing to a panel near the fireplace where the wood was stacked.

'Have you got a saw?' asked Memed.

'Yes,' put in Mother Kamer. 'Yes, we have, my boy.'

'Good, then it's easy,' said Memed.

Kamer handed him the saw, a billhook and a hatchet, and Memed put them down on the floor near the panel.

Old Osman, with his hands on his hips, watched him in the half-darkness.

'Try not to make too much noise, my hawk, or they'll know we're at home. They're already smelling a rat. My eldest son came and said to his mother, "Something's up with father. What's up?" he said.'

Memed smiled and took hold of the hatchet.

'Shall I start here, Uncle Osman?' he said, pointing to a place at about the height of a man.

'Yes, cut it there,' said Old Osman. 'I'll repair this door. Why don't you measure this door, and you can make the opening to fit it?'

Memed bent down and measured the old, cracked, sun-dried door which lay beside him, and than taking the hatchet he cut the opening as evenly as he could. Then he picked up the saw, and tidied up the rough places. A little later there was an opening in the brushwood-and-plaster wall. Memed was clever with his hands. Old Osman brought him the old door he had repaired, he fitted it into the opening, then he opened and shut it, and it was finished.

It was noon. A few cocks were still crowing. At this moment. there were two knocks at the door, but they did not open it. Memed was sweating. He handed back to Mother Kamer the

54

hatchet, the billhook, the saw and the pot full of nails.

'Congratulations, my boy,' said Old Osman. 'You've made a good job of it, my hawk, my boy,' gently patting him on the back. His hands trembled and shook as he did so. Then he bent down and whispered into Memed's ear:

'Now get along with you and make yourself comfortable in the stable. Mother Kamer, bring the boy a ewer of water. After his bowels have been opened we'll have a good meal together. Sitting facing one another. I'm longing for your company, my boy.'

Memed took the ewer from Mother Kamer, went to a corner at the other end of the stable, squatted down and relieved himself. What Old Osman had said was true. He had felt very awkward relieving himself into the petrol can. Some days he could not manage it, and waited till evening. And that was awkward.

When Memed had come back from the stable, he poured water with one hand over the other and washed it by the chimneypiece. Mother Kamer would have poured the water over his hand, but he would not let her. Mother Kamer did not insist.

'I didn't light the fire,' said Mother Kamer. 'But there's some beestings from the red cow. And I can put some sugar on it. Or there's honey if you wish.'

'Bring the beestings with honey,' said Old Osman. 'That'll be good for my boy. It gives strength.'

Old Osman was set on making this frail, puny boy eat and drink until he became a fine figure of a man. If only his hollow eyes would fill out, his stature increase, his shoulders broaden, his neck thicken like a wrestler's, if only the sight of him scared people . . . One was ashamed to reveal that he, that puny boy, was Slim Memed. Even if you swore by God and with your hand on the Koran that he was Slim Memed, you couldn't make anyone believe you. 'And here I am,' he said to himself, 'afraid and hiding this little man! Why, if I let him out into the village now and say "here is Slim Memed come to visit us" nobody will believe me. Even Mother Kamer only half believes that this child is Slim Memed. Every little while she narrows her eyes and looks at me and her eyes seem to say, "I don't believe it, Osman. I don't believe this is our hawk. God grant that you are not mistaken." You can see suspicion in Kamer's eyes. If I hadn't seen him, I wouldn't have believed it was him,

55

either. Him you call Slim Memed can't be like that . . . It's a good thing no one can see him. It would be a great pity if they saw him sleeping like a baby, dribbling at the mouth, and snuffling. One day Mother Kamer saw him crying in his sleep like a baby.'

'The child is crying in his sleep, Osman.'

'All right, let him cry.'

'Like a baby.'

'Very well, Kamer.'

'He shouldn't be carrying a gun. A slip of a boy like that.'

'What do you mean, Kamer?'

'I don't mean anything. A slip of a boy. Only children cry in their sleep.'

Mother Kamer doesn't believe it. If I hadn't seen him with my own eyes, I shouldn't have believed it myself. Was this the boy who had killed Abdi Agha, and right in the middle of the town too, in full view of the Government officials? Was it this boy who took Kalayji's life and brought all that trouble on to Sergeant Asim's head, who made the whole of the Taurus Mountains tremble and quake?

'Eat up, boy, eat plenty. Take some big mouthfuls, my little hawk. Beestings and honey makes people strong. You must eat that for three days on end . . . And then you must eat food with plenty of fat in it. You haven't eaten anything . . . What will Kamer say?'

Memed smiled, and to satisfy Old Osman he took some mouthfuls that were two or three times bigger than usual.

'Look, my hawk, I couldn't find an opportunity to tell you before. The land that the villagers bought you has passed into Ali Safa's hands. You have no land apart from that. As for your house, it's still there. Maid Seyran is living in it. She's a very angry woman, and doesn't talk to anyone but Mother Kamer. Seyran loves her. Every night, when people go home and even the birds go to rest, Seyran begins to intone laments. Her voice rings out clearly . . . The villagers know when she's going to sing, and they don't go to sleep, but stay listening to her songs. Memed, my boy, Maid Seyran is a real beauty. May what happened to her never happen to any other human being . . . May troubles like hers never happen even to one's enemies. But Seyran bears up;

56

her face is rather sad and troubled, but she holds her head high
... Her anger is like a flame inside her. And her anger makes her
more beautiful. You can hardly bear to look at her.'

Like the whole of Chukurova Memed knew what had happened
to Seyran. He sighed.

'Did you ever hear of Seyran, my boy?'

Memed, with tears in his eyes, and his face tense, replied sadly,
'Yes, I heard about her, Uncle Osman. I know her.'

'Because we bought land for you, and built a house, Ali Safa
has treated us abominably. It is a good thing you didn't come,
child. If you had come down from the mountains at the time of the
amnesty, the Chukurova aghas would have plotted against you.
They wouldn't have let you live. You are like a huge, sharp thorn
in their flesh. Whether you come down to the plain, or wander
about the mountains, or are locked up in jail, or go right away, or
die, you are still a thorn that has sunk deep into their flesh. If you
had gone to them to be their slave, they would still not have
pardoned you. Take some big mouthfuls, eat plenty of beestings
and honey.'

Memed looked up, his face grave. He put a huge mouthful into
his mouth. A steely gleam came into his eyes.

'What happened to Yobazoghlu?' he asked, in a voice as sharp
as a knife, which startled his hearers.

Mother Kamer thought to herself, 'So this is the Slim Memed
they talked about, this voice! What an angry voice he has, bless
the boy!'

'Yobazoghlu took his leave and went away,' replied Old Osman.
'He was disgruntled, terrified, finished. He went away. A complete
wreck.'

'If only he hadn't left the village,' said Memed emphatically.

Old Osman bowed his head.

'If only he hadn't,' he said. 'Eat up.'

Then Osman got up, went to the place where light was shining
through cracks round the window, took out his pistol from its
holster and began to oil it. After being silent for some time while
he was oiling the pistol he said:

'You left the village of Deyirmenoluk like a gust of flame. You
flew away. You disappeared from sight. When you went, an

immense light burst forth on the summit of Alidagh, a light as tall as a minaret, which burnt for three days and nights. The whole village was amazed, and watched the light for three nights without sleeping. I watched it too. Then every year on the night of the day you went that light shone. The whole landscape was lit up for three days and nights. Then what happened?'

'Then I ...' said Memed, and his voice was hoarse. 'Well, Uncle Osman, I had your horse under me ... I rode without stopping. One night I slept at the foot of a huge mountain, and on the second day I met a Turcoman nomad family who lived in a goat's hair tent. They realized at once that I was Slim Memed. They welcomed me warmly and gave me hospitality ... I asked them about Kerimoghlu ...'

'He was a brave man, a fine man, was Kerimoghlu,' commented Osman, pushing his pistol into its holster.

'The Turcoman tribe's Bey was a venerable old man like Kerimoghlu,' continued Memed. 'When I entered his tent, he shot three times into the air, then sacrificed a goat on the spot...'

9

'His name was Müslüm Bey. It was a banquet ... They kept the fire going in front of his home until morning, a huge fire four times as large as the tent. The flames lit up the sky.'

Would Müslüm Bey ever do you any harm, my child? Any more than I myself would, now ... Why, he was proud that you should come to him, bursting with pride ... Would a man ever fear such a one? Wouldn't he trust him implicitly? These nomads are brave, strong men. They cling more closely to their own customs than people who live in villages. There is a handful of long hair on our heads, Sefché's and mine ... This is objected to by those bastards who always know better than everyone else. But among the Turcomans the elders are all like that. And the youths, too, they all keep a wisp of long hair. It is a Turcoman custom, a sound custom. It is a custom that denotes manliness. If someone comes to you for shelter, and says you are my support, you are my fortress and I've come to your fireside, what do you do to that man? Do you take him in or throw him out? You didn't do right not to trust him. One must have trust in mankind.

'It was a very dark night. Dark as the pit. The tent was full of the scent of plants, the pungent scent of flowers. The cushions smelt of mint gathered in the hills. I had been Müslüm Bey's guest for two days. I hadn't had a wink of sleep for two nights. "If I go to sleep, Müslüm Bey will kill me in my sleep," I thought. I was on the watch every minute. I had never known such worry, such mistrust. That night it was raining gently. I got up out of bed. I hadn't undressed. My rifle, my ammunition, everything, field-glasses, fez, I left them all, and even the horse tied up at the door of the big tent, I left that too, and set off on foot . . .'

Would the Bey have killed you for a horse? However degenerate a Turcoman may be he would not kill a man who has taken refuge in his tent for the sake of a horse. You didn't come out of the cave where you hid until the following night. You thought you were naked, unsupported, alone against the world, didn't you? No longer being a brigand, you thought that the ground had given way beneath your feet, didn't you? You were sick with worry, weren't you? You were shaking with fright in that cave. It happened to me too. It happens to everyone. The braver a man is, the more he's frightened. And the more frightened a man is, the braver he is. A man only understands that this is so when he gets to the age of eighty.

The stones in the cave were reddish. If you touched the red stones, they crumbled. A strange blue flower grew over the red stones; it was straggling, ugly, and quite unlike any other flower or plant. The mouth of the cave was also covered with germander, which smelt fresh and green.

People always think they themselves are brave. They can't accept the fact that they are afraid. They die, or go mad with anxiety about it. Why am I afraid? they say; I must be going off my head. They don't realize that fear exists in men's hearts. They don't understand that they cannot eliminate fear. The germander is a fresh, sweet-smelling flower. It scents your skin, your hair;

it penetrates to the marrow. Its scent can revive a man who is in a very bad way.

Below, far below, where the green streams flowed away into the distance, stretched a misty plain, with short, white, red and purple flowers, herds of sheep, gullies, a few stunted trees, and dense masses of thorn-trees dotted here and there. Flocks of crowned cranes were waddling about in the misty fields.

From the distance came the sound of shooting, as if there was a skirmish going on somewhere.

As the sun set, it cast a fiery glow over the plain. The sky, the mountains, the gullies and the big river which ran invisibly in the hollow of the plain shone red like the flames of a fire. For a moment the plain was filled with a torrent of fire. Then everything, mountains, trees, red earth, herds, plants and cranes turned a deep blue.

'I have never seen anything like it in my life. I dashed out of the cave into the fire. It was blazing over hills and dales and over me. I walked on, starving, through the blaze for three days. A shepherd gave me a black suspicious look and asked my name. "Black Mustuk," I said. He smiled at me. He gave me a piece of bread and a beaker of milk; I drank the milk at one draught, like a crazy thing, and ate the bread in one gulp. Then I ran away from him. The shepherd kept on smiling, and called after me. "Slim Memed, Slim Memed." I ran on until it was dark. The darkness was like a wall and the rain beat down upon it.'

All the animals set upon you, didn't they? And the plants, the trees, the insects . . . Did you ever see a snake changing its skin? It has a hard job. Killing.

First of all the snake finds a soft, grassy place. For a time it keeps twisting and turning on the grass. Then it stretches three times like a bow. It stretches, relaxes, stretches, relaxes. Finally it gives a mighty stretch and bursts open. If you look, you will see that at that moment the snake has lost its old, dry skin, and has left it behind in a thorn-bush. After this the snake feels bewildered, frightened, not knowing what to do or where to go. It goes stupidly round in circles. For a year after I came back from the army I didn't know what to turn my hand to. Even now I wake up every morning at reveille.

'The shepherd called behind me, "Slim Memed, where are you

going?" I heard it with my own ears.'

Now you have stripped off your skin, everyone will call to you. Everyone knows you are Slim Memed.

'How do they know?'

'They just know. Go on.'

There's a river they call the Euphrates. It's green and weeds float up over its surface. In the summer months it looks like the sea, and the wind whips it into white-capped waves. There is a village on the bank of the Euphrates at the foot of a green rocky hill. The flat-roofed houses are covered with green earth.

'What's your name?'

'Black Mustuk.'

'Do you want to stay and be a shepherd?'

'Yes.'

'Where are you from?'

'Long Pastures.'

'There are fine horses at Long Pastures. Fine horses at Urfa, and at Long Pastures too. They have lots of endurance. Especially the bays.'

'My name is Black Mustuk.'

There was a wedding festival. Two tall poplars had been tied together at the top, and everyone was firing at the decorated emblem hung between them. Old and young, soldiers, bandits, famous hunters, everyone was trying to hit the tiny target dangling from the poplars and so to win the prize. They used up a lot of bullets, and got angry and ashamed. The target was very small, the bullets couldn't hit it. If no one hit the target it would be a bad omen for the wedding. All eyes were upon it. The bride in her wedding dress, the bridegroom, the village maidens, the young wives were all looking at it . . . Bullets came whistling from all directions. The spangles on the target sparkled in the last rays of the setting sun.

Take off your cape. You have been sitting hunched up in a corner, not looking at anybody, a frail little fellow, scared stiff. Your eyes are darting about in their sockets with fright, like a squirrel's. Take off your cape, Shepherd Memed, Shepherd Mustuk!

'I took a German carbine from one of the youths. He looked

at me resentfully. All the men there looked at me suspiciously. The girls and women smiled at me. My hands and legs were shaking, and the gun in my hand shook as if it were going to fly into the air. I aimed. I hit the target. It fluttered to the ground.'

'What's your name?'

'Black Mustuk.'

Everyone said it was Slim Memed; they recognized you. You said Black Mustuk, they said Slim Memed. You fled from there too. You felt naked in the middle of the village. Everybody knew everything. Your mother's death, Hatché's being killed. Sergeant Asim's having captured you in the cave and let you go. Your killing Abdi Agha, your leaving the horse at Müslüm Bey's tent, leaving the weapons too, your flight, everyone knew it all. The burning of the thistle fields, the village of Aktozlu, Sergeant Rejep, everyone knew it all . . .

'Slim Memed, who hunts deer on the steep crags, Slim Memed . . .'

The darkness was like a wall. It was drizzling. Not a ripple moved on the surface of the river. Not the faintest breeze stirred. In the night, the warm drizzle was steamy. He undressed and went into the water. He held his clothes in his left hand, and swam with his right. He struggled across the Euphrates for maybe one hour, maybe two. When he reached the opposite bank streaks of light were appearing in the east. He was tired, exhausted. His body, with the water dripping from it, lying on the sandy bank, smelt of river-weed. He dressed and walked on.

He was recognized in every village. He could not stay more than a month in any village. In one, he said, 'I'm Slim Memed. Yes, indeed, I am that Slim Memed you've heard of.' No one believed him. They scoffed at him so much that he could not stay in that village, either. The darkness was like a wall. It was drizzling.

'Let's have your name.'

'My name is Black Mustuk.'

'Ah! Is Slim Memed Black Mustuk?'

There was nothing you could do, my child. Everyone knew you now on the banks of the misty Euphrates, among the eagle-like Kurds of Dersim, among the Turcomans of white-earthed Birejik.

Someone was bound to hand you over to the bloodthirsty Government. They would have made you pay for Abdi Agha's blood. And what about Hatché's blood, and your mother's, what about the blood of Iraz's Riza and Sergeant Rejep? What about their blood? The Government does not expect anyone to pay for that. But they want you to pay for Abdi Agha's blood. Everyone knows you now in this world. It is always like this, always. And you too, you hanker after the mountains. You will always be Slim Memed, do what you will.

It is a pity you didn't see Müslüm Bey when you returned. You could have gone to get your gun, not at night, by day. Is it fitting for a man to steal his own gun from Müslüm Bey's tent? You went and you found the rifle just where you had left it. And didn't the women give you a warm welcome? Didn't they tell you that the Bey had not allowed anyone to ride your horse after you'd gone? Müslüm Bey wouldn't let anyone mount your horse as long as he lives. If you hadn't gone near him for ten years, nobody would have touched your guns in those ten years. I'm giving my horse to Müslüm Bey, let him enjoy riding it, you said. But do you think Müslüm Bey would ride a horse entrusted to him?

'I came to the gorge of Meryemchil. I had my rifle and ammunition. Temir came up to me. A very small, stout-hearted man, And a good man. He'd stand up against an army. I came to Kayranli and Duldul mountain and saw that there were soldiers all over the place. Then I came to Alidagh, the soldiers were like ants . . . And villagers with their whole families into the bargain . . .'

Those who surrounded Hizarji, and riddled him with bullets were not soldiers, but peasants. Those who tied a rope round Big Memed's neck were not soldiers but peasants. If they'd caught you, they'd have done the same to you. They'd have tied a rope round your neck, and would have riddled you with bullets. They wouldn't have said this is Slim Memed, the friend of the poor. And they'd have done the same to Captain Faruk and any other Government men if they could. Worse even. They'd have made good sport of them. You have to let them know you're strong, that's the thing. If not you're lost.

You were left alone in the mountains, weren't you? Naked, helpless in the middle of the world . . . weren't you?

'I was left alone, Uncle Osman, naked, helpless ...'

The darkness was like a wall. It was raining on the night, a warm steamy drizzle ...

10

OLD OSMAN, his lips moving soundlessly, went into the stable and out again. He raised his bushy eyebrows and stroked them, looking as if he was searching for something in every corner, and now and then he bent down and polished his boots, or stroked the mane of the horse in the stable; then he went in to Memed, and trying hard to smile said, tearfully, 'Memed, my child.' His voice was gloomy, pain-ridden.

It was still half-dark; day had not yet dawned. The cattle were going to the pastures. A dark mist lifted very slowly from the crags of Anavarza.

The brown horse stood on top of a rock, straight and motionless as though frozen to it.

Seyfali the Headman came from behind a hut. Old Osman's worried expression first brightened, then became gloomy again. In a moment or two Sefché was seen behind Seyfali. He had a bunch of flowers in his hand, with narcissi as big as roses.

'Mother Kamer, take these narcissi, I picked them for you,' he said, and held them out to Kamer, who was milking a cow nearby. She blushed like a young girl, and said bashfully.

'Thank you for thinking of me, Sefché Agha,' and smiled.

'I couldn't sleep last night, so I walked round the edges of the reed-beds. Yobazoghlu's crazy horse was galloping round and round the plain until morning. The narcissi are knee-deep.'

They squatted on the threshold of the door.

Old Osman said angrily,

'I promised, but I shan't go. Even if he is an Agha, even though he's got the Government behind him. I'm eighty years old. And behind me ... !' He broke off, then said again, 'Behind me ...'

He was consumed with impatience. It was painful for him not to be able to speak out. 'Behind me is mighty Allah,' and as he said this he looked at the corner where Memed's sleeping-place in the closet was. 'Who is behind us, nobody knows. Kalayji got his deserts, so will Ali Safa Bey. We settled here before Ali Safa Bey was born. And behind us . . .'

Then Old Osman's eldest son Hüsam arrived. Afterwards Reshit came. All the village came to Osman's house, in ones and twos, and squatted down on their heels. The women came too, and assembled in a corner of the courtyard with Mother Kamer, who had finished milking and had put the pail of milk aside. They did not say a word.

Old Osman kept getting up and shouting. Then he would sit down again and fall silent. Now and then he took off his hat and took hold of a handful of hair, then he would angrily put the hat on again. He grasped the butt of his gun firmly.

'A curse on that Yobazoghlu,' he said. 'He has sold the whole village out of pure bravado. For a horse. Simply to scoff and swear at Ali Safa. Now get out of this mess if you can. A curse on you, Yobazoghlu. In the end he ran away from the village.'

Their faces wrinkled with anxiety, the peasants said, 'Curse him.'

'His running away's the last crippling blow for us. Now Ali Safa will get bolder and bolder. See how he'll hammer away at us now.'

'That he will,' they all concurred.

'Yobazoghlu must come back.'

'There's no other way, he must come back,' they agreed.

'Osman, my son,' said Sefché the Warden, 'you must go and see that pig again. See what he says.'

Some of the villagers said, 'You go with Osman Agha too, Warden Sefché. Perhaps he'll say something.'

'What will he say?' objected Old Osman. 'He'll simply try to frighten me again. He'll again say, get out of the village. I'll do this and that to you, he'll say. Do you want to leave this village, and go and settle elsewhere?'

Zeynel, at the edge of the crowd, was sitting on a square marble stone bearing an ancient Greek inscription.

'This village is no good to us,' he said. 'We brought experts here five times; we brought the District Governor, and the Sergeant of Police, and five times they proved the land belongs to Ali Safa Bey. They proved it.'

Nobody in the crowd raised his head or looked towards Zeynel.

'Let's give up trying to drive nails into the sky!' pursued Zeynel. 'Everybody's scrambling for land in Chukurova. Let's get out of Ali Safa's village and find a village of our own without more delay.'

'You shut up, you son of a bitch,' said Osman. 'You're just one of Ali Safa's lackeys.'

Zeynel, offended, said,

'Don't say that to me, Osman Agha. I'm not anybody's lackey. But we'll get nothing out of staying on this land. He has the title-deeds. He's got the Government behind him; in the mountains he's got the bandits, and a whole large village of relatives. He'll force us out, sooner or later. We ought to find a home before more time passes, before Chukurova is completely divided up. We can't stand up against Ali Safa. Osman Agha, wasn't it you yourself who said recently that these lands were no use to us under these conditions? Wasn't it you who said we must talk it over with Ali Safa Bey and find ourselves some other land, another place to build a village? Since Ali Safa Bey loves Anavarza, let's leave these marshes, this malaria, these calamities. Let's move to the country around Memetli village where the pomegranates grow, or somewhere near the foot of the mountains. It was you who said it, wasn't it?'

'It was you, Osman, my son,' said Sefché the Warden, 'it was you. So why have you changed your mind now?' he said, backing up Zeynel.

Bald Arif, a very tall man, was drawing strange shapes in the dust with a stick.

'Osman Agha,' he said, 'it's true, what you say now doesn't tally with what you said before. We either get out of here and go, or we insist on staying. We've been in this uncertainty for years, and that's what's ruined us. Half the villagers have gone. To somewhere behind Dumlu Castle. Barren land. They can hardly keep

66

body and soul together. What we say now doesn't tally with what we said before.'

'We'll both go and see Ali Safa Bey,' declared Seyfali the Headman, 'I will talk to him again. It's essential to settle this business once and for all. Uncertainty has been our undoing.'

Old Osman snorted with fury. He lit his pipe, got up, and began to pace up and down the courtyard.

'Ali Safa is very much in with the Government. His hatred of us has grown and grown. And we have got weaker and weaker. After Kalayji died we thought the black clouds around us had lifted, didn't we? But that didn't stop him. He stirred up all sorts of trouble. Losing hope, I said we'd better go. When Kalayji died, he set the Government against us. That mountain of oppression. What was I to do? He set that mountain of death before us. The long arm of the Government stretches from west to east. And as for us, we got weaker and weaker. What was I to do? Let's leave here, I said. Let us leave the land of our fathers, I said, this land where the yellow narcissi grow, where the purple-flowered mint reaches stirrup-high, where one seed yields a hundred-fold. We have no alternative, I said. Half the people who left the village did so through fear, and half through weariness and hopelessness. Ali Safa gave a few of them five or ten kurush. Some of them left here thinking that they were going to find some good land. Now things have changed. And how they've changed! You don't know it yet, but I'm telling you. And beside there isn't a single foot of land in Chukurova where one can go and settle.'

Hüsam said to his father, knowing that he was going to make him violently angry,

'What's changed, Father?' he asked. 'Didn't Ali Safa Bey destroy Yobazoghlu's house and exile the poor man? Didn't the police beat him until he passed blood? What's changed, Father? This? Go and fetch Yobazoghlu back if you can. Bring him back so Ali Safa can kill him . . .'

He thought his father was going to swear at him. But Old Osman didn't swear, didn't get angry. He walked to and fro, thinking. He puffed at his pipe, thinking hard. He looked at the villagers one by one. He stopped and looked deep into their eyes, as if searching for something. He pulled up a nettle root from the hedge, crushed it in his hand and threw it down. He seemed to be talking to himself. His expression brightened and darkened by turns. His lips, the hairs in his beard trembled, and his blue eyes alternately shone from under his thick brows, then clouded. It was evident that he was in a state of great indecision. He made as if to talk, but thought better of it. Everyone perceived that Old Osman had something on his mind, but what? Everyone waited impatiently for him to speak.

At last Old Osman burst out.

'I'm not going to see that son of a bitch,' he said. 'Let him throw us out of our village if he can. Let him do his worst. If he's got the Government behind him, if he's got the bandits for him, we've got someone too, who . . . Someone.'

A voice asked,

'Who have we got behind us?'

Old Osman stiffened, and angrily straightened his bent back.

'Someone,' he thundered.

Then he began to walk up and down again. He was undecided. Gradually he began to feel tired. His old body was too weak for the great struggle going on within him.

He thrust his right leg forward and swayed forwards and back. Then he smiled and put his right hand on his waist. His face darkened, but he smiled again.

'It happened at the top of Mount Kaf,' he started off, 'at the top of that vast Enchanted Mountain. The darkness was solid, bullet-proof. The travellers lost their way. There wasn't a gleam of light anywhere. Morning did not come. It thundered on the Mountain. Still morning did not come. They could not walk on in the darkness. They couldn't breathe in the darkness. They lost hope. They said it would never get light on the Mountain. They huddled up to each other, unable to take another step. A brigand chief with forty men was pursuing them, pursuing those travellers. They ran their heads against a wall of darkness. Yes, they came up against a wall, just like us. Let's not stay on the Mountain, they said. They huddled together helplessly, just like us . . .'

The villagers waited, all ears, wondering what he was trying to say. The women in the crowd, with all the talk of the Enchanted Mountain, began to giggle. Old Osman rambled on, unable to

68

come to the point. The Mountain, he said, the darkness you couldn't cut with a sword, the darkness like a heavy weight on our shoulders . . . Just like us . . . It was impossible to make head or tail of what he was saying. He was getting tired.

'Well,' he concluded, 'the darkness was suddenly rent by a blaze of light and the travellers were able to find their way again. They managed to pass over the wall of darkness. Our darkness too has been rent by a blaze of light.'

He paused for breath:

'That's all I have to say. I'm not going to humble myself before Ali Safa Bey. I've told you why. You can go if you want to, I'm not going. Because into our darkness . . .' he licked his lips – 'into our darkness has come a blaze of light. Our night has been turned into day.'

Sefché the Warden leant towards Hüsam, and whispered into his ear,

'Hüsam, my boy, that father of yours must be in his dotage. What's he saying, do you understand?'

'I didn't understand anything, Uncle,' said Hüsam. 'It's obvious that something's happened to Father. He has got a lot older, poor thing.'

The villagers, not knowing what to do, began to move away in ones and twos.

Old Osman said finally,

'You can go and tell that thug of a Bey that I'm not going to talk to him. And if he attacks us again, he'll see. Go and tell him just that.'

He went inside and quickly shutting the door behind him, rushed up to Memed.

'Did you hear what I said, my son?' he asked.

'I did, Osman Agha.'

'I spoke well, didn't I?'

'Very well,' said Memed.

'Did they understand who was the light that will burst on the darkness?'

'Who knows, perhaps they understood,' said Memed with a sigh.

11

AT the sound of rifle fire, Old Osman jumped out of bed and rushed outside. The noise of firing passed like a sudden squall. From all sides of the village came the clattering of horses' hooves, the horses were madly careering round the village without a moment's pause. Another volley swept through the village, and immediately there was a reply. Five shots rang out from the inscribed marble stone just in front of Osman. As more bullets hit the ground at his feet, he jumped back three paces.

'Memed my boy, is that you?' he asked. And then, 'You frightened me,' he said.

Memed replied almost inaudibly:

'It's me, Uncle Osman.'

'Go inside at once. Don't come out again unless I tell you to. Don't worry. If they bombard the village, don't take any notice, promise me, my boy? It's not your turn yet.'

Memed stood up from behind the stone, and went inside. Old Osman whispered behind him,

'Get into the closet straight away. Get in and have a good sleep.'

Then he was overcome with pity for Memed. 'Poor thing, from morning to night in a closet the size of a hand. My house is a worse prison for him than a real prison. My hawk, Slim Memed, came to my house as a guest, but just look how badly I've treated him. When the wolf grows old he becomes the plaything of dogs. But you, Old Osman, you . . . you're not even that, you're a dog yourself, a miserable dog. For heaven's sake, a fine welcome you've given Slim Memed, your mountain eagle, your hawk; a fine way you've treated your guest, for goodness' sake,' he thought to himself. 'If it had been twenty years ago, would you have treated your boy, your hawk in this way? Wolves . . . dog . . . for heaven's sake.'

He brushed the tears from his eyes. The horses were still galloping madly round the village, and at short intervals volleys were fired over the houses. In the darkness of the night a fine drizzle was falling.

He went inside. Kamer was squatting beside the fire, bent double.

'Is there anything wrong, Mother, that you are all huddled up?'

'What is it, Osman. What's happening to us?'

'Ali wants to frighten the villagers, of course! That's an old custom.'

'What are the villagers doing?'

'Sleeping. There isn't a sound to be heard.'

Old Osman dressed, sat down by the fire, and loaded both barrels of his gun.

'Mother Kamer!' he said, assuming a bold manner. 'I've loaded both barrels of my gun with dum-dum bullets. Whoever they hit, by God they'll come in one way and go out the other! Woe to the man who comes up against me! Woe to him, Mother Kamer. Look, my hand doesn't tremble, it's just like old times . . .'

He stretched out his right hand with the gun in it, closed one eye and took aim, and the hand did not waver. The noise of firing came from very near, behind the hut.

'They've entered the village,' exclaimed Osman, and rushed outside.

Outside in the darkness excited horses were streaming through the village. If for a moment the sound of horses' hooves ceased, a volley of shots rang out. It was raining in big slow drops.

'It mustn't come from our yard,' thought Osman. 'If I bring down one of those thugs, the police will come and search our house. You'd upset the applecart, Osman, old man. We've treated our guest, Memed, badly enough by locking him in a closet. We can't hand him over to the police into the bargain.'

He left his own yard and went into his son's yard. 'If I shoot those dogs from here, they'll search our house as well as Hüsam's,' he thought, so he jumped over the wall into the yard belonging to Kurdish Kerem. The horses were galloping madly through the village streets. Osman squatted down behind a stone, pointed his gun towards the street, and waited. He felt a wave of confidence.

'If I hit one and bring him down, my hawk is going to be delighted. He'll understand that Uncle Osman hasn't become a cowardly dog as he has got older. A brave wolf is still brave even in old age. Now if only they'll pass this way,' he thought. 'I'll teach them to ride their horses through the village! I'll teach them to spray the village with bullets . . . !'

Bullets began to whistle over Kurdish Kerem's hut, and the sound of horses' hooves drew nearer.

'Curse them,' said Osman, grinding his teeth, 'they've gone along the other street.'

The sound of horses' hooves stopped for a while, the firing ceased, and the village sank into a deep silence. Osman listened attentively. Not the slightest sound, not a sign of life. 'They've all died, old man, they're all scared stiff. Tomorrow morning you won't find any of them. They'll be scrambling to leave the village. Our village of Vayvay, our home with its yellow narcissi and purple mint will be empty and deserted. There isn't a sound. They're scared stiff, my friend. If only they knew that Slim Memed is in the village, they would take heart, and would not listen to Ali Safa or anyone. If only they knew . . .' He smiled to himself. 'What happened to those thugs?' he said. 'I've got my fine clothes all wet. Let them come so we can get this business over quickly. Can they have left already? No, they wouldn't, never, not till morning.'

It was not long before firing burst over the village again. Horses neighed and the shadowy figures of galloping horsemen passed in front of Old Osman. The riders went so fast that Osman could not take aim at them. His hands and body shook. They'll come again, he said to himself, and what he expected soon happened. As the riders began to loom up in front of him, he rose to his feet and instantly pulled the trigger. There was a deafening report followed by a shrill cry of pain. Almost at once the horsemen galloped off and out of the village. For some time the screams of the rider whom Old Osman had hit could still be heard coming from somewhere in the direction of the marshes.

When Old Osman, rejoicing, went back to his house, he found Slim Memed there fully dressed, with all his equipment. He had even slung the field-glasses round his neck.

'Did you hear it, Memed?'

'Yes, more power to your elbow.'

72

'He bellowed like an ox. I wonder where I hit him.'

'In the knee-cap,' answered Memed. 'It hurts a lot in the knee-cap, it kills you. Chaps who bellow like that have usually stopped a bullet in the knee-cap or the shoulder.'

Old Osman looked Memed up and down.

'What, my son,' he said, 'you've dressed as if you were going on a journey!'

'Forgive me, Uncle,' said Memed apologetically. 'It's the way I'm made. If ever I hear the sound of firing I must be dressed and ready.'

Osman sighed and said, 'I'm tired, my son, I'm old. I realized that today. I almost missed the fellow. Almost . . . I should like to know who it was I hit. Who do you think, Memed?'

'Who was it?' wondered Memed. 'Can we know who it was? What a good thing if it had been Ali Safa.'

Old Osman drew near the fire. 'My goodness, how wet I am,' he grumbled. 'You see these clothes, my hawk? It's the first time they've seen rain in all these twenty-five years.'

Then he turned to Memed and said, 'Ali Safa wouldn't have come here, my boy. He sends his thugs to places like this. I'd like to know who I hit.'

He took off his clothes, and handed them to Kamer saying, 'Mother, see you hold these clothes to the fire so they get thoroughly dry.'

'Do you think they'll come again tonight?' asked Memed.

'Why do you ask?'

'Nothing,' said Memed. 'I was just asking.'

'They would certainly have gone on riding round the village till morning, but I stopped them and they won't come back tonight. That fellow is still bellowing, and maybe he'll go on shouting for a week. The year you shot Kalayji Ali Safa had the village shot up from night till morning. When you killed Kalayji it was a slap in the face for Ali Safa. That's how it is . . . To-morrow night Safa will send some men again to shoot up the village. When we oppose him, he thinks up a lot of dirty tricks to get the better of us. If we oppose him, and are not frightened, Safa will be daunted. But if we oppose him and are scared of him at the same time . . . I'll hit another one tomorrow.'

73

He clapped his hands with delight, like a child, and said, 'I'm old, and in the darkness they were only moving shadows, but I hit one. I hit one, my friend. Tomorrow I'll shoot another one. And the next day another. However many come, I'll polish one off every day. Until they're sick and tired of it. This time it was a knee-cap. Next time I'll put a bullet into their guts. Don't you agree, my boy? They've maddened me. These villagers are chicken-hearted. If half of them hadn't gone off to Dumlu Castle, all these things couldn't have happened to us. If they hadn't left the village empty ... If Yobazoghlu hadn't gone away, this wouldn't have happened to us. I must go and bring Yobazoghlu back, I must go and find the villagers who migrated to Dumlu. I must beg them to come back. Mustn't I?'

Memed was lost in thought; he only nodded.

Osman turned to Kamer who was holding up his breeches to dry before the fire, her face drawn with sleeplessness and anxiety.

'Mother,' he said, 'I'm very tired. Hand me that gun. And my powder-horn. And a few dry rags. I'm going to load my weapon once more, for there'll be work for it tomorrow night.'

Old Osman rammed the powder well into the gun.

There were no more whistling bullets, nor pounding hooves that night. He sat opposite Memed all night long, Osman talking, Memed listening.

12

OLD OSMAN went to Seyfali's house before daybreak. Seyfali was sitting on his haunches close to the fire, thinking. When he saw Osman he got up, and from the way he swayed on his feet one could tell he had had a sleepless night.

'Come in, Osman Agha,' he said gloomily. His voice was cracked and timid. 'You see they've begun to attack us again.'

Osman gave him a beaming smile, and said, 'What else do you

expect from Ali? To sit down and pray for us? If like women we hide in our houses and don't say a word, if half the villagers are terrified and leave for Dumlu or Yüregir, if Yobazoghlu, after riding the man's horse for a year, two years, and insulting him, gives up and runs away just because his house is burnt down and he's been beaten up a little, then of course Ali Safa will do this to us . . .'

'Sit down, Osman Agha, do sit down.'

Old Osman sat down on the cushions on the other side of the hearth. He was still smiling confidently.

'Don't worry, Headman,' he said, lighting his pipe with an ember from the fire. 'Don't worry. When the light blazed forth on the night of the Enchanted Mountain it poured forth on our night, too. Only Allah is free from the vicissitudes of Fate. From every peak a new day will dawn. There is only one God, but he has a thousand doors. The Prophet Hizir* doesn't come to help if you're not in dire straits. And he will come to us in the shape of a white dove. Don't worry, Seyfali, don't fret, every day comes to an end.'

Seyfali cast a doubtful look at Old Osman. Osman saw the look and was hurt. He emphasized every word. 'Every night has its dawn. My dear Headman, don't look at me like that,' he exclaimed at the top of his voice.

Seyfali, startled, said gently, 'You've got something up your sleeve, Uncle, everybody in the village is bursting with curiosity about it.'

Old Osman jumped to his feet as if impelled by a spring. 'Curse them,' he shouted, 'let them burst. I've got something up my sleeve; maybe I have and maybe I haven't. I grasped the hand of our Lord Hizir; maybe I did and maybe I didn't. Last night a gun went off, maybe it did and maybe it didn't. A rider bellowed like an ox, did you hear him. Maybe he did and maybe he didn't. That village looks like a thousand-year-old graveyard. Maybe it is and maybe it isn't. Tell us what to do. You're the Headman. Maybe you can and maybe you can't.'

* The Prophet Hizir is the equivalent of Elijah in Jewish and Christian texts. He is mentioned in the Koran and is a well-known figure of Turkish religious and folk lore. He is frequently invoked for help.

At that moment the Imam Ferhat came in. He was a tall, sunburnt, healthy man, with a long face and long eyelashes, who looked about thirty years old. Years ago he had come to Vayvay and settled there. He settled, and got married. He and his wife Eshé had two sons and two daughters. No one knew where he had come from, and a lot of rumours circulated about his origin.

When Seyfali saw Ferhat *Hodja** he got up: 'Come and sit down, Hodja,' he said.

When Old Osman saw the Hodja he softened a little and sat down, saying, 'Maybe I have and maybe I haven't,' once again.

As Ferhat Hodja sat down, he asked,

'Osman Agha, what is all this about maybe I have and maybe I haven't.'

Osman looked at the Hodja and said, 'Something about which my lips are sealed.'

'Then it's true,' said Ferhat, with a mixture of amazement and curiosity. 'For some days you have seemed a bit odd. You are keeping a secret.'

Old Osman straightened up from where he was sitting.

'Yes,' he said, 'I was asleep one night. I heard a voice in my sleep. "Old Osman, Old Osman", it said. I jumped up and opened the door. A white dove glided in. Its eyes were two drops of light. In an instant it had shed its plumage and I saw before me the Prophet Hizir himself. His white beard was bright with light. He took me by the hand. I was neither sleeping nor dreaming. Over the travellers in distress in the darkness of the Enchanted Mountain there came a blaze of light. You don't believe that, you don't believe in miracles, do you, Hodja?'

'No, I don't,' replied Ferhat Hodja.

'And in my secret?'

'I believe in that,' said Ferhat Hodja unhesitatingly.

'Oh, Hodja,' sighed Old Osman. 'If only I could tell you what is nearest my heart! Where were you all these days, for goodness' sake, Hodja? You'd disappeared again. Were you here last night?'

'Yes, I was.'

'What did you do?'

* *Hodja* is equivalent to priest.

76

'I didn't leave my bed.'

Old Osman was almost bursting. What stupid people they were. He was explaining and explaining, and even a quick-witted man like Ferhat didn't understand. 'The Prophet Hizir is in my house,' he had said. 'A blaze of light came into our darkness, our hopelessness,' he had said. 'I have something up my sleeve,' he had said, but they didn't understand at all. How could a fellow say it more openly? Straight out that Slim Memed arrived at our house one evening? How could he say that? Should he have said it? Should he have said it in order to put fresh heart into the villagers? Supposing he'd said it, and some scoundrel had gone and informed an agha or to the Government, what would have happened then? Wouldn't the Government and the aghas have thrown in all the soldiers, policemen and helpers they had? He pictured Memed being shot, his corpse curled up like a child. They would have pierced his handsome body, his warm heart, with a hundred bullets. He imagined them photographing Memed's body propped up against a wall, fully dressed and equipped. He pictured the crowd of villagers, weeping and sobbing, their necks bowed like oxen. He pictured the smiles of the aghas and beys. You couldn't entrust Memed's secret to anyone. But it was impossible not to tell someone. What about Ferhat Hodja, should he tell him and make him swear an oath on the Koran? He wasn't much like a hodja. He was a brave man, Ferhat Hodja, a man of standing and experience. One man, at least, must know . . . Yes, one man must know . . .

Old Osman got up, saying, 'Come outside with me for a moment, Hodja.' His tone was resolute.

Ferhat rose to his feet at once, and taking Osman's arm, led him outside.

'Hodja,' groaned Osman. 'The villagers will leave the village. They won't hold out.'

'I agree,' replied Ferhat. 'If they burn a few more houses, and have horsemen firing volleys over the village, no one will stay. One after the other . . . The ones who left have been cowardly. They did not find hearth or home where they went, they're eking out a miserable existence. Ali Safa is here, but isn't there an Ali Safa where they've gone to? There's an Ali Safa under every stone,

Osman Agha. Either the villagers oppose these Ali Safas, or they become slaves. Man is God's servant; His servant may not enslave others. A man who doesn't oppose injustice is against God. Tell me your secret.'

Old Osman did not reply at once. He was thinking. He was longing to tell, but he also felt an intense longing that such a secret should be his and his alone. They walked on and on until they were out of the village. They came to the juniper wood. They were walking very slowly, but Old Osman was panting in a fever of indecision. Ferhat could read in his face at each moment his changing moods. He had made up his mind to tell, Ferhat waited eagerly to hear what he was going to say. A moment later Osman's expression changed. Now he wasn't going to tell. This increased Ferhat's curiosity.

In the end Ferhat lost patience, and said, 'Don't tire yourself out, Osman, you aren't going to tell anyone the secret at present. You grudge anyone the knowledge of this secret. Don't wear yourself out. You are guarding it even from yourself.'

'Yes, I am guarding it, Hodja,' said Osman tearfully, and then he gazed into the Hodja's eyes, saying, 'Do you swear on the Koran not to tell anyone, Hodja?'

'I do,' replied Ferhat.

Old Osman was silent, and again gazed deep into Ferhat's eyes. He seemed to be in a trance.

'Forgive me, I've changed my mind, I won't tell you,' he said. 'Only I want you to know that the Lord Hizir is in our village. A blaze of light rained on our darkness, and there was a great miracle.' He again took the priest's arm, and the walked on. The effort of making up his mind had made Old Osman sweat and his whole body was damp. When they reached the village and Seyfali's house, day was breaking, and a slight summer haze was rising from the earth.

Seyfali was awaiting them at his door, and with him were Hüsam, Zeynel, Mother Kamer, and other villagers, with arms folded, and faces that gave evidence of a sleepless night.

Seyfali said, 'Now five or six of us will ride to the police post and make a complaint. First to the police and then to the District Governor. After that we will send a telegram to the Provincial

Governor. And after that we'll send one to Mustafa Kemal Pasha.'

Old Osman laughed hugely at this, holding his belly and coughing, 'Friend Seyfali,' he said, 'I knew you were naïve, but it never occurred to me that you could be so naïve. Friend Seyfali, if the judge insults your mother, who will you complain to?'

Ferhat Hodja frowned and said,

'Don't laugh, Osman Agha, if there were a judge who insulted our mothers, we should still have to complain to the judge about the judge. They attack a big village, they fire volleys of shots all night long, they burn down the houses. Let us make a complaint, even if they take no notice.'

'All right, let's make a complaint,' agreed Osman, with a smile. 'We'll see what the judge who insults our mothers will say, we'll see what verdict will come from the judge.'

Shortly afterwards, they mounted and rode off, Osman in front and Ferhat behind him, then Seyfali and three men from the Council of Elders, all making for the police post. This post was a long mudbrick building which stood at the edge of the road outside the village. Over it there waved a torn, drooping, faded flag.

They dismounted in front of the police post, tied their horses to the fence, did up their buttons, and went in. Corporal Dursun met them at the door, and Headman Seyfali, bowing, asked,

'Is the Sergeant inside?'

The Corporal changed colour and looked confused, as if not wanting to reply, but then he said,

'The Sergeant got shot last night. By bandits.'

Old Osman's eyebrows rose, and his eyes gleamed from beneath.

'Is it a bad wound?' he asked. 'Where did they hit him?' He sounded anxious to know.

'It was a dum-dum bullet, the kind used to hunt wild pigs. It blasted the Sergeant's knee-cap to pieces.'

Old Osman smiled and said, 'Where did the Sergeant encounter the bandits last night and get shot?'

The Corporal got very confused. He could not find an answer at first. Then he said,

'We got news last night that a gang of brigands had gone up to Anavarza. Captain Faruk drove them down into the plain, and that was how they wounded the Sergeant.' He sounded upset, and his voice shook.

Osman winked at Ferhat, and the latter said, 'Well, let's go to the town, to the Governor, and we'll send a wire to Ankara.' He was dark with rage.

'Something's happened?' asked the Corporal, unable to suppress a derisive look.

'Nothing's happened, boy. Thanks to you all is quiet with us. They fired a few shots at us last night, though. We thought the bullets were meant for us, but it seems it was the Sergeant clashing with the brigands . . . Good day to you.'

They left the police post, Osman in front, the others behind, and mounting their horses they turned towards the town.

'Hodja,' said Osman as they went along. 'Come close to me.' The two riders hung back a little.

'Well,' asked Osman, 'did you realize where the dum-dum bullet came from that shot the Sergeant's knee-cap to pieces and sent him off bellowing like an ox?'

'I did,' said Ferhat. 'More power to your elbow.'

'If we'd all done what I did last night instead of crouching like scared rabbits, do you think Ali Safa would ever dare raid the village again? He burnt down Yobazoghlu's house; if we had burnt down Ali Safa's the next night, what would have happened? Would he have dared to attack us again?'

'No, he wouldn't.'

'So why don't we hold out against him instead of leaving the village empty and deserted? Are we going to sit with our arms folded while they spray us with bullets every night? What do you say, Hodja?'

'A frightened man does not find favour with God,' said the Hodja. 'A frightened, shrinking man is the worst thing the Creator ever created. A frightened man will never get out of hell, he's a creature that will burn for all eternity. A coward is the lowest of God's creatures, a coward is a source of shame to mankind. I'm glad about the Sergeant, but how shall we explain it to the Governor? How shall we explain that it was the Sergeant who raided our village?'

'We can't explain it,' said Osman. 'We can't tell anyone that I shot the Sergeant, either. They'll raid us again tonight. And I'll hit one again tomorrow night.'

'Good. I hope so,' said Ferhat.

'The Lord Hizir told me,' said Osman, 'that in order to win this battle those who have left must come back. I'll go and see them again, and tell them to return to the village. I'll tell them the situation has changed.'

Ferhat Hodja gave a deep sigh.

'Aaah! Osman Agha,' he said. 'You won't be able to persuade them. They may live in misery, or die, but you won't be able to get them back. The Lord Hizir said the same to me, Osman Agha, aah . . .'

They reached the town. Taking Ali Safa Bey's enemy Halil Agha to precede them, they went into the District Government headquarters. They related how the village had been raided, and shot up all night long. The Governor said he would find a solution. They got Fethi Bey, a public scribe, to write out a telegram for them, which they despatched to Ankara.

The town was buzzing with the news. Everyone was talking about how Ali Safa Bey had sent his men to raid Vayvay, how Sergeant Remzi was one of the men, and how eighty-year-old Osman had hit the Sergeant in the knee-cap, firing an old pistol in the dark.

Sergeant Remzi had been transported to the Military Hospital at Adana that very day.

As they passed through the market place, Old Osman at the head, the others behind, the grocers, drapers, coppersmiths, shoemakers and ironsmiths came out of their shops and looked at Osman in amazement. Women and children also came out into the street to look at him. Osman kept his head bent until he got out of the town. He felt shrunken and crushed by the gaze of hundreds of eyes. He was embarrassed by the town that day.

13

ADEM was a very short man, with a round, unsmiling face. He had a short neck, and three-cornered eyes. His thin lips were always tightly closed. His arms, legs, hands, fingers, and trunk, everything about him was short and stumpy. His tawny, yellow-streaked hair bristled like the spines of a hedgehog.

With the handsome German carbine he possessed, Adem could stay for days sitting in a hide, without moving and without eating. He never missed his mark.

He had gone into Ali Safa's service six years ago. Before that he used to shoot hares, partridges, francolins, bustards, or cranes, and bring them to the aghas or beys of Anavarza plain, and in this way he used to eke out a living. He was out on the plain the whole twelve months of the year, winter or summer, rain or shine, night or day. Sometimes he would shoot a rare bird and this he would bring to Ali Safa, and although Ali Safa was a mean man, he was pleased and would reward Adem. One day Adem came with some rare birds, which were blue, shot with green. Their beaks and legs were long and thin. Ali Safa Bey had never seen such birds before. He was delighted. 'It's a pity you couldn't catch a live one,' he said.

The sun was setting. Adem slung his rifle on his shoulder and went off to Ahjasaz. In the morning he had one of the long-legged birds in his arms. It lay there as tranquilly as if in its nest. There were markings on its head, and it had red eyes. After this, Adem stayed at Ali Safa's farm. Adem did not say to Ali Safa Bey, 'I would like to stay on this farm, may I do so?' in so many words, nor did Ali Safa Bey say, 'You are needed here, stay.' Adem settled down, as if he had been born and grown up there. There was a small empty hut behind the main farmhouse, which he appropriated. A few months later he brought a woman to live with him, a woman exactly like him, short and stumpy, silent, with large clear blue-grey eyes which looked at you as if she were moving in a dream. Adem was very fond of her.

After this Adem became the Bey's most trusted henchman. Whether it was terrorizing people, raiding villages, taking messages to brigands, brigandage itself, or any other difficult jobs, the Bey would always send Adem. Adem repaid this confidence, for whatever job he took on, he came out of the affair creditably. In a short time Adem the Hunter had become the scourge of the villages in the Anavarza plain. The village that had had most to put up with from Adem was Vayvay. They were frightened and weary.

Adem was upset and angry, after chasing the brown horse for days and never even getting close enough to fire. It was as if this horse had a thousand eyes and ears. From a long way off he could pick out the slightest movement or shadow, hear even the faintest sound.

For some time now Adem had been hiding in this clump of reeds hoping that the brown horse would pass near by. But there was still no sign of him. Adem was experienced and patient. He could have waited five days, a week, ten days, without moving from this place. But this horse shook him out of his usual composure. Twice he had come across him on the plain, and each time before he had had time to raise his gun, the horse had disappeared. What had become of the stallion? Where had he gone? Adem had begun to think there was something strange about a horse that could vanish like that, in the twinkling of an eye! It wasn't normal. Adem began to feel afraid.

Towards midnight he heard the clatter of hooves. He came out from the reeds. Far off, the shadowy shape of a horse was galloping swiftly uphill towards Topraktepe. He went back into the reeds. He hadn't slept for nights, and as soon as his head touched the roots, he fell asleep.

When he awoke, it was daybreak. Over Ahjasaz floated a haze, half mist, half cloud. Anavarza was almost completely hidden; only its vague outline could be discerned. He came out of the reeds and stopped short, hardly able to believe his eyes. There was the horse, standing motionless on a mound, only a short distance away, now vanishing, now visible again, as the thick mist eddied around him. Adem's heart was in his mouth; for the first time the

83

horse had come within shooting range. Quickly he raised his gun, took aim, and pressed the trigger. For a moment everything disappeared in the mist. Adem ran to the mound where the horse had stood. He expected to see him kicking and struggling on the ground. He thought how he would cut the head off and take it straight to Ali Safa Bey, saying, 'Bey, may the same fate overtake your enemies, the village of Vayvay.' And how the Bey would reward him with whatever he wished. He would ask the Bey for fifteen dunums of land. Would he give so much? But when he reached the mound, what did he see? The horse was already a long way off, galloping up a gully towards the Anavarza crags. He was going so fast that his belly seemed almost level with the ground. Adem stood still watching the horse as he went up the gully as if on wings. The mist was slowly lifting. He followed the horse with his eyes until he was a small black spot at the foot of Anavarza. Then he sank to the ground, clenching his teeth with rage. Then he became frightened. There's something strange about this horse he said to himself. Could it be that a fairy, a djinn, or some good spirit had taken on the shape of this horse? To miss at that distance! Impossible! There was only one way to kill this stallion. He must go and ask the Bey for a fast horse and pursue him.

Adem's feet were swollen. The thorn-bushes had torn his shalvar-trousers which hung in tatters below the knees. His face and hands too were scratched by the thorns. He made his way to the farm reluctantly. The Bey had just risen and was in the upper gallery, washing his face and hands with water that a young girl was pouring from a ewer. Adem stood stiffly down in the yard waiting for the Bey to notice him. But Ali Safa Bey did not see him. After drying himself thoroughly on a towel he went into the living-room. Adem went up the steps and stood waiting on the landing. The Bey had sat down to breakfast with some other people at a long table. Suddenly he saw Adem on the landing.

'What's that?' he called. 'Come on in, Adem.'

Adem walked up to the table. He could not look the Bey in the face. Ali Safa realized that he had not shot the stallion. He turned to the others and said:

'This is the champion huntsman, Adem, I mentioned to you. Nothing escapes him, on the ground or on the wing. But I see

84

now from his face that this time our champion huntsman has missed his mark. How could this happen, Adem? Tell me!'

Adem raised his head. His eyes were swimming with tears, at a touch they would have brimmed over. His voice shook.

'That horse has a thousand eyes and ears. He becomes wind and flies through the air. He turns into a bird and takes wing. I could only approach him once, and that because he came by himself. I fired. I thought I'd hit him. I looked, and there he was far away, going towards Anavarza. That horse is not a horse, Bey.'

Ali Safa Bey sighed.

'He is a horse, Adem, he is indeed. He is a horse, but cleverer than men.'

'If he is a horse, if he is not a fairy or a djinn in the shape of a horse, if he is not a thing of magic, then I will kill him, Bey.'

Ali Safa smiled, as did the others at the table.

'That horse has been too much for you, Adem,' he said. 'What's the matter with you?'

'Bullets can't touch him, Bey.'

'It's a very fast stallion. It's not easy to hit such fast horses, Adem.'

Adem bowed his head.

'Let me have a horse, Bey. Maybe I'll catch him that way . . .'

'Go to the stable and choose one. But I have no hope Adem, that you'll catch that horse with any other horse. Anyway go ahead.'

Adem went out sheepishly and made his way home, overcome both by the Bey's kindness and by the undertone of mockery in the Bey's voice.

There was a large white horse in the stable. He'd take that one to pursue this accursed brown stallion. But the fear in him was growing fast. In all his life that horse was the only living creature he had taken aim at and missed. That night sleep would not come to him. His wife never asked him questions. They did not talk.

14

FERHAT HODJA'S black, curly beard trembled. There was an expression of deep anxiety in his tawny eyes. His long, sunburnt, handsome face lengthened still further. Old Osman's wrinkled face was also full of sorrow.

Yobazoghlu Hassan had found shelter in a deserted hut with a dilapidated reed-thatched roof and sagging walls, on the outskirts of Narlikishla village. Inside there was nothing but a pinewood jar, a single pallet, a couple of copper dishes and a saucepan. His three children lay sick and moaning on a rush mat in the corner. Yobazoghlu was shrunken and wasted and the wounds on his face and hands were still festering. Yet he still laughed and joked, and made as if nothing was wrong. But his wife had an air of mourning about her.

Old Osman felt a lump in his throat:

'Hassan, my child,' he began in his quavering voice. 'We've come to you, Ferhat Hodja and I, to put an end to this misery of yours away from home. You'll die of hunger if you stay here. Whether a man lives or dies it should be among his own kin. We've come to take you back. We'll hire a cart and put your family on it and go back home.'

His head bent, Hassan never gave them a glance. It was impossible to tell what he was thinking. His face was quite expressionless.

Ferhat Hodja tackled him next. He talked and ended by saying, 'So now you're coming back with us, Hassan.'

When Hassan raised his head his face had changed beyond recognition and his eyes were full of tears. He looked like a helpless child.

'I can't go to that village,' he said.

'Don't be afraid of the Sergeant,' said Osman. 'Somebody in our village put a dum-dum bullet through him as thick as my finger, and with a two-hundred-year-old pistol too! Now he's lying on his back in Adana Hospital bellowing like an ox. You know, friend Hassan, only when a knee-cap is shattered by a dum-dum bullet do they bellow like that. And we sent a telegram, a fine telegram, to Mustafa Kemal Pasha. Now here is God's own man to tell you. Tell him, Ferhat Hodja, for God's sake, what was in the telegram. Tell him about Fethi Bey the scribe, that learned man, that son of the brave Kozan tribe, tell how he wrote a telegram for us fit to melt a heart of stone. Did you save the fatherland for this, he wrote, so that policemen, sergeants and petty feudal lords should come and raid our village every night? Isn't it shameful, he wrote, for the Government to back those aghas who attack us like this? Oh he wrote, and wrote well, this Fethi Bey. So you see Hassan, you must come back now. You're the son of a Kurd. Your father was a brave man. You belong to the Kizilbash sect as well, and the Kizilbash don't know the meaning of fear. They're like eagles on the high mountains. They sing stirring songs that leave you breathless . . .'

Old Osman talked on till he was hoarse. He told the story of Mount Kaf, how the despairing travellers had come up against a wall of darkness, and how a light had rent the darkness like a sword.

'What do you say to that, Hassan?' he asked. He was sweating; he opened his shirt, and passed his hand over the long white hairs. His fingers came away with the sour smell of sweat. 'Will the Lord God who brought Joseph out of the well, refuse to look after us, do you think?'

'The Lord God who brought Joseph out of the well never abandons his faithful servants in difficult straits,' Ferhat Hodja emphasized. 'If we are summoning you to the village, it is because we know something. You heard what Osman Agha said about Mount Kaf and the lost travellers. I'll tell you about three other people who got lost in the desert and were dying of thirst. The sun was relentless and the three of them were wandering about with their tongues hanging out of their mouths. Quite near them was a green oasis with a well of ice-cold water. Yet they could not see it. Then they saw a white bird in the air. One of the travellers was a wise man like Old Osman. "Let's follow that bird," he said. "That bird is looking for water too. See the beat of its wings? It is also suffering from burning thirst." So they followed the bird and came to the green oasis and found the well. They drank and their lives were saved. Now listen, Old Osman has seen this white bird and he tells you it will lead us to water. What do you say, Hassan? Are you coming back to the village or not?'

Old Osman was pleased. 'That's a good parable, Hodja,' he said. 'Do you see, Hassan? That white bird is flying to the spring from which comes the water of life. Come back to the village.'

But Yobazoghlu was not to be persuaded. At last, with heavy hearts they left the tumbledown hut and rode off side by side without talking.

They spent the night at the village of Hadjilar. At daybreak they set out towards Dumlu Castle.

'Is anything wrong?' asked Ferhat Hodja. 'Why are you so silent, Osman Agha?'

'I'm silent, but I am thinking; do you know anything about my white bird? Have you seen it?'

'I didn't see it, Osman Agha. But you have hope and I trust you. And if you have hope, it means you know something.'

'Yes, Hodja. I know.'

He was burning to tell Ferhat Hodja. His expression brightened and became sombre by turns. At last he said.

'A white bird, but what a white bird, Ferhat Hodja! Aah it's well worth seeing! A white bird that's really a white hawk, Ferhat Hodja.'

As soon as he'd said this he was sorry. At the word hawk Ferhat was sure to guess everything.

But Ferhat seemed abstracted. 'Well worth seeing,' he murmured.

The next day they reached Saricham, where the villagers who had run away from Vayvay had settled in a deserted stone quarry. There they had built a few ramshackle mudbrick and reed huts. Some had found only old goat's hair tents to shelter under. Their clothes were in rags; they were all thinner, mere skin and bone. Almost all the children had caught malaria.

At this sight Old Osman was moved to tears.

'I heard about the terrible state you're in. My heart bled for you and I asked Ferhat Hodja to come with me so that we should take you back to our village.' No one said a word at first, then Abdur-rahman spoke.

'How can we go home? With our houses burnt down, our fields ploughed up, our daughters kidnapped, our animals slaughtered and our people killed . . . ? How can we live there again? Is Ali Safa dead, or has he suddenly become a friend? Has the Government come over to our side? Has Slim Memed appeared again? What has changed that you should tell us to go back?'

At the mention of Slim Memed a fresh hope stirred Osman, but alas how could he speak out! His eyes met Ferhat's. They exchanged a meaningful look. Should he tell?

He began to speak. He talked on and on, begging, threatening, wheedling. He told the story of the light that pierced the wall of darkness, he went over everything again and again and ended up with the wonderful tale of the white bird.

After him the Hodja began to argue with them. His voice, trained to chant the *Mevlut* prayer, moved the people to tears. He quoted verses from the Koran in Arabic and then explained them in Turkish to prove to the villagers that they should return to their lands.

They kept on all day but the villagers would not change their minds. By evening Old Osman was shaking with rage. He refused the meal they offered him and sprang to his feet.

'A curse on people like you!' he shouted. His face was as white as paper. Ferhat Hodja calmed him down and helped him on to his horse. Then he mounted himself and before riding off he spoke to the stunned villagers. His voice was deep and calm, emphasizing every word:

'You have incurred God's wrath. And now I tell you He will punish you. Stay here then, on these barren stones. Stay till you rot. You have ruined Vayvay.'

The peasants were struck dumb. They remained there rooted to the spot.

The moon had not yet risen, and they rode on through the darkness, in silence, side by side, until late in the night.

Old Osman was wondering whether Ferhat Hodja had guessed about Slim Memed or not. Should he tell him? Ferhat Hodja would never betray them. The next minute he had changed his mind. The son of man has sucked raw milk, he would tell himself. You can't trust anyone. In the end he could bear it no longer:

'Slim Memed . . .' he said, and stopped.

'What about Slim Memed?' asked Ferhat quickly. Osman hesitated.

'Ferhat Hodja . . .' he said, and stopped again. After all where had this priest come from? Who was he? He had married at Vayvay, and had chosen the daughter of one of Osman's relations, but who was he? Could he be trusted?

'Ferhat Hodja!'

'Yes, Osman Agha?'

'Ferhat Hodja, if Slim Memed were alive now . . .'

'What makes you think he's dead, Osman Agha?'

'I mean suppose Slim Memed were back in the mountains, would he have helped us, d'you think?'

'He would,' answered Ferhat Hodja with great conviction. 'He was a brave, good, honourable boy.'

'Wouldn't he be the light that pierced the darkness, Ferhat Hodja?'

'Yes, he would,' said Ferhat Hodja.

'Like the white bird?'

'Men like him are all white birds. And as sure as he killed Kalayji, so he would seal Ali Safa's fate.'

'If only he would come again,' said Old Osman. 'And deal with Ali Safa in such a way that he would never straighten his back again . . .'

15

THEY had given the house that was to have been his to Maid Seyran after her misfortune – a misfortune one would not wish upon one's worst enemy. Memed was curious about that house. He was longing to see it. The Vayvay villagers had set aside some land for him, but now Ali Safa had seized it. What sort of man was this Ali Safa? What did he want, what would he do with so much land? Did he want to found his own kingdom in the plain of Anavarza? Old Osman had told him that on top of the Anavarza crags there still stood the ruins of a citadel built by Armenian kings, who had ruled the whole of Chukurova in those days. Perhaps Ali Safa Bey wanted to do just that.

Ali Safa was ruthless, cruel, inhuman, but he had the Government behind him. Old Osman had made Memed sit by his side, and for three days and nights he had told him all about the aghas and beys of Chukurova. It is true that Memed knew a great deal about them already, but Osman explained events to him in even greater detail. Now he could see everything clearly. As time went on, his indignation against the aghas increased. Every one of them was worse than Abdi Agha. Especially Ali Safa Bey ... The mere mention of his name made one shudder. And the whole bunch were enemies of his, Memed's. The man who had taken Abdi Agha under his wing was Ali Safa Bey. However much the aghas and beys might hate one another, they stuck together against him. The death of Abdi Agha had infuriated them. On that account they had formed bands, and had searched the Taurus Mountains hole by hole and village by village. If he had not got clean away they would certainly have killed him. The thousands of peasants and hundreds of policemen combing the mountains never bothered about Big Memed, Hadji Duran and other bandits. The one they were looking for, the one they were furious at not finding, was himself. Wherever he went they would find him and kill him. It wasn't Abdi Agha he had killed, it was them. What was killed in the person of Abdi Agha was the aghas themselves. For this reason they would never pardon Memed.

Since Ali Safa Bey had treated these villagers so cruelly, why had nobody come forward and shut his mouth with a bullet? Everybody was cowed. Today many of the villagers of Chukurova, perhaps half, had left their homes on account of his cruelty. They were constantly wandering about the plain, looking for a place to settle. The village of Vayvay was half-deserted. They were so terrified of Ali Safa that one morning you might wake up to find nobody in the village. Old Osman did not know what he should do to hold them back; he was in a fluster about it. Osman had told him that there was a man called Idris Bey at a village called Akmezar, and that he was in a pitiable state. The man who held this Idris Bey in a stranglehold was a close friend of Mustafa Kemal Pasha, called Arif Saim Bey. This man had a motor-car, and he was in the habit of driving over the dusty tracks of the Chukurova in his motor-car. Memed had never seen a motor-car, and was longing to see one. In the whole of the great Chukurova plain, only one man had a motor-car, and that was Arif Saim Bey. Both the villagers and the aghas, including Ali Safa, were terribly afraid of Arif Saim Bey.

Memed was sitting in the corner of the dark hut, his rifle on his knee, thinking these disconnected thoughts. From the edge of the closed wooden shutter came a long sunbeam, which stretched to the earth floor of the hut. Thousands of particles of dust were dancing in the sunbeam. Memed stretched his right hand into the path of the sunbeam, and his hand seemed to grow larger and stronger in the light. Memed was in a strange mood. The cowed and hopeless attitude of the villagers had gradually affected him, too. Like the villagers he had come up against a wall of darkness and was battering his head against it.

He had seen Ferhat Hodja twice through the crack in the door. He didn't look like a hodja at all. With his curly black beard, his big tawny eyes, his curly hair and his aquiline nose, he looked like a man you could trust. According to Old Osman, he had come into the village from the direction of Anavarza one day of Ramadan, weary, carrying a bundle on his back; in the bundle were books and linen; that very evening he made an empty house into a mosque, he held a Ramadan service for the villagers, and he had stayed as the hodja of the village, ever since. He scarcely ever spoke about religion. He conducted the prayers for the villagers and then went about his business. He married a girl from Vayvay village who had a little land. He took no tithes for his work as priest, and sowed and reaped his own fields.

At first the villagers were a little wary and shrank from him, but gradually they got used to him, and now considered him as one of themselves. But there was still something supernatural about him in their eyes, and most people credited him with having magic powers . . . Old Osman trusted and loved him, but also respected and feared him. The aghas of Chukurova heard that a hodja like this had come to Vayvay, and at first they were very curious about him; then they too got used to him, heard he was harmless, and forgot all about him. But news spread through the Chukurova about the handsome hodja and the women gossiped about him. Young girls and women came to see him from far-away villages, from Adana, Kozan, Tarsus, and even Mersin and Alexandretta, with the pretext of getting him to make out a charm for them. Ferhat would accept no money for writing out those charms, and his reputation gradually spread throughout the whole of the Chukurova district.

Memed felt a hundred conflicting emotions within himself. Sitting in the darkness of the hut, he turned things over and over in his mind.

Would this village be his last resting-place? If he were shot, where would the shot come from? What kind of death would be his? And if death was like darkness, what sort of darkness was it? Was it like sleep? Would the death-wound be very painful?

Sometimes he was frightened to death; he felt death, emptiness, right to the bottom of his heart, he trembled, a deathly shudder went over him from head to foot. He had condemned himself to death a long time ago, and yet he could not imagine how death would come. One thing he knew; he would not be captured, he would not fall into the hands of the police, he would not go to prison, he would not be brought to trial. Hatché had told him about policemen, prison and the trial, and when she related it to him, 'Death is preferable by far, Memed,' she had said.

At times Memed was shaken by a wave of anger, and would shout to himself: 'I will die fighting.' Within him there was an unquenchable desire for vengeance. Abdi Agha had not fulfilled this. This feeling for vengeance did not settle at any one point. His anger was directed at the Sergeant of Police, at the Sergeant who had beaten up Yobazoghlu ... At the Government, at Ali Safa, at Arif Saim Bey ... His vengeance hovered from one to another.

Sometimes Memed would fight with Ali Safa, whom he had never seen or met, he would kill him, bring his head to Vayvay, and withdraw to the mountains. Old Osman would then embrace him tearfully, saying, 'My hawk, you have saved us, you have given life to the villagers.' And the people of Akmezar, too, would celebrate with a great feast after Arif Saim Bey's death! Only thinking of these things – firing, killing, and cutting off heads – threw Memed into a cold sweat.

Then at times he would beat his head against a wall of hopelessness. He couldn't expect Old Osman to hold his tongue much longer. Ever since Memed's arrival the old man's behaviour had been such that everyone in the village suspected something. One day Osman would burst and tell the great secret to everyone at the top of his voice. And the next thing they knew the aghas, the beys and the Government would be informed. He had been here quite a while. A long time. He must not stay here any longer.

He got up, went to the door, and looked out through a crack. Behind a hen, fifteen or twenty chickens, yellow balls of fluff, were rolling in the dust of the yard. In the lane across the yard a young girl was passing; she was short, broad in the hips, and her hair, done in tiny plaits, was spread out over her shoulders. A dog, its tail between its legs, was slinking along the foot of the wall. The memory of Koroghlu came to Memed. After thinking of the legendary outlaw, he thought of his mother and Hatché. And Mother Hürü, what a brave woman she was! If there had been a Mother Hürü in every village in the Chukurova, Ali Safa and Arif Saim Bey would have had their deserts. Then there was old, stout-hearted Durmush Ali ... Then there was Lame Ali, resourceful, faithful Lame Ali ... Sergeant Rejep, Jabbar ... Jabbar had forgotten his days as a brigand and had settled down in a village, planting lots of maize. He was married, with two children.

Hatché, his mother, Abdi Agha, the mountains, the cave, Kalayji, all flashed through his head in disconnected images, sometimes bright and clear, sometimes dark and blurred, a world of dreams, painful, sweet, magical, harsh as stone ... Now he was happy, now he was plunged in deepest gloom. The heady, warm scent of the acacia tree floated towards him at the door. Thousands of bees, intoxicated by the strong scent, swarmed over its flowers. He recalled the tall, wind-racked plane-tree ... And then crimson anemones, that somehow had sprouted. They were in the middle

94

of a red rock, like a flame seen burning from afar. For a while their brilliant crimson swam dazzlingly before his eyes. Then he saw his village clearly, down to its smallest stone, its brook, its huts, the children, the flowers and bees, the mountains, rocks and birds. An unbearable longing gripped his heart. Anyway, I shall soon be killed, he thought, so let me see my village once again with my earthly eyes.

The police and peasants held all the roads to the mountains. They were sweeping across the Taurus like myriads of ants, hunting for brigands from one hole to another, from one cave to another. Wouldn't some village or other up there speak out and betray him? But here too they might speak, he thought. Anywhere. The brigand is betrayed by a bird in flight, by the stone under his feet. Sooner or later the life of the brigand ends with a bullet. But it must be a good, pleasant, manly, honourable death when it comes . . . 'As soon as Old Osman returns I shall ask his leave to go on my way.'

While he was talking to himself and meditating, Mother Kamer came running back to the house. She put the key into the lock and turning it twice opened the door. She saw Memed standing close by the door.

'What is it, my boy?' she asked. 'What were you doing here?'

'I was looking out, Mother,' replied Memed. 'I was feeling depressed.'

Mother Kamer bent towards him, and said gently. 'The villagers know. They guess that there is something going on, but it hasn't occurred to them that you might be here. Everybody's eyes are on our house. Oh, that childish Osman of mine, he drew everyone's attention to our house. Our children are all pressing us to tell them what is going on, what their father has got up his sleeve. I tried to put them off the track but they wouldn't believe me. I'm sure they'll search the house today. Or they'll keep a watch on it. You mustn't come out of the closet until Osman comes back, promise me.'

'I promise,' said Memed, but his heart misgave him. If it came to a skirmish on this flat plain of Chukurova what would he do? It could only end in death. He had to wait until nightfall, and then slip away. There was nothing else for it. How long would it be till nightfall? He looked at the light through the cracks in the door. The sun was setting. It won't be long, he said to himself thankfully. He would go but he was full of regret. How could he go without bidding goodbye, without asking forgiveness of someone who loved him so deeply? Old Osman loved him as much as his own mother had loved him, as much as Hatché . . .

16

ALI SAFA BEY, furiously angry, was walking up and down his hall, muttering to himself.

'My plan isn't working,' he moaned. 'How much longer is this struggle going to last? The fields are lying fallow. Those good-for-nothing peasants will neither work their land nor leave it to us.'

Zeynel was sitting huddled up on a couch at the other end of the hall. His expression changed according to whether Ali Safa Bey's indignation waxed or waned. He portrayed distress, rejoicing, or hopelessness by turns.

Ali Safa Bey stopped before him suddenly.

'Well?' he said mockingly. 'Well, Zeynel? So Vayvay village was to migrate this summer? You know everything! How well you understand things! Not only has no one moved but Old Osman and Ferhat Hodja rushed off to Yobazoghlu to bring him back to Vayvay! Then they went to Saricham, and begged and pleaded, trying to get the people there to return. You said that there'd be nobody left in the village by this summer. But instead . . . What's happened, Zeynel?'

'Really, Bey, I don't know. I've been trying to puzzle it out, but I can't find an answer. After Yobazoghlu's house was burnt down, and the village had been showered with bullets night after night, I never expected the villagers to stay, but what happened? I don't understand it, Bey. First, Old Osman stood up in the middle of the village. Then Ferhat Hodja . . . Everything changed all of a sudden. Those frightened desperate villagers came to life

96

again. Something's happened Bey, but I swear I don't know what . . .'

'Surely that snivelling Governor, or the Captain or any other Government chap isn't inciting them against me? No, that's impossible. They're all my men, all under my orders. Could it be that Arif Saim Bey . . . Surely it isn't him! If it is, I'm done for. If Arif Saim Bey's got his eye on the land here . . . Can he be stirring up the Vayvay people against me?'

'I thought of Arif Saim Bey and made a lot of enquiries. He spoke to Old Osman once ten years ago. But he's never met or talked to anyone else from the village since then.'

'What about Ferhat Hodja?'

'No.'

'What's the matter with this Ferhat? He's always minded his own business up to now.'

'They say he's very angry. Angry about the horse, about the village being shot up every evening, about what happened to Yobazoghlu . . . At the sight of the horse wandering about the country, tears fell from his eyes like rain. They say it was Old Osman who shot the Sergeant. If it is, then he's certainly changed! He wouldn't have put his head out of his door during the firing, much less have shot the Sergeant!'

'In my opinion Old Osman's at the bottom of all this. Arif Saim Bey wouldn't be so petty. He doesn't need the Vayvay lands and he's fond of me. If he wanted the Vayvay property, he'd tell me . . . No, no. I can't think of anybody. Perhaps it is Ferhat Hodja who is stiffening their resistance.'

'Perhaps, but I couldn't find out. I know that the opposition first came from Old Osman.'

He related at length how one day Old Osman in his best clothes, his pipe in his mouth, had strutted through the village smiling, without saying a word to anyone, how he had smoked his pipe and laughed when Yobazoghlu's house was burnt down. He told the whole story down to the smallest detail.

Ali Safa Bey sank on to the divan.

'I don't understand this man Osman at all,' he said.

'He's a very courageous man,' replied Zeynel. 'And shrewd too. He's survived fifteen wars and bears the scars all over his body . . .

He can be very meek and mild, and then suddenly so angry, you can't get near him. I simply can't understand the man at all.'

Ali Safa Bey put his hand to his chin, and scratched his chin and neck.

'I've seen many wars too, but I never interfered with anybody's rights like this old scoundrel. I never occupied anybody's land, I never endangered the future of the nation like this senile old man. I didn't shoot sergeants in the national police force. I'll make him pay for it, the old dog! And that fellow as well, be he hodja, imam or bandit. I'll trample on them, Zeynel. I'll prey on them. I'll persecute them till they're worn out, sick of it, till I've made Vayvay a hell on earth. Either they hand me over my land, or I make it a hell on earth for them. Now let's see, where shall we start, Zeynel?'

'I have an idea, Agha,' said Zeynel. 'Let's go to Yaghmur Agha, and have him steal all the horses in the village.'

'A good idea,' said Ali Safa Bey, delighted. 'And I'll give Yaghmur Agha one lira for every horse that's stolen. Besides, my men will help them. You can help too, Zeynel.'

'Very well, Bey.'

'The horses will be a beginning. Either they'll come to their knees, those villagers, and cry for mercy, and pack up and go, or . . . Or they'll see. They'll have their fill of calamities.'

Zeynel closed his eyes and licked his lips with pleasure.

'Calamities,' he echoed.

'I'll go and see Yaghmur Agha tonight. You go to Mehedinli village, and to Chikchiklar . . . Tell my relatives to raid the village again tonight. Like that people won't know it was the Sergeant those other times.'

'I'll go now, Bey,' said Zeynel, and descending the steps, he mounted his horse and rode off.

Ali Safa Bey was thinking. If Arif Saim Bey was backing the opposition against him, if he had his eye on the land, it would be hard to stand up to him. He was well acquainted with the man. Arif Saim, a Kurd from Bingöl, had been Superintendent of Police in the District. He was a reckless, bold, ambitious person, a dare-devil. When the French occupied Adana, he had played a double role with the French and the Nationalist Forces. He was very intelligent. Nowadays the Government in Ankara was Arif Saim Bey. He was Mustafa Kemal's closest comrade and his favourite Member of Parliament. Ali Safa hoped to God it wasn't Arif Saim Bey who had stirred up Old Osman. Anyone else he could deal with, but Arif Saim Bey . . . Yet Arif Saim Bey would never incite the villagers secretly. What he would do would be to send a message to Ali Safa, saying, don't meddle with the villagers or meddle with them at your peril. What about the District Governor? He was a poor-spirited man, but he was cunning; and might well be a man given to secret intrigues. He must get rid of this Governor quickly, and find someone more reliable. The Captain of Police . . . He always minded his own business. He didn't understand anything, and went about the world in a dream, poor chap . . . He could stay. They'd be lucky to get anyone better.

Gradually his satisfaction increased. He pictured the people of Vayvay waking up one morning to find not a single horse left in the village. Only their donkeys would be left them. On the whole of Anavarza plain just one horse would be seen, the dark-brown horse . . . Had Adem managed to shoot it? When he thought of the brown horse, it pained him. Then there would be other games, other tricks . . . until they came and said, 'We did you wrong, Bey. But don't punish us. These fields are yours. We did you harm. Please give us two days' grace and we will put our things together and go.'

All the Vayvay villagers, young and old, would crowd around the gate of his mansion and he would look down on them from the balcony, and say, 'All right, go. I give you two days' grace. No more. Don't let me see you any more round here after those two days. You've persecuted me on my own land. Why should a man suffer such injustice, eh, my friends?'

After the villagers of Vayvay . . . He had to clear the thornforest. There were five thousand dunums of thorn-trees . . . Then bit by bit he had to reclaim the land from the Ahjasaz marshes . . . Then the farms . . . To own a huge farm or farms on the Anavarza lands within the Chukurova, was like owning a whole state.

'Ah you Vayvay fellows, you scoundrels, you've stood out against me like the heights of Alidagh or Duldul mountains . . . Get out of my way. For me this is a life-and-death struggle, for

you it's nothing at all ... Take yourselves out of my way ...
Chukurova is full of empty land. Long live Yobazoghlu ... You
did me a great favour ...'

He drew out from his wallet the title-deeds of the seventeen
dunums ceded to him by Yobazoghlu, and holding the document
he gazed at it and smiled. If he had not laid hands on this, his task
would have been more difficult.

'Veli,' he called downstairs. A tall, swarthy boy, wearing large
shalvar-trousers, came up.

'Veli, when is the valuation of the Vayvay land coming up?'

'On the eighteenth of this month.'

'Are the valuers ready?'

'Yes, Bey.'

17

THEY were returning home empty-handed, but Old Osman was
happy. Osman's horse was in front, and Ferhat's behind. Ferhat's
expression, with his mystical face, and his curly black beard tinged
with green in the sunlight, was that of a man deep in thought. His
eyes were half-closed, as if dozing. They followed the dry bed of
a mountain torrent uphill. The horses' ears and eyes were plastered
with black midges.

All kinds of hornets, wasps, bumble-bees and honey-bees,
hovered in swarms over the breast-high narcissi that grew on the
edge of marshes, and over the mint, brambles, dog-roses and bog-
myrtle. Their buzzing was heard in rumbling waves coming from
the immense Ahjasaz marshes. In the gully, greyish snakes slipped
from under the horses' hooves. The cool, bright-green frogs puffed
their bellies in and out like bellows, and breathed in the warmth
of the sun. At every step the horses took, a crowd of grasshoppers
sprang out like popcorn.

'Oh dear, oh dear,' lamented Old Osman. 'How frightened the
poor wretches were! Terrified! Oh dear, oh dear ...'

100

From the further side of the Anavarza crags came the song of a francolin. It sang and sang, then for a time it was silent, then its call began again and went on and on.

A white cloud sent its dark shadow over the plain of Anavarza, and passing over the bubbling waters of Ahjasaz, the bright-green reeds, the thousands of wild duck scattered over the water, then over the fields of wheat, and the beds of wide-open wild tulips it floated, solitary, like smoke, from Sülemish to the River Jeyhan, from the River Jeyhan to the bare slopes of Bozkuyu, and from there to Öksüzlü.

A gentle breeze played with the hairs in Old Osman's beard.

'Oh dear, oh dear! How frightened they are, damn them! They have no livelihood, they've been driven out, into exile, but they won't turn back and come home. There's nothing worse than a frightened man. Just put fear into a man and you can make a slave of him for ever. A man with fear in him isn't a man any longer. Isn't that so, Ferhat Hodja?'

Ferhat Hodja did not answer. It was doubtful whether he had heard.

'A man with fear in him isn't a man any longer. He's some different creature, not a human being any more. Let him go to the wall, eh, Ferhat?'

Ferhat again made no reply. Osman turned to him, and said again:

'What do you say, Hodja, perhaps you think a coward is a man. But I think a frightened cowardly man is no longer a human being. Don't you agree, Ferhat?' This time he shouted out the hodja's name. Ferhat looked up, and in a harsh, deep, impressive voice, emphasizing each word, said,

'A terrified man is not a human being.'

Osman was pleased at this.

'But there are people who will not be cowed. Whatever is done to them they are not afraid. Isn't that so, Hodja?'

'It is.'

'A man who is very small in stature. His body is as small as a child's . . . A twelve-year-old child . . . They kill his mother, but he is not frightened. They kill his sweetheart, his beloved, but he is not cowed. The Government, the villagers, the aghas all attack

him with a hail of bullets, but he remains undaunted. The mountains cannot hide him, he cannot take refuge in gullies or hollows,
or caves, or with people, but he remains undaunted. Undaunted,
Ferhat! He does not cringe like us. He stands like a giant resisting
the injustice of a thousand years, of two, three, ten, a hundred
thousand years.'

'He crushes injustice personified, you mean, Osman Agha?'

'He slits open the belly of injustice, and beats it to the ground,
Hodja. Then he comes and takes shelter in the house of a poor
eighty-year-old man, old as Methuselah. This tiny boy comes and
takes refuge with this failing old man. This tiny boy knows that
the old man will protect him at all costs.'

As Old Osman talked, he kept turning to look at Ferhat Hodja's
face, to see if there was any change in expression. Ferhat did not
show any reaction, and not a muscle of his face moved to indicate
that he had understood.

Well, thought Old Osman, how else can I say that Slim Memed
came to our house? Ferhat Hodja is a quick-witted man. Usually he
catches at the slightest hint. How is it he doesn't understand something said as openly as this? The brave man who looks like a tiny
twelve-year-old child is Slim Memed, isn't it? The pure-hearted
hero whose mother and sweetheart were killed, who could not
find refuge in the hills or the ravines or with people is none other
than Slim Memed, isn't he? My rejoicing, my shooting of the
Sergeant, my courage, the change in me is all on account of Slim
Memed, isn't it? Why don't they understand? Nobody understands anything. Ah, if people were not so stupid, the world
wouldn't be what it is.

'Look here, Ferhat Hodja, have you understood anything of
what I've been saying, for heaven's sake?'

Ferhat Hodja guided his horse to Osman's side, and they began
to ride side by side.

'I understood a little, Osman Agha,' he replied. 'There's something you know, but you cannot say it openly. I gathered part of it.'

'About the light that pierced the darkness. And about the well
in the desert. And about hope . . . And . . . When we reach home
you shall see. You'll be beside yourself with delight. You'll see
that Prophet Hizir has come to my home. Spur on your horse.'

Ferhat Hodja was madly curious about the secret Osman wanted to tell and couldn't, about the light and the Prophet Hizir, but he knew that people in the sort of mood that Osman was in would refuse to say another word, if pressed. Whereas if you paid no attention to them, they'd come out with their secret of their own accord.

'Spur on your horse, Ferhat Hodja, hurry!'

He whipped up his own horse. He was out of breath with emotion. His horse was going at full speed, and the hodja also forced his horse on to keep up with him.

'At home you'll see a child who has suffered a great deal. At home you'll see a hawk, the handsomest in all Chukurova. At home you'll see a lion that is all courage. At home you'll see a hero who is a real man. At home you'll see a man who is a friend . . . And a brother. He is like the golden eagle that lives among the purple crags, Hodja . . . He is as gentle as a lamb. Yet Ismet Pasha, our army commander Stern Ismet, would be afraid of him. Stern Ismet is a brave man, who fears nobody. Even Mustafa Kemal asks for his opinion. The brain of the army is Ismet, and the sword is Mustafa Kemal. Now do you understand, Hodja, who is staying in my house?'

'I don't understand, but I'm very curious, Osman Agha . . .'

'What do you say, what do you say?'

'I'm very curious, very. I want to know about that man. I'm dying to know.'

'You're dying to know? Really?'

'Dying to know, Osman Agha,' shouted Ferhat.

'Then urge on your horse, whip it up and you'll see my hawk all the sooner.'

Ferhat Hodja whipped up his horse, and they rode side by side at top speed towards the village.

Old Osman was the first to dismount in the courtyard. As soon as his feet touched the ground, his knees gave way, and he fell to the ground. He was dizzy, but he pulled himself together and got up.

'Mother Kamer, Mother Kamer, we're here,' he called. But there was no answer from within.

'Mother Kamer, Mother Kamer, for heaven's sake, we've come

back, Ferhat Hodja and I . . .'

Ferhat Hodja had also dismounted, and had tethered his horse to the nearby fence.

Old Osman went to the door, which was not bolted, and disappeared inside.

'Mother Kamer! Where are you?'

No reply came from anywhere. Suddenly, he ran to the closet, and called gently.

'Memed, my hawk, where are you? Please answer.' Then he stopped and listened. No reply came. He opened the door of the closet, and felt Memed's bed with his hand. It was empty. He must have gone to the stable, he thought, and rushed to the stable, calling softly.

'Memed, my hawk, answer me. It's only Ferhat Hodja with me, not a stranger.'

He listened, but there was not a sound from anywhere.

'What has happened?' said Old Osman, beginning to turn dazedly round and round. Ferhat Hodja found him in this state. Puzzled, he put his arm through Osman's, and guided him back into the house.

'What's the matter with you?' he kept asking him, but got no reply from the dazed old man, who was now damp with sweat. Ferhat made him sit down on the pallet in the corner, brought him a bowl of water from the barrel, and tried to get him to drink it. Osman's chin and hands were trembling so much that the water got spilt all over him.

At this stage Mother Kamer came in, her face drawn with worry.

'Tell me quickly, what happened?' groaned Old Osman. 'What has happened to him?'

'Nothing's happened to him,' she replied in a sad voice as if intoning a lament.

'Where is he?' asked Old Osman, a little relieved. 'Where is he now?'

Kamer looked at Ferhat Hodja, then at her husband, and said nothing.

'Speak,' said Old Osman. 'Ferhat Hodja knows someone's disappeared but he doesn't know who.'

'He was longing to see his village again,' said Kamer. 'He's gone to his village. I begged and pleaded with him. Wait for your Uncle Osman before leaving, I said, but he wouldn't. I'm longing to see my village, was the only thing he said, and at midnight he put on his clothes and equipment, and off he went. He left you his greetings. I kiss his hands, he said. I'll see him again in this world, he said. I may even be back in a couple of days, he said.'

'He won't come back, he's gone,' groaned Old Osman. He's broken my arm and my wing with his going . . .'

He took Ferhat Hodja's hand:

'I so much wanted you to see my hawk,' he said. 'But fate has willed otherwise.'

He said no more, and in a little while was asleep.

18

SHE wore a green kerchief round her head. She was tall, black-haired, golden-complexioned. Two thick plaits hung down to her hips. She had a longish face, with dimples, and melancholy eyes. There was a tender crease at the corner of her lips, and she had long, black, curling eyelashes . . . There were three tiny moles a little below her ear, which gave her face a strange fascination. Seyran was like a sacred creature, an inhabitant from other worlds, untouchable, solitary and without compare in this world. Neither women nor men could look at Seyran's face for long. And no one could look into Seyran's eyes. They made you feel a strange emotion that wrung your heart, that brought sadness and unbearable pain. She was like an ancient melody, a melancholy song, tender, yet harsh, that came from beyond the mountains and the night. She spoke very little, and almost never laughed. Her voice was like a thousand-year-old lament. And when once in a thousand times she laughed, the whole world became brighter, sunnier and more hopeful. When she laughed, she laughed with her whole being, and became twice as beautiful. She looked about twenty-five or thirty. No one remembered how long she had been in the village. She was as much a part of it as if she had been born and bred there. Everyone in the Anavarza region was very considerate towards her on account of her terrible misfortune and in Vayvay she was accepted as a daughter by every household. For Maid Seyran to leave this village was unthinkable, it could not have existed without her. At least so it seemed to them. After the unheard-of disaster that befell her, Seyran's brothers and cousins and other relations, from the Pazarjik mountains had come to take her away to her native place, but they did not succeed in taking her from Anavarza, from Vayvay village. Seyran had never said anything. She remained silent for long years. The brothers and cousins who had failed to take her back to the Pazarjik mountains, unable to bear her mother's laments, came down from the mountains in a large tribe. They settled on the rich lands of Vayvay village. They were wealthy. They were bold, strong, healthy men, good shots and good riders. They were generous and affectionate. They became fond of the Chukurova Turcomans, and the Chukurova Turcomans liked the bold mountaineers. Within a few years, the mountain people had mixed with the Turcomans, giving and taking their daughters in marriage, and becoming close friends. They were different in temperament and constitution, but their fine tradition of friendship, generosity and respect united them. Maid Seyran would never speak to her brothers or relations, or even to her mother; she could not forgive them. Her mother said, 'If only Seyran would open her mouth and speak, and call me mother, just for once, I would gladly die.' But Maid Seyran took no notice, and remained impassive. The first person she spoke to was Mother Kamer. The affection that existed between Kamer and Seyran was greater than the love between mother and daughter.

Seyran heard from Ibrahim, a neighbour's child, that Old Osman had fallen ill.

'Old Osman got home,' explained Ibrahim, 'and there was something in the house that he couldn't find. When he couldn't find it, he was taken ill. He fell down in a faint. He was terribly ill. Ferhat Hodja was terribly alarmed. An evil spirit has afflicted Old Osman. What with Yobazoghlu getting beaten up and all those villagers running away, he's terribly upset. Terribly . . .'

Without waiting to hear more from Ibrahim, Maid Seyran hurried to Old Osman's house. Kamer was seated at Osman's bedside, holding his hands in hers, kissing them and weeping. When she saw Seyran, she said,

'Uncle Osman is dying, my daughter. Even if he doesn't die, this grief will exhaust him. His pride has been hurt. Uncle Osman's pride has been hurt. Why should this have happened to the poor dear in his last years?'

Osman opened his eyes, and his beard trembled. 'Has Seyran come, has my girl come?' he asked.

'Yes, Seyran's come, your girl's come,' answered Kamer. 'When she knew you'd been taken ill, naturally she came to see you, Osman.'

Seyran squatted down beside Kamer, and took Osman's hand in hers.

'Get better quickly, Uncle Osman, get better soon,' she said, in warm affectionate, sincere tones.

Old Osman raised himself a little, and looked long at Seyran's face from under his thick white eyebrows.

'I shan't get better. I shan't get better, my beauty. Wars, the Yemen, malaria – those things couldn't kill me, but this grief will.'

He lay back quietly, and began to weep a little.

'I'm a hawk. An old, broken-winged hawk, with worn-out talons, who cannot fly. Besides, I'm a hawk that has had its chick taken from the nest, snatched from me, a hawk that has lost its hope and its light. They will kill my hawk, my little chick, the hope of the world, the light of my eyes. They will kill him, Seyran dear.'

The hand in Seyran's hand twitched and quivered with fever. Tears trickled down his cheeks, and Seyran wept with him.

As if talking in his sleep, Old Osman said,

'Go and find my hawk. Go and find the beauty of the world, the light of my eyes, the centre of our hopes, don't let those brutes kill him. Don't let the wolves and the infidels tear him to pieces. Ferhat, you are a very fine hodja. A fine man, a brave man . . . I entrust my hawk to you, if I die. Don't let ravening wolves attack my hawk. Did I say something that made him angry, Kamer?'

'I've told you a hundred times, Boy Osman,' cried Kamer, 'he didn't go away in anger.'

'Then why didn't he wait for me? He was afraid. Afraid I'd betray him. He didn't trust me, was that it?'

'That wasn't it at all,' said Kamer. 'The boy trusted us greatly. He trusted us enough to stay as long as he did. But if only you hadn't proclaimed it to everybody.'

'Who did I proclaim it to, Kamer?' he asked slowly.

'Who did you proclaim it to? The whole village!'

'Who did I tell? Who did I open my mouth to?'

'You didn't open your mouth,' said Kamer crossly, 'but you dressed in your best clothes, you put your pipe in your mouth, you thrust your pistol in your belt, you put on your silver watch-chain, and after polishing your boots, you paraded around the village for three days like the victorious Kozanoghlu himself, didn't you? Of course the villagers asked why you were walking about like that, of course they thought about it, and of course the boy was alarmed to see you in that crazy frame of mind!'

'Be quiet, Kamer,' said Osman, 'be quiet, I beg you. Don't kill me! Don't torture me! Seyran dear, tell her to let me die in peace,' he pleaded.

'I won't be quiet, Boy Osman,' said Kamer sharply. 'Wasn't it you who wanted to show him to Ferhat Hodja only yesterday, that boy who had come to your house and had taken refuge with you?'

'Be quiet Kamer, I beg you. Seyran dear, this old hag is killing me. She's torturing me, please make her stop.'

'I've finished,' said Kamer, getting to her feet angrily.

'Ferhat, my friend,' said Osman. 'Please do something for me, find my hawk,' and he turned restlessly in his bed.

Ferhat Hodja, with his black, curly beard, said agitatedly,

'Don't worry, Osman, nothing will happen to him. He has come out of lots of tight places unscathed. Don't upset yourself. If he said he'd come, he will come. Nothing is too difficult for him. either he got bored here, or he had some work to do. Otherwise he'd never have gone without taking leave of you. He'll come back,' said Ferhat firmly.

'Are you telling me the truth?' said Osman, raising himself in bed. 'Ferhat, you saint, you man of God! Nothing's happened to him, has it?'

'No,' said Ferhat Hodja confidently.

'But if he's angry with me?'

'He isn't angry,' said Ferhat Hodja in the same tone.

'Will he come again?'

'He will,' said the hodja.

'If you'd seen his face you couldn't have mistaken him. He's unmistakable. Ah, if only you'd seen his face.'

'I shall see him,' said Ferhat. 'Sooner or later I shall see him.'

His voice rang out hopefully and confidently. The faith and hope that could be heard in his voice brought Old Osman gently to his senses.

'If only you'd seen his eyes, Hodja, they're like a piece of steel. You can't look into them. His eyes are like him.'

Osman's sons and daughters-in-law arrived. Seyfali, other villagers, Sefché the Warden, Seyran's brothers, cousins and mother, Zeynel and Selver also came. Everyone came when they heard that Slim Memed had been hidden in Osman's house for some days, and that on arriving home and finding him gone Old Osman had taken to his bed.

There was a great stir in the courtyard at the entrance to Osman's house. Sefché the Warden said happily,

'So our friend isn't in his dotage. So he had a secret that he couldn't reveal to anyone. Thank God!' and with his hands behind his back he strutted to and fro, a proud smile on his face.

The villagers, hearing about Slim Memed, had first been pleased and then bewildered, and now they swung from bewilderment to delight, and from delight to terror.

Zeynel, getting to know what was going on, stayed for a moment at Osman's bedside, then pressed his hand and slipped away, without calling attention to himself. Ferhat Hodja followed him and caught up with him in front of Kurdish Kerem's house. He put his hand heavily on Zeynel's shoulder.

'Look at me, Zeynel,' he said in a very harsh, slow, emphatic way. 'You are not to tell anyone, including Ali Safa Bey, that Memed came to the village and went away.'

Zeynel stopped, his lips quivered, and his face looked as if he were about to cry. He thought for a while.

'Look, Hodja,' he said, stretching his long neck a bit further. 'I won't tell anyone. But the whole village knows. The news must have reached the nearby villages, in fact in the whole plain, by now. If Ali Safa Bey and the other aghas hear of it from someone else, I can't help it. It's not my responsibility. So, with you watching me, I'm not going, I'm returning.'

And walking behind Ferhat, he returned to Old Osman's yard.

That day the villagers all talked of Slim Memed. They were hopeful and depressed, angry and joyful in turns. A few young men and girls hummed tunes from songs that had been composed about Slim Memed.

Then they began to feel angry with Old Osman. Slim Memed comes to his house, and he doesn't say a word to the villagers! He just strides about the village arrogantly smoking his pipe! Impossible old man! He should at all costs have told the villagers about Slim Memed, he should have told everyone so that they could feast their eyes on Slim Memed.

Their anger, irritation, disappointment and fears were all turned against Old Osman.

At least twenty people claimed to have seen Slim Memed entering the village, or walking on the edge of Ahjasaz or in the village at night or riding like the wind on a white horse towards the crags of Anavarza.

It was also Slim Memed who had shot Sergeant Remzi.

Everyone had something to say about Slim Memed, some new invention and story about him.

That night Mother Kamer and Maid Seyran stayed by Old Osman's bed. Osman wanted nobody but them, and sent his sons, daughters-in-law and everyone home. Ferhat Hodja went of his own accord.

Old Osman related to Seyran what Slim Memed was like, his courage, his eyes, his hair, what his hair was really like, his voice, his way of speaking, his humanity, his friendliness, his goodness and his gentleness.

'Don't imagine I'm afraid,' he said enthusiastically, 'he would fight an army. Single-handed. Just like a hawk. He's so quick and agile that when he is fighting you can't see his face. If he were here now, he would be over there in the twinkling of an eye. Otherwise he wouldn't have managed to protect himself against his many enemies. Brigands like him find that animals, trees, stones, thickets, snakes, a myriad creatures, are all their enemies. Extremely so . . .' and he stopped.

'But what if they surround my boy in the Akarja mountains? A squad of police, a thousand lowdown peasants with sticks in their hands, or the aghas' creature, Black Ibrahim, with fifteen men . . . A single man, a tiny handful of a man, how can he stand up to them, so many thugs?' he said anxiously.

Then he turned to Kamer and asked for the hundredth time, 'Did he have plenty to eat before he left? Did you give him plenty of food to take with him? Enough for three days?'

Mother Kamer replied patiently. 'He ate until he was full up. And I got ready a huge bag of walnuts, cheese, hard-boiled eggs, a sugar loaf, flaky pastry and spring onions, and tied it on to his belt. Enough for three days, five even . . .'

Old Osman fretted at the ruin of his hopes.

Towards morning he dropped off, and sank into a deep sleep.

The news spread over the whole of the Anavarza plain that he had come to Old Osman's house, that he had hidden for six nights in Old Osman's house, that only yesterday he had got offended with Old Osman and had withdrawn to the mountains; the news spread like wildfire from Vayvay to Kesikkeli, from Kesikkeli to Hemite, Bozkuyu, Akmashat, Narlikishla, Öksüzlü, Chiyanli, and from there to Hadjilar.

No one mentioned the name Slim Memed; they either said 'he' or 'the hawk'.

The legend of his reputation and courage was repeated daily all over the plain of Anavarza, in the Chukurova villages beyond, and also in the six Kozan villages, yet not a single agha or Government man learnt of his presence. The villagers of the plain concealed Slim Memed's name as if they were keeping the holiest of secrets. If Osman had known about this he would have been beside himself with delight.

19

SEYRAN was from the village of Harmanja with its red crags, in the Pazarjik district. Harmanja stood on a rocky outcrop which was knife-edged, made sharp by white, green, purple and red flints, a strange place, like a forest. Some fine horses were reared there. Water bubbled from between the flinty rocks, and splashing, crystal-clear, sparkling with a thousand points of light, it descended into the plain. Above Harmanja village flocks of migrating cranes, flying very low, used to pass four times a year. From among the flinty rocks sprouted big, tall, brilliant flowers with a pungent smell. The wheat sown in small patches among the crags was very hard, abundant and nourishing. Cows, horses, oxen and all the animals that were bred at Harmanja were slim, tall, strong and handsome. As for the people, they were the handsomest on earth. Among the people of the lowland plain and the villages round Marash, the people of Harmanja were well-known for their pure beauty and attractiveness. The birds and insects of Harmanja were long and brightly-coloured. They sang more sweetly and shone more brightly than other birds and insects.

Maybe they were not very rich, but they were thrifty. Want was never seen. They did their own weaving, their own dyeing, and they embroidered, cut and stitched their clothes. You never saw anyone from Harmanja wearing dirty or ragged clothes. They were hard people, touchy about their dignity. A lot of blood was spilt in Harmanja. This was traditional, and it meant that very few people ever knew what fear was. Whether it was because of the air there, or the water, or the soil, everything was hard and crisp. There was nothing soft or pliable. People's faces were copper-coloured. And both women and men had large eyes.

Seyran was the daughter of Halil, the Mullah or Moslem judge, and was the youngest of five children. The Mullah was considered to be the man with the best ancestry in those mountains. His genealogical tree went back for centuries. And his house was a haven for guests. The Mullah's house had specially good manners and a special tradition.

One day a tiny child happened to come to Harmanja. He was five or six years old, not more. Nobody knew where he had come from or where he was going to, or which village he was from. Only the child himself provided a clue. Wherever he saw a drop of blood he would begin to cry and would run away at once. And if he saw a person actually bleeding, he would cry and be upset for a long time. The child grew up in Beardless Veli's house. Beardless Veli was a neighbour of Seyran's people. At one stage the child went bald. Whatever was done to cure this, with a lot of medicines and ointments, was done by Seyran's mother. The villagers gave the child the name of Aziz. Seyran was two years older than Aziz. As they were neighbours they were always together. Seyran became like a mother to the orphan boy. She did not let anyone touch Aziz, neither child nor grown-up, nobody. Seyran would fly into a rage if anyone tried to harm Aziz or to tease him. She was like a fierce leopardess prowling the flinty crags of Harmanja and would hurl herself savagely upon anyone who attempted to harm her cub. Aziz was just like a child born to a wild Seyran. If there was any food at her own table that Aziz did not have, she would take some to Aziz. As they got older, their friendship got closer. They were scarcely ever apart.

Seyran and Aziz reached adolescence. Seyran was tall, Aziz was short and small-boned. His face was sweet and sad, and handsome when he smiled. There was a scar that ran down his left cheek to his chin, which gave his face a strange beauty. But in spite of his smallness, Aziz grew up to be as hardy as the people of Harmanja, as good a horseman, as good a shot, as good as they at climbing steep crags. And as daring, as brave as they.

When Seyran and Aziz reached adolescence, the village began to gossip. It was not proper for a teenage girl and a youth to be together from morning till night.

The gossip spread from Harmanja to villages both near and far. While the news of Seyran's beauty was on everyone's lips, the news of her love for Aziz also spread, increased and became legendary.

Seyran's father drew her mother into a corner one day:

'Have you heard what is being said?' he asked.

'Yes,' said the mother, 'I have heard, but Aziz is just like Seyran's child. They're closer than brother and sister.'

Halil the Mullah said,

'I know that very well, but how can you explain it to other people? Tell the girl to keep away from Aziz.'

The mother told Seyran what had happened. Seyran was dumbfounded. She had never imagined that anything of the sort could occur to her. When the first amazement had passed, she laughed, but then she became anxious. She argued with her mother and father. Once she did not see Aziz for three days. She almost died of grief. Of grief and worry. Her mother, father, brothers, cousins, friends, the whole village remonstrated with her. But Seyran could not do without Aziz, and she neither ate nor drank, laughed nor cried.

They sent Aziz to other places, other villages. Seyran went and brought him back. They betrothed Seyran to an attractive youth from another village. He was the son of Hurshit Bey, who had lots of horses, flocks and land. When he tried to kiss her one evening, she almost shot him.

Seyran struggled against the villagers and her relations for two years. She suffered for it.

One day Aziz disappeared. They said he had gone to Chukurova, to a faraway unknown land. One day Seyran, losing hope that Aziz would come back, took a horse from her father's yard, mounted it and rode away. She searched and searched, and asked and asked, and everyone who saw her was overcome with admiration of her beauty. She found Aziz in the village of Vayvay. He had taken refuge with Seyfali, the Headman. The Mullah Halil was a friend of Seyfali's father. He had sent Aziz to them. Seyfali and his father welcomed Aziz. The romance of Seyran and Aziz became legendary among the Turcomans of Chukurova. The Turcomans, adhering to their traditions and customs, gave what help they could to the young lovers. So they were the happiest lovers in all the world. But soon an unexpected disaster came upon them.

Ali Safa Bey had an elder brother. And the brother had three sons. They lived on the farm, but were educated people. They were infected with town life, and had turned their backs on Turcoman

114

traditions and customs; they did evil things and had become inhuman. They gambled, they trifled with women in the villages and they drank. They were people such as the Turcomans had never seen, and had never believed existed. They robbed and they killed.

These men heard about the beauty of Seyran, who was living in Seyfali's house, in the village of Vayvay, and then they would not leave Vayvay alone. They were there morning and evening. When the villagers saw how they pestered Seyran, they got angry with these evil men. Several times there were fights between them and the villagers. At one stage the police sergeant, Sergeant Zulfo, joined them. They walked around the village continually, but could not get near Seyran. Seyran was very beautiful, and had no relatives with her, and Aziz was like a child, but even so they could not get near her. Seyran did not even look at them, let alone encourage them. They could get no further, so one night they attacked Seyfali's house. Some of the attackers and some of the villagers were wounded, but they abducted Seyran. After the abduction, a great many rumours went round about Seyran. Some said that Ali Safa's eldest nephew had fallen in love with Seyran, and was dying of love for her, and that Seyran would not give herself to him; some said that they all raped Seyran every night, first Zulfo and then the others. However that may be, no one ever knew the truth of the matter, and never will.

When his wife was abducted, Aziz went crazy. Somehow he got hold of a very good German carbine, and a lot of cartridges. He took so many that he could hardly stagger with the weight of the cartridge-belt round him.

One day towards morning, Aziz surprised Sergeant Zulfo, the three brothers and some other people in a mudbrick house in the village of Bozkuyu. He opened the door, squatted down on the threshold, and began to shoot the people there one by one. No one was left alive inside but Seyran. When he had finished, he coolly took Seyran by the hand, raised her to her feet, gazed deep into her eyes, kissed her on the forehead, then turned and ran down into the village of Bozkuyu. When he reached the police station it was noon. He shot the first policeman who came out towards him. The others, shutting the door of the police station, began to shoot at Aziz. The battle lasted three hours. Then Aziz, very coolly, got up, asked one of the villagers who was standing some distance away for matches, paraffin and rags. The man could not refuse him, but very soon brought the things that Aziz had requested, and gave them to him as if under a spell. Aziz, equally coolly, went and set fire to the door of the police station. Then he stood by, ready to fire. Soon after this the policemen rushed out, and Aziz shot and killed them as they came out of the door. When he had killed the last of them, a detachment of police from the neighbouring town, where news of the affray had been received, surrounded Aziz. There was a long fight, and in the end, when a number of policemen had been shot, Aziz ran out of ammunition, and, rising from the trench in which he had been lying, marched on them and fell. His body was riddled with bullets. Nobody knew how many.

They took Aziz's body to the town and exposed it to the public gaze for two days in front of the police headquarters. The people looked with admiration and affection at the tiny corpse. Looking at his body, which had shrunk still smaller in death, was like looking at a holy relic.

They threw Seyran into prison. No one came forward to claim Aziz's body. The policemen threw it into a hole outside the town, and heaped a few spadefuls of earth on top of it. The head and feet were left exposed. When the police had gone away, the people came, and taking the body out of the hole, removed it to the mosque and washed it, and after a great ceremony buried it in the graveyard.

The terrible news reached Seyran's father, the Mullah, some days after the event. It had such an effect on him that he fell ill, and died a few days later.

Seyran's mother, brothers and cousins came down to Chukurova and visited Seyran in prison. Seyran would not open her mouth to say a single word to her mother or brothers.

They let Seyran go not long afterwards. As soon as she came out of prison, she went to find Aziz's grave, which was on the highest hill above the town in a clump of myrtles. In her beautiful voice she intoned the most affectionate, heartfelt, moving prayers beside Aziz's grave. A few days later she left the town and went to Seyfali's house at Vayvay. Her mother, brothers and cousins wanted to take her back to Harmanja. Seyran took no notice; she would not listen to them, did not even see them. Her mother, brothers and cousins returned to their homes without her. After this they came to fetch Seyran every three months. One day, realizing that Seyran would never return to the mountains, her mother packed up her goods and chattels and moved to Vayvay. In her wake came the brothers and cousins and they all settled in Vayvay. They had money, so they sold their horses and flocks, and bought land from the Turcomans at the edge of Ahjasaz. They were very hard men, and, though few in number, no one ever dared challenge them about anything.

Seyran did not go to their houses, and would accept nothing from them; she never spoke to any of them, including her mother. She did not even turn and look at the houses where they lived.

The hill-folk had difficulty in accustoming themselves to the air and water of Chukurova. Both Seyran and the others suffered from malaria during the first year. Then they gradually got used to the heat and mosquitoes of the low-lying plain.

Seyran went to the town, to Aziz's grave, on the first Friday of every month. She would sit by the grave intoning prayers in her beautiful voice, like a bird singing in the night.

Seyran lived alone in a separate house, and worked by herself, like a manual labourer, not accepting anything from anyone.

After Aziz's death, no one proposed marriage to Seyran. She was so beautiful that the villagers of Chukurova looked upon her as they might have looked upon a holy creature. No one thought of looking upon her as a woman.

After Kalayji's death, when Memed disappeared, the villagers gave Memed's empty house to Seyran, fully furnished. Seyran did not make any show of refusing Memed's empty, ownerless house. Like a bird singing, she intoned in this house the most beautiful laments composed in honour of Aziz. And young men and women of the village would stand all night at the corner of the house simply to hear these laments. They became known all over the plain of Chukurova.

After Aziz was killed, Seyran only once smiled again. That was at the moment when she heard that Slim Memed had killed

Kalayji. Since coming to Vayvay, she had not wanted to see anything or anyone, and had not shown the least interest in anything. But after Kalayji was shot, deep in her heart she cherished a desire to see Slim Memed.

Now that he had slipped away, she regretted the lost opportunity, turning things over in her mind. 'I knew, I guessed that something was going on in Old Osman's house. Mother Kamer was continually on the move, she didn't stand still a moment; she was always looking back at the house, at the closed door. I wish I had gone there,' she said to herself. She had been going to go several times, and then for some reason changed her mind. So now she was sorry. She wondered what he was like. What sort of a man was Slim Memed?

As if Old Osman divined this curiosity of hers, he began to tell her again all about Slim Memed the moment he woke up.

'He has such eyes, big, enormous eyes. When you look at his face, you don't see anything but those big, bright, flashing eyes. They are so hard and bright that you can't look at them for long, without your heart going pit-a-pat. Nobody can kill him; if he were killed I could not bear it. I couldn't go on living. I should die. Ah that trigger-finger of his, how quick it is! So quick you can't see it. And bullets cannot touch him. He'll come back again.'

When he said, 'He'll come back again,' he gazed up at Ferhat Hodja's face, appealingly, and waited. Ferhat summoned up all the faith deep within him, and tried to convey it in his voice as he said,

'He'll come back again.'

20

THE sun was fierce, the air was hot. The dark shadow of the horse fell along a bright green pond that was as deep as a well. In the remote distance of the sky a mass of white clouds floated in glaring white light, so high up that wherever they cast their shadow it was nowhere to be seen.

At the edge of the green pond grew mullein, brambles and blue water-mint and bees had made their nests there. Thousands of them were buzzing over the pond. There were big green dragonflies, too . . . And large spiders' webs were stretched out in the sun.

There was the sparkle of broken glass on the tracks. In the distance, from where the River Jeyhan flowed across the plain, came a dazzling reflection. It flashed like a sharp sword across the plain, now this way, now that.

The stallion stood immovable as a rock. Slivers of light were reflected in his eyes. The skin over his shoulder-blade quivered continually. Black flies settled on it all the time. The stallion raised his head, distended his nostrils and sniffed the warm air for a while. Then he lowered his head towards the ground, snorting as if to expel the earth and dust from his nostrils. He raised his head four or five times, and breathed in air, then lowered it again. A great cloud of flies were buzzing round his head. A little later the brown horse began to shake and swing his head, as if to get rid of the flies. Then, for some reason or other, he reared up on his hind legs. As he did so, he turned round twice in his own length, and hollowed his rump. He galloped madly three times round the green pond, then stopping, gave a long, long whinny that rang out all over the plain. After this whinny he again stood motionless by the edge of the pond. The whites of his big, black eyes were bloodshot. The shapely white sock like a bracelet on his right leg was invisible in the long grass. He had lost the shoes from his two hind feet.

A light breeze sprang up. In the distance a small but rapid sand-devil moved across the plain. The skin over the horse's shoulder-blade twitched, and there were no flies left. When he felt the breeze and saw the sand-devil gleaming he began to twitch his tail gently.

Adem, mounted on the white horse, had been looking for him for three days. He had looked into every hole, and explored every thicket. He had not seen the brown horse anywhere, and the fear inside him drove him mad.

Adem said to himself, 'It's impossible, there's something uncanny about that horse.' And he could not get this thought out of his mind; what is more, it gradually absorbed all his waking moments.

'I've been looking for three days; I haven't left any place un-explored in the whole plain. I've searched everywhere in the reed-beds that could be searched, and still there is nothing, nothing, nothing . . .'

Adem conjured up that night before his eyes, just as if he were re-living it, that night when they had set fire to Yobazoghlu's hut, and the brown stallion's stable. Once alight, the hut had melted like snow. The door had caught fire immediately. Unless there had been a miracle, that horse could not have escaped from the fire. How was the brown horse saved from the fire? How was it that he had not been seen for three days? 'It must be by divine dispensation.'

For a moment an incredible wave of terror came over him, clutching at his heart, at his whole body, and sapping all the strength from his limbs. I cannot shoot that horse, he thought to himself. Nobody can. If I shoot him, I shall be struck with paralysis.

He believed that if he shot the horse, some great disaster would befall him. On the one hand he did not want ever to find the horse, on the other he was desperate to see it.

Swallows swooped and darted in front of the white horse as he rode along. He was now going to the farm at Tarsuslu, below Kerimli. Here, on the edge of the Ahjasaz marshes, the canes rose to the sky, each as thick as a tree . . . This was a forest of canes.

Adem thought to himself, I must go into that cane-thicket. Somewhere in the middle of the cane-thicket, near a mound, there must be a cold, pebbly brook, he said, searching his memory. He dismounted, tied the horse to a willow-tree, and walked to-wards the cane-thicket. Then he stopped; the feeling of terror had come over him again. There was water all around the edge of the cane-thicket. He waded in, not stopping to take off his sandals or to roll up his trousers, and moved forward into the canes. There were lots of hornets' nests and wasps' nests, and lots of spiders' webs. His feet touched some spiny hedgehogs curled up in a ball. He passed near to a long-legged bird, as tall as himself. Adem passed so near he could have stretched out his hand and grasped it, but the bird took no notice; it did not even move. It only opened one eye for a moment, and at once closed it again. Inside the cane-thicket, it was cool and dark. Adem walked with care. There were many poisonous snakes in the cane-thickets.

Adem said to himself:

'If he is not here either, where can he be, that stallion? That limb of Satan hasn't gone to Heaven yet. He must be somewhere.'

He found the spring, and stretching himself out to the place where it bubbled forth, held his lips to it, and began to drink thirstily. Then he took a deep breath, and lifted his head from the spring; his knees were muddy, and he slapped at them.

That stallion could never be found. If he were found, he could not be shot. Even if he were shot, the man who shot him would not find salvation. Maybe he would not die, but would drag on miserably year after year until he would cry out to Death and beg him to come.

He searched the cane-thicket, and was fearful and glad at the same time; he went right to the other end, to the marshes themselves, and saw more of the motionless birds. When he emerged from the cane-thicket, the sun was sinking fast. He saw a huge orange and red flower. It was so wide open that it looked like a bird.

The brown horse had taken on the shape of a bird. It had become a swallow that swooped in front of him. I barred your way, I befouled your moustache, Adem, it said.

Over and over again, it kept repeating: I have taken on the shape of a swallow. I have taken on the shape of one, two, three, five, ten swallows; I barred your way, I befouled your face.

He could not get rid of this repetition; he got angry, furious, but the voice within him repeated: I barred your way, I befouled your face.

For a moment he dozed off, and continued walking in his sleep. That long-legged green bird must be the brown horse. He aimed his gun at the green bird, but he was afraid and lowered it again. He raised it again, but was even more frightened the second time. His hand was like a machine, first aiming, then lowering. The movements became quicker, as if Adem's hand had a life of its own. Suddenly the gun went off. As soon as it went off the long-legged green bird fell lifeless to the ground, and lay stretched out there without moving. Adem went and picked it up; its large wings, twice the length of Adem, were open. He threw it to the ground, and began to go swiftly out of the cane-thicket. His thoughts too moved swiftly. The horse was passing before his eyes at the same speed. The brown horse faded away, and became a slim gazelle with sad black eyes, a white gazelle. The white gazelle vanished and became a girl, a fairy girl . . . Then the horse became a bird. A dove. From a dove, it turned into a plover, a beautiful blue plover, with a well-shaped bill. After the blue plover, a blue mist floated over the plain of Anavarza. The horse had become mist. The mist collected together, and became a poplar. A silver poplar, standing alone in the middle of the level plain . . . The poplar became water, flowing white over the earth, the water became a grassy copse, the copse became a cloud, the cloud, rising over Anavarza Castle, became a dragon. Adem was terribly afraid of the dragon. The dragon approached, stretching out its seventy-two tongues, crimson, flame-coloured. Adem took to his heels and rushed out of the cane-thicket. The bright light struck him sharply like a stone, dazzling him. He had to rub his eyes, and when he opened them the white horse was not far in front of him. He mounted hastily, and rode away like the wind. Hundreds of swallows again began to swoop and dart in front of him. I barred your way. I befouled your face . . . Adem urged on his horse with whip and spur. To give it its due the white horse was swift enough. But still the swallows flitted in front of it. And the inner voice repeated the words. The white horse entered a ravine, then went through a pool. It entered a swamp, it leapt over a chasm. It gradually got slower, and then it ran into a thicket as tall as itself. It could not break through this obstacle, so it stopped there.

The brown horse became a bird. I barred your way . . . It was a red-legged stork. I befouled your face . . . It became a golden-eyed, huge-winged eagle, or a slim greyhound. I barred your way . . . It became a black snake, slithering up the trunk of a huge plane-tree in order to eat the young birds in their high nest. It was stretching out its head towards the nest, its red, flame-like, forked tongue almost touching the chicks. Adem sprang into action at this moment, and with a bullet brought the snake down to the foot of the tree. How long it was! I barred your way . . . Adem was paralysed. His limbs were shaking like Trembly

Ismail's. His hands went one way, and his legs, head and trunk the other. Trembly Ismail had been a good shot and an attractive young man. He could shoot a crane in flight. One day, when he was out hunting, a deer crossed his path, a delicate, graceful deer. Something inside Ismail said, don't shoot it, Ismail. The plants, flowers and stones seemed to say, have mercy on it, don't shoot, Ismail. But Ismail could not restrain his trigger-finger. When he looked again, in the place of the deer there was a small, shimmering patch of mist! At that very moment the gun dropped out of his hand, and he began to tremble; he shook so much that he foamed at the mouth.

Adem could not believe his eyes. He shaded them with his hand and looked again, and again he could not believe it. But there, motionless, stretching towards the sun, head raised, was the brown stallion, none other. For a moment he could not think what to do. He took aim; the horse was a long way away, but he pressed the trigger. His limbs and whole body trembled. For a moment he thought, I have become like Trembly Ismail. He looked towards the place where the horse was. The stallion was rearing up, straining, his forelegs stretched towards the sky, as if he were rising into the sky. Just as if he were climbing into the sky. He looked like a legendary bird with wings stretching into the heavens. How long he stayed like that Adem had no idea. The horse pawed the ground with his forelegs, and then once more leapt skywards. He was playing a strange, mysterious horse game. His legs, and his long, slim thoroughbred body stretched as if in flight, and then once more relaxed.

Adem would have taken the gun and fired at the horse again, but his hand trembled so much that he could not hold the gun steady.

The stallion reared once again, and again relaxed. Then he gave a long, ringing whinny.

The whinny rang out over the whole plain of Anavarza, and echoed against the Anavarza crags. Then the brown horse began to gallop towards the setting sun, towards the village of Anavarza. When it saw him, Adem's white horse also began to gallop. Otherwise, Adem would have been in no state to pursue the brown horse. The brown stallion galloped so fast that he seemed not to touch the ground. The white horse also galloped at a good speed, and as it galloped the wind of its passage gradually helped Adem to recover his senses.

In a little while the brown stallion passed behind the Anavarza crags towards the village, and then turned in the direction of the Hadjilar reed-beds. From there he turned at the same speed, and reached Ahjasaz. He gradually slackened speed, but he was still a good distance ahead of the white horse.

The brown horse went to a clump of willow-trees on the edge of the Ahjasaz marshes, and there he stopped. Adem was over-joyed when he saw that he had stopped there. Neither his hand nor any other part of him trembled. Taking careful aim, he pulled the trigger. He looked, but there was no sign of the brown stallion. He had disappeared. Adem felt angry, frightened, full of self-pity. He had been pursuing a horse for days. He had been pur-suing a horse, whether djinn, or fairy or devil. It was a dog's life. If he went back without having killed the horse, he would be disgraced and Ali Safa would throw him out. He and his wife would both have to go and labour in the fields. Their whole happiness depended on his killing the horse.

His self-esteem was shaken too. Whether the horse was a djinn or a fairy or a saint, whatever shape he assumed, why should he not be able to shoot him? He, Adem, who was known to shoot anything on the run ...

He approached the clump of willows where the stallion had paused, and dismounting, tied his horse to a tree. A misty twilight had fallen. He bent down and looked at the place where the stallion had been to see if there was any blood. Then he followed the horse's trail, and went into the marshy land on foot. A little further on some warm, deep waters bubbled up. Suddenly, he heard a whinny behind him, echoing through the darkness. Only fifty paces away in the other direction. He turned round, but could see nothing but the reeds. He began to run. The white horse and the brown were nuzzling each other. This was an opportunity not to be missed, so in a flash, he knelt down, took aim and pulled the trigger. From the sound of the bullet he realized that he had missed. He fired again four times. When he looked he saw the two animals galloping off together. The white horse, having broken its halter, was disappearing in the direction of Narlikishla, together with the brown stallion. Adem stood transfixed at the edge of the marshes, among the water-mint. The horses turned back from beneath Narlikishla and as they slipped by in front of him, Adem, raging with fury, dropped on to one knee, took careful aim and pulled the trigger. He fired five bullets one after the other. One of the horses fell. It whinnied feebly several times. It kicked and struggled for a long time in the darkness.

21

IT was a damp, misty, close night. Only a few not very bright stars shone in the sky. Shepherds' fires were alight on the slopes to right and left. Memed was familiar with the path he was taking. It was a narrow, rocky, goat-track, which came out at Yellow Ümmet's house. The wind was moaning in the trees; there was no other sound. In spite of the great weight he was carrying, Memed did not stumble or make any noise as he walked; he glided along as if his feet hardly touched the ground. He had three cartridge-belts round his body; two went over his shoulders to right and left. His rifle, dagger, field-glasses, hand-grenades and revolver – it was quite a weight. Memed was used to walking, to gliding along little paths like a partridge.

He had been in the mountains for two days. He covered the distances very fast. He had not met a single soldier, policeman or peasant, but all the same he was very much on his guard. There was something in the air. An ambush, something waiting. Down below, from the district of Nürfet he heard the sound of rifleshots. Perhaps there was a slight skirmish. As it did not last long the bandit who had walked into an ambush had either been killed or had given himself up. So Memed went along very cautiously, following the by-ways.

He was near Ümmet's house now. It was past midnight. From the vicinity of the house came the barking of big shepherd dogs.

At that time of night it boded no good.

Memed slid down the slope to Ümmet's mudbrick house. He tapped gently three times with his foot on the earth roof. Even if Yellow Ümmet were asleep he would hear the noise and come out. If he did not come out it was to be assumed either that he was not at home or that there was great danger. Memed got impatient, and tapped three times again, but harder, on the roof. Soon he heard footfalls approaching but they were very faint. A shape appeared above the wall, climbed the slope on all fours, and from the slope slid down on to the roof of the house.

'Lie down, Memed,' he said.

Memed at once lay down quietly.

'The house is full of soldiers,' said Yellow Ümmet. 'And Black Ibrahim's band is in the stable.' He spoke with his mouth close to Memed's ear: 'They're looking for you ... going from house to house, hole to hole, village to village. Everybody knows you've come back to the Taurus. Who saw you, for heaven's sake?'

'I don't know,' said Memed. 'I simply don't know who saw me. But there must have been someone.'

'This time they're really set on finding you. Ali Safa Bey and the other aghas have actually put a price on your head. I heard Captain Faruk talking about it. Leave the Taurus for a few months. They'll search and search and when they don't find you, they'll get fed up. Get away from these parts until the storm has blown itself out. Wait for me here, I'll find you some ammunition. You may clash with someone as you go.'

Yellow Ümmet slid down off the way he had come, and soon afterwards came back with a bundle of ammunition in one hand and a bag of food in the other.

'Take these,' he said, 'and don't call at your village. The police have been pestering them for two months.'

'What news is there of my village,' asked Memed, and Yellow Ümmet at once retorted,

'Don't stay here too long, and as for your village, it stands where it always did. For pity's sake, don't stop there. You would fall into a trap. The whole place is thick with soldiers, mind how you go. The peasants have gone crazy, they wouldn't mind if it were their father or their brother. Leave the Taurus tomorrow.

Goodbye and good luck.'

He stretched out his hand in the dark, and shook Memed's ice-cold hand. Then he slid down from the wall of the house.

In a moment or two Memed climbed the slope, went into the wood and groped his way to a hidden goat-track. He walked fast, the fear in his heart increasing, and his whole being full of distress. He felt friendless, alone, surrounded by a wall of darkness. The world was full of soldiers, and hostile peasants. Earth, soldiers, peasants, trees, plants, the birds of the air, the ants on the ground, everything, every living thing was against him.

A terrible hopelessness darkened his world. His inner longing for his village grew stronger and stronger. If he went, he knew what would happen to him. There was no hope of getting away safely. But he wanted to know about it madly, desperately. What had happened to the villagers? Did they still set fire to the thistle-fields with a special celebration? Did Uncle Durmush Ali still lead the merry *halay* dance in spite of his tired old legs? Had Mother Hürü got over her exasperation? She was a short-tempered woman. The earth trembled and the heavens shook at her rages. Had the villagers kept the oxen and the land he had distributed to them? He had learnt so many things in the last few years. So many . . . A man might live ten lives and not learn as much as Memed.

Ali Safa Bey, Arif Saim Bey and the other landowners of Chukurova . . . For a long time Memed simply had not realized why the landowners of Chukurova were hostile to him. He had killed Abdi Agha. But Abdi Agha was no relation of theirs. What had Memed done to them that they filled the entire Taurus with policemen merely on his account? He still did not entirely understand the reason. Why were they not so hostile to other brigands? Did they not even protect some brigands? But even supposing we understood the aghas and the beys, what about the peasants?

Where shall I go? he asked himself. I wandered all over the Euphrates region, and the land of the Kurds with their foreign tongue, and I found no refuge. This world is too small for me. I've returned to the mighty Taurus. No one knows where death awaits me. I've come to the Taurus to die. To the land of my fathers. The smell of death is in my nostrils. The world rejects a brigand, a certain Slim Memed who has been ill-used by the aghas and the beys, Yellow Ümmet. The earth and the sky reject me. Where am I to go, Ümmet? I am a broken-winged bird, a small bird, but every thicket rejects me.

He kept on thinking of somewhere to go to or to flee to, but in vain, and he grew more and more desperate. I took refuge in Old Osman's house; he is a good man, a pure man, a fatherly man, a sincere man, but a child-like man. He was longing to tell everyone I was in his house. Fortunately Mother Kamer was there . . . If you are caught by policemen in the plain of Chukurova, there's no hope for you. And how the Chukurova aghas would celebrate and rejoice then!

Suddenly he stopped on the goat-path in the wood, in the middle of the night. Whichever way he turned, there was nowhere to go. Which way should he turn? He stood stock still there in the darkness, for a while, thinking of many things. His thoughts passed through his brain at an incredible speed, and crowded in on him. His mother came before his eyes, Hatché, the baby, Mother Iraz, Old Süleyman. When he thought of Süleyman a warm, bright ray of hope shot through him. There was Kerimoghlu. And Jabbar. He was a brave man and a friend. He was married, with two children, a girl and a boy. Supposing he went to Jabbar's? They would not leave Jabbar alone. Nor Old Süleyman . . . Nor Kerimoghlu, either. It was no use staying in the mountains. But where should he go?

Wasn't there a cave near by? It would soon be daylight. He turned in the direction of the cave. At daybreak he reached a large rocky cave. At its mouth two eagles were perched, and on either side of the opening stood a mastic tree, with a blue-flowered creeper clinging to it. Memed went into the cave, and the tired eagles unwillingly opened their wings and flew to another place a little further on.

Memed unslung his rifle and holding the strap in his hand, placed it on the ground. As soon as he had put the bundle of ammunition on top of the rifle he fell asleep.

When he woke up the sun was setting. He was hungry and thirsty. The air was full of the scent of wormwood and thyme. The front of the cave was bedecked with anemones of an incredible crimson. The crimson flowers were growing out of the red rocks, which were spotted with white, black and green patches. Memed had never seen a mass of crimson flowers so wide-open, so flame-like and so dazzling, even from afar. He put on his rifle, picked up his package of ammunition and went outside. The eagles which had been there in the morning had come to perch again at the entrance to the cave. Unwillingly they flew off, and alighted side by side on the top of a rock ten paces away. They were very old eagles.

Further down a spring was bubbling from a crack in the rocks. Memed went to the spring, sat down in the purple water-mint, and opened the food package that Yellow Ümmet had given him and which he had strung on his belt. In the package there were three onions, six eggs, a lot of white cheese, a piece of Turcoman cheese, and plenty of wafer bread. And some pastries. He ate the food hungrily. It would last him for another two days. Memed was not a great eater. At times when he was worried it did not occur to him to eat.

He got up, and turned northwards. He was going to his village. He wanted so much to see it; a fire of longing had sprung up within him and was burning him up. He knew he was going to his death, but he could not prevent himself. He had to see his village. And what if he died without seeing it? The huge plane tree, Earless Ismail, his mill, the whirlpool by the big plane tree, the henna-red track, the thistly Plain of Dikenli, the houses, the patterned fields, the pebbly stream on the edge of the village, the trees, the thickets, the giant thistles, the village hens, even the tiny round yellow chicks running behind the hens . . . He could see it all, every bit of it, in his mind's eye. Durmush Ali, his warm, affectionate, friendly eyes, full of love, pitying, very kind . . . Mother Hürü, even kinder, much kinder . . . Rough and stubborn, but kinder than anyone. She would give her life for those she loved. One day she had stroked his hair in his sleep. Memed had never forgotten the warm, friendly, comforting, gentle touch of that motherly, friendly, sisterly hand. If Mother Hürü caressed you like that, you would give your life for her . . . Or if she did not, simply the way she said, from her heart and soul, 'my boy, my Memed', put new heart into you. What would she do when she saw him? She would be so wild with delight that she would hardly know what she was doing. Little Mustafa, Uncle Hösük . . . How dumbfounded Hösük would be. He would clap his hands for joy. 'Memed has grown a bit,' he would say. 'That's good. A sturdy man makes a better brigand and all the world's afraid of him. Everyone is already afraid of our Memed, but now they'll be even more afraid of him,' he would boast. What would Mustafa say or think? Would he be afraid? Perhaps he would. Would he tell the police? He had got married and had a child. If Jabbar heard, would he come? Memed smiled and said very firmly, 'He'll come.' And what about Lame Ali? Sly, fox-eyed Lame Ali? A loyal friend, and brother, and man . . . What would his reaction be? He would throw his head back and laugh. He would go on laughing like a stream of running water. He would laugh with his arms, his face, his body, his head, with every part of him. He would even laugh with his lame leg. He would be beside himself with joy.

In a whirl of joy and affection, Memed flew along. He walked so fast, it was as if his feet had grown wings. He did not think of misfortunes. He did not remember that the village might be full of policemen, or that he might be killed. It did not occur to him that, even if he were not killed, he would be up against tremendous difficulties. He even started singing. He knew very few songs. There had never been any time to learn any . . . but he had a melodious voice.

Day was breaking when he reached the head of Long Spring. The heart of Long Spring teemed with red-spotted trout. If you stretched out your hand you could catch one, but for some reason no one ever touched the Long Spring fish, and they increased rapidly. He sat down beside the water, took out his food packet, broke an onion with his fist, and began to eat it with the white cheese. Every now and then he threw some crumbs of bread to the fish, and watched them darting over each other towards the bread.

He ate his food very slowly, looking at the fish, and then stretched himself out comfortably on the ground. Since this spring belonged to his childhood, it never occurred to him to feel afraid there. Just as he had slept in his childhood, unafraid and unsuspicious, so he slept now. He had never slept so soundly and so uninterruptedly since the day he had become a brigand and taken to the mountains. When he woke up he was amazed. But this region was the land of his fathers, a land familiar to him. His inner gladness swelled and swelled as he waited for night to fall. As soon as it was dark he would go down to the village and knock gently at Mother Hürü's door, saying: 'Mother, I've come.' Would she know him by his voice? Of course she would recognize it! She was clever.

Slipping into the wood he descended the slope above the village. He sat at the foot of a high rock, and began to gaze at the village, and as he gazed lots of memories stirred within him.

In his childhood, when he was cross with his mother and escaped from the house he would come to the foot of that rock, and resting his back against it, would gaze at the village and think. This high rock was sooty. Memed had always known it thus. Peasants and shepherds liked to light fires at the foot of the rock.

He saw policemen in the village, walking to and fro. Then he made out his own hut from among all the others. The earth of which the hut had been built was red, green, blue and orange, it shone in the dazzling heat like fragments of glass. His father had brought this earth from a long way away so that the roof should not leak. His beautiful, gentle, warm-hearted, loving mother came before his eyes, and he felt a more acute loneliness than ever before in his life. On every side of him were tall asphodels. Thousands of bees buzzed in the dazzling heat, the white heat as Memed liked to call it, they hovered over the asphodels. On the thin, upright, immensely tall asphodel stems were hundreds of flowers like little white buttons.

He could not look at Hatché's house. He could not look at the huge tree in front of her house.

In the end he could not help himself, the tree came of itself and stood before his eyes, its branches extended as on that night. A young man, his heart beating like mad, had imitated the call of the whistler bird and had waited in a whirl of anticipation, feverishly. A gentle, warm-hearted, loving girl had come. There was a lump in Memed's throat, and two tears rolled down his cheeks.

In order to shake off this mood Memed fixed his eyes on Abdi Agha's house. Thick smoke was issuing from its chimney. Memed's anger boiled over: 'I haven't put out his hearth,' he said. 'I haven't

131

extinguished his fire. I haven't put out his light.' It was almost a groan. Bitterly he got up and walked on, then recovering himself, he smiled to think he was about to go into a village full of policemen in broad daylight. Returning to the foot of the tall rock, he saw a child's eyes gleaming in the depths of a thicket. The eyes were wide open, and were fixed on him in astonishment and admiration. In his childhood Memed used to come here and slip into that thicket and watch what was happening from the foot of the rock. Once, hidden in the thicket, he had seen Süleyman and the daughter of Lame Anshaja making love. He had never seen any brigands from that thicket. How he would have enjoyed watching a tiny brigand wearing field-glasses round his neck, bowed beneath a load of cartridge-belts and carrying a long silvermounted Circassian dagger, and hand-grenades at his belt. Standing there, Memed looked affectionately at the child. The child, realizing that the brigand had seen him, at a loss what to do, began to tremble.

Memed said smilingly, in a soft, friendly voice, 'My boy, don't tell the policemen you've seen me, I'm Slim Memed.' Memed was so pleased to see the child watching him like that, that he did not care whether he spread the news or not. At the sight of his village, Memed forgot that he was a brigand, that he was Slim Memed, that the police in the mountains had been sent by the mighty Government to catch him, and that the aghas' man Black Ibrahim was thirsting for his blood; he forgot everything, A child-like, innocent hope, a wave of affection and happiness welled up within him. He suddenly thought, 'I can't kill a bird, I can't crush an ant. I can't catch a bee, or a butterfly or a bird for fear of hurting it.' At that moment what most astonished him was probably the rifle in his hand, the dagger at his belt, and the cartridges round his body. He looked down at himself and laughed.

At that moment the child, having eluded Memed's gaze, came out of the thicket, as wary as a fox. He came out of the thicket a little way on all fours, and then took to his heels. As he ran he turned his head and looked back at Memed. This action of the child's made Memed even happier. He wondered who the child was. Who was he like? He had not had a good look at the child, so he could not imagine who he belonged to.

He was more impatient than ever. It seemed to him the sun would never set. Smoke continued to billow from Abdi Agha's chimney, and policemen continued to march to and fro between the houses. There was no sign of a woman, a man or any villager at all. Had they all been put in prison?

He was obsessed with the smoke coming out of Abdi Agha's chimney. It was on Abdi Agha's account that he could not enter his own village, that he could not walk freely in his own birthplace. He ground his teeth, and shouted, 'I'll put out that smoke. I won't leave a single one, not a single one . . .' He threw himself down at the foot of the rock, leaning his back against it with a thump.

Darkness had fallen and a breeze had sprung up from the north. The scent of wild mint and thyme and wormwood baked in the daytime heat, was wafted on the breeze.

He thought of that night. The night when Sergeant Rejep was about to kill Abdi's children; just as he was pulling the trigger, he had kicked the rifle and the bullet had gone in a different direction; the children were not killed. Should he have killed them? Innocent children? But what if they grew up to be as evil towards the people as their father? Well, we would see. Perhaps they wouldn't be at all like their father. All those sayings, 'A wolf-cub becomes a wolf,' or 'Like father, like son', were simply not true. He thought of old times, of Abdi Agha, Sergeant Asim, Captain Faruk and many other people. Captain Faruk had killed Hatché. As he said Captain Faruk's name he felt a sharp pain like that of poison within him and his hair seemed to stand on end. He could not leave this world without killing Captain Faruk and avenging Hatché. 'Mighty Allah,' he prayed, 'do not grant me death until I have killed Faruk.'

He got up and began to stagger down to the village as if he were drunk. Then suddenly he was in a happy mood. 'This autumn I'll come to the village again,' he thought to himself. 'I'll come on the day when the villagers begin to plough their lands, at the time of the celebration, and I'll be the first to set fire to the thistles. I and Mother Hürü . . .' As he got nearer the village, he grew more and more impatient and his heart beat more and more violently.

He stood at the door and if he had not leaned against the wall, he could not have remained on his feet; he would have fallen to the ground. Taking a deep breath,

'Mother Hürü, Mother Hürü,' he said, in a hoarse voice.

Mother Hürü was dozing inside, all alone. She could not believe her ears, she thought she was dreaming, so she opened one eye and closed it again.

Memed thought to himself, 'Perhaps Mother Hürü thinks I'm dead,' and he said again,

'Mother Hürü, Mother Hürü!'

Mother Hürü again thought she was dreaming. She opened one ye and murmuring a prayer, closed it again.

'Mother Hürü, Mother Hürü. It's me. I've come.'

Good heavens! It wasn't a dream at all, the voice was coming from behind the door, and it was like Memed's voice. But how could that be?

'Mother Hürü, Mother Hürü!'

Let me go out and have a look. She got up, only half-awake, picked up a pinewood torch that was already alight, and going to the door, whispered doubtfully,

'Who is it?'

Memed said quietly, just loud enough to be heard:

'It's me, Mother, Slim Memed, Deuneh's son. Open the door.'

Mother Hürü drew back the bolt and the door opened. Standing upright on the threshold was Slim Memed. Her mouth and tongue went dry and she could not utter a word. For a while they stood looking at each other. Then Memed took Mother Hürü by the arm and guided her into the house. He took the torch out of her hand and fixed it on the wall, and made Hürü sit down on the divan close by. For a long time they gazed at each other in silence. Then Mother Hürü, recovering herself, said very gravely,

'Welcome, Memed, my child, I'm glad you've come. We thought you were lost and gone for ever. Welcome, my child, I'm glad to see you. The village is full of policemen.'

'I know,' replied Memed.

'Did anyone see you entering the village?'

'A child saw me.'

At that very moment the sound of rifle-fire came from around the foot of the High Rock.

'Those bullets are meant for me, Mother. The child saw me at the High Rock . . .'

Mother Hürü smiled.

'Let them go on firing,' she said, 'let them go on wasting the bullets of that infidel Government and of those aghas!'

Memed smiled too.

He wanted to ask Mother Hürü a lot of questions, but he was tongue-tied and could not frame them. He would have asked where Durmush Ali was. Where had he gone? Was he dead? If he were, why was Hürü not wearing a black band round her head? Had they burnt the thistle-fields every year? Had they sowed and reaped their fields without anyone interfering from that day to this? But he could not ask. He began to be afraid that some disaster might have come upon them, and he could not ask a single question. He might wait a month, and look at Mother Hürü with wondering eyes every day, but he could not have asked a single question.

Hürü understood the expression in his impatient, questioning eyes, but she could not bring herself to give him bad news. She told herself that the poor boy was exhausted, at the end of his tether. His mother was dead, his sweetheart was dead, and it was not certain where his only child, whom he loved tenderly, had been taken, so if he heard some more bad news, what sort of state would he be in, the poor boy? What sort of state, Hürü?

When she looked at his face she saw his piteous, sorrowful expression. One could not refuse to tell him. Look at his face, God forgive me, look at his face, he looks like a baby whose mouth has been taken away from his mother's nipple, snuffling and crying.

I'll tell you, my child, I'll tell you. Hürü's heart has been turned into stone and iron. I'll tell you, my child. I'll tell you. If I'd been made of iron I couldn't have borne what has happened. I should have melted away, rotted to pieces. I became of stone and so I bore it. How will you bear so many sorrows and misfortunes? How will you bear them? I wish you hadn't come, my boy. You went away safe and sound, you slipped out of the village like a dark cloud. Why did you come back, my child? Some thought you had gone to join the Forty Holy Men. Others said you had gone to Mustafa Kemal, that you had become his chief of staff. And still others that you had been transformed into a huge bird and that you came to your mother's grave every night, and you hovered over my Deuneh's grave until morning, saying prayers in bird language. And over Hatché's grave too . . . How could you bear it, Memed, first your mother, beautiful Deuneh, and then beautiful Hatché? Why did you come back, child? How shall I tell you what has happened? Look at my hair. Have I a single black hair left? Look at my face. Is there any place without a wrinkle? Did I look like this when you went away, Memed?

With her eyes fixed on Memed's face, she continued her inner dialogue, just as if Memed could hear what was passing in her mind. She gesticulated, and her face now puckered, now brightened, now became sombre.

He'll hear in any case, she said to herself. He has borne so much grief that he can bear this too. He's not a child, he's a great man, Slim Memed.

Having decided to tell him, she broke into the laments that she had been suppressing. She wept and prayed and related her woes. At the end of every sentence she repeated that if she had been made of iron she would have gone to pieces, but as she had turned to stone she bore her woes. She wept for Deuneh, she wept for Hatché, she wept for Durmush Ali, she wept for the children, and she intoned laments.

Memed sat as if turned to stone, and listened to Hürü without moving a muscle of his face. The sound of firing came from outside, but it was as if neither of them heard it.

When Mother Hürü finished her tears and laments, she wiped her eyes and nose with her kerchief, and got up.

'I ought to be ashamed of myself, my boy,' she said. 'Seeing you made me forget what a long way you've come. Ill-fated Hürü ought to be ashamed of herself. I'm letting you go hungry.'

She fetched the cloth for meals and laid it in front of Memed. It was a beautifully embroidered cloth. She brought him a bowl of yoghurt and another of grape molasses. She also brought a little honey and cheese.

'There you are, my boy,' she said, 'please forgive me. Well, where have you been since you disappeared? Where did you go?'

Memed did not reply, he was plunged in thought, his face sternly set.

He took a piece of bread, and dipped it first in the molasses then in the yoghurt, and put it in his mouth. He chewed and chewed, but could not swallow it. It simply would not go down his throat. Durmush Ali had not died naturally, he had been killed, but he did not understand from the lament how he had been killed. The villagers had all become hostile to Hürü, and the villagers' houses had been plundered. That was what the lament said, but who had plundered them?

If he did not swallow some food Mother Hürü would be upset. He chewed and chewed and managed to swallow but then he began to cough. Afterwards, he took hold of Hürü's burning hand and said,

'Mother, tell me what's happened. However hard, what happens has to be endured. I can't swallow the food, please forgive me. I would have eaten your bread even if it had been poison, but I can't swallow it. Please forgive me, dear Mother, I've been through so much.'

Mother Hürü began her story tranquilly and calmly as if nothing had happened.

'Memed, my child,' she said. 'After you left the village . . . Everyone rejoiced at what you had done. Then they got frightened. They thought Abdi hadn't died. Then they found out that he was dead and that his heart had been pierced by dum-dum bullets. They were delighted. Then the five villages of the Plain of Thistles came together. They held a celebration. There never was such a celebration since the world began. The girls put on their best clothes. The old women put on their whitest kerchiefs. The drums beat in pairs. Even Durmush Ali, without regard for his health, took part in the dancing. Then at sunrise one morning men and women of the five villages, young and old, sick and well, went to the thistle-fields and set fire to the thistles. Never had there been such rejoicing since the creation of man. This lasted for a year or two. There was plenty of everything. The night of the day we set fire to the thistles, there was a blaze of light on Alidagh. It shone there on Alidagh for three nights. It was as light as day on the summit for those three nights. The villagers were even more delighted about this. Thus one year went by. In the second year the celebration was even better and more joyful. The Plain of Thistles burnt even more brightly. The blaze of light from the mountain-top was even more splendid. In the third year the celebration was even better and more joyful ... Durmush Ali danced – you remember how well he danced – and brandished a pinewood torch in his hand. He was going to set fire to the thistles. Suddenly in the distance three shots rang out, and we all looked in that direction. A rider came galloping along, raising the dust, and rode straight at Durmush Ali, who was near the heap of thistles. Durmush Ali fell to the ground and the rider made his horse trample on him. Behind him came ten more riders, riding over children and shooting. Many people were hurt. Five children, two of them girls, were killed. Uncle Durmush Ali lived for two days. He sent you his greetings. "Tell my son," he said, "that although it did not end well, he did a good job. Yes, he did a good job." So that year the thistles didn't burn. Nor did we see a blaze of light on Alidagh. Uncle Durmush Ali died. He remembered you in his last breath. Who was the rider, do you know? You remember Bald Hamza, Abdi's brother? Abdi had chased him out of the village, and he couldn't set foot here again while Abdi was alive. You remember Bald Hamza, Memed?'

'Yes, I do, Mother.'

'Well, that Bald Hamza has settled in the village now. He has his own armed men and he's brought in the police too. He's made us regret even Abdi Agha ...'

Mother Hürü went on and on relating what the villagers had had to put up with from the bald man, stopping now and then to gaze long and dolefully at Memed's face.

Bald Hamza was Abdi's own brother, but Abdi hated him and drove him out of Deyirmenoluk at the age of fifteen forbidding him to ever come back. Only once did Bald Hamza come back; he was caught and taken to Abdi Agha; Abdi had him beaten for three days and nights and then taken out of the Plain of Thistles, half-dead, on a horse, and cast away like a dead dog. After this terrible experience Bald Hamza did not recover for a long time; some nomads found him on the road and nursed him and he worked as a shepherd with them; then he eked out a living on a farm near Telkubbe, in Chukurova. He was not like Abdi Agha, short and scraggy; he was a tall man with a thick neck and great strength. When he heard about his brother's death, he was overjoyed; he was beside himself with delight; he rode round the farm for three days in a state of intoxication, telling everyone his brother had been killed. Then he forgot the event and continued his former way of life.

One day Pitirakoghlu came to see him at the farm from the Plain of Thistles. He was a very garrulous man.

'What a fool you are!' he told him bluntly. 'Haven't you heard that your brother has been killed?'

'I heard. I was overjoyed to hear someone had put paid to him.'

'You were right to be glad. Did you hear that the villagers have shared out his lands among themselves?'

'Yes, I heard,' said Bald Hamza.

'And that every year they go and set fire to the thistles in a great celebration?'

'Yes, I know.'

'And that there is a blaze of light on the top of Alidagh?'

'I know.'

'And that Abdi left two widows behind him?'

'I know.'

'If so, what are you doing here, scraping a living, you idiot!' shouted Pitirakoghlu. 'While you could be the Agha or the Pasha at Dikenli, what are you doing here? You stupid idiot.'

Pitirakoghlu was a very old man.

'You are right,' said Bald Hamza.

'If I'm right, you'll let me choose a well-watered field for myself at Dikenli, and give it to me.'

'All right,' said Bald Hamza.

They made preparations that very day. With the money he had saved up from his work on the farm, he bought a pair of boots, a fine pair of shalvar-trousers, a jacket, a hat, and, on credit, a handsome, slim four-year-old English horse. He also bought on credit a German carbine, with a hundred cartridges. He found half a dozen hardened jailbirds and with Pitirakoghlu leading, they all set out for Dikenli.

The peasants were just setting fire to the thistle-fields. Now they would be taught their lesson! Later he'd use the Government too . . . But not yet . . .

The peasants put up no resistance. They bowed their necks

like sheep. Many of them even went and apologized. They blamed Slim Memed, swearing at him and cursing his father's bones.

The same day Bald Hamza summoned Green-Rifle Hodja and had himself married to both of Abdi's widows. He slept with one in the evening and the other in the morning. The women were immensely grateful to Bald Hamza.

Then he brought policemen to the village and feasted the sergeants and corporals on roasted sheep and *raki* every day.

'It's better I shouldn't tell you, Memed, my child, what happened next and much better you shouldn't hear. Bald Hamza sent a message to the villagers saying, "You've sown and reaped for three years without giving his tithe to the Bey. Now for three years I shall take whatever you have in your houses." Flanked by a sergeant and a dozen policemen he went from house to house taking away everything we had; flour, wheat, oil, horses, cows, and donkeys, and heaped everything into Abdi's granary. That year the villagers went hungry. They howled like hungry wolves. The nearby villagers heard about our plight and brought us a few loaves of bread. Many people went away to nearby villages. That winter fifteen people swelled and swelled from hunger and died. When you came did you see anyone in the streets? You couldn't, my child. They're all half-naked . . . They can't go out . . .'

'Lame Ali?' asked Memed. His voice was almost inaudible.

'He's become Hamza's henchman. He helped to take the villagers' goods to the granary . . . Didn't I tell you to kill him? Didn't I tell you to stick that big dagger of yours into his belly?'

Memed, swaying, and pale as death, got to his feet. He could not stand, he had to hold on to the post. He tottered outside and made his way down to the Plain of Thistles as if he were drunk. His teeth were locked together and he was trembling all over.

The first ray of sunlight found him standing motionless, frozen, in the middle of the thistles. His face was dead white and expressionless. His shadow stretched ahead of him.

At noon Memed had still not moved; but his shadow had shrunk into a dark circle around his feet. The afternoon came and went.

Mother Hürü had run out after him and had looked for him everywhere. She searched all over the plain until sunrise and even

140

after sunrise she went on searching. In the afternoon she suddenly thought of looking in the thistle-field. She looked and there, sure enough, was Memed standing like a post in the middle of the thistles. Stumbling, half-running, she reached his side. She found Memed exhausted, his teeth clamped together.

'I've killed you, my child. Come along quickly. The policemen will see you, someone will see you.'

She took him by the arm and dragged him towards a nearby gorge and made him lie down in a thicket of chaste-trees. She sprinkled water on his face, and talked to bring him round, joking and smiling. After a while Memed recovered.

'Mother,' he said, 'you are the bravest of mothers. I've done you a lot of harm.'

He took Hürü's hand in his and pressed it to his lips. Then he smiled.

'Mother,' he said, 'tell Lame Ali to come here.'

Hürü was about to object, but she changed her mind.

'Very well, my boy,' she said, and bowed her head. 'I'll go straight away and have him come to you tonight. But please, Memed, don't trust that infidel. He'll do you a bad turn. The village is full of policemen. He's hand in glove with the police and Bald Hamza. Forgive me, but do be careful . . . I've only you left . . .'

If I'd been made of iron, I would have rotted away. I became earth and I endured . . . I became earth, earth, earth and I endured.

22

IDRIS BEY appeared to be about thirty. He was thin and tall. With his yellow eyes, aquiline nose and long face he looked like a wild untamed creature that did not inhabit this world but had happened to alight here. An enchanted, sacred creature . . . He had long drooping moustaches. His fingers were long and beautiful. When you met him for the first time you didn't notice his body or his beautiful golden eyes, or his fair, glossy moustache, or his hair. The first time you met him you would only notice and admire his long, fine fingers.

His father, who was a Chechen chieftain, had come from the Caucasus with his tribe in Ottoman times and had settled on the south bank of the River Jeyhan, opposite Anavarza Castle. The village they founded was called Akmezar (the White Tomb). At first they sickened and wasted away with the flies, malaria and heat of Chukurova. After three or four years they became acclimatized, but their numbers were reduced by half. The horses they had brought from the Caucasus and their other animals were also decimated. But later on, when they were used to the conditions in Chukurova, they began to breed fine horses. They tilled the land. At that time Chukurova did not know what an orchard looked like. They planted fruit-trees and tended orchards in the heat of the plain. In contrast to the Turcomans' reed huts, they built two-storey houses made of wood and stone, and laid out streets and avenues in their village.

On the fertile lands they founded a happy way of life. They became famous all over the plain for their beautiful horses, their huge fruit and their brave deeds. They did not engage in horse-stealing like the other Circassians of the Taurus. They obeyed their chieftains. They preserved the traditions and customs of the Caucasus.

This peaceful, contented existence had been going on for years when one day a new black Ford motor-car came and stopped in front of the door of their last chieftain, Idris Bey. The motor-car was covered in dust. Its big headlamps, though dusty, sparkled in the Chukurova sunlight. Until that day the peasants of Akmezar, with the exception of a few who had done military service, had never seen a motor-car. The peasants, men and women, young and old, looked at that huge, shining-eyed strange creature in bewilderment and admiration. Some felt in their hearts a bitter, ominous fear. Others were delighted to see this strange creature.

Two people got out of the motor-car. One had big, thick black eyebrows. He was all in black. He had on a broad brimmed black hat. The man with the thick, black eyebrows wore a gleaming gold watch-chain across his stomach. He stood stiffly, leaning back, and shot condescending glances around him out of the corner of his eye. He looked as if he were the maker of heaven and earth and the whole creation. He gave this impression with every gesture he made. Even Idris Bey was unusually impressed, and bowed low before this demi-god. The old Circassians were surprised at his gesture, and angry too. After the man in black, another man, dressed in grey, got out of the car, doing his jacket buttons up. His hand fiddling with his buttons, he followed the first man, waiting like a bird of prey on the watch.

It did not take the Circassians long to realize that this was a new, great man, like the Czar. Who and what was he? They wondered.

Idris Bey invited him into the house, rather surprised and still more afraid and curious. The guest said nothing. As he entered the room the man who was following the big man whispered a name into Idris's ear. Idris Bey's face paled, and his agitation increased threefold. He said,

'Welcome, welcome, welcome, this is a pleasure, Bey. You have honoured our village, Bey. Honoured it greatly.'

The big man slowly stretched out a plump hand towards Idris Bey, and Idris took it but did not kiss it, thus causing an expression of displeasure to cross the big man's face. Idris Bey saw this, guessed the reason, and was ruffled. 'Our tribe has never kissed anyone's hand, even a Pasha's or a Czar's,' he said to himself. 'Let no one expect hand-kissing from us.'

The big man, who appeared to be about thirty years old, looked like a statue of Fear personified. He did not speak. To the man standing with his hands on the button of his jacket, waiting respectfully, and to Idris Bey, who was waiting politely, the big man gave a jerk of his head indicating that they were to sit down. They sat down on the edge of the sofa opposite him and put their hands on their knees. A young girl, tall, fair, beautiful, with a neck like a swan, brought coffee on a silver tray. The big man looked her over out of the corner of his eye. The sombre expression on his face lightened a little, and then returned to its former impassiveness. Slowly he took a gold cigarette-case out of his pocket, opened it and drew out a cigarette with the tips of his fingers, then equally slowly he closed the case with a snap and put it back in his pocket. Idris Bey in a flurry took out flint and steel and prepared the tinder, in order to strike a light, but the guest equally slowly took a petrol-lighter out of his pocket and at once lit the cigarette. Idris Bey had never seen a petrol-lighter until that moment. In Turkey there were only a few people who had such a lighter. It too was made of gold.

When he saw the flame spring from the lighter Idris Bey smiled shamefacedly. The ghost of a smile passed over the big man's face too. 'A gift from the Pasha,' he said. 'He loves to give his friends beautiful, valuable gifts. The English Ambassador brought this for the Pasha.'

The big man finished his coffee and cigarette in silence and sat there a little longer. Then he got up, very straight and in full majesty, stretched his hand out and touched Idris Bey's, shaking it twice, and said in a loud voice, 'Goodbye.'

Without looking to one side or another, he walked, very upright, down the stairs, and walked to his motor-car. The chauffeur, bowing till he was bent double, held the door of the car open. He got in, bolt upright. The engine started. The man in grey got in next to the driver. The motor-car moved off. The big man did not even turn and look at Idris Bey.

The motor-car went off in a cloud of dust, sinking up to its axles in the dust of the track, and left the village.

Idris Bey said to the assembled villagers,

'That was Arif Saim Bey, Member of Parliament for Kozan.'

The villagers had often heard the name.

An old Circassian, with years of experience and battles behind him, said,

'He's Mustafa Kemal Pasha's right hand, one of his guards. He and the Pasha are close friends. At Diyarbakir I saw some men he had hanged; their bodies were hanging from one end of the town to the other. He is the president of the High Court. But how young he is! Not even thirty.'

The whole of Chukurova knew Arif Saim Bey very well. When the French occupied Adana he was the Police Commandant at Sis. At first, he came to an understanding with them. Then he realized that the French would not be staying, and went over to Mustafa

Kemal's side; in a short time he became Mustafa Kemal's most trusted man.

He came from Bingöl and was the son of a poor Kurd. He had some difficulty in getting through his studies and only graduated from the Military Academy by the skin of his teeth. Anyway he had no great inclination for studying. But he loved using a rifle. His greatest boast was that he could hit silver coins with a revolver from a great distance.

Mustafa Kemal Pasha took him away from Kozan and sent him to a southern province to organize the people against the French. Months before he arrived, the people there had organized themselves against the French, and had begun to clash with them. In several places, the French had been routed. The brave people of that province were driving the French towards the desert, without any help from anyone. Arif Saim Bey took over the leadership of the people's forces; the French, defeated in all the southern provinces, were routed in this one too, and evacuated their troops. Arif Saim Bey, like the other officers who took part in this campaign, had the Independence Medal conferred on him, and was proclaimed a hero. He became one of Mustafa Kemal's most intimate companions. Furthermore, he was at once elected to Parliament as a member for the place where he had been in command of the police.

When Arif Saim Bey was elected to Parliament and went to live in Ankara the first thing he did was to buy a car. Then he built up a fortune. When the period of the founding of the Republic was over, and things were settling down, his first move was to come to Chukurova which he knew well. He had a great passion for the golden land of Chukurova. But it never occurred to him that if the War of Independence had not taken place, he would not have owned a foot of that land. Most of this land had belonged to Sultan Abdul Hamid, to feudal lords, to the Arabs who were known as Egyptians and to the Armenians.

When Arif Saim Bey came to Chukurova he brought with him in his car an expert in agriculture and land. The man in grey who had come with him to Akmezar, the man who kept his finger on his button, was this agricultural expert. His name was Ahmet Bey, and he had done his training in Budapest at the Higher Agricultural College. He was one of the few experts in the country.

As they left Ankara Arif Saim Bey said,

'Ahmet Bey, my friend, they recommended you to me as being a great specialist in land. We'll go to Chukurova now in the motor-car, we'll drive over every inch of the plain; you will examine the quality of the soil and determine the most fertile land. I will acquire that land and will establish the largest and most modern farm in Turkey.'

First of all they drove over the plain of Yüregir and in the neighbourhood of Tarsus. They went to the marshes of Karatash and Aghba. Ahmet Bey looked at the land, enquired about the crops, talked to the peasants, took measurements, and wrote in his notebook. All he said was, 'Yes, sir, we can go on', and all he did was to button up his jacket and bow. It was evident throughout that he had done and would continue to do his work very well. From Aghba they went to Yumurtalik where they stayed three days. From Yumurtalik Arif Saim Bey drove to the Aptioghlu farm. A parliamentary colleague of his, who had once been Minister of Education, had acquired this farm. Arif Saim Bey was madly envious of him. That member of Parliament had never served on any battle front, or risked his life like others; he had just sat quietly in Ankara. How and why had he obtained a farm? What right had he?

When the expert had examined the soil of the Aptioghlu farm, the Bey hissed at him between his teeth,

'What's it like?'

'Perfect,' said Ahmet Bey.

'The land you find for me must be better than this.'

'At your orders, sir.'

'The best land must be mine. I have a right to it. I shed my blood at the front; while I was risking my life, he was sleeping in his wife's arms.'

'Yes, sir, we'll find some, sir.'

'Of course you will.'

He spoke with a slightly Kurdish accent.

From Aptioghlu they went to the town of Jeyhan. They went up to Dumlu. They toured the Osmaniye region for four days, then came to Kadirli, and wandered on the fringes of Ahjasaz.

There Ahmet Bey found a nice piece of land.

'Bey, this soil is inexhaustible,' he said. 'It will never yield less than fifty to one. Maybe even seventy-five.'

Arif Saim Bey asked,

'Fifty to one, seventy-five to one, what does that mean?'

Ahmet Bey answered,

'If you sow a single seed, you will get fifty seeds.'

'What about middling or bad soil?'

'Bad soil would give you a return of one, two, three or at the most five.'

'Where is there soil like that?'

'The whole of Central Anatolia is like that.'

'Pity.'

'A middling soil yields ten or fifteen to one.'

'Very good . . . What does inexhaustible soil mean?'

'If soil is used too much it loses its fertility, and its strength decreases. We call soil inexhaustible if the strength of the soil scarcely ever decreases. Such soils do not become exhausted. Soil that nourishes itself, pure silt, alluvium or marshy soil is inexhaustible.'

'Is this soil inexhaustible?'

'Yes, it is.'

The soil that Ahmet Bey had found belonged to an old farm. It belonged to the Akhodja family, who were Turcoman Beys in olden times. Nowadays the Akhodjas were scattered, and their broad lands had been divided up. The land that Ahmet Bey liked had fallen to Selim Bey. He did not concern himself with the farm or the land, but had joined Yaghmur Agha's gang and was engaged in horse-stealing. Arif Saim was delighted to hear about this. When he went to the town he immediately called the Land Superintendent into his presence.

The Land Superintendent said: 'Selim Bey's land does not belong to the Treasury, but in that neighbourhood there are three hundred dunums of Treasury land, confiscated from the Armenians. The documents referring to these three hundred dunums can include Selim Bey's farm.'

And he explained in detail how this could be done. Arif Saim was satisfied.

'Go and put it up for sale at once without letting anyone know.'

Mazlum Bey, the Land Superintendent, put the land up for sale by auction at once. The day of the auction came round but no one attended it. The ownership of three hundred dunums fell to Arif Saim Bey for twenty-three liras.

As Arif Saim Bey drew up the boundaries to his farm, including within them the farm that had belonged to the horse-thief Selim, the Akhodja family got to know about it. The oldest, most experienced man in the community was tall, white-whiskered Aziz Agha. When he heard about the situation he flew into a rage. The land was going. It was not a question merely of his own land; if Arif Saim Bey obtained Akhodja land in this way, they would soon not have a foot of land left in their possession. So he bestirred himself, mounted his horse and went to see the important long-standing landowners of the province of Adana. One of these was General Secretary of the People's Party, the Government party. These two ancient families had been friendly for many long years. Their interests had coincided for decades.

The General Secretary, after hearing what the situation was, went straight to the Pasha, and told him the story of Arif Saim Bey's conduct. What the Pasha said about the matter is not known. But Arif Saim Bey withdrew from Selim Bey's farm, and never set foot in that region any more. The three hundred dunums he had obtained for twenty-three liras were forgotten.

After this terrible setback, Arif Saim Bey went to Dörtyol with Ahmet Bey. They stayed there a week. At Dörtyol there were some large orange groves. While he was staying there Arif Saim Bey spoke to rich citizens and notables. Here too, some Armenian estates and orange groves had fallen to the Treasury. Arif Saim Bey ordered that one of the most beautiful of these estates and some orange groves should be given as a present to the Pasha.

'What?' he said in great fury. 'Is it possible that there is no orange grove here belonging to the saviour of our fatherland?'

The rich citizens and notables were longing to make such a gift to Mustafa Kemal Pasha. But they were afraid that the Commander-in-Chief would not appreciate their motive. It had been the custom in the last days of the Ottomans that the feudal lords should present land, gardens or pavilions to the Sultans.

They liked Arif Saim Bey's proposal enormously.

After this Arif Saim Bey found a pretext for pillaging land. If the Pasha heard about the stratagems he was using over Chukurova and was angry, Arif Saim would say,

'Pasha, the people made me a present of a little piece of land, just as they made you a present, they gave them in recognition of our services. The feudal lords complained because they were envious of me. How could I not accept this token of regard from the people?'

The second piece of land in Chukurova that Ahmet Bey approved of was a small farm near the village of Akmezar. When the Armenians had been driven out, the Armenian owner of this small farm had sold it to a Turcoman friend. The Turcomans and the Armenians had very close and friendly relations with each other.

'If I come back again, my friend,' said the Armenian, 'you can give me back my land. If I don't come back the farm is yours. You need have no qualms about accepting it; may it be your lawful property.'

Arif Saim Bey asked Ahmet Bey again and again,

'Is it inexhaustible land? Is it better than Selim's land?'

'Yes,' said Ahmet Bey with complete confidence. 'It's better than Selim's land. Plots of land as fine as this one only exist in very few parts of the world. Even on the banks of the Nile they would be hard to find.'

Arif Saim Bey made enquiries in the town that very day and heard the story of the farm. He had the poor Turcoman brought over, and threw down ten liras in front of him.

'Make over that Armenian farm to me,' he said.

Having to get into the motor-car, and being hustled by two policemen into Arif Saim Bey's presence had frightened the poor Turcoman. As he was being taken there, he imagined that he was going to be killed, imprisoned or at the least sent into exile. Everyone throughout Anatolia knew Arif Saim's reputation ... Nobody who opposed him could survive. When the Turcoman saw that instead of being hanged or thrashed he was having ten liras put before him he could hardly believe his eyes. First he looked at the ten liras, then at the hard face of Arif Saim Bey, with his thick black scowling brow. As if thinking 'There must be a snag in it', his suspicious eyes went from the ten liras to Arif Saim Bey, and back again from Arif Saim Bey to the ten liras.

'Take it, Mahmut,' said Arif Saim Bey, understandingly. 'You have a right to this money.'

Mahmut, delighted to hear the Bey calling him by his name, took courage.

'Take it, I tell you, Mahmut! Take it, my friend, you have a right to it. How long have you had that property round your neck?'

'Ten years,' cried Mahmut.

Arif Saim very slowly picked up the ten liras between his fingers and thumbs, screwing up his face as if with loathing, and held it out to Mahmut.

'Take it,' he said, 'you've carried the title-deeds in your pocket ten years so it's one lira for each year.'

Mahmut took the money and thrust it into his breast. Then he threw himself down at the Bey's feet. The people standing by raised Mahmut from the ground. The Bey slowly drew out another five lira from his pocket, and gave it to Mahmut. Mahmut's behaviour had touched him.

'Were you ever in the Army, Mahmut?'

Mahmut immediately stood to attention stiffly in front of Arif Saim Bey. He stood as straight as a ramrod, without moving. He fixed his eyes on a spot in the distance, without blinking.

'I was, Commandant,' he said, as if responding to the roll-call.

'Did you fight?'

'I did, Commandant.'

'Whereabouts?'

Mahmut recited breathlessly,

'Galicia, the Dardanelles, Mesopotamia, Greece . . .'

'Were you ever wounded?'

'I was, Commandant.'

'Where?'

'In the neck, groin, arm, leg.'

'So you're a hero? Did they give you a medal?'

'No, Commandant.'

'Mahmut!'

'Yes, Commandant.'

'I'm going to reorganize the farm soon. I like you. Will you come and work for me?'

The Land Superintendent was waiting with his register in his hands. The handing-over of the title to the property began and finished there and then. Mahmut appended his thumb-mark, and the Bey added his pretentious signature with innumerable flourishes. He shook Mahmut's hand and Mahmut left him, full of delight. As he went back to his village, he tapped his heels together behind him, as if celebrating his happiness in rhythm.

In this way, with the handing-over to Arif Saim Bey of the farm belonging to the Turcoman Mahmut, there began the events that affected the village of Akmezar. It was from that day on that unexpected troubles began to happen to young Idris Bey.

The farm property that Arif Saim Bey liked and bought measured only two to three thousand dunums. Was that amount of land sufficient for a man like Arif Saim Bey who had shed his blood in the war, who was a close friend of the Pasha, who had reached the rank of national hero? Really it was shameful. It was a beggarly amount. One could not let a national hero sink so low. The villagers of Akmezar had a lot of land. What did the Chechen people know of farming! Let them breed horses, or join Yaghmur Agha's band and steal horses.

Arif Saim Bey said mockingly,

'Let them give up their land to those who know how to cultivate it and love it, and let them carry on with the kind of work they like. Let them follow their ancestors' calling.'

At first it was easy to obtain land from the people of Akmezar. It was easy since our young hero of the War of Independence was clever enough to adapt himself to the times and to make use of circumstances. He made careful enquiries about the Circassians of Akmezar. He found out their preferences. The old ones, even after two or three generations, still loved the Caucasus and Caucasian traditions. They had run away from the Caucasus and yet for them it was a dream world, a paradise. Every time they spoke it was about the Caucasus, their homeland. And the sacred trust which remained in their hands from the Caucasus was their horses. They loved their horses better now than they had in their homeland. When the Bey learnt this he summoned Yaghmur Agha and invited him to stay one night at his mansion. They spoke at length of the old days. Arif Saim Bey knew Yaghmur Agha from the days when he himself had been the Police Commandant of the district. He had captured him and his gang five times, and had released them five times.

He pretended that he had released Yaghmur Agha solely because of his friendship for him, but this was a lie. He had undertaken some jobs in co-operation with Yaghmur Agha. It did not suit either Yaghmur Agha or Arif Saim Bey to mention this co-operation now . . . They were mysterious matters. They did not even mention them, and were embarrassed by each other.

Once Yaghmur Agha made a slip. He was just saying, 'Bey, we and the French . . .' But the Bey interrupted him.

'What French?' he shouted.

Yaghmur Agha understood. Even between the two of them, Arif Saim Bey, the national hero, did not want it said that he had collaborated with the French. They never spoke about it again. But the whole of Chukurova knew about this collaboration.

'Well, Yaghmur Bey, has your troop grown? How many horses a day can you steal?' asked Arif Saim Bey quite seriously, and the other man answered with equal seriousness,

'The troop has grown a lot, thanks to you, Bey. Thanks to our Republic. Nowadays the troop is made up of experienced horse-copers, and there are three hundred and thirty-six useful members. They also have some assistants. And the assistants have other assistants. I am now at the head of an association of one thousand five hundred men, Bey.'

'An army.'

'Yes, Bey, it's an army now. There are fine horses in the Caucasus and Iran. We take those horses and sell them on the shores of the Black Sea. Horse-stealing is rather difficult in the Caucasus and Iran, but I've sent the most able men, especially Circassians, to those places. I send the horses stolen from the Black Sea area to the East, to the Fourth Army. Horses cannot stand too great a change of climate. One year I took three hundred horses down into Chukurova from the Caucasus, and they all died. They could not stand the flies and the malarial fever. I send the horses we get from Syria, Iraq and Urfa to Western Anatolia, for example, Smyrna, Aydin, Denizli and Manisa. Horses were depleted by the war there. They're very expensive now and those coming from the places I mentioned adapt themselves well to that climate. The horses I steal from Western Anatolia are sent to Central Anatolia. I think I can extend our organization for the development of horse breeding right into Iran, Afghanistan and India. I'm working on a plan.'

'I'll tell the Pasha about your great energy, Yaghmur Agha. I think they ought to elect you to Parliament. Your services to the Turkish nation are important.'

Talking seriously in this way, with grave faces, they suddenly burst out laughing.

Having had a good laugh, and joked about the gang and horse-stealing, they now turned to serious matters.

Yaghmur Agha loved horse-stealing, and every year he was responsible for the movement of hundreds, even thousands of horses from one region to another, from one country to another. He did all he could to improve the breed of horses in the Middle East. If all the Circassians from Uzunyayla and a large part of the people of Chukurova had very soon joined Yaghmur Agha's band it was not to be wondered at.

At the large old farm that belonged to Yaghmur Agha, old and famous horse-thieves gave lessons to the young ones in the art of horse-stealing; they would take the ones that caught their eye to Yaghmur Agha and say, 'Make good use of him, Bey.' Üzeyir, a bold, strong, eighty-year-old horse-thief, would train the most promising ones, showing them how to remove chains and tethers and steal the most well-guarded horses.

Everyone in Chukurova, indeed in the whole of Turkey, knew about Yaghmur Agha's activities. There was no secret about this large, strong band; they carried on their work openly, before everyone's eyes.

The year before, a beautiful horse was stolen from an Arab sheik in Iraq. The sheik, who was devoted to the horse, set out at once and hastened to see Yaghmur Agha at the farm. Weeping bitter tears, he related what had happened. 'I can't bear to live without my horse,' he said. Taking out a purse of gold coins, he said, 'Take all this, but find me my horse.' Yaghmur Agha was a decent man, and would not take the sheik's money. He felt sorry for the man, and taking him by the hand, led him to the stable. As soon as the sheik looked the horses over from a distance, he said, 'Mine isn't there.'

Yaghmur Agha sent one of his most renowned horse-thieves with the sheik, saying to him, 'Don't come back until you've found the sheik's horse.'

Six months later they found the sheik's horse with a nomad chief on a mountain near Marmaris. They greeted him in the name of Yaghmur Agha, and the nomad chieftain gave the horse back without even asking for any money.

Arif Saim Bey said to Yaghmur Agha, 'I want you to find me at least a hundred horses that can stand the climate of Chukurova, within two months.'

'Very well,' said Yaghmur Agha. 'Must they all be the same colour?'

'I would prefer different colours. Ten bays, ten greys, five whites, five dun and so on . . .'

Within two months more than a hundred horses had been brought to Arif Saim Bey's farm.

Then Arif Saim Bey sent for a Circassian called Yakup. He was a very old decrepit man, yet he never left the saddle. He always wore boots and his beard was still red. He would tell everyone that his own father not Idris Bey's had been the real Bey, and that Idris Bey's father had been their servant.

Arif Saim Bey said,

'Yakup, how much land have you?'

'A hundred and twenty dunums.'

Arif Saim Bey took him by the hand, and led him to the stable, which was full of horses.

'Make over to me the rights to your land, and you can take whichever two horses you want from here.'

Yakup's eyes opened wide:

'Do you really mean that, Bey? But these are thoroughbreds.'

'Choose the ones you want, whether they are thoroughbreds or not. All the better!'

Yakup the Circassian spent a week in the stable examining the horses, and finally selected two splendid three-year-old white

on his face, neck, hands and legs. He even felt their bites on his back through his thick jacket and shirt. Adem was lost in thought. Was it his own white horse he had shot, or the brown stallion? It was the brown stallion, he said to himself again and again. When it fell to the ground it rolled over like a black treetrunk. Quite black. If it had been the white horse it would have shone in the sunlight, like a white cloud. Thinking about this, he cheered up. I'll go to the Bey tomorrow, I'll take the head of the brown horse and throw it down in the yard. I'll say, thus may thine enemies perish, Bey. If you wish, I'll bring Yobazoghlu's head, and Old Osman's and Slim Memed's. Kemal Pasha's too, if you say the word. He laughed to himself and gazed towards the place in the darkness where the dead horse lay; he could see the black shape of a horse. Look! he said to himself. Look! It's a black body lying there. The brown horse, I said, and I took aim. Do I ever miss? He waded into the narcissus-beds, crushing the flowers, and drank some cold water from the brook. I've succeeded, he said. It was no easy task but I've managed it . . . He emerged from the reeds and went to the plane-tree, but could go not a step further. I must go and look, he said, but he could not bring himself to take a step towards the horse's carcass; an icy dread came over him, preventing him from moving his other leg forward, so he retreated again. Suddenly the thought came to him, if it was the white horse I killed, the Bey will never look at me again; never, never, he groaned. I shot his most beautiful horse, poor man . . . I chose the best one from the stable, then with five bullets . . . If only I could go and look at the carcass, and escape from this torment.

A clammy mist weighed on the night. His hands, full of mosquito-bites, his clothes, cap and legs were all damp with the mist. A clammy mist. He sweated constantly. There was not a breath of wind. The heat was suffocating. Adem tore open his shirt down to his belly. He felt acutely uncomfortable, and could not keep still.

For a while he tried to sleep, putting his head on a mound, but sleep would not come to him. Usually, only yesterday, he would have fallen asleep as soon as he laid his head on the pillow. He tossed and turned for a time, and then got up. He walked towards Anavarza Castle. Even in the night the swallows still flitted mockingly before his face. As he got further away from the dead horse he felt more cheerful, and a quiet contentment came over him. He walked like that till morning. It was not until the sun was up that he stopped, turned round and looked towards the place where he had fired the evening before. He could not see the dead horse, but the tall plane-tree with its wide branches was visible. A little way beyond the plane-tree, high in the sky, a group of eagles was wheeling.

For a time Adem stood motionless watching the flight of eagles swooping down towards the plane-tree. He stretched his hands out, appealingly, like an innocent child.

'Please God, let it be the brown horse I hit,' he said. 'If it wasn't the brown horse I can never look anyone in the face again. Oh God, you know how much I love my wife, but I can never see her again.'

He realized that he was longing passionately for his wife. He remembered the last time he had slept with her; her large taut breasts were warm.

'If the one that died wasn't the brown stallion, I shall die. Oh God, please help me!'

Near the plane-tree, the eagles kept hovering in the sky, swooping down and hopping on the ground with open wings; then they were lost to view in the grass.

He began to run towards the dead horse. When he got to the plane-tree he would close his eyes, then when he got to the dead horse he would open them.

It was very hot. The blazing sun beat down on the plain of Anavarza scorching it. The sun belched forth fire. There was not a single creature out in the open; horses, donkeys, wolves, birds, bees, flies, spiders and snakes had all taken shelter in shady, cool places.

Breathless, he reached the plane-tree. He was too tired to stand, and sank down in a heap at the foot of the tree. He was worn out with lack of sleep, totally exhausted. He rested his head on a tree-root, watching the swooping eagles out of the corner of his eye. Absorbed in this he fell asleep, still clutching his rifle tightly in his right hand.

Eagles descended from the sky in their hundreds. There was a

157

flapping of eagles' wings on all sides. Black, grey, reddish eagles. Old and young vultures. The vultures could not draw near the horse's carcass but stood at a distance waiting for the eagles to withdraw.

Around the carcass there was a beating of wings, a confusion of eagles that lasted for some time; the eagles alighted one on top of another on the carcass, in a heap of flapping wings. Other eagles glided down one after the other. Between the carcass and the plane-tree under which Adem was sleeping, under the tree and all around Adem there came black fluttering eagles.

Then, in the afternoon, the eagles began to withdraw. The last of them, finding not a scrap of flesh left on the carcass, went away. Only the head and a piece of the tail were left, and some shreds of the mane, hanging from a clean white skeleton.

After the eagles came some scraggy dogs. They pulled the horse's skeleton into the shelter of the reeds, into a thicket of willow saplings, and began to lick the bones at their ease.

The sun rose above Adem. In the heat of the sun he was scorched and dried up, and bathed in sweat. At last he woke up. As he awoke the first thing he saw was that where the horse had been there were no eagles, nothing . . . Where were the horse's bones? Instead of bones all he saw were three or four old, bald vultures stepping here and there. Adem was glad it was like that. To himself he said, to hell with it! I did kill the brown horse. The eagles have eaten the flesh, and the dogs have taken away the bones.

He advanced to the place where the horse had been. There was not the smallest trace left. On the earth and in the grass there was not even a patch of blood or a halter, or a piece of saddlecloth. The eagles and dogs had devoured every bit. Adem knew that this would be so. 'I thank you, God,' he said. 'You have saved me from disaster. You vouchsafed me the power to kill the brown stallion. Thank you. When I get home I will sacrifice a fine cock to you. But how shall I find the white horse? And the head of the brown horse? How shall I convince the Bey that I killed him?'

He was very hungry. Below the marshes lay a deep gully, and in the gully grew a lot of water-mint. There was a mulberry tree there, too. The water was cool. He descended into the gully, and undid the bundle of food tied to his waist-belt. The cloth round the food was damp as if with water. His sweat had soaked even the bread. The bread had got dry and hard as stone. The sweat that had soaked the hard bread had not softened it.

Adem put the bread, black as clay, into the spring; he held it in the cold water for a time; when the bread got a little softer he began to gnaw it. He munched at that black clay until he had finished it. The white cheese he put bit by bit into his mouth. Then he went on his way. The cool of the evening descended. The afternoon wind had risen and to the south some big white clouds were piling up. Dust rose over the tracks; sand-devils whirled from south to north.

He could not go home. What would the Bey say? Would the white horse have returned to the farm?

Suddenly he grew angry with the eagles. Foul, disgusting creatures. They had not left any of the horse's carcass for him to see. They had even eaten the bones. Foul birds, whoever heard of birds eating bones? You aren't birds, you're dogs . . . Filthy curs . . . Filthy curs . . . Reptiles. Carrion-eaters. I'll show you. As he walked along, his anger grew and grew. When he reached the crags of Anavarza it was twilight. Over a reddish hole in the rocky area four or five eagles were standing with wings folded and necks drawn in. He raised his gun, aimed at the largest and pressed the trigger. The eagle he had aimed at immediately began to roll down the rocks. Adem climbed up to the place where the eagle had fallen. It was not yet dead and was clawing at the rocks. He took it by the tip of its wings and began to drag it behind him down the hill.

He was not thinking about anything, but the anger inside him boiled up. He stopped, and in his fury crushed the head of the dying eagle under his heel.

His legs took him straight to the house of his friend from army days, Kurdish Sefer, in the village of Anavarza. When he suddenly looked up, he found himself at Sefer's door.

Sefer saw him, and came down the ladder of his *chardak.**

'Welcome, Adem my friend. I thought you'd forgotten all about us. Look how the children have grown!'

* A *chardak* is a shelter built of branches and set on stilts

He saw the eagle that Adem was holding by the wing-tip and dragging behind him.

'What's that? Why have you brought an eagle here?'

Adem glanced at the eagle which he had dragged with him, and at once dropped the wing he was holding.

'I shot it as I was coming along,' he said.

'Come up to the chardak. You look tired.'

He called to his wife:

'Bring a ewer quickly. Fill it so that Adem can give his face a good wash. Fancy seeing him here!'

Adem washed and dried his hands and face thoroughly, and climbed up into the chardak. There was thick soup, flavoured with mint. Adem had been longing for a hot meal for days, so he devoured the soup greedily. Then reclining against a cushion, he related at length to Sefer what had happened, the struggle with the brown stallion and the eagles.

'What do you think of it, Sefer?' he ended up. 'Give me some advice.'

Sefer thought hard. Adem asked Sefer another question,

'Do you think it was the brown stallion I killed?'

'I don't know,' said Sefer. 'Nobody can know. You'll have to go on looking for whichever one's alive. You can't go to see Ali Safa Bey empty-handed as you are now. You'd find it too awkward. You'd be a laughing-stock. Don't tell anyone, not even your wife, that the horse was eaten by eagles and that for this reason you haven't seen him. Everyone would jeer at you.'

Adem could not sleep all night, but kept on brooding. Before daybreak he came down from the chardak and went on his way. Fortunately Sefer's wife had prepared a bundle of food the night before, and this he took with him. He was in no state to think about provisions.

He walked along the bank of the River Jeyhan in an easterly direction; he passed the tip of Anavarza and wandered along on the other side. A sound reached his ears like the sound of hooves; he raised his head, and came face to face with the brown stallion. Perched on the top of a rock the stallion switched his tail gently to and fro. Adem was dumbfounded, his knees gave way and he collapsed on the ground.

A few moments later the horse moved, and fearlessly glided down from the rocks. After turning on itself it was lost to view above Kesikkeli.

Adem said to himself, 'How was I to know?' as he struggled to get up from where he was sitting. He put his right hand on the ground, 'How was I to know?' he said. 'Ah, how was I to know? . . .'

24

THERE was a visible change in the village. Everyone was in better spirits. They went from house to house laughing.

They all heaped reproaches upon Old Osman. 'Damn that old man,' they grumbled. 'He was jealous and didn't let us see Memed. Damn him, at least he should have let us have a glimpse of his handsome face. But no, he had to keep it for himself alone! Mean old man!'

'He's a dog in the manger.'

'When people grow old they get mean . . .'

'He kept stalking around the village with his pipe in his mouth for three days. He thought he was Sultan Süleyman, he was so above himself.'

'Serve him right . . . When his hawk flew out of the nest he was taken ill.'

'Let him!'

'I don't care whether he kicks the bucket, or not.'

'Nor do I. Why shouldn't we catch a glimpse of Memed's handsome face?'

'If he'd told us, if he'd said he'd come to his house . . .'

'Why did he hide it from the villagers?'

'Taken to his bed. I hope he never gets up again.'

'Who knows what he looks like?'

'Who knows what a fine face he has?'

'They say when he goes into battle, his gun grows twenty cubits longer.'

'They say that bullets cannot hit him.'

'They say that Sergeant Asim took him prisoner one night when he was asleep.'

'He was so sound asleep . . .'

'He didn't know a thing about it, poor chap.'

'Sleeping like a child.'

'Sergeant Asim gave the order to a squad of soldiers: "Empty your bullets into his belly . . ." '

'They emptied them.'

'Then they looked . . .'

'And just imagine what they saw!'

'Bullets can't pierce him.'

'They can't!'

'Never!'

'Curse that mean Old Osman, you didn't show us our Agha . . .'

'Our soul . . .'

'Our child . . .'

'Our hawk . . .'

'Our darling . . .'

Still they were proud. They were cross with Old Osman, and angry, but the fact that he had come to their village was enough. And if they'd only been told about him and had had a glimpse of his face, what harm would there have been?

They began to feel more confident. The fear of Ali Safa had disappeared. They completely forgot that such a man existed. There was an atmosphere of rejoicing and festivity in the village, which put fresh heart into people.

'Osman Agha, why didn't you tell us he had come to the village?'

'I was afraid, my little ones, terribly afraid.'

'What could we do to him? We would have guarded him like our life.'

'The peasants are angry with you. See how even after he's gone, they've taken heart? Just his coming here . . .'

'I couldn't have told anyone. If an agha or the Government had got to hear about him – they would have raided the village and killed my hawk. I didn't dare.'

'Why, we wouldn't have handed him over even to the Shah or

the Padishah! No one would have taken him from us but over our dead bodies.'

'How could I know! A bird came and sheltered in a thicket . . .'

'But no bullet can pierce him.'

'He can resist a whole army.'

'A hero.'

'If only I had known, my children.'

'But you didn't even let us see the tip of his nose.'

'He didn't let me. There was a whole army of police after him. He hadn't eaten properly for months and was nothing but skin and bone. Don't show me to the villagers in this state, Uncle Osman, he said to me.'

'We would have given him food, we'd have fed him on butter and honey.'

The peasants kept on lamenting the fact that they had not seen him. They cursed Old Osman, and cross-questioned him. Why on earth had he not shown him to them? Would ever such a chance come again? The nearby villagers were also annoyed with Old Osman. They were disappointed and angry.

Then some people came forward saying they had seen him, and related how they had seen him. At this Old Osman on his bed of sickness was forgotten. Everyone who had seen him told his story in his own way.

First of all it was Veli who narrated how he had taken him to Osman's house.

'I was sound asleep, and very tired,' he began. 'I had a dream. In my dream water was flowing, very bright daylight it was, not water. From the water there came a tall man, with cartridge-belts crossed on his breast, and a bright-green gun. A voice came to my ears, saying, "Osman Agha, Osman Agha!" I awoke, wondering whether I was imagining things or dreaming. When I looked, I saw someone at the door, so I opened it. A man, a tall man was there, so covered with cartridges that you couldn't have found room for a needle. His field-glasses were of shining gold . . . His revolver and the handle of his dagger were also made of gold. Every bit was gold. I invited him in. He came in and I lit a light. He sat down with his back to the wall. He had such eyes . . . if you looked at them for a little while, you would begin to feel frightened.

Flashing eyes . . . eyes like a fierce wolf. He said his prayers. As he did so, I saw that his hands were a sacred green colour up to his wrists. I brought out some food, and he ate some. He did not speak, but remained deep in thought. Please tell me your name, I said. I asked him three times, but he paid no heed. He didn't seem to hear me. Then he got up and his head almost touched the roof of the hut. He was so tall that he had to bend low to pass through our doorway. When Seyfali goes out of it, quite upright, there are several inches to spare. He walked to the door. I'll take you to Osman Agha, I said. Show me his house, he said. He also said to me that this village was suffering from tyranny. People shouldn't be treated so cruelly, he said. I showed him Osman's house. It was drizzling. I was curious, and waited in the doorway. At Osman's door a huge firefly flashed its light on and off, on and off. Since that day the same light has shone at Osman's doorway.'

Veli told a wonderful new story about him every day. Then Selver said she had seen him. Mullah Mustafa from the next village had seen him. Jabbar from Anavarza, Blind Ahmet from Hadjilar, Kurdish Jimshit from Narlikishla, Zeynel and Kurdish Temir from Vayvay and Muttalip from Öksüzlü. A lot of people had seen him there in Osman's stable, on the night the riders had raided the village, when they were shot at from Kurdish Kerem's yard, and the Sergeant was hit and bellowed like an ox.

Others had seen him in the darkness wandering along the edges of Ahjasaz and round Anavarza Castle. He was sitting on a rock, with his head in his hands, thinking. Around him hundreds of eagles were hovering, coming close and perching on his knee. He stroked the back of those huge eagles, as one would stroke a lamb . . .

Once they had seen him mounted on an enormous white horse. The horse had galloped so fast that its hooves did not touch the ground. Its mane was like a cloud.

In the end there were very few people in Vayvay and the nearby villages who had not seen Memed.

The Vayvay villagers who had taken refuge at Saricham heard that he had been to Vayvay and lamented not having seen him. If only we had been in our old homes and had seen his handsome face, his blessed face, they said. Why didn't we listen to Old

Osman? Why didn't we come back to the village? Yobazoghlu also regretted his stupidity. He came and apologized to Osman. 'I am terribly sorry I didn't come back that time,' he said. 'If only I had known! You didn't say a word . . .'

All the children in the village had seen him. They told stories about him from morning to night, they lived his life, and played games about him. Like the grown-ups they did not mention his name, but gave him different nicknames. In their games the aghas and the police trembled before Memed. They could not stand up before him and would sink to the ground, plead and kiss his feet. The children would play a game in which they wriggled along the ground, blowing their noses and sobbing.

Every day a new song would be composed about him just like that, out of the blue. Piteous laments, awesome legends, laughable songs, playful songs . . . The children even made up a game with songs.

The attitude of the villagers towards Memed delighted Old Osman and speeded up his recovery. If things had been different he might never have got up out of his bed again, such had been his distress.

The delight and gladness of the villagers did not last long. For the past three nights there had been raids on the village, but the villagers were unaffected. It would take more to daunt them now. Let them raid as much as they can. They'll see. Old Osman, only just able to stand on his shaky legs, on the evenings when raiders rained bullets on the village, came outside and let fly with both barrels of his pistol shouting at the top of his voice:

'Come on, you dogs, come and shoot, we're ready for you!'

The villagers began to think the nightly raids were simply a game that Ali Safa Bey renewed every night.

But one morning they woke up and were dumbfounded at what they saw. They could not believe their eyes and ears. All the horses in the village had been taken away during the night. Not one was left. They had thought of every possibility but this. What were they to do without horses?

Their gladness and pride were blighted. They spent the whole day wandering aimlessly round the village, not uttering a word. Everyone was deeply depressed.

165

On the second day some terrible news went through the village from one end to the other: the horse-thieves had not taken the old horses away, they had killed them. They had filled the ravine of Chikchiklar with them. When they looked into the distance, and saw the eagles wheeling over Topraktepe, they hurried there, and saw a heap of carcasses.

That very morning two people packed up their things, said goodbye and went off to Saricham. A lot of other people were making ready to go. Ferhat Hodja tried to stop them.

'Not to oppose tyranny is against our religion,' he said. 'Not to protect one's children's bread and one's parents' hearth, but to leave and go to strange lands is wrong. Not to oppose tyranny is to become an accomplice of the tyrant. To be afraid, and to give in from fear is wrong.'

If he had not prevented them, the village would have been half-empty.

'Allah will send us a leader,' he said. 'Think how *he* came to the village! We could not hold him. We let the hawk flutter out of our hands. If he'd been here, do you think all those things would have happened to us?'

Zeynel listened to Ferhat Hodja, but then said defiantly: 'Nonsense. This is only the beginning. You'll see what'll happen to us yet! You'll see! You'll see if to be afraid is wrong! Don't be afraid then, Ferhat Hodja! You'll see!'

Ferhat did not answer. He merely said,

'Allah will not leave his poor servants quite alone,' putting all his faith into his voice. 'Allah will always be with those who oppose tyranny. If he were not, would tyranny have diminished so much on the face of the earth?'

They assembled in Seyfali's house, and after a long discussion they decided to go and ask Yaghmur Agha for the horses. The whole world knew that only Yaghmur Agha could steal all the horses belonging to a village. Ferhat Hodja, Seyfali and Sefché the Warden set out for Yaghmur Agha's farm. Yaghmur Agha was a close friend of Sefché the Warden. They had been deserters travelling together in the Taurus Mountains during the war. Three years they'd been together. Yaghmur was very young in those days.

As soon as Sefché got off his horse, he said,

'Yaghmur, isn't it shameful what you have done? You steal horses all over the place, all right. But what did you want of us? What filthy beast put you up to this?'

Yaghmur coming out to meet them on the steps of the house, smiled at Sefché's words, and said,

'Who stole your horse? Who stole it? If your horse has been stolen, whose is the horse you're on now?'

Sefché shouted, 'You dog, I got these horses from Memidik Agha at Narlikishla in order to come and see you. Do you understand? You didn't leave a single horse, blind, lame, mangy, sick, you stole them all. And you had the old ones killed. You dirty rascal . . .'

'Come up here and let's talk.'

They sat down on the sofa, drank coffee and ate some food. Yaghmur was very courteous but he did not give back the horses. They begged, they threatened, they raged, they raved, but they could not get the horses back.

Ferhat Hodja said to Yaghmur Agha,

'God brought Joseph out of the well; do you think he won't look after us? Do you think Allah won't send us a leader, Yaghmur?'

Sefché finished off what he had begun:

'Allah sent us a leader, but we were blind and did not keep him. Otherwise, do you imagine your thieves could have got so close to the village?

Yaghmur Agha smiled. Smilingly he saw them off.

They returned to the village crestfallen and empty-handed.

25

ALI SAFA BEY looked out of the window and saw the shapes of three riders waiting outside in the yard. One of them was tall and sat very upright on his horse, and stood ahead of the others. The riders had been there for some time silent and still. Ali Safa, standing at the window, was preoccupied.

The farm hand at the door asked,

'What am I to say to Idris Bey? He's been waiting there a long time.'

Ali Safa was thinking. Should he see Idris Bey or not? Idris Bey was insisting on an interview. This was the sixth time he had come to the farm this month, and he had refused to see him each time. Now he was thinking. Could this be useful in his dealings with Arif Saim Bey? He wondered about it. One could never know with Arif Saim Bey. He was a hard man. Perhaps he would be angry if he learnt that Ali Safa had received Idris Bey at his farm and had talked to him.

The sun had sunk and would soon be gone. The twilight was slowly spreading over the plain. The last rays of light were reflected from the silver ornaments on Idris Bey's rifle, dagger, cartridge-belts and bridle.

'What did Idris Bey say?' he asked the man again.

'I must see Safa Bey, he says. On a matter of great importance,' he said.

Ali Safa Bey thought a little longer. He looked again at the riders out there, the three armed Circassians. The light was falling on Idris Bey.

The last rays were slowly disappearing.

'Call Idris Bey in,' he ordered. 'Do not fail to treat him with respect.'

The three men dismounted. They climbed the stairs slowly, Idris Bey in front and his companions behind. Ali Safa Bey awaited them at the head of the stairs.

'Welcome, my friend. Welcome, Idris Bey,' he said. The two men embraced.

Idris Bey's men came behind him. Ali Safa acknowledged them with a nod of his head.

They entered the room, Idris Bey in front and Ali Safa Bey behind him. Ali Safa did not invite the men into the room. He knew something of Circassian traditions. Armed men do not sit with beys, they stand at the door, waiting.

Idris Bey said in his innocent, frank, childlike way,

'I've come to see you many times, Safa Bey. Maybe ten times. I've been unable to see you. Do you know what it means for me to come from so far away, outlawed as I am, to see you? It means the odds were a hundred to one I should be killed. I faced death.'

'Sit down, sit down, and then we'll talk. Sit down, my friend, and have some coffee. You're running grave risks; you mustn't wander about Chukurova in broad daylight like this.'

Idris Bey sat down on the divan and said,

'I hate coming down to the plain at night like a wolf. A month ago we had a clash with the police in the gully below Bozkuyu. The fighting lasted four hours. Fortunately night fell and so we escaped. We got away and came to you but again you were not at home. So we went to Kurdish Ali's house, and stayed there a week. He gave us shelter.'

'I'm wondering where all this will end,' said Ali Safa Bey pityingly.

Idris Bey, as if he had envisaged everything, said cheerfully,

'I know where it will end. I know very well where it will end as far as I am concerned. Arif Saim Bey must know too. This is what I came to tell you.'

*

Arif Saim Bey was furious, mad with rage. What was the meaning of this? A Circassian good-for-nothing had come to Chukurova and had set himself up against him. A Circassian fellow who wasn't even thirty and didn't know Turkish . . .

'I'll show you, you miserable Circassian,' he shouted to himself. 'If I don't send you crawling back to the Caucasus, among those Bolsheviks, my name isn't Arif Saim.'

He was very annoyed with the Pasha too. 'Ah, Pasha,' he grumbled to himself. 'What sort of understanding is this? Does a man give so much of himself to his fatherland? Can a man be so idealistic? Did we shed our blood in order to go hungry and thirsty and to find ourselves a pawn in the hands of the Circassians? Did we risk our lives and save the fatherland just for this? Law and order . . . I understand, that's all very fine. But our children will go hungry, and we shall be beggars, Pasha. Wretched Circassian, I won't let you ruin a hero and if the Pasha wishes, he can have my head! If the Pasha only wants us near him for our *beaux yeux*, let him leave us alone; if he does not need us, let him leave us alone, let him get off our shoulders. Then we can look after our own interests.'

He summoned the leaders of the Akmezar villagers one by one, and put before them a little money on one side, and a heap of cherrywood cudgels on the other. 'Choose, you slave of Idris Bey. Choose between the money and the cudgels.' Some chose the money, others chose the cudgel. Those who chose the cudgel were cursed and given a terrible beating. After the beating they were placed, half-dead, on a horse, and left in the middle of Akmezar village.

There was a large clump of thorn-trees in front of the big house belonging to the farm. Finally Arif Saim Bey had the Circassians stripped and driven towards the thorn-trees by five men with whips. Behind them the whips cracked, lashing their backs, and in front of them were the thorns which pierced their naked bodies. This torture lasted until their bodies were steeped crimson with blood, and until they said, 'Take the title-deeds and the land, Bey.'

In this way Arif Saim Bey came into possession of a lot of land. But he could not obtain Idris Bey's land or that of his relations or of those who agreed with him. Arif Saim Bey's land now completely surrounded the land of those stubborn few. The land belonging to Idris Bey and his supporters was left like an island in the middle of Arif Saim Bey's land. If Idris didn't give up that land now . . . If they didn't give it up, he would see!

'All right, don't give it up, you filthy beasts,' Arif Saim growled. 'Plough your fields, if you can, and as for reaping, we shall see!'

The black Ford came once again to Akmezar village and stopped at Idris Bey's door. It was dirty and muddy and was buried up to the axles in dust; its huge headlamps seemed to have grown even larger.

The villagers and Idris Bey greeted him with greater respect than before. As before, Arif Saim Bey sat down solemnly and did not speak. Only when he was leaving he said, in a loud voice,

'Idris Bey, your land and your friends' land has been surrounded by my land. You are not to trample on or go across my land. I forbid it. Will you sell me that land, which has been left in the middle of mine? What do you say?'

Idris Bey said his final word in a firm voice:

'With regard to the land that is inside yours . . .'

'In the middle.'

'. . . in the middle of yours, I and my friends will not sell it'

Arif Saim Bey offered his hand, and said, with a bitter smile, 'You're very young, very brave, very manly. I should like to have been friends with you but it's too late. Goodbye.'

Arif Saim immediately armed ten men. He had them dressed in private guards' uniforms. Green.

'If anyone goes across my fields, or tramples on my land, shoot,' he ordered.

It was autumn, the season for ploughing, and a young Circassian called Fehmi took his plough and went to his field. Arif Saim Bey's guards told Fehmi to go back; Fehmi took no notice and walked on. The guards shot him without more ado. Fehmi's corpse was left for three days in the fields. Idris Bey complained. They arrested one of Arif Saim Bey's guards and put him in prison. He stayed there three months. Arif Saim set out for Sivas. In those days the highest court of law was at Sivas. He got the guard acquitted. Then he went himself to take him from the prison, brought him to the farm and made him head guard.

That year they shot three more men who trespassed on Arif Saim Bey's land in order to get to their own land. For days no one could approach the bodies of the Circassians. They lay and rotted on Arif Saim's land. The men who shot them stayed only three months in prison. Another journey to Sivas solved everything.

That year the land that had been surrounded by Arif Saim Bey's land could not be ploughed or sown. The next year the same thing happened. It could not be sown, but this land, in the middle of the farm, was like a tumour, like a bleeding wound. In the coming year the Circassians would again go to plough and would again be killed. In the end the Pasha would be bound to hear about it and say, what kind of a scandal is this? He was terribly afraid of the Pasha. He could not say to the Pasha, I am in such-and-such a situation, peasants, backward peasants are treating me badly. He must deal with the gaping wound very soon.

The black Ford, its headlamps huger than ever, stopped again at Idris Bey's door. Arif Saim Bey had grown a little fatter and more imposing. The Circassians and Idris Bey again greeted him with the same respect. This time Arif Saim did not go up into the house.

'Idris Bey,' he said. 'I've come to talk about the question of that land. The land that has been left like an island in the middle of mine, what use is it to you?'

'The land that has been left within yours . . .' began Idris Bey in a harsh voice.

Arif Saim gave him his hand and said with a bitter smile,

'What a pity. You're very young. We should have been friends.'

And the black Ford never went to Akmezar again.

Fazli Bey, Clerk of the Court, was acting as notary in the town, a small, wily, timid, drunken man. Being a relic of Ottoman times, he was terrified of the new Government and its men.

Arif Saim summoned him to the farm.

'Fazli Bey,' he said, 'you remember you drew up the note that says that Idris Bey of Akmezar owes me one hundred and fifty thousand lira?'

'Yes, sir, I remember. Have you lost the note, sir?'

Arif Saim Bey, with a fatherly smile and a look of pride, placed his hand on Fazli's shoulder, and asked,

'What will a new document cost?'

Fazli made a calculation on his fingers, and said,

'Two hundred and ten lira two kurush. Including a witness and all that. Including the stamp, too . . .'

'Here's three hundred lira. Now tell me where you want to live and in what district . . .'

'I'm quite content, sir,' said Fazli suddenly nervous. 'I'm contented with this district and the bread, the water, the butcher, the baker, and the people.'

The demand note for the hundred and fifty thousand lira reached Idris Bey three days later. And as he would not pay the debt Arif Saim Bey immediately brought a court case against him. When Idris Bey heard this he said,

'I was expecting it. I knew he would do something like this. We'll settle accounts with him in court. I'll prove that the IOU is a forgery and show what a scoundrel he is.'

For years he had been sending telegrams to Ankara, to the

Pasha, to the ministers and to members of Parliament he knew. He again threw a few telegrams into the bottomless pit at Ankara. They had no result, but he was used to this.

Arif Saim Bey heard about what Idris Bey had said.

'What a pity; he is very young,' he said. 'We could have been friends.'

That very evening Arif Saim Bey summoned Hidirinoghlu, who was one of the most savage brutes in the district.

'Can you find someone who has a feud with Idris at Akmezar, Hidirinoghlu?'

'If you so command, Bey, I will not find, I will create someone. My life is at your service.'

'You will kill that man.'

'I'll kill him, Bey.'

'You'll kill him and bury him somewhere on Idris's ground, in the yard or by the gate.'

'I'll do so, Bey.'

A few days later the police searched Idris Bey's stables and found the body. At once they arrested Idris Bey, but as he was being taken to the district gaol he escaped. Hidirinoghlu had arranged everything as Arif Saim Bey wanted it. Everything fitted in pat.

The case did not last long. As Idris Bey was a fugitive he could not come forward and prove that the promissory note was false. He was saddled officially with a debt of a hundred and fifty thousand liras.

Then some eminent lawyers took up the case of the man whom Idris Bey had shot. Six months after the man's death he was condemned to twenty-four years.

Idris Bey was informed about these events day by day. He was furious, mad with rage. He was so angry that one night he came down to the town, took can after can of petrol from the filling-station and set fire to the law court. He would not let anyone near it until it was reduced to ashes. In any case it was an old building and in a short time it was burnt to the ground. It was high noon, yet Idris Bey and three men fought their way out of the town and took refuge in the mountains.

All the newspapers reported the smallest details about the

burning down of the district criminal court by Idris Bey. This was also what Arif Saim Bey had wanted.

When he heard about the fire, he said,

'What a pity; he's very young. We could have been friends.'

Thus Idris Bey became a furious wolf in the Taurus. A mad, raging wolf.

*

'I have come to make a request to you. The whole world knows that I don't owe him a penny. The whole world knows that I didn't kill the man. I burnt down the law court, and I'll bear my punishment for that. I'm not going to give a foot of my land to Arif Saim Bey. Tell him to tear up the IOU. I don't owe him a hundred and fifty cents, even. Not even five cents. I've never killed an ant. Everybody knows that – the whole plain, even the judges who have condemned me. So tell them to get me acquitted. If he doesn't do what I say, Arif Saim is doomed. What the consequences will be he knows better than anyone, better than I. You are a close friend of his, go and tell him this.'

Then he got up and walked to the stairs.

'Goodbye, Ali Safa Bey,' he said. 'That is all I had to say.'

Idris Bey sent the same message in the same words to Arif Saim Bey by whatever messengers he came across in Chukurova or the Taurus, and patiently awaited a reply. No answer came.

Idris Bey's words came to Arif Saim Bey's ears several times. He nearly split his sides with laughing. He had already added the lands belonging to Idris and his men to his farm a long time ago.

This visit served Ali Safa Bey's purpose. He at once mounted his horse and went to see Arif Saim Bey. He would talk both about Idris and also about his own affairs.

It was evening when he reached the farm. Arif Saim Bey had a father, Zeko Bey, who knew no Turkish and who was as bulky as two men. Ever since his youth, Zeko Bey had sported long up-curled mustachios. He had been a town-crier in the market of Harput. He was extremely proud when his son became eminent, and had at once left the job he dearly loved in the market and hastened to join his son.

He sat in a chair in front of the door of the house. He was wearing wide, blue shalvar-trousers, the edges of the pockets and the legs being embroidered with silver. The watch-chain which dangled across his green silk jacket was three fingers thick.

The labourers, tired from the fields, dressed in rags, thin, shrunken, and with lips cracked with fever, came and went down on their right knees to pay their respects to Zeko Bey, then they kissed his hand three times, bowing their heads, before going home.

This ceremony in which the labourers kissed his hand was held twice, morning and evening. For the hand-kissing Zeko Bey would get up before dawn, light his *nargileh**, order his coffee and sit down at the door; then, closing his eyes with delight, he would stretch out his hand to the labourers. One group after another would kiss his hand and pass on.

Zeko Bey was delighted to see Ali Safa Bey. He closed his eyes and ostentatiously stretched out his hand to the workmen.

'Guro hesbè bigirin,' he ordered in Kurdish. His voice was thick and booming.

A few hefty men hurried to hold Ali Safa's horse's head. Ali Safa dismounted and hastened to Zeko Bey. Zeko Bey had his legs stretched out, his large belly protruding, his neck swelling, and his mouth open in a wide smile showing his gleaming gold teeth. He waited, turning towards Ali Safa Bey for his hand to be kissed. Ali Safa Bey took his hand, knelt down in respect, kissed the hand and placed it to his forehead three times.

After this ceremony Zeko Bey said to him again in Kurdish:

'Lavo Ali Safa, du serseran hati, sercavan hati, vira rune!'

He made Ali Safa sit down next to him:

'Chayani?'

Those in attendance said,

'He is asking you how you are.'

'Du hati bal Bege?'

'He's asking if you came to see the Bey.'

'Beg viraye!'

'He says the Bey is here,' they said.

On the one side Zeko Bey had his hand kissed by the passing

* *Nargileh:* a hookah

labourers, on the other he talked to Safa Bey in this manner. Their conversation lasted until Arif Saim Bey saw Safa Bey from upstairs and called down,

'Father, if you'll allow it, I'd like Safa Bey to come upstairs. I have some important business to discuss with him.'

His son's words were translated for Zeko Bey. His face grew tense and his lips drooped, but he once again stretched out his hand stiffly.

'Here lavo jorè,' he said.

Ali Safa Bey again knelt down on his right knee respectfully, kissed the large, long-fingered, plump hand and pressed it to his forehead three times.

The two friends, the two new landowners, the two veterans from the War of Independence had a meal together. There were different kinds of game on the table. Francolin, plover, partridge, hare ... Four good hunters went after game every day from morning till night for Arif Saim Bey's table. They drank fine French wines with the game.

Ali Safa Bey found an opportunity to mention Idris's threats. Arif Saim Bey was highly amused. He nearly split his sides with laughter. Ali Safa Bey joined in his delight, and laughed with him.

Finally Arif Saim Bey stopped laughing, and his face took on an expression of great regret, while he sighed heavily:

'What a pity,' he said. 'And he so young. We could have been friends.'

26

MEMED gradually realized where he was, and sensed some danger. He made an effort to remember what had happened. Everything was confused in his mind. In the distance a yellow light revolved, mingled with the darkness, then broke out into showering sparks. His whole body felt bruised and hot.

He got up, and shading his eyes with his hand looked towards the village. It lay in a hollow. He could see nothing but some wisps of smoke floating above the village and rising into the sky. Everything was very still. Not the slightest breeze stirred the air. The spring earth stretched under the sun, and slight crackling noises came from it. High above it, a host of butterflies flew by. A jet-black butterfly, with reddish tips to its wings, alighted on a big blue flower. It was the first time Memed had seen such a big black butterfly. Something like fear or pain gripped him. 'Your end is in sight,' he said to himself. Then, 'It's better so,' he said. 'Well, it's fate. I caused Hatché's death, and my mother's too . . . I escaped to the mountains. As for the villagers, look how I ruined their lives . . . They're groaning under tyranny. Before I came each of them managed to lead his life in his own way. I've done no good. I must disappear.'

It came into his mind that everything had happened after he had gone to the town and spoken to Corporal Hasan in the room at the inn. 'If only I'd broken my leg rather than gone to the town. If only I'd gone blind before I set eyes on Coproral Hasan. If only I'd been deaf and never heard him speak. Just look at what a wretched state the village is in now!'

He recalled the day they had gone to set fire to the thistle-field, how the villagers and the whole of nature had danced for happiness. Even the flames that rose from the burning thistles had danced all over the plain in a whirl of joy. He could see Durmush Ali, bent as he was, lifting his old legs into the air in an old Turcoman dance. He went twisting and turning in harmony with the flames, so that he seemed to mingle with them. It must have been while he was dancing, embracing the fire, that Bald Hamza, not being able to stand the sight, trampled him down under his horse's feet.

Two big tears welled up in his eyes. He smiled to himself. Then he got up, slung his rifle on his shoulder, and began to climb up towards the rocky outcrop that topped the valley. He had to have his back to the huge crags. He hurried along, keeping well under cover.

He had just reached the head of the valley when a volley of shots rang out. There was a spring there gushing forth over bright coloured pebbles. Memed lay face downward and drank deeply of the ice-cold water. Bullets whizzed high over his head. At once he threw himself down behind a purplish rock, dotted with lichen.

If the heights had not been occupied, he would be safe now. Then he saw Mother Hürü. She was hurrying towards him screaming and waving her arms.

'Run, Memed, that infidel Lame Ali has given you away. Kill him, didn't I tell you to kill him?' she cried.

Memed felt easier now, hidden in the rocks. He looked about him for a better spot where he could hold off the attackers till nightfall. Then he crawled over to where the rocks were steeper, and leaning his back against a rock, stopped to take breath.

The policemen were advancing from below. A shower of bullets hit the crags, and the encounter began in earnest. Memed, very coolly defending himself on the right and the left, was taking things slowly. He did not want to hurt anyone. If he had wanted to, he could have shot ten policemen in no time at all. They were advancing openly, not seeing the need to keep under cover. Memed fired some shots to frighten or distract them. The policemen reached the foot of the rocks. Captain Faruk was at their head. Memed caught a glimpse of the Captain, then lost sight of him. He saw Lame Ali, holding a rifle, standing behind a rock. He looked calm and collected, and one could almost make out a vague smile on his face. At least so it seemed to Memed.

Mother Hürü was still coming on, waving her arms and calling out like a screaming wind. She stopped for a moment, hands on her hips, looking at the policemen who were spraying Memed with bullets from where they lay behind the rocks.

'Policemen, my good fellows,' she said, 'don't kill my Memed. Look, is he shooting to kill you? If he'd wanted to he could have killed you all. Look where you are and where he is. Bullets can't touch my Memed . . . Policemen, dear lambs, don't waste your efforts. Let my boy go and don't stop him from going on his way. If not, you'll get hurt. My Memed has a lot to do. He's very angry, very! He's upset at what has happened. You policemen, my boys, my lambs, you too are oppressed, groaning under tyranny. Don't put up with it. Don't put up with the Captain, that infidel, that Ottoman . . . Don't trust him!'

Bullets whistled to right and left of her, but she took no notice. 'What!' she yelled during a pause. 'You sons of infidels, are you trying to shoot me?'

She walked towards the crags. The firing became more intense. Memed waited and waited, and then replied to their fire with a sharp burst; then again he waited.

One of the policemen whom they called Payasli was shooting recklessly from a standing position; Memed hit him in the leg.

A hail of bullets surrounded him, making a puff of smoke as each one hit the rocks. The face of the rocks was enveloped in smoke.

Bullets whistled past Mother Hürü to right and left, deafening her.

'Shoot then! Kill me, you filthy beasts! See what you'll get, just see!'

Payasli was writhing on the ground, scrabbling in the dust with pain.

Hürü went up to him and said,

'Poor lamb! Well, if you hadn't been so foolish my Memed wouldn't have hit you. Don't be afraid. When we get back to the village I'll put on a plaster and we'll have you up and about in a day or two. And in return you'll never shoot at my Memed again.'

Leaving the policeman there, she went further forward.

'Mother, Mother,' came Memed's voice, crying out in agitation, 'sit down where you are. Those infidels will kill you!'

'Let them kill me, my boy,' said Hürü. 'What does it matter if I live on or not after this! Let them kill me, my boy, I'm coming to you.'

The bullets whistled. Mother Hürü walked on as if nothing were happening, as if she'd gone out for a walk, or to drive the calves to pasture.

Captain Faruk asked Sergeant Asim who was at his side,

'Who is that mad creature?'

'Memed's Mother Hürü,' replied Sergeant Asim. 'You know, the one who hates Lame Ali. The one who refused to see you.'

'But she's a brave one. Is she crazy?'

'Very clever,' smiled Sergeant Asim.

Mother Hürü stumbled, and fell to the ground. Memed was terrified. Hürü got up, and again stumbled and fell. Memed called out,

'If you hit her I won't leave one of you alive. Not one of you will get out of this valley alive.'

Hürü got up again, and said,

'Don't worry, Memed. Those thugs can't hit me. I shall see you again before I die. I prayed to God and he won't let me be killed before I see your handsome face and stroke your head once more.'

Memed stopped firing. The policemen also stopped. In an unspoken agreement between them, they waited for Mother Hürü to get out of the way.

The Captain said to Sergeant Asim,

'Shall we be able to catch him?'

'I don't think so, Captain. He slips out of your grasp like a snake. He's gone before you know it. Just now he could have shot us all. If we'd engaged him down below, in the gully, before he reached the crags, maybe we could have captured him.'

'Why did he shoot Payasli?'

'He was standing up, taunting him and cursing.'

'And if you taunted and cursed him wouldn't he shoot you?'

'No, he wouldn't,' said Sergeant Asim positively.

'Is that certain?'

'He did not fire at me even when I pursued him into the tightest corners. He was face to face with death, and he didn't fire at me.'

'What is the reason, Sergeant?'

'I have no idea, Captain.'

'Let them take Payasli to the village.'

'They're taking him now, Captain.'

Mother Hürü reached Memed's side quite out of breath. Her hands and feet were torn and bleeding. Her new skirt hung in tatters from beneath her sash.

'Mother,' said Memed. 'Are you hurt, Mother?' He got up and walked towards her.

'Keep down,' shouted Mother Hürü. 'Keep down, darling!'

Memed smiled, took her by the hand, and drew her into the shelter of the rock.

'You're not hurt, are you? Don't say you want to move from here. If you move you'll kill me.'

'I'm not moving. Don't stop. Go on firing. Look at Lame Ali there behind the tree. Shoot him, mow him down! This is your chance.' She stopped, then she said: 'Oh dear, I shouldn't have come, now I'm a nuisance to you. Do as you think best, my boy. Go on, fire. Don't stop!'

Memed started firing. The other side started too. With the bullets hitting the rocks the air was filled with dust and dirt; the chips of rock detached by the firing whistled like bullets and were scattered all over the place. There was a deafening noise.

As the minutes passed Captain Faruk said to Sergeant Asim,

'Well, Sergeant, what about it? There are a hundred and eighty of us and only one man is holding out against us . . . Shall we take him by storm?'

'It's very steep, Captain. While we are climbing the rocks he could shoot us all. Not a single one of us could get there.'

'Evening is coming on. As soon as darkness falls he'll slip away.'

'Yes, he will, Captain. He's got us in a bad position. Just to go on firing is useless. And Memed's got plenty of ammunition.'

As time went on the Captain began to get angry. How was it he had missed this opportunity? If they had taken action half an hour earlier . . . Just half an hour earlier . . . This was the second time the Captain had clashed with Memed. The first time was when they had shot Hatché.

A bullet passed within a hand's breadth of the Captain's head and buried itself in the earth. Then another.

'He's had us in sight for some time,' remarked Sergeant Asim.

'Let's take cover,' said the Captain.

'We can't find any cover. He can hit us whenever he wants to. That's what he wants to tell us.'

'Yet we shot his wife . . .'

'He's a strange man,' said Sergeant Asim. 'Not like a brigand at all. More like a djinn, a fairy, an angel. He should have been a saint, not a brigand.'

At that moment they heard a voice cry out, 'I've been hit!' Then followed another, and another. Memed had now hit four policemen in the leg.

'How's that!' screamed Mother Hürü. 'How's that! Don't trust Bald Hamza I said, didn't I?'

Then she pointed out to Memed a policeman who was in the open,

'Go on, quick . . .'

And Memed responded at once. When the bullet found its mark and someone cried out, Mother Hürü clapped her hands like a child.

Memed's face was dark with sweat.

The sun was sinking low in the west. Soon it would set. Twilight was falling, Memed's rifle had grown red-hot, so he only fired at intervals, wounding a policeman now and then to gain time and to let his gun cool a little. He also kept an eye on the setting sun.

All at once the policemen stopped firing. Memed, surprised, also stopped. Then he saw Sergeant Asim. Holding a white handkerchief aloft in his right hand, he advanced, shouting out,

'Memed, my boy, I'm coming up to you. Give yourself up! I don't want you to be killed.' He was walking straight as a ramrod, up the hill towards Memed.

'Go back, Sergeant.'

'Memed, my boy, you can't stand out against the Government. The whole area's full of soldiers. You'll either be killed or wounded. The Captain will see that your life is spared.'

'Go back, Sergeant!' Memed shouted. There was fear, despair, helplessness in his voice. 'Please Sergeant, don't come on!'

'Shoot him! Finish the job! You tell him to go back and he keeps coming on. Shoot him.'

The Sergeant was coming on, very upright, undeterred.

'Sergeant, go back. I shall shoot. Sergeant, don't make me do it, I implore you. Don't do this to me, Sergeant . . .' There was a tone of fear and desperate entreaty in his voice. 'Sergeant Asim, Sergeant, my dear Sergeant, have you no pity, no compassion?'

The Sergeant's right hand was raised, stiff and straight, holding the handkerchief. He pressed on.

'You'll surrender to me. Today. You know that if there's one man in the whole world that I really like and respect, it's you.'

'I know, Sergeant, my goodness, I know. Don't make me do it. I have other work to do.' His voice grew louder. It rang out and echoed back from the rocks. His voice had changed completely. 'Sergeant, I'm telling you. Listen to me carefully. I would have surrendered to you, but . . . Everything you've said is true, you're right. They'll kill me, I know. But I have a little job to do before I die, Sergeant. If I hadn't had this job, I wouldn't have hurt you, Sergeant. Please forgive me. If it had been a question of my life I would have sacrificed it for you. Go back, Sergeant.'

Two shots whistled past the Sergeant's ears, but he took no notice and walked on. Memed fired two rounds over the Sergeant's head. He took no notice.

Memed's whole body began to tremble.

'Captain,' he shouted. 'I have a job to do. Otherwise I would never kill Sergeant Asim; order him to stop.'

He took aim . . . and his trembling stopped. He pulled the trigger. Sergeant Asim called out. The white handkerchief fell out of his right hand. It was stained with blood.

'Come back, Sergeant,' ordered the Captain.

The Sergeant stopped and gave a bitter smile. Darkness was closing in. Very slowly he turned back.

Memed, with a groan, said,

'Forgive me, Sergeant. You've ruined me. I'd rather you'd killed me than brought this upon me.'

The Captain gave an order and the firing started again. Memed did not reply. He kissed Mother Hürü's hand, and she embraced him.

'Mother, forgive me and wish me godspeed.'

'May God be with you, my child. Don't forget Lame Ali. Kill him. He is the origin of all these misfortunes, remember.'

Memed slipped away in the darkness like a pole-cat, and in the twinkling of an eye had made his way to the next valley, which was steep, rocky and wooded. He knew these parts like the palm of his hand. Not just a platoon, but even a regiment of soldiers could not catch him in these mountains.

The police were still firing. By now Memed was so far away that he could only just hear the sound of firing.

Mother Hürü had not moved from where she was, but crouched there in an ecstasy of delight. She kept shouting at the policemen:

'All right, use up the Government's bullets! Fire on, you infidels! Fire on! The bird has flown long ago.'

Then she added,

'And now you'll all be coming to me, won't you? So I should

dress your wounds? "Mother, Mother Hürü," you'll say, eh? If it hadn't been for my boy, if you hadn't been afraid of him, you'd have killed me, you infidels. You'd never have thought about who would dress your wounds then! Memed shoots you, and then I'm to dress your wounds, eh? Indeed, my little lambs, indeed! . . .'

27

HUGE, green snakes' heads, with flickering tongues of flame, descend from the mountain in a great booming clatter. A black cloud looms over the plain and from the heart of the black cloud coral-eyed snakes emerge. Their long tails strike the ground, raising the dust. Hundreds and hundreds of coral-eyed heads with flashing forked tongues . . .

A sword strikes one of the heads, and two heads appear in its place, with bigger, more brightly flaming tongues, that dart out to their full length. A sharp sword comes and cuts off those two heads, whereupon four new heads spring up. The heads are cut, they grow and fall again. A thousand-headed dragon. Its heads grow steadily bigger and more numerous as the swords rain upon them. Floating on the clouds are many dragons. They rise to the sky, then descend towards the roads below. Masses of cloud, shot with black, white, grey, orange and gold, float down on to the dusty roads and plains. Thousands of swords strike at the snakes' heads in the clouds. And still the heads multiply.

Beyond the Enchanted Mountain there are lofty crags, eagles as big as aeroplanes, dragons as long as trains. Suns, moons, and dark nights.

Memed's arm was numb. The barrel of his gun had at last got cool. There was a moon and its light shone on Memed's rifle and cartridge-belts. His knee hurt where he had bruised it on a rock. His hands were bleeding. For a moment he thought he had been wounded. Then he realized it was simply his hands bleeding. Blood soon dries. The sound of rifle fire could be heard in the

184

distance. The policemen were still firing. Evidently there was someone replying to this fire; who could it be? Could it be Lame Ali? Memed wondered. What a sly one he is! How he's wormed his way into their confidence!

Memed felt better. He decided not to hurry. Leaving the steep crags, he took a goat track. He was sure now that it must be Lame Ali lying behind a rock who was firing at the police.

Captain Faruk said to Sergeant Asim,

'Sergeant, night has fallen. Why is that man still firing, why doesn't he give up and go?'

'I don't know,' replied the Sergeant. 'Maybe he thinks we have surrounded him at the rear as well.'

'If he stays here tonight, his fate is sealed.'

'Who knows what he's planning, Captain?'

'Do you think he has gone mad?'

Bullets whistled past them continually.

'In my whole life,' said Sergeant Asim, 'I've never met such a difficult customer, such a cool, agile fellow. You know the saying, stealing a man's nose off his face . . . Well, he's as clever as that. He must have something up his sleeve.'

'If he'd wanted to, he could have killed half of us. What can he be up to?'

'His voice sounded resigned. Like someone who is resolved to die.'

'That was why I made you come back. He would have killed you, Sergeant.'

'He would have killed me,' said Sergeant Asim with a sigh. He's changed, that lad, he thought to himself. There's something the matter with him.

So that Memed could escape and hide, Lame Ali had slipped into the place he had occupied and taken cover; from there he was sending a hail of bullets down on to the police. There was a strange mad smile on his lips. He would keep up the firing until it grew light. Then he would stop and go and mingle with the police, and join in the search among the rocks for that Memed who had been firing on them all night.

'Sergeant Asim,' said the Captain in some agitation, 'he might be wounded. If he's wounded he couldn't get away.'

'Maybe, Captain.'

'Sergeant?'

'Yes, sir.'

'He might have left one of his companions as rearguard.'

'Memed wouldn't do that,' replied Sergeant Asim. 'He knows that the companion he leaves behind will either be captured or shot in these circumstances. Memed wouldn't cause anybody's death.'

'Then he must be wounded.'

'Maybe.'

*

They were descending upon a hot plain now, the snake-like dragons with their hundreds of tangled heads . . .

'Lame Ali's a sly one,' smiled Memed. He'll go on firing at the police until daybreak. In the morning the police will look for my body. They'll go on for a day or two, among the rocks, and when they don't find it they'll be alarmed. Every policeman will wonder whether I'm a saint or a magician. Lame Ali will enjoy this. But if they catch him . . . Then he's lost. They'll break his lame leg into pieces, into little pieces . . .'

He sat down to rest for a while with his back against a big plane-tree. He listened to the distant sound of firing. He could tell which report was that of the policemen's guns and which was Lame Ali's.

His head felt confused. Bald Hamza, Chukurova, the runaway horse, the fire, Idris Bey . . . Old Osman had related the story of Idris Bey to him . . . Mother Hürü, what a fine, friendly, affectionate, sincere face she had. Lame Ali, what an unfathomable man he was. The Ahjasaz marshes, Seyran, whose beauty was said to be beyond compare, the cowed, frightened villagers. The old people were very brave, Mother Hürü, Old Osman . . . They had more self-respect. And the women were much braver and more bellicose than the men. They stood up against injustice. Mad Durdu the bandit . . . How he had been killed . . . A thousand-headed dragon . . . Cut off the thousand heads and a whole forest of heads emerged. Cut those off too and a still bigger forest appears . . . A crowd, hundreds of people swoop down like eagles

186

over Mad Durdu. In a moment they rise again but Mad Durdu is not there . . . Only a leg, a booted leg lies bleeding in the dust. In Chukurova plain, up in the mountains, in the whole world, there are many people, but few aghas. So why don't people swoop down on the aghas like eagles? If they did, what would happen? Memed asked himself. A thousand-headed dragon, a huge cloud . . . A sword cuts at the thousand-headed dragon, it slashes again and again until it is blunt and worn out, and yet the heads still multiply.

Confused images . . . The palace of the king of the Taurus in Anavarza Castle . . . Once the whole of Chukurova . . .

A shadow moved just in front of him. Memed started, but it was only a fox sniffing at the earth. Seeing Memed start it turned, with a flick of its long brush, and ran off. Memed's heart was pounding.

After resting a while, he got up. His body ached all over, and he was tired out. Bald Hamza's dealings, Uncle Durmush Ali's death, Mother Hürü's distress, the state of things at Deyirmenoluk, the thistles, the fields, tyranny, hungry villagers, the thousand-headed dragon . . .

He walked down the valley, which seemed darker and deeper in the night. The forest on his right hand rustled. In the moonlight, it looked like a black rainstorm beating down upon the earth. The valley rumbled and murmured, and opened and closed in upon him. Trees, streams, rocks met and joined and then cleared again. The forest was pressing down upon him, pouring, rumbling . . . Memed's head whirled. The forest, the valley, the streams, birds, flowers, thickets, Anavarza Castle mauve and glinting in the heat, Alidagh, the lights, the fire, endlessly spiralling horses . . . Horses thundering down the valley . . . A confused world was churning in Memed's head. There was a roaring sound in his ears. He was struggling in a mighty torrent. Someone was holding him by the legs and dragging him down, down into the valley. The pungent smell of a plant reached him. Then the sharper smell of gunpowder. And of sweat . . .

The moon disappeared; the darkness raised its voice and enveloped Memed. Wolves, birds, jackals, bears, gazelles, wild goats, fallow deer, roe deer, leopards, dragons, horses, both wild and domestic creatures came clamouring down in the darkness to the dark bottom of the valley. Memed's head whirled and his eyes were blurred. The stars and the forest swayed, and flowed down into the valley, into the darkness.

Beneath Memed's feet stones rolled away down the slope like a river in spate. Memed too was swept away on top of the river of stones.

He tried to remember Bald Hamza; he called up a vision of him, but all at once it faded. There were sore places on his head, he remembered that. His arms were very long, and came down to his knees, he remembered that. He used to sit in a corner in the sun, not speaking to anyone; out of obstinacy he stayed in the sun, hot and sweating. His face was like leather. His skin was thick like the hide of a water-buffalo. The villagers used to say 'that is bullet-proof skin'. When or why Abdi Agha drove him out Memed could not remember. There was a bright light on the surface of a large sheet of water. Dragons on clouds floated on its surface. Masses of pure white clouds . . . White and dazzling . . .

All at once the murmuring and thundering stopped. Memed was suddenly plunged into an incredible silence. The world was so silent that it seemed empty. It was a strange sensation. Everything around him, the darkness, the night, the lights, the forest, the ground on which he was standing, his thoughts, everything was wiped out. It was as if he did not exist, either. Memed took a deep breath. The silence went on and on. He looked around him; there was unbroken darkness. He took a step forward. A tiny sound reached his ear, just a rustle. Then he heard a sound like a cough. A door opened, and a beam of light sprang out. Memed's eyes were dazzled. He heard a voice. Someone took him by the arm and pulled him inside.

A long white beard flowed before his eyes like a stream of water. 'What's happened to you, my boy?' said the white beard. Then he felt a woman's gentle hand. Her voice was warm and sounded like a lullaby. Memed did not hear what she was saying, but he let himself be lulled by the charm of the voice.

'You're bleeding, my child,' said the sweet voice of the woman. 'There's blood on your clothes.'

Memed's teeth were clenched. He tried to open them, he struggled, but they would not come apart. This always happened to him when he was in great distress.

He became conscious of what they were saying, but the voices came from a great distance.

'Let's put the boy to bed.'

'Has he been shot?'

'There's no wound.'

'What's happened to him?'

'Heaven only knows . . .'

'Where shall we hide him?'

'Will the police look for him here?'

'He's only a boy still.'

'He never grew up.'

'What is this blood?'

'He grazed himself on the rock, or got caught up in the thorn-trees . . . There's no bullet wound.'

'Be sure you look carefully.'

'There isn't a wound anywhere.'

'How does he come to be here in this state?'

'How did he find our house?'

'In this state . . .'

The voices faded away. Several times Memed turned from side to side, and groaned, trying to say something, suddenly his teeth unclenched. He began talking in his sleep. 'The dragon . . .' he babbled. 'Black Hamza . . . Bald . . . What's going to happen? What, what? Kamer . . . Seyran . . .' he was babbling incoherently.

He became silent. He fell asleep. His sleep was peaceful. He breathed easily.

He slept until afternoon. Then suddenly he started up, snatched the gun which lay near him, and began to stagger out, but at this point Süleyman caught hold of him. Memed opened his eyes, and seeing Süleyman, smiled, relaxed, and gazed around him in utter amazement. Süleyman's elderly wife came in, and said calmly,

'Welcome, my child.'

When Memed heard her gentle, sweet voice, like a lullaby, he remembered everything.

Süleyman said, 'Eh, my child, but we're glad to see you! How was it you thought of us? As you see, we've only got a sparrow's life left in us. It's good to see you once more.' Then he turned to his wife, 'What are you waiting for? The child is hungry. The poor boy is starving.'

The woman said,

'The tarhana soup's on the fire. I've got it ready.'

Süleyman embraced Memed:

'My big boy, my big son, where have you been all this time?' he said, hugging him. 'Where have you been, where?'

The woman quickly spread the meal-cloth. Süleyman said, 'Sit down, my big boy,' and released Memed. The soup steamed in a deep bowl, it was sprinkled with melted fat and red pepper. There was plenty of mint in it and garlic, too. A long blue wisp of steam rose from it towards the roof. A delicious smell of tarhana soup spread through the hut.

The woman handed Memed a spoon:

'Drink it up quickly,' she said. She wondered if Memed would realize why she said it. Years before she had set before him a steaming dish of tarhana soup. Memed looked at her smilingly. He remembered the old days, his childhood.

'I will,' he said.

Old Süleyman burst out laughing, and said,

'Slim Memed, you'd do well to listen to me. It's hot. You'll burn your mouth, you know.'

Memed said delightedly, 'Would I ever burn my mouth?'

Memed, Old Süleyman and the woman looked at one another and smiled.

Then Old Süleyman became serious.

'Listen, Slim Memed,' he said. 'Don't worry. This morning I made careful enquiries. Lame Ali took the police, and with them behind him, he's following your tracks in the direction of Chichekli valley. So drink your soup calmly.'

Memed smiled again.

'I'll drink it calmly.'

Old Süleyman pursued this gentle trend,

'Well, guest, where have you come from and where are you going to?'

A spark sprang into Memed's eyes; a sheaf of yellow light pierced his head and shone within it. The steely glint his eyes used to have returned to them. He bent his head.

'I've come from Deyirmenoluk and I'm going to that village, Uncle,' he said.

'I know Deyirmenoluk, but where is that village?'

A deep sadness came over Memed, but he did not show it, in order not to upset Süleyman.

'Oh, it's just that village. I'll go there and find that man, Uncle.'

'Will you be able to find him, son?'

'I'll find him,' said Memed confidently. Did he know about Deyirmenoluk?

'Who did you see at Deyirmenoluk, son?' asked Süleyman.

'I didn't see anyone or anything, Uncle Süleyman,' he said, with tears in his eyes.

Süleyman realized that Memed knew all that had happened, and not wishing to dwell on it, he changed the subject.

'Well I hope you go to that village and find the man.'

'I'll find him,' said Memed.

Ah, that village is not to be found, Old Süleyman said to himself. I've been looking for it for seventy years. That village and that man . . . That village doesn't exist in this world, my boy. But you go on looking for it. Since the world began everyone has been looking for that village and that man.

Memed finished drinking the hot tarhana soup.

'Oh, I'm full up,' he said.

Then a silence fell between them. The woman removed the plates and the silence continued. Süleyman's sons and daughters-in-law came in and looked at Memed apprehensively. They had heard about the previous night's battle. Memed looked down at the floor. Old Süleyman waited for him to speak.

After a while Memed raised his head. His eyes were gleaming and full of questions. He began to talk. He began to tell his story, what he felt, what he thought; he told it all openly and coolly. He told them all about Old Osman, the people of Vayvay, Seyran, the people of Akmezar, Idris Bey, Ali Safa, Arif Saim Bey, Mother Hürü, Bald Hamza; he poured it all out.

'We killed Abdi. He was a cruel, pitiless man. My mother died, Hatché died. I took to the mountains. I've lived with death every day. And the result? Bald Hamza came. It had never occurred to me that Bald Hamza would come and descend upon the village, that he would take back the land, and make the villagers' existence a worse hell than before. What do you think of it, Uncle Süleyman, please give me your advice.'

'The world is like that,' said Süleyman. 'Water fills a crack. People are born and die. The sun rises and sets. Trees grow and rot. Waters flow, clouds rise. If you kill one agha, another one comes in his place. If you kill another one, another one comes.'

'If you kill another one, another one comes,' repeated Memed. 'Another one, another one comes. Abdi goes, and Hamza comes. Hamza comes, Hamza comes,' he said, as if reciting a verse. 'Hamza comes, Hamza comes, Hamza comes . . .'

'Yes, Hamza comes!' shouted Old Süleyman. 'That villain Hamza.'

He jumped up, and then sat down again. His long white beard waved in the air.

28

LAME ALI was following a trail. He had put on his hand-woven striped woollen shalvar-trousers, dyed brown with walnut juice. A black sash was wound round his waist, and a pistol without a holster was thrust into his sash. Ali walked along, his lame leg dragging behind him, and followed the trail in the direction of Kesme village. Everyone knew that Memed had gone that way. Lame Ali knew it only too well. Moreover, he knew that Memed was at Süleyman's house. With Ali was another tracker, a very famous one from Elbistan, who went by the name of Swift Musa, an elderly man, tall and swarthy, all skin and bone. One morning he had materialized at Captain Faruk's side. He was an old acquaintance. When the Captain undertook the pursuit of Slim Memed he sent word to Elbistan and had Swift Musa brought to him. Swift Musa was well known in Chukurova, Marash and Antep. His fame had even reached Aleppo. As for Lame Ali, he was well-known to the villages of the Plain of Thistles and to some of the Taurus hamlets.

Swift Musa was not a talkative man. It had not taken Ali long to realize that here was an expert tracker, and he began to be afraid of him.

They had started off from the rocks where Memed had hidden the day before. It was a bright day. The scent of the flowers was strong in the summer heat. A light breeze, like the dawn wind, was blowing, making the wings of the bees quiver as they flew from flower to flower. The short green grass between the rocks was dotted with squat brightly-coloured yellow crocuses, violets, orchises, and anemones, of a strong razor-like red. The scent of fresh thyme filled the air. Plains, mountains, fields, springs, gullies and forests all have their own plants and their own scents. In rocky places the plants and scents are very different. Especially in the spring their scents and colours are intoxicating. And if the day is bright and sunny, if a gentle breeze is blowing, if a pungent scent comes wafting in, if there is a faint mist over the rocks . . . if spring is in full bloom . . .

Among the closely packed plants, the varied asphodels, flowers and colours, the rocks took on an added beauty. Beneath the flowers there were strangely-coloured tiny birds' nests. And from one flower to another, from one asphodel stem to another, little blue or red or bright green spiders had spun thousands of webs, as big as a hand, and were stretched out in a corner of the web in the spring sunshine.

Some tiny white rock toadstools, like grains of wheat, had pierced through the rocky soil.

Lame Ali was frightened and very worried. That scoundrel Musa was terribly hot on the trail, never losing it even for a minute. If things went on like that the trail would come to an end at Old Süleyman's door.

Once or twice he tried to mislead him, to take up the trail and to lead him in another direction. But Swift Musa darted a terrible look at him, a contemptuous searing look. Ali was silent. He tried to think of another solution . . . The affair was hopeless. The damned fellow would find Memed. Captain Faruk, Sergeant Asim, Hamza Agha, and policemen were advancing along a goat-track below them.

On this beautiful spring day, bathed in sunshine and scents, Lame Ali was sweating. He had never been in such difficult straits in his whole life. There was only one way left, and that was to send a warning to Memed at Süleyman's house. If Musa had been an average tracker, he could have misled him, drawn him in another direction, delayed him till nightfall, and while he was sleeping he could have gone and taken Memed away from Old Süleyman's house. But that was quite impossible. Not a single footprint failed to catch Musa's eye.

At one point in a space surrounded by rocks the tracks were more numerous and straggled off in several directions. Swift Musa hesitated some time over these tracks. He measured directions and footprints. Ali, thinking that it was a good opportunity, drew his attention to a track that went up into the mountains. Swift Musa, for some reason agreeing with Ali, began to climb the mountain. Ali's heart almost stopped beating with joy.

Musa followed the tracks as far as some earth which lay at the foot of a white crag, and which was as fine as flour; brown, virgin soil. There were hundreds of footprints on this earth. Ali identified the footprints one by one. Wolf, fox, jackal, horse, leopard . . . Eagle, pigeon, polecat, vulture. Hundreds of prints dotted the soft earth. A man's footprints came in and went out towards the top of the white crag.

Ali began to talk. He talked on and on without a break, about Memed, Memed's childhood, his courage, Abdi Agha, his cruelty, how he was killed, Hatché, Iraz, the thistle-fields, the light that blazed over Alidagh, and how Memed disappeared – all this he related, hoping to bewilder Musa. Ali knew that if he did not confuse him sufficiently, a tracker like Swift Musa would not be put off, and would not follow the trail to the summit of the peak.

As Musa followed the trail towards the top of the white crag, Ali did not stop talking for a moment, but, gasping for breath, went on relating Memed's adventures: 'No one who did him the slightest injury has ever benefited by it. They have always come to grief. I am afraid of him, my friend. He is like a saint. He is not easily found, he vanishes; no one can injure him. Anyone trying to harm him gets an unpleasant surprise from his unseen protectors, the Invisible Ones. If someone does find a chance to harm him, then beware! There is no salvation for him. Why did Osmanja go blind? Do you know why? Because ... Well, because when the light blazed forth on Alidagh and burnt for three days and nights, Osmanja saw Memed near the Monk's Spring and went and informed the Captain. Then the Captain surrounded Memed, and made his red blood flow on to the black earth, for he was slightly wounded. Osmanja got up next morning, and imagine it ... He was blind in both eyes. Then there's that business of Dumb Duran. He too was one of the people who betrayed Memed's whereabouts to the Captain and caused Memed's wife, Hatché, to be shot. Hatché's red blood mingled with the black earth. The policeman who shot her was killed there and then, a black storm arose on Alidagh. Flashes of lightning were followed by thunderbolts. Earth and sky were in chaos. Alidagh rose and fell, rumbled and rattled. A furious rain poured in torrents and the rivers overflowed, sweeping away Dumb Duran, his relations and acquaintances, sweeping away their cows and horses too. Even their bodies were never found. And then there's what happened to me. When Memed eloped with Abdi Agha's nephew's fiancée, he ran away into the forest with her. It was a rainy day. I was summoned to track them down. I started off from those crags over there. When I was halfway across the crags "Beetroot" Hösük appeared before me, a great hodja whose healing breath cuts sickness like a sword. He said to me, "Beware Ali, beware of finding Memed and separating the lovers! That boy, whom they call Slim Memed is no ordinary man, and he will cause you trouble." As soon as he had told me this, Hösük Hodja disappeared from sight. Ah, I didn't heed him, I was just a headstrong youth. I tracked them down ... Memed shot Abdi and wounded him, he shot the nephew and killed him. When I was still on my way back I felt a pain in my leg. An unusual, unbearable pain ... I cried out at the top of my voice. I kept on crying, night and day for a month, then "Beetroot" Hösük could not bear my wailing and came and read prayers and breathed over me, and the pain diminished. But as you see, I was left with a lame leg. I'm not going to track down Slim Memed. I've been punished enough by him. I'm not tracking him down, but as the Government wouldn't leave me in peace, I'm letting it be thought that I'm on his trail. I appear to be tracking him, but if Memed has gone one way, I lead them another way. Memed is no ordinary creature. On the top of Alidagh ... Three days and three nights ... A huge ball of fire ... as tall as a minaret. It burst forth, and the whole place was as light as day. All the Taurus villagers saw it. This Memed boy is no ordinary being!'

Swift Musa reached the top of the white crag, and squatted down. Ali was out of breath with talking. He sat down opposite Musa, stretching out his lame leg right under the other's nose.

Musa looked at him so scornfully that Ali did not know what to do or say. He put his hands on his knees, then on the rock. He picked a flower and shredded it. He got up and sat down again. He looked at Musa and again saw on his face a stealthy, mocking smile. He bent his head, and began to pour out a torrent of words. Musa looked at him in astonishment and said nothing.

His breeches were of white handwoven cotton, now greyish with dirt. His red Marash shoes were rubbed, and full of holes, like a pock-marked face. His long grizzly beard hung scantily. With his deep-set eyes, his long curved nose, his slanting eyebrows and his pointed chin, he looked like some strange bird. An old, brooding, melancholy bird ...

He flapped his arms two or three times like a bird and got up. Ali followed his every movement with his eyes. Musa first turned in the direction of the summit of the mountain, then climbed down the crags. Ali was almost dead with excitement. He followed Musa down in transports of delight. Musa fixed his eyes on the mountain peak and scanned the cloud-capped summit. In front of him a mullein plant as big as a tree, with large yellow flowers, was growing. Musa took a few steps upwards, then at once turned downhill and began to descend the mountain in haste, almost at a run. Ali's heart sank. He looked at the sun, it was only just noon. The man would be at Old Süleyman's door before evening.

I'll kill him, I'll kill him and save Memed. I'll go to prison. Anyway Memed will come and get me out, and I'll take to the mountains. I'll become a brigand too. Let them see what kind of a brigand a tracker makes, he thought to himself. Should I tell this man everything, he wondered. Should I plead with him? Will it be any use? Yes, I'll do that first, and if he goes on with the tracking, I'll draw my gun and shoot him. I'll pretend I did it out of jealousy. Or I can tell them he was following the wrong trail, that he was Slim Memed's man.

Musa came down back to the open space. At a glance he found the right trail and plunged straight ahead, following it down into the darkening valley. He walked very fast. From far down below the Captain called to them,

'Trackers! Come here, you've done enough! Come and have some food. You can go on later.'

The Captain repeated his call several times. Musa did not hear, or pretended not to hear. This infuriated Ali. He grasped his arm and pulled him back,

'Can't you hear the order?' he shouted. 'What sort of a tracker are you? The Captain's calling.'

Swift Musa stopped, and looked him in the eye obstinately, as if he could kill him, then shook himself free.

'I shall find Slim Memed,' he said. 'I'll risk being paralysed or going blind. I'll even risk death, but I'll find him.'

Lame Ali said nothing in reply; he was petrified.

He thought to himself, before you find Slim Memed I'll kill you, Take that, you master tracker.

They made their way to the place where the police had stacked their guns, and were sitting down. Musa, striding along in front, flapped his arms like the wings of a bird.

Four people, the Captain, Sergeant Asim, Hamza, and an old brigand, seated by a spring under the pine-trees, were drinking raki and eating the meat that was being cooked by a policeman on spits over a charcoal fire near by.

'Come on,' said the Captain, 'come on, you trackers who follow the trail of birds' wings! What have you been doing?'

Musa stood to attention and saluted like a soldier:

'I have got on to the right trail, sir, and I'll find our quarry before nightfall.'

Ali had expected him to tell the Captain what had happened. But Musa just glanced at him out of the corner of his eye. They sat down, and started to cook their meat over the charcoal embers. Musa was quick at everything. He walked quickly, he ate quickly, he cooked quickly. And when he spoke the words tumbled out of his mouth. Ali tried to keep up with him, and swallowed the meat without even chewing it.

Musa, with his mouth still full, jumped to his feet.

'Many thanks,' he said. 'May the Prophet bless you.'

He started off. Lame Ali set off behind him, but by the time he caught him up he was sweating.

'Why are you running?' he yelled. 'Are there horsemen pursuing you? Why all this haste? I can hardly keep up with you.'

Musa had found a clear imprint on the earth. He circled it a few times, and then set off. Five paces further on he saw another footprint just as clearly outlined, at the foot of a mossy rock.

The shadows lengthened. They came and went. The sun still shone. Above Musa's stockingless feet, between his shalvar and his shoes, his legs showed bare, wrinkled, scratched, and covered with dried blood. Musa alternately bent down and straightened up. He stopped at the foot of a white boulder on which a small pine-tree was growing. There was no soil, nothing. The roots of the pine-tree could be seen on the surface, clinging to the white boulder. Musa passed rapidly down the valley. The police would spend the night at Kesme. 'Trackers,' the Captain had said, 'we'll await you there. If you find a trail let us know.'

Even the Captain doesn't care. Has the task of finding Slim Memed fallen to you, you scoundrel?

Suddenly Ali planted himself in front of Musa. His eyes were red with fury.

'Musa,' he said, 'listen to me. The trail is leading towards the forest. Straight into the forest . . . Or are you following a false trail because you're afraid that Slim Memed will cast the crippling spell on you?'

Musa did not answer. He placed his stick on a mark scratched in the dust. Then he walked on.

Lame Ali began to tremble.

'To the forest, I beseech you, Musa, the trail is leading to the forest.'

Musa took no notice. He walked on obstinately. They were above the village now. The sun was setting. The policemen could not yet have arrived. They must be drinking in the forest, thought Ali. The village of Kesme was quiet. If the policemen had arrived there would have been a hubbub in the village. Smoke rose from the chimneys.

'There's plenty of smoke coming out of Süleyman's chimney. Our foolhardy boy's there, taking it easy and enjoying himself. If he only knew what I've been going through . . .' he muttered. He could have wept.

If Musa went two hundred paces further downhill, it would be all up with Memed . . . He drew his pistol out of his sash, and slipped in some cartridges, but when he was about to take aim, Musa faced about with incredible agility. He looked distraught.

'Don't kill me, Ali, I have a wife and family,' he pleaded, raising his hands. 'Don't kill me . . . The footprints lead to the forest. I didn't know you felt like this. I thought you wanted to give me the slip so as to catch Slim Memed yourself. The footprints lead to the forest. All right?'

Ali thrust the pistol into his sash. They stood facing each other and trembling.

At last Musa said,

'Ali, Memed is in that house,' and he pointed to Old Süleyman's house.

'Yes, in that house,' said Lame Ali.

They advanced side by side towards Old Süleyman's house. As they walked they stopped every now and then, looked at each other and laughed.

29

T HE District Governor was a fat man, with a double chin, swollen, protruding eyes, cold, purplish thick lips, big ears, and thick eyebrows. The eyebrows made a curving line across his forehead. He was short in stature and very cold in manner. He had only recently discarded the fez, and wore a hat as if it were a makeshift; he was a real Ottoman.

He was secretly furious with Kemal Atatürk, and his rage increased because he could not express his rancour openly. He was angry with the peasants too, because they were soldiers with Kemal Atatürk, they drove the Greeks into the sea, and they drove out the Sultan. He vented his rage on them. Sometimes when he came across someone suitably fanatical, who understood his hostility towards Mustafa Kemal, he would unburden himself to him, and go on talking to him for hours about the Ottomans, Sultan Abdul Hamit, and Vahüdettin, and he would renew his hope that one day they would be delivered from that green-eyed devil.

'Our beautiful fatherland whose rulers were the Lawgiver and the Conqueror will not be left abandoned in their hands,' he would shout. 'In the hands of these nonentities, these bandits . . . these Bolsheviks . . . This state of affairs is only temporary. Allah is great . . . It will not be left to them! That green-eyed fair-haired monster will be destroyed! The English, French and Americans will come and occupy these territories. They, those Bolsheviks, that rabble, those crawling scoundrels will not be the rulers of this country. Those infidels.'

He spread immense hope among Mustafa Kemal's enemies. He performed the prayer ritual five times a day punctiliously.

He hated the peasants, and as far as possible avoided seeing their dirty faces. Whenever he saw a peasant, he would pucker up his face, mutter a prayer to avert the devil, and spit noisily on the ground.

'Whenever I see one of those peasants, it is just as if I see that blond tyrant. And I shudder, my good sir, I can't help myself.'

If Arif Saim Bey was with him he would jump through all sorts of hoops; he would walk at least five paces behind him, and if he opened his mouth he would rush forward as if shot from a gun. It was he who finished off all Arif Saim Bey's dirty jobs.

'It's these men, these lions, these rascals who'll destroy the blond devil,' he would say to himself. 'He's got lots of Arif Saims with him. Every one of them is worse and viler than Arif Saim. They'll ruin the blond devil. We shall see, we shall see what happens. A single Arif Saim can destroy him. And a thousand Arif Saims . . . Wait and see.'

When he went to bed he would imagine what it would be like

to wake up the next morning and hear the news that the blond devil had fallen from power, and the Ottoman Sultan had been restored. He would imagine his embroidered clothes, braid and medals in great contentment, and so he would go to sleep peacefully.

'These people cannot last in the land of the glorious Ottomans. A jackal does not sleep in the lion's den.'

Every night he went to sleep in the belief that next morning he would be a pasha. He had great faith in the English. Would those who ruled the empire on which the sun never set abandon Anatolia to those Bolshevik vagabonds? Had they not already occupied all the Arab lands and restored the sons of our Prophet to their throne? He would not stay another minute in this town then, this rubbish-heap without roads, without water, without houses, without light, this town wallowing in mud and filth. The blond devil's government held only by a thin thread.

Ramiz Bey was fed up to the teeth; he drank from morning to night, and played cards with the remnants of the feudal beys. He had prostitutes brought from Alexandretta, and all night long there was gambling and roistering.

Since his appointment to this district he had never gone out into a village. It was more than he could do. He could not bear to see those peasants who had been the blond man's soldiers. But this was just an excuse. Under his skin and in his heart it was the fear of the peasants. He used all sorts of pretexts in order to disguise this fear.

Ali Safa Bey had begged him to come, again and again. This Ali Safa fellow was just another of the blond devil's henchmen. During the War of Independence he had gone up into the Taurus, had taken the name of Typhoon, and had campaigned in the mountains against the French, and just because of this the blond devil had awarded him a medal. He had a lot of tin medals, that blond devil! And gave them away to all and sundry! Yes, this Ali Safa was one of the blond devil's henchmen, a double-dealer, a scoundrel. But on the other hand he persecuted the blond devil's favourites, those dishonest, stupid, cringing soldiers, that is to say, the peasants. Not long ago he had made Yaghmur Agha steal all the horses in one village. He raided the villages every night, shooting them up and making the villagers wish they were dead. Ah, they are rotting away, my dear sir, disintegrating. So you drive the ruler from his beloved fatherland after seven hundred years? Then this is what you get! People like Yaghmur Agha, people who in the seven hundred years of Ottoman rule could never have existed.

'I leaned over and watched him. He was like a green snake in the deep flow of time, drowning, rotting, my dear sir. He's a strange, conceited man, the blond devil. His nose does not perceive this powerful smell of rottenness. A lot of Yaghmur Aghas will come into existence, a lot of Arif Saim Beys, a lot of Typhoons ... They will spread rottenness.'

Ali Safa Bey said,

'You simply must come, your Honour. They occupied my lands without any right, and built houses there. Dirty houses made of grass and reeds. Did we shed our blood for this? As Allah is my witness, your Honour, a piece of me was left on every rock in the Taurus. I fought at Hachin, I was with Shahin Bey at Antep, with Sinan Pasha at Karaisali. While we were fighting and dying, deserters from the army were taking over my land, stabbing us in the back. Now they've become our masters. Please come and see with your own eyes the kind of tyranny under which we are suffering, and bear witness to it. You'll see the kind of men we are having to struggle with to serve the fatherland. It was easier to fight the French. They were our declared enemies. Now we have to fight the treacherous enemies of the fatherland at home. I have asked Arif Saim Bey for his motor-car in order to take you to the village. The car and the driver are waiting at the door.'

The Governor, who was sitting at the table, immediately jumped up, and did up his buttons.

'Is Arif Saim Bey's motor-car waiting for me? Quick, let's go. Did you ask the Bey for it for me?'

'Yes, for you.'

'We haven't made it wait too long, have we?'

'No, sir.'

'What about the clerk, the police and the Sergeant?'

'They went to the village last night, sir. I have made everything ready.'

He got into the car, radiant, and lit a cigarette. His double-chin bulged more than ever.

'Drive this way, my boy,' he instructed the driver, pointing out the direct opposite of the way they had to go.

Holding his long, thick, amber cigarette-holder in his mouth, he looked about him proudly.

The driver did as he was told and drove through the market-place. He blew the horn three times. This delighted the Governor. All the artisans and tradesmen came out of their shops, and greeted the Governor by bowing low from the waist. Ali Safa Bey was pleased too. The fact that the people were seeing him riding in Arif Saim Bey's motor-car, beside the Governor, increased his influence tenfold. Ali Safa Bey had calculated well ahead how many birds he could kill with one stone. It had taken some bowing and scraping with Arif Saim Bey, but he had got what he wanted.

The driver understood the Governor's desire. At the end of the market, he turned and drove back again under the admiring gaze of the shopkeepers.

'Shall I go round once again, your Honour?'

'Yes, do, my boy.'

This opportunity to ride in Arif Saim Bey's motor-car would perhaps not come his way again. If he hadn't been ashamed to do so, he would have asked Ali Safa Bey if he could sit enthroned like that in the car all day, driving round the market followed by the surprised, admiring or apprehensive looks of the shopkeepers. Yes, till night.

He smiled at the people who stood by obsequiously, and dispensed gracious waves of his hand to each of them individually. Then, sighing, he said,

'Drive on, my boy, drive on, and we'll have a look at that village.'

It was mid-morning when they reached Vayvay. All the villagers, young and old, met the Governor outside the village. Seyfali had brought a drummer and a fife-player who were playing away.

The Governor darted a look over the crowd.

'How poor they look!' he said. 'But it serves them right . . .'

'Yes, indeed,' said Ali Safa Bey. 'They have victimized me, and that is why I went bankrupt. They neither plant my fields, nor let me plant them. If they would give me my fields and would agree to be labourers on my farm I would look after them beautifully. There wouldn't be any poverty or anything like that.'

'They don't understand, my dear fellow. They're not people really. And yet His Excellency Mustafa Kemal Pasha declares them to be our masters!'

'Masters!'

'If he came and saw this melancholy lot . . .'

'Our masters are different creatures, quite different from ordinary men!'

The people were a heap of rags. Each of them looked like a dry stick. On their faces was a greenish-yellow corpse-like look.

The car stopped in the middle of Vayvay under the huge tree. The villagers stood around respectfully, their heads bent.

The Governor said in a harsh, rumbling voice,

'Are the experts here?'

'Yes,' said Ali Safa Bey.

'Silence,' shouted the Governor, for no reason at all.

The buzzing of flies could be heard in the air. Everyone was holding his breath in terror.

'Clerk, read the deeds.'

'At your service, Bey.'

'Ali Safa Bey, who are your experts?'

'Surmelioghlu Mahmud from the village of Chikchiklar.'

A bent man came forward. He had a long white beard, green eyes, a big face and a large head; he could not hold his head up straight and it was tilted to one side. His shalvar-trousers were in tatters. He wore a white sash round his waist . . . A holster was tied in his sash and an old-fashioned pistol thrust into it.

'Duran Hadji from Chikchiklar.'

Duran Hadji was an old man too. He was tall, with a scanty beard.

'Abdurrahman Hodja from Topraktepe.'

He too was old. He was dark-skinned, and had a round white beard.

'Kölemenoghlu from Chankaza.'

Kölemenoghlu came forward. He was bent, emaciated and trembling.

'Headman, where are your experts?'

Sefché the Warden, Old Osman, Memed the Mullah and Corporal Ali came forward.

'Clerk, read on!'

The Clerk read:

'Ali Safa Bey holds a title to seventeen dunums of land. To the south, the high road . . .'

'Where?'

They pointed to a white road some distance from the village.

'That's the road we've been using for thirty years . . .' said Surmelioghlu.

Sefché the Warden, Old Osman, Corporal Ali and Memed the Mullah pointed out a distant track to the left of the village. The experts broke into a violent argument about this. The Governor interrupted the argument:

'To the east the gully of Yalnizdut.'

Ali Safa Bey's experts pointed to a dry gully above the village. The Vayvay experts pointed to Yalnizdut in the distance.

'To the north Ahjasaz . . .'

Again the experts pointed in the wrong direction.

'To the west the Inscribed Stone . . .'

They pointed a long way down, to a place below Anavarza.

The experts again began to hold a long discussion. The Governor was silent.

'Have you finished your discussion?' he said at last, harshly.

They were silent.

'From what the experts have said it is understood that Ali Safa Bey's rights include the village of Vayvay. As the evidence of the experts proves, the Vayvay villagers came only a short time ago and built shacks out of brushwood and grass on Ali Safa Bey's land. It is clear that the Vayvay villagers have occupied his land illegally. It has been decided to put an end to the occupation and to remove these flimsy shacks the villagers call houses.'

Then he turned to the villagers, and said,

'You have opposed the Government. You have occupied a man's land illegally. I cannot take someone else's land and give it to you. I'll give you a month's grace. If you have not vacated this place and gone in a month, I shall send the police in, and I shall pull your grass huts down on your heads. You have become so insolent that you recognize neither your betters, nor the Government nor God. Neither right, nor law, nor justice . . .'

The villagers said,

'No one knows how long ago this village was founded. It was built in the time of our grandfathers' grandfathers, in the days of the reform party.'

'Are you setting yourselves up against me?' thundered the Governor. 'Are you raising objections to what I have said? Do you think you are going to browbeat me? This village is a hundred years old, you say? I suggest you put up these houses just a day or two ago in order to invade Ali Safa Bey's land. Who do you think you're taking in? Does this village look as if it were a hundred years old, or ten, or even ten days old? Is it a village at all?'

He shouted louder and louder. He foamed at the mouth, and swelled up. He was quite beside himself, rolling his eyes, stamping his feet, and waving his arms.

'Liars, cheats, scoundrels, unbelievers, infidels! If you don't get out of this village in a month, look out! I'll crush you, crush you like ants . . .'

He stamped his foot violently and rubbed it over the ground.

'Like that, like a snake's head . . . I'll crush your heads, I'll crush you.'

The villagers were frightened, disconcerted, cowed.

'I'll show you the advantages of a Republican Government!'

Shaking with fury, he strode about under the plane-tree, shouting, reviling, cursing and giving orders.

Eventually Ali Safa Bey and Seyfali approached him.

'Bey,' said Ali Safa Bey, 'the villagers have killed a ram in your honour. Seyfali the Headman says that it is noon and he invites you to eat, asking you to forgive any deficiencies.'

The Governor stopped and thought; then suddenly he shouted at the top of his voice,

'Tell them to throw their offering to the dogs, those shameless liars! Trying to take me in with that bare-faced lie about their ancestors having founded this village a hundred years ago! This heap of grass . . . Listen, you filthy lot, tell the truth, how many days ago did you throw those grass shacks together? If you put up those huts a hundred years ago, if you've been living in those shacks for a hundred years, I despise you; I ought to spit in your faces. Let the dogs eat that ram of yours!'

Holding Ali Safa Bey's arm he dragged him towards the motor-car and pushed him in, then he got in himself.

'Start the engine, my boy,' he said gently. 'Please, my boy, don't let Arif Saim Bey hear that I got so angry with the villagers. I know he loves the peasants. I love them too, but not the ones who tell lies, or seize other people's land.'

He was still shaking with anger.

The chauffeur set the car going with three turns of the starting-handle, then he got in and the motor-car moved off.

The Governor stretched out his hand, and grasped Ali Safa Bey's, saying,

'That's the only way to deal with those scoundrels, isn't it, my dear chap?' and he pressed his hand warmly. 'I have a request to make of you.'

Ali Safa Bey was on the alert at once:

'What is it, sir?'

The Governor put his mouth to his ear:

'I beg you. If the chauffeur lets slip to Arif Saim Bey what happened today, my violent but righteous anger . . . I do entreat you . . . Can you find some way of keeping him quiet?'

'Don't worry about that, Ramiz Bey. He'll keep quiet.'

The Governor could not be reassured. His fears grew. If Arif Saim Bey heard of this . . . What if Arif Saim Bey's chauffeur was a spy?

Putting his mouth close to Ali Safa's ear, he said,

'My dear Ali Safa Bey, what if our friend here was sent secretly to keep a check on my activities? To find out how I behaved towards our villagers . . . Isn't it possible?'

Ali Safa Bey said firmly,

'No, it isn't.' This reassured Ramiz Bey for a time, but then once more his inner fear overcame him. If it should be heard that he had treated the villagers like that, had cursed and insulted them, they would dismiss him from his post.

Again he bent towards Ali Safa Bey:

'Wouldn't it be all right if those people remained in their

village? Couldn't you find a way? Perhaps you could drive them out without my intervening, by your usual method of intimidation?'

'No, I can't,' said Ali Safa Bey. 'Not now that things have been set in motion. Besides, it would weaken the Government's authority. It would be flouted. You cannot do this to the Government of the Turkish Republic. You cannot make a permanent official of the Republic eat his words.'

The Governor said firmly,

'I'd make him eat his words, Ali Safa Bey. And how! Not only the District Governor, but the Provincial Governor, the Minister, and the Head of State . . . ' Then he realized he had gone too far. 'Well, speaking for myself,' he corrected himself, 'I'm ready to eat my words . . .'

Why should a man like Arif Saim Bey lend his private motor-car to a petty agha, and why should that agha persuade a district governor to get in the car and go with him to wipe out a village? With a chauffeur too. Was it likely? Was it normal? And this chauffeur was obviously a sharp-witted fellow. Why he might even be a superintendent from public security!

'Did you study in Europe, my good sir?'

The chauffeur heard, but took no notice.

'I asked you if you studied in Europe?'

The chauffeur half turned round, smiled, and said in a pronounced Black Sea accent,

'I've never been to Europe, I can't read or write.'

This reply made the Governor even more suspicious. He's hiding something, he thought. He's from public security that's certain. Would a man like Arif Saim Bey have an illiterate chauffeur? Is it possible that he's never been to Europe? He's given himself away properly. What a good imitation of a Black Sea accent he gave. Bravo, they train these police spies well. If the last Sultan had had capable people like these, wouldn't they have spotted Mustafa Kemal's intentions long before? It wouldn't take this devious, clever assistant more than a day or two to get to know all one's business.

'My good sir, you drive excellently well. Only someone who has trained in Europe could drive a motor-car so smoothly and nicely.'

The chauffeur grinned from ear to ear, and let out such a guffaw that the motor-car shook.

'Our boss, Halil from Erzurum, has travelled a lot in Europe. He said to me, "Jemal, there's no one like you in Europe. You're the god of the machine".'

'My dear sir, you speak with a very charming Black Sea accent.'

'So I do. It's my mother tongue.'

Well, well, bravo! They have trained him well.

'My dear Jemal Bey, I suppose you are very fond of the peasants?'

'Yes, I am. The peasants are my motherland. Anyone who doesn't love his country is a great bastard.'

'I treated the peasants very harshly today, didn't I?'

'No, sir, not harshly. You treated them very gently, very humanely. Our Arif Saim Bey has them trounced with cudgels. Arif Saim Bey says the peasants only understand blows, nothing else. The Bey was very angry with the villagers of Akmezar. He had them beaten to death, a lot of them.'

'Very proper.'

The Black Sea accent grew stronger.

'Yes, they asked for it.'

He's mocking me, said the Governor to himself. I am ruined. How is it I didn't realize that the Bey's chauffeur might be a member of the security police?

'My good Jemal Bey, how would you like to drink a glass or two with me tonight? If I asked you? You would make me very happy, very honoured.'

'I might make you feel honoured, but if my master heard about it, I wouldn't half get it . . .'

He's laughing up his sleeve at me, the scoundrel. But if I'd come across such an idiot, such an imbecile as I . . . I too should have laughed up my sleeve.

'Please do come, my dear sir. Arif Saim Bey won't hear about it.'

'We won't let on, Jemal, don't worry,' said Ali Safa Bey.

The Governor was furious. The unmitigated ass, he said to himself, addressing a police superintendent with such familiarity! He doesn't realize who he is! He'll see! I'll take back my decision. Yes, it is a hundred years since Vayvay village has been a place of residence in this mud, this quagmire, these flies, this hell. Historians know about it. I won't make use of Government authority on behalf of a beast like Ali Safa. He can drive out the villagers by whatever methods of his own he likes to use, but he won't get me involved officially.

'My good Jemal Bey, I too am very fond of the peasants. My ancestors were peasants.'

The motor-car lurched into a hole, shook, and climbed out again. The red-tiled roofs of the town, its mud-brick houses, the panes of glass reflecting the afternoon sun, made it look like an enchanted city. It clung to the slopes of the mountain. High up and far away.

30

LAME ALI knocked at Old Süleyman's door.

'Hey there, Süleyman Agha, Uncle Süleyman, open the door. It's me, Lame Ali,' he called.

Old Süleyman's thick white eyebrows rose, and bristled. He began to mutter angrily to himself. 'So it's you, you lickspittle belonging to Bald Hamza. And he thinks I'm going to open the door to him! Be off with you, you shameless rogue! Go and shit your lame leg. You lackey, you tyrant, you torturer of Deyirmenoluk.' He prowled about the house.

'Uncle Süleyman, I know you're inside, open the door. I'm in a hurry. I must see your guest.'

Süleyman went to the closet, and took out a beautiful old rifle, which he slowly loaded.

'You want to see my guest, you lame dog! You've followed his trail then . . . Now I'll show you how my guest is to be seen.'

He drew near to the door. He placed the muzzle of the gun to a knot-hole in the door, and looked through a chink in the panels. He took aim, drew back, and would have pulled the trigger if Memed had not come up behind him, and said,

'Stop, Uncle,' and he pulled him by the arm. 'Open the door. Lame Ali's one of my men.'

Old Süleyman did not understand anything at all.

'Open the door, Süleyman Agha, I expected him here.'

'But I was going to shoot him.'

'It would have been a mistake.'

'You don't know that Lame One. It wouldn't have been a mistake.'

Old Süleyman unlatched the door, grumbling all the while, and Lame Ali came in, followed by Swift Musa. Memed and Lame Ali embraced each other.

Old Süleyman looked at them in wonder.

'There's something about this boy of ours,' he muttered. 'He's not a brigand, he's a general staff strategist!'

Quickly Lame Ali explained the situation to Memed and then introduced Swift Musa. Old Süleyman and Memed had both heard Swift Musa's name before. Süleyman, smiling, said,

'Ask Memed, you lame villain, if I didn't nearly kill you. I knew you as one of Bald Hamza's followers. I swear by God I would have killed you. There would have been one unbeliever less in the world and Swift Musa would have had a free field. It's his right to be unique.'

'I saw for myself. It's his right,' said Lame Ali.

'If I had acted a moment later, it would have been all up with you,' Memed reproved him. 'Are you mad? You have become so notorious in these parts that if the peasants had got hold of you, you would have had a hot reception. Why are you taking such risks?'

Old Süleyman added,

'He planted himself right in front of the door. But for Memed that lame leg of yours would have been blown to pieces by now . . .'

'It's the good deeds I've done stopped you, and saved my life,' said Ali.

They went on joking for a time. Then Old Süleyman asked,

'Musa Agha, is it true what they say about you? That you can leave Marash at daybreak and be in Adana by sunset? That you are faster than a bird on the wing?'

Swift Musa smiled.

'Yes, it's true. Or more correctly, it was true. I've grown old, Süleyman Agha.'

Old Süleyman was extremely curious. 'There's never been a trail you couldn't pick up – is that true?' he asked.

Swift Musa became as shy and bashful as a child, and said hesitantly,

'Once in the place they now call Jeyhan I picked up a trail. It was a brigand's trail, but not the one I was supposed to be tracking. That one was hidden among the Anavarza crags. Later I rectified the trail and found the man, but at one point I had made a mistake.'

Lame Ali said,

'I've been watching Swift Musa and I'm really afraid of him now! I tried hard to mislead him, but he followed Memed's trail right up to this door. Memed, my friend, you saved my life but I saved yours too.'

He related what had happened on the way there, and told how he had decided to kill Musa. Swift Musa turned pale and his eyes became glassy.

'Would you really have shot me?' he asked in astonishment, his face showing consternation.

'Well, tell me,' said Lame Ali, 'what else could I have done?' He pointed to Old Süleyman. 'He was going to shoot me, and it wasn't my fault or my doing.'

'My goodness, yes, I would have shot you,' said Old Süleyman. 'And a good thing too. Anyway it is my bounden duty to send Lame Ali's soul to hell next time.'

After they had eaten a meal, Lame Ali took Memed aside, and said,

'They'll search every house in this village. It's Captain Faruk's custom. He'll beat up everyone from the Headman downwards, old and young, women and children. Take a horse and get away from here at once.'

'Where can I go?' asked Memed.

'The mountains around here are full of policemen,' said Lame Ali. 'And there are the bandits too who will give no quarter. That Black Ibrahim, for instance. I don't know what he wants of you. "I'm out for his blood," he said, and didn't say anything else. What have you done to him?'

'That filthy beast!' shouted Memed. 'What have I done? Destroyed his stables, burned his harvests, raped his wife and daughters-in-law and daughters! What did I do to him? Where shall I go now?'

Ali thought deeply.

'You can't stay here. It's too dangerous. Everyone knows you would come to Old Süleyman's house. You can't hide in the forest. You would die of hunger. Everyone who sees you would inform on you. The old Slim Memed doesn't exist any more. Don't let anyone from Deyirmenoluk get hold of you, they would tear you limb from limb.'

'Where shall I go, Ali?'

Ali thought and thought, but could suggest nothing. 'You can't live in the mountains nowadays. If only you'd stayed in your hideout for another year or two, so that people would have forgotten all about you.'

'I was in Chukurova,' said Memed, and sitting in a corner of the house he told Ali the story of Chukurova, Vayvay, Ali Safa Bey, Arif Saim Bey, Idris Bey, the other Chukurova aghas and Seyran.

'If only you hadn't come to the mountains,' said Ali. 'Old Osman and the Chukurova villagers wouldn't have given you away. They were in great trouble and expected help from you. None of those villagers would have given in or betrayed you. But here . . . they're out for your blood. Old Süleyman is different. He loves you . . . But how can you escape? I can only think of Yellow Ümmet's. He would give his life for you. When you went away he was miserable for months, and wept bitterly. But his place is full of police, we can't hide you there.'

They called in Old Süleyman, and appealed to him. He thought hard, but could find no refuge for Memed. Swift Musa pondered. 'Ah, if only we could get him to Marash!' he said. 'I could hide not only little Slim Memed, but a whole army there.'

The four experts, the four old wolves put their heads together and considered the matter until midnight. In the meantime the police had come to the village, eaten their supper and even gone to sleep. The Captain, Hamza, and Sergeant Asim were drinking raki with roast partridges at the Headman's house. News was brought to Old Süleyman every now and then.

Finally Memed yelled,

'I've got it! I've got it! I'll go to Earless Ismail's mill and no one will think of it.'

'They'll think of it,' said Lame Ali, 'but there's no other way out. Stay there a few days and we'll think of something; that's the most suitable place for the moment.'

'Yes, that's the best,' said Old Süleyman. 'We'll think of something later on with Lame Ali.'

Memed remained deep in thought by the fireside. He did not even hear Old Süleyman giving orders to his sons and daughters-in-law: 'Saddle the horse, and prepare his rations. Put in some honey and fat and a roast chicken.' But in a moment or two he raised his head, and said,

'Ali, my friend, listen carefully.' He turned to Swift Musa. 'You listen too. And you too, Uncle Süleyman.'

He swallowed and prepared to speak. He assumed the attitude of someone who is going to say something important or to make his will:

'You are people who have a lot of skill in your hands, your eyes and your minds, you are very experienced, and you have lived a long time. You are all three here together.'

He was silent, trying to collect his thoughts. Ali saw the steely glint in his eyes once more.

'You all know the things that have happened to me,' he began. 'I can't say that what has happened to me never happened to any other human being. Human beings go through things that are hard to believe. But to me unbearable things have happened. You know all about them. In the end I killed Abdi Agha, in the hope of saving the poor . . . They were saved . . . After Abdi Agha died the people were very happy. The land was divided up among them. Both the people and I thought that things would go on like that . . . Then what happened? Bald Hamza appeared. A thousand times worse than Abdi, he made the people spit blood. What will be the end of all this? Abdi went, Hamza came . . . Worse than a thousand Abdis . . . Where has it got me, what I did, what I suffered? You have a lot of intelligence, a lot of skill, a lot of experience; tell me, please, what am I to do? Give me your advice.'

'I told you,' said Old Süleyman harshly. 'All rivers flow downhill. To the Mediterranean. Have you ever seen rivers that flowed uphill?'

'You mean that when Abdi goes Hamza will come, always?'

'That's it,' replied Old Süleyman, his beard trembling, angrily and hopelessly.

'Aghas go and aghas come,' Swift Musa said, 'It's like that everywhere. Allah created the world like that. Birds fly with wings. The wind blows without wings. Men walk on two legs. The sun and moon rise and set.'

Memed, his face contorted, interrupted,

'Abdi will go and Hamza will come, is that it?'

'Yes,' said Swift Musa, bowing his head.

Lame Ali had not spoken so far. He had evidently thought a lot about this question.

'After you went and Bald Hamza came, I thought about all this. I couldn't sleep at nights. I couldn't find a way out.' He sighed deeply. 'I thought and thought but I didn't get anywhere. I couldn't find a firm foundation.'

'Abdi will go and Hamza will come. Hamza will go and Süleyman will come. Ali will go, and Veli . . .'

'It's always been like that,' said Old Süleyman. 'Ali went, and Veli came. Grandfather went and Father came. Father went and you came. You will go, and your son will come . . .'

'Then, why do we struggle so hard at the risk of our lives, you, I, Ali, Swift Musa?'

'We struggle,' Süleyman said confidently. 'It is right to struggle.'

The horse had been ready for a long time and was waiting at the door. Memed stood up and embraced the three of them in turn.

'God be with you,' he said, and going outside he mounted the horse. 'To struggle, to fight, to give one's life blood . . . uselessly . . . And it is right to struggle.'

This question, revolving in his mind, gradually overwhelmed him.

'To struggle, to struggle for nothing. How can that be right?'

He was undergoing an emotion he had never experienced before. He felt passionately through his whole body the process of thought. His helplessness hurt. It weighed upon him.

He had reached the mill. He was at the door but it never occurred to him to dismount. He stayed there on the horse, brooding. He did not understand what was going on in his head. The Idris Bey incident had confused his mind. Idris Bey who had risked his head for his people, who had taken to the mountains where death stalked him constantly.

He loved watching the break of day. The blue rim of the mountain peaks grew deeper and clearer. Then the blue rim silvered. The mountains gleamed with moisture, and then were enveloped in mist. The morning-star like a freezing sun, flashed on and off, on and off. Then everything grew light. Memed did not even notice. The dew fell on him, but he sat rigid on his horse. The sun's rays struck him and as he felt the heat on his neck he came to his senses and dismounted. He walked to the door of the mill and touched it with his foot. It fell back with a creak. At the sound a voice called out, a sleepy voice from the hollow darkness within,

'Who's there?'

'Uncle Ismail, is it you?' replied Memed.

A tired, cracked, sleepy voice said,

'It's me, my friend, but who are you? Have you come to have your flour ground? Where did you get wheat? Has Hamza shown some pity at last? I'm coming. Wait a minute. I'm putting on my trousers.'

Pulling at his trousers he came to the door. The light of day dazzled him and he rubbed his eyes. Then shading them with his right hand he could just see Memed.

'Are you a traveller?' he asked.

'Uncle Ismail, it's Memed.'

Earless Ismail began to pull himself together, and shake off the effects of sleep.

'Which Memed?' he asked mildly. 'Which Memed are you?'

'I've come, Uncle Ismail,' said Memed. 'I'm Slim Memed.'

'Oh, Slim Memed. Which Slim Memed?'

'How many Slim Memeds are there, Ismail Agha?' said Memed.

Earless Ismail looked him up and down.

'You're the Slim Memed that goes in for banditry?'

'That's me,' said Memed.

Earless Ismail stared at him, then rushed back into the mill and reappeared with a cudgel.

'Infidel,' he said, shaking the stick at Memed. 'You filthy infidel! You shit on our homes, you leave five villages to starve to death, and then you dare to walk about here of all places, saying "I'm Slim Memed"!'

If Memed had not caught hold of him straight away and taken the stick out of his hand, Ismail would have split his head open.

Earless Ismail, unable to free his wrists from Memed's grasp, began to shout at the top of his voice,

'Help, help, can't anybody save me? That brigand Slim Memed has attacked my mill. He's killing me, help, help! Save me . . .'

Memed would not let go of his wrists, and the whole district rang with his cries. The voice of one who had never suffered from malaria rang out from hill to hill and echoed from the crags.

As Earless Ismail shouted and struggled, Memed only said,

'Have you gone mad, Uncle Ismail, have you gone out of your mind?'

'Help, he's killing me! Killing me!'

Ismail threw himself to the ground, struggling and kicking and raising hell. Memed was infuriated; he gave the writhing miller a violent kick and drew out his revolver.

'You black heathen,' he said. 'Be quiet! Be quiet, or I'll take away your voice for good.'

Earless Ismail became silent at once, and did not utter a sound. He stayed curled up on the straw and dried dung. He was shrunken, his neck was longer than ever and all wrinkled. His bare feet had cracks in them into which you could put a finger. His clothes were tattered. Here and there were glimpses of wrinkled, shrivelled flesh. His long dirty white beard was stained with soot.

As Memed gazed at him his heart swelled and a lump came into his throat. He went and picked him up and took him inside. He took the pinewood jar and washed his face thoroughly. Then he brought in the horse that had been standing outside and tied it up.

Earless Ismail, his back against the wall, was weeping. He was crying and sobbing, but at the same time he was talking:

'Who told you, you snivelling Slim Memed, to kill our Agha and leave us to the mercy of Bald Hamza? Who told you? . . .'

'Don't weep, Ismail Agha, don't weep. Listen to what I'm telling you.'

'I don't want to. It's two years since anything went through these millstones. No wheat, no corn, no barley, no millet, not a grain has gone through the mill. It's you who brought us to this pass. The peasants of the Plain of Thistles have been beggars for two years. They're naked . . . Yes, it's you who brought us to this pass . . .'

'Don't weep, Ismail Agha, don't weep. Listen to what I'm saying!'

'What will you say, infidel, unbeliever, murderer . . . You struck down our handsome, conscientious, brave, merciful Agha and plunged up to your wrists in his blood, so what else can you say, infidel? Our children have shrivelled and died of starvation. Bald Hamza's barns and storehouses are full. He took everything the villagers had, yes, everything. He didn't leave a single grain of barley or millet or maize. He didn't leave a grain. People died of hunger. They suffered terribly. We gathered grass on the mountains and ate it. We ate bark, and nettles and sorrel. We ate whatever we could find. Bald Hamza took all our cows, oxen, goats, sheep, horses and donkeys, everything. He used Government forces to do it. One week he would have his men beat the villagers, one after the other. Then the next he would bring in the police to beat them. With so much beating the people's backs got sore and calloused, Memed, my dear brigand, eagle of the high mountains! Tell me who's to weep if I don't? I haven't had a decent meal for six months. And all because of you . . . You extinguished my hearth, you ruined my home. You destroyed our village. You planted fig-trees in our hearths. You annihilated us. Who told you, who told you to kill our precious Agha, the apple of our eye, who told you to make orphans of us, who told you!?'

He began to praise Abdi Agha. He wept and wailed over Abdi Agha, extolling his kindness and humanity.

'Don't weep, Ismail Agha, that's enough,' said Memed. 'Come and let's have a bite or two.'

He untied his package of food, and opened it. In the package, wrapped in wafer bread, was a large roast chicken.

Earless Ismail looked at the food out of the corner of his eye, then he got up, went to the millstone, and washed his face, splashing it noisily.

'Here you are, Ismail Agha,' said Memed.

Earless Ismail fell on the chicken like a hungry wolf. Memed watched him as he swallowed the chicken ravenously, hunched up, eating with his two hands, his mouth, his nose and chin and eyes. In a short time he had finished the chicken and began to crunch the bones. No sooner had he crunched one than he picked up another. In no time at all he had polished off everything in the package. Then, after a long drink of water, he said,

'Oooh! I've come back to life. Bless the soul of your dead ones. Oh, thank goodness, I've eaten my fill. Excuse me, my boy. I was very fond of your father. He was a good man. He minded his own business, a very gentle, mild man. You did not act wisely, Memed. You did us harm. Excuse me, my boy. You are welcome, indeed! If there had been a cigarette to finish off with . . . Where have you been, my friend? Welcome, welcome.'

31

THAT night there was a terrible downpour, just as if rivers were pouring from the skies. The wind blew hard, tossing and breaking things; roofs flew off, branches broke, tall poplar trees snapped in two. Lightning flashed and the thunder rolled continuously, reverberating from mountain to plain, from plain to peaks and valleys. It was one of Chukurova's disastrous rainstorms.

The rain thinned off towards morning. Gorges and valleys were flooded and impassable.

At daybreak the rain stopped. The burning sun rose, shrouded in moist, clammy vapour, vaguely shining through the mist.

At Tuvarasi the police had shot Zala's boy and his band, eight men in all, with the help of the former brigand Black Ibrahim. Zala's boy was a seventeen-year-old youth, tall and handsome, with an aquiline nose. He had killed a townsman who had seized his father's land by force, and had taken to the mountains.

His mother loved him dearly, and as a child would always keep him at her knee, saying affectionately, 'Zala's sweet little boy, sweet little boy.' So he was nicknamed Zala's boy, and people even forgot his real name.

The police had flung the bodies over some horses' backs. The legs hung down on one side and the heads on the other. Zala's boy's long body hung down, his head swinging against the horse's belly.

They took the bodies to the police post and threw them down in the big yard. The eight corpses lay there in the heat of the morning. Big green flies at once began to buzz round the heads of the corpses. The sky was grey and burning. The sun had a strange misty glare.

Zala's boy wore black homespun shalvar-trousers and a jacket of fine black contraband English cloth. Three bandoliers crossed over the jacket, ornamented with chased silver, Circassian work. His silver-handled Circassian dagger hung down low from his belt. His field-glasses were small brown ones. On his feet he wore Marash shoes with thick soles, and knitted Kurdish stockings. The handle of his pistol was inlaid with mother-of-pearl.

The other brigands were similarly attired. One of them was bald – it was probably the famous Bald Brigand . . .

The police-yard began to fill up with townspeople. Those who had heard the news came to see Zala's boy. The people from his village also heard about it. They all set out, men and women alike, his mother in front, chanting laments. Other villages near by also turned out to see the corpse. But the police would not let anyone approach. Cries of lament rang out from the crowd. The women beat their breasts.

Zala's boy was stretched out at full length, his head turned to the right. In the misty brightness of the watery sun he looked as if he were sweating. A childlike smile was frozen on his face. His wet clothes clung to his well-formed body. Steam arose from the bandits' clothes as the day grew hotter. More and more greenish flies began to buzz round the corpses, alighting on them every now and then.

Zala fluttered like a bird in the vicinity of the body that she was not allowed to approach. Zala's little boy, Zala's pet, how was it they killed you? Zala's pet! The flies are settling on your face, Zala's little one ... Even with a kiss I wouldn't have touched you and they have smeared you with crimson blood ... Even with a kiss I wouldn't have hurt you, and now they've thrown you into the mud and dirt. Why are you lying there, Zala's darling, in the heat of noon? Why are you lying in front of the police station?'

Zala went on chanting, and beating her breast until her voice was hoarse and she was exhausted.

Then Glass-eyed Emin the photographer came along. They picked Zala's boy up, and tried to prop him against the wall. He was riddled with bullets, and his clothes were smeared with blood and mud. They brushed him down.

'Don't hurt my darling, don't hurt him,' cried Zala with the little voice she had left.

Two strong men held Zala's boy up against the wall. A policeman came along and put his tasselled fez on his head. Glass-eyed Emin took a photograph. It was his job to take photographs of all the bandits who were killed. Then the men dropped the body, which fell in a heap at the foot of the wall. The head drooped over to the left shoulder, smiling.

Zala began screaming again.

Then they got hold of Bald Brigand. They put him against the wall too and held him by the arms. The police brought his fez and stuck it on his head which made everyone laugh. After his photograph had been taken Bald Brigand also was left lying at the foot of the wall. His head hung over his breast.

The brigands remained two days longer in the courtyard of the mosque. The corpses gave off a stench and swelled up until they were bursting out of their clothes.

Crooked Ahmet the Town-crier, with a cup instead of a medal attached to his collar, went around from morning till evening shouting:

'Oyez, oyez, oyez! Zala's boy's band is lying at the entrance to the police station. Let the sight be a warning to you. Go and see ... go and see what they were born to ... Zala's boy will only be there a day longer. He smells, he's getting swollen ... Let everybody hear! Oyez, oyez, oyez!'

Zala stayed in the police-yard without eating or sleeping for three days and nights; she sat there like an inert bundle, her eyes fixed on her son. No one could get her to move.

After three days they handed the body over to Zala. She threw herself on her son like a wounded eagle, and embraced his stinking swollen body.

The corpses of the seven brigands were claimed by their relatives. But Bald Brigand had no relatives. The police threw his corpse into an old lime-pit outside the town, and the dogs ate it.

Sergeant Hanefi was an old white-haired policeman from Gedik. He was one of those who had shot Zala's boy, thinking he was Slim Memed. He strutted about the market-place relating the incident with the exuberance of an old bard.

'We thought we'd surrounded Slim Memed, so we were feeling very pleased with ourselves. In that gorge at Tuvarasi, even Slim Memed couldn't have escaped. There were rocks on every side,' he began. 'The brigands were at the foot of the rocks. The battle lasted an hour. I looked and there was Slim Memed, with a handkerchief tied to his gun, coming towards us shouting that he surrendered. His men were behind him . . . The Captain said, "Stop, I won't take Slim Memed prisoner. Let him come a little nearer and we'll fire . . . " We killed the lot. Only one of them called Bald Brigand did not hold up the flag of surrender. He fought till evening. Then his ammunition ran out. We caught him and killed him. How pleased we were, thinking we'd got Slim Memed at last. Then the villagers looked. "This isn't Slim Memed, it's Zala's boy," they said. The Captain was in the depths of despair. "What is there about this Slim Memed? Why can't he be caught?" he kept repeating.'

This town had seen many brigands' corpses. A few years earlier the Government had sent word to the mountains: 'Let those who are in the mountains come and give themselves up. Those who do so will be pardoned.' Thirty brigands surrendered, including the renowned Hadji Veli. They were shut up in Kozan gaol. One morning they bound these brigands, tying one to the other by the wrist with rope. We're taking you to Adana, they said, and set off.

There is a place called Saricham between Kozan and Adana, a place with poor soil and stunted trees. They shot the thirty brigands in the ravine at Saricham. Then they drew up a report saying that they had been shot while attempting to escape. They buried the corpses in the ravine. All the villagers in that district saw and heard what happened.

The Governor was delighted to hear this story.

'Let them break the law, let them! Their downfall will be all the quicker,' he said. 'Cruelty and oppression are never lasting. On account of being very young our Republican gentlemen do not know this, and sweep over the people like a conquering sword. Yes, just like the sword of tyranny, my dear friends.'

He was very curious about Slim Memed. Who and what was he, and where was he from? He was very young, or so they said. After remaining in hiding for a good while, he had now come back into the arena.

'Our Republic is very powerful. They'll catch him too very soon and shoot him. We shall see that, my dear sir, and very soon,' he said, closing his eyes with delight, and rubbing his hands.

And the townspeople he talked to listened to him with fear and astonishment while he expounded his views about Slim Memed.

'He's a very cruel, ruthless, inhumane creature, my dear sir. The Turkish peasant, my dear friend, is a very peculiar creature, not a human being at all. Just give them a chance and they'll turn against their own fathers,' he said.

Slim Memed came to raid the house of a rich landowner in the village of Tasholuk one night. I haven't any money, said the landowner. Is that so? said Memed. He told his men to shut the door and wait. The landowner had three daughters of sixteen, eighteen and twenty-three. First he made the sixteen-year-old lie down in the middle of the room, and raped her in front of her father, mother and sisters. He laughed and raped her at the same time. The father, mother and sisters covered their faces with their hands. Then he left the girl to his men, and they began to rape her too. Then Memed took the middle daughter. Then the eldest one too ... The eldest one fell in love with him, and said, I will not leave you, Memed.

After this treatment Memed said to the landowner, if you don't bring out your money I'll do even worse to you than to your daughters.

'He is cruel, my dears, my good friends, very cruel. The Turkish peasant is the epitome of cruelty . . .'

The man brought out everything he had: gold, silver, diamonds . . . After Memed had taken everything, *au revoir*, he said, and left. But the eldest daughter who had fallen in love with that unbeliever, followed him up into the mountains. Memed looked back and there she was! madly in love. He turned his gun on her and that was it!

'He will get his deserts . . . if our Republican Government managed to get the better of the mighty Greek nation, it isn't going to be stopped by a handful of brigands, my good sirs! Wait a little while.'

Once he went into a house; he found nobody there but a baby sleeping in its cradle. It was smiling at the angels. What did that infidel do? He drew out his dagger and cut off the child's head:

'Impossible, impossible, my dears! *Merci*, don't tell me any more. A tragedy . . . A man's heart cannot bear these things, my friend. It tears your heart to pieces. Such cruelty is found only among the Turkish peasants, among our so-called masters.'

He went into a big village with a band of ten men. He made the whole village, men and women, children, youths, bedridden and crippled, assemble in the village square. He ordered everyone to bring their trivets and ploughshares. Everybody did so. Then that infidel ordered them to bring all their wood and heap it up in the square. They did so. Light the firewood, he said, and they lit it. The wood burnt and turned to glowing embers. Throw the ploughshares and trivets into the embers, he said. They did so. When the pieces of iron had grown red-hot, he told them to take them out. Now put the trivets round your necks, and tread on the ploughshares with your bare feet, he said. A few people hesitated. He shot them there and then, and had their bleeding corpses thrown on to the burning coals. When the villagers saw this they put the trivets round their necks, and trod on the embers with their bare feet. A sizzling noise and a smell of burnt flesh filled the village. Weeks afterwards, the village still smelt of burnt human flesh.

'Unbelievable, my dears, unbelievable! But absolutely authentic. He is cruel . . . The Turkish peasant is the epitome of cruelty . . .'

The District Governor and the townspeople continued in this strain, inventing incredible, black legends about Memed, and these spread from that town to other towns, and even as far as Adana and Ankara. But they had no effect on the villages of Chukurova and Anavarza. The villagers listened and were silent, apparently unmoved. 'Strange,' they said, and secretly they scoffed at the townspeople.

'Our crazy lad has put the fear of God into those scoundrels,' they said to themselves, delighted.

Who was he, and what was he like, the man they called Slim Memed? He was thick-set, coarse, big, pig-like, ugly, pop-eyed. The world had never seen such an ugly man, nor would again. 'Slim Memed has such long arms that even when he stands upright they nearly touch the ground. His nose is curved right over his mouth. His eyes are red-rimmed and bloodshot, and bleary.'

The person who talked most about Slim Memed's appearance was Ali Safa Bey's wife. From morning to night she went from one house to another, describing him in detail.

A terrible fear had settled over the unlighted, dark, muddy, dilapidated town, with its streets smelling of dung and running with filth. This town was like a corpse. It was a nest of gossip, a witches' cauldron. Everyone knew everyone else's innermost secrets, and nobody would overlook the slightest backsliding on the part of anyone else. All kinds of tittle-tattle was invented every day. Everyone was a victim of gossip, and everyone strove to impose himself on those around him by means of gossip. In this sluggish, boring town everyone cheated or laid traps for everyone else. If it had not been for the brigands the townspeople would have died of boredom, or would have drowned one another in the dung-smelling puddles in the middle of the town. The tales about the brigands were related with both fear and relish. The men were bad enough at all this, but the women were a thousand times worse. Their tongues were never still. Ali Safa was at the head of the men, and his wife led the women. The story she had made up about Slim Memed was as follows:

'A big, thick-set, coarse peasant lad from the mountains came to see the Bey. The Bey asked this monster whether he had come to work. "No," said he, "I've come to be a brigand. In the mountains every agha has a brigand, and even the Government has brigands, so let me be your brigand. I'll do whatever you say, I'll kill anyone you want," he said. Safa Bey said to him, "Forget those ideas, you are strong and fit, come and work on my farm." He turned up his nose. "If you want I'll be your brigand," he insisted. "I don't want a brigand," said our Bey. "I'm a man who helped found the Republic, and I'm not going to use a brigand against the Republic." So the huge peasant, a gigantic ugly fellow, but hunchbacked, went away. Two days later he was back again, and said, "You'll be sorry, Bey. When I shoot I can hit a coin in the air. Give me a gun, and watch me!" Our Bey refused. For a whole month he came and went. The Bey still said no and made an enemy of him. In the end it was Abdi Agha who engaged him as a brigand, and see what the result was! Abdi Agha gave him a rifle, a new one, and plenty of bullets, and a lot of money, too. He went up into the mountains, and became renowned there, and took the name of Slim Memed. Then he went to the villages and told them that if anyone did not speak against Abdi Agha or curse his wives, he would kill him. So, out of fear, everyone began to curse Abdi Agha with one voice. Ah, if you nourish a serpent in your breast, it will bite you first. Abdi Agha sent word to him telling him not to do this. He got angry and attacked Abdi Agha's house, setting fire to it. There were two wives. The huge man raped first one and then the other, he raped them both all through the night. As soon as Abdi Agha got a chance he came to us, trembling like a leaf, the poor man. Safa Bey gave him hospitality, hid him in our house for a week. One day I heard that Slim Memed was still looking for him. "Mercy on us," I said to the Bey, "send him away. Otherwise he may raid our house, that gorilla." The Bey put Abdi Agha in the house next to the police-station, but he couldn't save him. Everybody knows how Slim Memed raided the house one night, how he put a bullet through each of Abdi's eyes. Our Bey says it is a good thing he didn't engage Slim Memed as his bodyguard. He is an enemy of civilization and humanity, he says. Just let me get those Vayvay people out of my land and I'll see that not a single brigand's left in the mountains . . . Not even

Yaghmur Agha. I'll eliminate that horse-thief too.'

As Ali Safa Bey's plump wife narrated this story, with a new variation each time, her pink cheeks would get pinker with excitement. She described in detail, in piteous tones, how Memed had hunted Abdi Agha from one village of Chukurova to another, how he had driven the poor old man from one house to another in terror of his life. Sometimes she could not keep from weeping herself. At the end of the story she would say,

'But he got what he deserved. Why did he have to engage that huge brigand, that giant? He is a blood-thirsty monster. Our Bey is the bravest man in the world, but even he was afraid of taking on Slim Memed as a bodyguard. Abdi Agha deserved it, he deserved what he got. He caused his own death, and brought great misfortune on the people through that monster.'

Strange news came to the town from the mountains. Three times a day the police would have him surrounded and three times a day he would slip out of the circle like a snake, and vanish like a bird. When the police saw him their mouths grew dry with terror. Their hands were paralysed, and they could not pull the trigger of their guns. His eyes were so terrifying that they nailed you to the spot . . .

One night he came to the Governor, all muffled up, 'I'm Slim Memed,' he said, 'don't oppose me; I shall destroy all the aghas and rich men there are in the mountains and in Chukurova, I shall destroy them root and branch.' The Governor swore not to oppose him. That's how things are now.

He killed his mother, his wife Hatché and his child so that they would not fall into the hands of the police. They say he also killed his father, but that's a lie. His father died earlier, and Slim Memed grew up as an orphan. He had a brother, who fled from him to another district, because Memed would have killed him too.

He placed himself on the road beneath the castle, and raped the women who passed along, and cut off the right hands of the men.

He sent word to Mustafa Kemal Pasha, saying, 'Don't hunt me down; I'm cleaning up the feudal lords and hodjas you didn't manage to get rid of. I'll fill train wagons with their heads and send them to you.' So Mustafa Kemal Pasha won't touch him. He's even sent him a firman which runs as follows:

'You are granted immunity. Enforce your authority over old

Chukurova and in the lofty Taurus Mountains.'

'We have to look out for ourselves, my friend. We have to look out for ourselves.'

They brightened, they despaired, they feared, they took heart. They were worried to death, they talked, they did their utmost to believe the most improbable stories.

If one day, one rainy day, Slim Memed were brought to the town hanging over the back of a horse ... They did not know how they would react. Would they rejoice, or would they weep?

The rain poured down, the earth steamed, rivers streamed from the sky over the plain of Chukurova and towards the Mediterranean sea; lightning flashed. The sun glimmered. The sad, lonely corpses of the brigands lay near the white marble stone in the police-yard. They lay shoulder to shoulder, soaked through.

Under the rain and the sun.

32

AFTER the Governor's visit nothing special happened at Vayvay, but a certain fear had crept into the villagers' hearts. Every day they awaited some action from Ali Safa Bey, and when nothing happened they felt completely at a loss.

Then one day Idris Bey, accompanied by two riders, came to the village and dismounted in front of Old Osman's house. He expressed the admiration, affection and respect he felt for him. He was very pleased at the firm attitude the old man had taken with Ali Safa Bey, and praised his courage.

'We did not stand up against Arif Saim Bey,' he said, 'we sold ourselves. So in the end we have fallen very low. And we have had to take to the mountains.'

He sighed. His young, handsome face was pale, and his eyes sunken.

'But we shall take action. I have sent Arif Saim Bey a warning "Do not touch my land," I said. "You invented those twenty-four years, just as you invented the hundred and fifty thousand lira debt. Undo what you have done," I said. "I am waiting. Otherwise I know what I shall do." Kurdish Ali says that Arif Saim Bey is thinking. Thinking very seriously. Let him think. I am a patient man. You must be patient too.'

The villagers, hearing that Idris Bey was visiting Old Osman, hastened to the house. Seyfali, Sefché the Warden, and Ferhat Hodja came too.

Idris Bey looked at them and his eyes filled with tears.

'I envy you,' he said. 'Ali Safa is oppressing you. Much more than Arif Saim Bey did in our case. We did not stand out against Arif Saim Bey, but sold him our forefathers' fields one by one. We were frightened, we sold them and became outlaws. We were stupid, we sold them. And so we took to the mountains. I admire you because you are holding out. However big, strong and healthy a tree is, it will die if you uproot it. They uprooted us, and we shall wither and die. I admire you.'

On their side the villagers were full of admiration for Idris Bey's way of speaking, for his big mild eyes, and his long slim fingers. They felt very sorry for him. As he mounted his horse and rode away they were moved. Nothing but misfortune awaited him. They knew it. Yet here he was riding openly on the plain. They would soon bag him, like a partridge.

Suddenly Idris turned back and spoke to Old Osman.

'Will you walk a little way outside the village with me, Osman Agha?' he said, and getting off his horse, he took Old Osman by the arm and led him out of the village. 'Do you know why I came to this village, Osman Agha?' he asked. 'They told me that Slim Memed had come here, and was staying in your house. I came to see him. If I could meet him it would be useful for me, and for him too.'

Old Osman pondered a little on what to say. He thought to himself that as the villagers had told him about Slim Memed, this man must be a good man, a man to be trusted.

They sat down under a tree, and Osman told Idris Bey every detail of what had happened.

When taking leave, Idris Bey kissed his hand and said,

'Don't worry, Osman Agha, I'll find him for you.' He leapt on his horse, and rode away across the plain.

Very soon after Idris Bey had gone, some policemen arrived at the village. Realizing that Idris Bey had left only a short time before, they remounted and set off in pursuit.

Two days later news came that there had been a clash between Idris Bey and the police on the crags of Anavarza. The fight had lasted a long time; Idris Bey had fought so bravely, so daringly, that the police had been routed, and he had ridden away in broad daylight.

Summer came, and the yellow heat submerged the plain. The waters of Ahjasaz marshes bubbled. Hundreds of sand-devils rose skywards, and began to whirl giddily across the plain like strange giants. Storks and other migrant birds, herons, kingfishers, doves, thousands of different birds filled the Ahjasaz marshes and the sky above. To the south, cumulus clouds massed over the Mediterranean far away. South-west winds blew. Big wild boars came down from the hills to the plain and scraped the earth with their long tusks. Grasshoppers grew bigger. The earth, plants, birds and insects all brought forth offspring in plenty and abundance. The earth of Anavarza became more lively, it teemed, and everything multiplied two and three-fold. Spiders and spiders' webs, bees and bee-hives increased greatly, grew wider and bigger. The earth of Anavarza was teeming with a rushing tumult of new living creatures.

That year the Vayvay harvests were hardy and abundant. The wheat reached the height of a man. In some places the crop was leaning over with the weight of the ears. The water-melons grew to an unheard-of size. The melons were big and yellow, and gave off a honeyed scent in the heat. People passing at quite a distance could smell the heavy, heady melon smell, wafted into the air and over the earth. White summer butterflies, big as birds, began to fly high in the sky. Big, shining black ants got together to carry the heavy grains of wheat. Red ants, grouping in sevens or eights, could only just manage to drag away some dead beetle with its hard wingcase and shimmering body. Spiders' webs were plastered with flies. The fat, well-fed spiders had retired to the corners of their webs to digest this ample banquet. And the flies accumulated in front of the sleeping spiders, and the webs got heavier as the day went on, so that they sagged from the branches like ripe fruit. Sometimes the webs got so heavy that they would tear apart. Then the spiders would at once set to work to spin the torn web again, and as soon as it was spun it would be black with flies and the spiders would again retire to their corners and fall sound asleep.

Honeycombs weighed down the branches of the trees. In the combs millions of bees, heaped one on top of the other, their shimmering wings folded over their bodies, waited lazily.

Old Osman was reaping the firm Chukurova wheat, with its dark ears bowed down to the earth.

'Thanks be to God,' he said, raising a sheaf, 'What a wonderful harvest . . . The threshers won't be able to take all the wheat this year. The threshing-floors will be overflowing,' he cried. 'Thanks be to God!'

He was beside himself with joy, and imparted his joy to everyone he met. The whole village of Vayvay was dizzy in the heat with the same kind of joy. A lot of people were suffering from malaria, and clouds of mosquitoes were coming from the marshes, nobody could sleep well at night, and yet their rejoicing grew greater and greater, and the whole village took on the air of a gay festival. Actively, zestfully, hopefully, they began reaping the harvest and preparing for the threshing. The evil days, the oppression were forgotten. The stolen horses, the Governor's unkind behaviour, the raids and the firing were forgotten. They usually used horses to pull the threshing-sledges, but they never even thought about what they would use to pull them this year.

Ali Safa Bey too rejoiced at the abundance the year had brought. Yet, when he looked at that fertile, productive soil, he gnashed his teeth and clenched his fists.

'Ah, you filthy wretches!' he exclaimed. 'You miserable villagers! I'll show you. Just wait!'

The news given by Idris Bey was true. Slim Memed had appeared in the mountains again. Almost every day news about him came down from the mountains to the plain, and in a moment it spread from the Kozan villages to Jeyhan, from Jeyhan to Osmaniye and the villages round Kadirli, and from there to Bulanikbahche.

In Vayvay, songs were passed on from one field to another. Songs about Slim Memed, the landowners, the beys and the

231

police. The songs about Slim Memed were lyrical, enthusiastic . . .
Those about the landowners, the beys and the police were mocking,
full of defiance.

All kinds of stories sprang up, incredible stories. Memed is
fleeing up into the mountains, a crowd of policemen at his heels.
And peasants too, curse them, curse their hearths, those stupid
asses . . . What do you want of Slim Memed, you stupid creatures,
what harm did he ever do you, you brainless asses, you ignorant
peasants? They are spreading out over the mountain slopes. They
are encircling the mountain on every side, and hunting Memed.
Memed is fleeing desperately. He has no hope of escape. Once he
reaches the mountain top, where will he go? He has no wings to
fly . . . In hot pursuit comes Captain Faruk, laughing and shouting:
Not long now, Slim Memed, not long now. It is not far to the
summit. We're coming up from below. There's no way beyond the
peak. I shall catch you and tie a rope round your neck; then we shall
go from village to village, and I shall make you dance like a bear.
Memed is sweating. He stumbles. On the summit he slides behind
a rock, and begins to fire. The battle between the police down
below and Memed on the summit lasted two days and nights.
Memed has not had a bite of food for three days. He is starving.
But in the excitement, he has forgotten his hunger. Memed is not
shooting to kill, neither at the police nor at the peasants. If only
he'd put a bullet through the head of those base, cowardly peasants!
If only he would . . . Then Memed's ammunition gives out. What
can he do, poor Memed, only one against so many . . . He has no
bullets, nothing. Suddenly an idea occurs to him, and he begins to
roll stones down the hill. He rolls stone after stone . . . Stone after
stone after stone . . . All hell is let loose on the peak and on the
slopes. An avalanche of stones rolls down without ceasing. The
police and peasants only draw breath when they reach the foot of
the mountain. There is not one policeman or peasant who is not
wounded, serve them right, those scoundrelly peasants, serve
them right. I hate them.

There was tumult in the sky, and the thunder rolled as if it
were the end of the world. All that night an avalanche of stones
crashed down the mountain without stopping.

*

According to the stories, Memed and the police were fighting another battle. He was again in a tight place, but in the end he managed to break out. It was a little before morning, almost daybreak. Memed escaped at full speed. The police got on his trail immediately. At daybreak he was going along a path when he saw an old woman. The police had killed her donkey the day before, as she was returning from the mill with flour for her grandchildren. The donkey had fallen on one side, and the sack of flour on the other. The old woman was beating her breast in despair.

'If you want to know my name, it's Zeynep and my village, well, I'm from that village over there. I have five grandchildren who have no mother or father. I begged a little wheat from the neighbours, borrowed a donkey, and went to the mill to have the wheat ground. As I was coming back the police shot the donkey here, see? I don't know why. How can I get to the village, and what am I going to say to my neighbour? What a dreadful thing to happen to me! The children are waiting hungry at home. Brigand chief, please don't shoot me. If the police shot my donkey, a brigand's sure to kill me. Don't kill me, my boy.'

Memed lifted the sack of flour on to his back.

'Get up, mother, let's go,' he said. 'I'll give the owner of the donkey some money.'

The old woman seized Memed's hand and said, 'Are you a djinn or a good fairy, or the Prophet Hizir himself?' Memed, bent under the weight of the sack, walked on. And all the while the police were firing in the vicinity, on the look-out for him.

Then the old woman realized that this was the man they were looking for and firing at. She began to wring her hands, and say,

'Give me the sack of flour. Forgive me, brigand my boy, leave it and run. The police will come and kill you like my donkey. Nothing will happen to my children. They won't die of hunger. Dear brigand, you handsome boy, don't get yourself killed on my account. Run!' she begged.

Memed took no notice. He walked to the village, bent double under the sack. He gave some money to the donkey's owner. The mountain villagers realized that he was Slim Memed, and they wanted to capture him and hand him over to the Government. Memed spat in their faces.

'I spit in your faces, you dogs,' he said. 'What good did the Government ever do you that you should hand me over to them? I spit at you,' he repeated, saying everything he had a mind to.

They regretted what they had said, and were ashamed. Memed was so angry with them that he did not eat a mouthful of their food.

*

He was a gentle creature, as meek as a lamb. He spoke quietly. From bashfulness he rarely lifted up his head and looked a person in the face, but kept his head bowed. When he spoke he blushed like a girl. But if you saw him from afar, he was awe-inspiring like a mountain. When he was angry, fire darted from his eyes and his beard bristled. His hair too stood on end and he grew in stature. He was often sad and preoccupied. But he could also be very gay. Then, too, he was proof against bullets. He was blessed, he bore a charmed life. He could not be cut by a knife, or burnt by fire, or drowned in water. When he killed Abdi Agha and reached the village, he got the villagers to light a huge fire in the thistle-fields on the Plain of Thistles. He went into the fire and sat down in the middle of it. People who had been there said they had seen this happen, and added, 'May my eyes fall out if it isn't true.'

'Only in one place can a bullet pierce him. And that is in his eyes ... If they are open, a bullet, or knife, or fire could harm them.'

'Memed's eyes must be saved.'

'They can't be saved. When he is firing how can he not have his eyes open? He wouldn't be able to take aim.'

'Memed's eyes must be saved.'

'If you're thinking of goggles, they can break. A bullet would shatter them.'

'Memed's eyes must be saved.'

'If a remedy can be found then he'll stand up against whole armies.'

'Memed's eyes must be saved.'

'Then he'll rise and walk openly into the armies without hiding himself. He'll fire at them and to their amazement the bullets fired at him will flutter to the ground like cotton wool.'

'Memed's eyes must be saved.'

'Memed hates to kill the humblest creature. He even spares those who are out to kill him.'

'Memed's eyes must be saved.'

'On a horse, on a big, handsome bay horse, he flies from peak to peak.'

'Memed's eyes must be saved.'

'A hawk always flies above him. At a great height. When Memed sees the hawk above him, he is glad. He knows that while the hawk is flying above him no living creature can do him harm. One day he was in a tight corner, his ammunition was all used up, and the police had hemmed him in. His friend Jabbar was by his side. Jabbar said, "It's all up, my friend, they'll capture us. Let's give ourselves up." Memed raised his head and looked up. Far, far away in the sky the hawk was wheeling. "Get behind me, Jabbar," he said. "Make a shield of me. Nothing will happen to us." And they escaped. His talisman is the wheeling hawk with its outspread wings.'

'Ah, Memed's eyes must be saved . . .'

*

'This is the kind of man Memed is.'

The child was asleep. He had just fallen asleep. All the lights in the town had been dimmed. In another quarter a few dogs were barking and watchmen's whistles could be heard. Memed had been in that town for six months. He had been given shelter in a two-storey house belonging to Shemsi Bey. So that nobody should notice, his food, water and other necessities were brought to him by an eight-year-old boy called Mustafa, who was the orphaned child of Shemsi Agha's sister. Jabbar was with Memed too. Mustafa brought them both food, and became friendly with them; he narrated in detail everything that happened outside, and what he heard and saw. These three became very fond of one another.

The child was asleep. Memed woke him up.

'Goodbye, look after yourself, Mustafa,' he said.

Mustafa hugged him.

'If I come back, what shall I bring you, Mustafa?' asked Memed.

Mustafa had always dreamt of having a pair of red shoes from Marash.

'Memed Agha, bring me some Marash shoes from Marash. Soft red ones . . .'

And he fell asleep again.

Memed went up into the mountains. He fought. He had all sorts of problems in his head. He was hungry, thirsty, ill, he was hunted, but he did not forget Mustafa's shoes. He did not ask anyone else to bring the shoes, but was determined to bring them in person from the big bazaar at Marash. In order to get the shoes he went from the mountain of Berit to Marash, bought them and came back, and then for months carried them with him like a sacred trust.

'That is the kind of man Memed is.'

Then one day the police were hard on his trail. They hemmed him in at Watersmeet. He slipped away to Tuvarasi. With him were Jabbar and an old brigand they called Sergeant Rejep. Hizarji also joined them. They were again surrounded at Tuvarasi. Slim Memed's band slipped down to Chukurova, above Akarja.

Here they were lodged at Duran Hasan's house. Memed said,

'I'm going down to the town tonight and I'll be back.'

Said Duran Hasan,

'Not just a brigand, but not even a slithering snake or a winged bird could get into that town . . . It's chock-full of police.'

'I'm going to the town tonight.'

'Rubbish, man,' shouted Sergeant Rejep. 'Listen to what he's telling you. Haven't you any sense?'

'I'm going to the town.'

'They even shot two travellers who were entering the town last night.'

'No one can go to the town tonight, man,' cried Sergeant Rejep. 'Or if they do, they'll never get out alive.'

'I'm going to the town. Maybe I won't get out alive.'

So that night Memed went to the town. It was wrapped in a deathly silence. He found Shemsi Agha's house in the darkness. Mustafa was asleep; he had not the heart to wake him, so he put the shoes by his pillow, kissed him and slipped away.

'That is the kind of man Memed is.'

On his way back the police met him below Akarja. There was a violent clash. It was here Sergeant Rejep got his wound. How he cursed Memed! The police chased them down into Chukurova plain, and they hid in the Ahjasaz marshes. Here Memed caught malaria. So did Jabbar. The wound in Sergeant Rejep's neck swelled up until it was enormous. He could not turn his head. He struggled on in the fever-ridden marshes, but the swelling grew so big that his eyes and mouth were hardly visible. Sergeant Rejep cursed all the shoes in the world, all the children called Mustafa and all the Memeds. Then he died and was buried in the Ahjasaz marshes. Memed mourned the Sergeant and wept bitterly.

'That is the kind of man Memed is.'

*

Ali Safa Bey called Idris Bey to him.

'I want to ask you for your help,' he said. 'Slim Memed has appeared again.'

'Let him,' interjected Idris Bey.

'I don't mean that,' said Ali Safa Bey. 'As soon as he appeared in the mountain villages, the peasants round here began to dance for joy. He gives them the strength to resist us. We shall never have any peace while he is at large. To speak frankly, Idris Bey my friend, to put it in Abdi Agha's words, he puts the donkey in mind of the water-melon rind . . .'

Since the news of Slim Memed's return Ali Safa Bey had not dared to go out. If he did, he took six armed guards with him. Slim Memed haunted his dreams. In his agitation he sent one telegram after another to Ankara, saying, 'Send help, Slim Memed has been seen in the mountains, our life and property are in danger, send help. Send a battalion, anything may happen, a regiment, anything may happen, a division, anything may happen. Send a lot of soldiers . . . The scoundrelly peasants of the entire plain of Chukurova are behind him. Give us your help quickly. The snake must be crushed while it is small. Once the peasants rise up, and they're as numerous as ants, it will be impossible to cope with them. Help, help!'

He had sand-bags put at the windows and doors of his house,

and there were armed watchmen at the door all night. But still Ali Safa Bey couldn't sleep, and tossed about all night in terror of his life.

'Memed, my brave one, my hawk, my lion.'

'Yes, Idris Bey, all the Chukurova aghas and landowners, and the property-owners of villages and towns, got together. We came to a decision. If you will kill Slim Memed, we will all go to Arif Saim Bey, and demand your rights from him. You're a Bey too. One day that accursed man may also turn your villagers against you. And you're the only man in Chukurova who can get the better of him. If you kill Slim Memed all the aghas and landowners of Chukurova, and the Government as well will be grateful to you. Ismet Pasha has recently said that this snake must be crushed. When Ismet Pasha hears that you have killed Slim Memed what can't you expect! We will support you. He is a wicked, an evil man. If you heard what is said about him in the town . . . If you were told what he has done . . . It makes one's hair stand on end.'

'Don't kill Memed, you infidel Idris, you are like Memed. Don't kill him!'

'This is an opportunity for you. If you miss it, the Government will not be able to save you later on, Idris Bey.'

'Well, I'll think about it, Safa Bey.'

'What does it mean, to kill Slim Memed? The man who kills him will be a hero.'

'Well, I'll think about it, Safa Bey.'

Idris Bey thought hard, racked his brains and deliberated. He realized that it was either Memed's head or his . . . If he did not kill Slim Memed he could not live in the plain. If he killed him, he would be in a better position than ever before. Memed was an innocent youth. It would not be very difficult to shoot him.

'Have you thought, Idris Bey?'

'I have.'

'When are you setting out for the mountains?'

'Tonight.'

Big lizards live among the reddish crags of Tuvarasi. The soil near there shades from red to purple . . . There are deep valleys, deep and barren, and only the red anemone blooms there. In each valley the soil is a different colour; green, yellow, dark-green, with narrow red stripes, or patches of blue. The Turcomans use this earth for their dyes. The steep red crags are fiery, and sharp. Even the big-eyed owls are red here, and cannot be distinguished from the colour of the rocks.

Memed and Idris Bey had a meeting at Tuvarasi in a deep rocky valley. Behind Memed, in the shelter of a rock, his three companions waited, their hands on the trigger. Memed knew why Idris Bey had come. He would kill him and take his head and throw it into Ali Safa Bey's yard.

They seated themselves without shaking hands. Memed took a fancy to Idris Bey. What an attractive man, he said to himself. And as innocent as a child. How had he managed to be an outlaw as long as this? Such innocents can never last even three days in the mountains. Memed knew Idris Bey's story down to the smallest detail and his heart bled for him, but he could not spare the man who came to kill him; he had to kill him. Memed's melancholy eyes became even sadder.

They began to talk. Memed asked him why he had come to see him, and suddenly Idris Bey was at a loss. Eventually he said,

'I was passing this way, and I said to myself, let me go and visit Slim Memed. I shall see what sort of a hero he is.'

Memed was surprised at his awkwardness and naiveté.

The hawk in the sky swooped to the earth like a lightning-flash, till it was only man-high over the crags, then ascended at the same speed. It continued to do this, weaving black lines between sky and earth. The times when the hawk flew thus angrily were times of great danger for Memed.

Idris Bey's right cheek twitched. His brow was furrowed. His legs began to tremble violently. Memed gazed for a time at the trembling, twitching man facing him. He was awaiting the end of it all. Suddenly he saw that the man was calmer, that his trembling had stopped and that the colour was gradually returning to his face. The hawk above Memed had turned towards the wind that blew from the south, and with outstretched wings hovered tranquilly in the sky, its small black shadow gliding over the red crags.

Idris Bey lifted his head, and fixed his eyes on Memed. Then suddenly he rose, and Memed rose too. Idris Bey drew his dagger from his belt, and made a cut in his forefinger, then he took Memed's hand, and made a cut in it. Memed smiled. Idris Bey licked Memed's blood. Then he held out his own bleeding finger to Memed, and Memed too touched it with his tongue.

Idris Bey embraced Memed with a joyful child-like innocence.

'I came to kill you, my friend,' he said. 'But now we have become brothers.'

'I knew you had come to kill me,' said Memed. 'I was ready for it. Before you killed me I would have killed you. Look,' he said, and made a sign behind the rocks. Three men emerged, all three with shining rifles.

'Well, Idris Bey, do you approve?'

'Yes, I do,' said Idris Bey. 'But I must tell you that anyone who sees you or gets to know you cannot raise his hand against you, cannot kill you. I did not know you. Whereas you knew me. You must have known that a decent man could not bring himself to kill you.'

Memed stretched out his hand, and gently took hold of the little finger of his right hand, and pressed it.

The hawk glided smoothly through the air, its pointed wings stretched, as if it were stuck to a cloud.

The crags of Tuvarasi were dotted with clusters of blue and pink spiky verbena, apart from the anemones.

Idris Bey explained to Memed exactly what had happened. Memed gave him some advice. He told him that he wouldn't be able to live in the plain and had better come to the mountains.

Idris Bey said, as he left,

'I'm leaving you now. I have a job to do in Chukurova, and when I've completed it I'll come to you, my friend. You're my blood brother now, and I won't leave you until I die.'

Memed offered him a good meal of game by the Tuvarasi spring. They parted.

Memed reflected that he would never see him again. He grieved in his heart for the frankest, purest, bravest man he had seen in his life, and a deep melancholy settled upon him.

The hawk hovering in the sky flapped its wings and like a dark lament flew after Idris Bey, seeing him off on his journey.

*

A fine summer came, with abundant crops. It brought joyful, hopeful tidings. Old Osman looked twenty years younger. Ferhat Hodja became gayer. He was quick at reaping, and this year he had even time to help his neighbours. Malaria was raging. Women, children and old people shook with fever in the heat of the sun. But this year people did not mind. This year they had their stalwart rock up in the Taurus Mountains. This year hot, burning Chukurova was different. This harsh earth had put on a gay festive apparel.

There was a lowering sky, and thick clouds weighed heavily over the Chukurova earth. It was a starless, silent, humid night. Suddenly a great clamour, tearing the night and the clouds, cut the Anavarza plain like a sword. At the same moment fires were seen to break out all over the plain, growing and spreading. All the ricks and stacks of Vayvay were alight. The villagers, their hands on their hips, lined up at the edge of the ditch that bordered the village and stood watching silently. From Vayvay to Ahjasaz marshes, from Ahjasaz to the black thorn-forest and from there to the ravine, the whole of the Anavarza plain was on fire. Grain stacks ready for threshing, standing maize-stalks, dried grasses all went up in flames and were consumed. The flames even reached as far as the ditch. Thin cries rose from the fields. Beetles, snakes, spiders, birds, tortoises, jackals, foxes and other animals darted here and there and got caught in the flames.

All through the night the peasants stood watching the fire as it careered madly through the plain. They did not speak, they did not curse, they did not think, they were so completely numb that if you had cut them not a drop of blood would have flowed.

Towards morning a breeze sprang up. It drove the flames towards the foot of Anavarza Castle.

Old Osman, holding his side painfully, tottered back home.

'So be it,' he said, 'do your worst!'

A few people behind him mocked him in desperate tones:

'Do your worst! But what shall we eat this winter?'

The summit of Gavurdagh began to pale. Beams of light spilled on to the burnt black earth in the strange, wavering twilight, which was pale on one side and dark on the other.

33

WHEN Hamza appeared on that day of the first ploughing, when he rode his horse over the people who were burning the thistle-fields, and then when he married his brother's wives, the villagers took it all very lightly at first. Hamza held a feast in honour of the marriage, a grand celebration, to which all the villagers were invited. Only one person did not join in the celebrations, and that was Mother Hürü. Her husband had been killed, and she could not forgive the peasants for taking part in Hamza's wedding feast. She nourished great resentment against all those who had joined in the celebrations, who were friendly towards Hamza, and took orders from him. She did not look at them or even pass in front of their houses. She lived on in the village, as if in an uninhabited desert. People came and begged and coaxed her but Mother Hürü would not open her mouth. She could not even bear the little boys, the birds or insects belonging to that village. 'Let them kill me,' she said. 'If they wish they can spill my blood on this earth, but I say that what they have done is a filthy shame. Rather than live with a mean-spirited lot like them I will go to join Durmush Ali, Slim Memed, beautiful Deuneh and Hatché.'

Now and again a neighbour would taunt her.

'Why doesn't she make a complaint about the people who killed Durmush Ali? Is she afraid? Daren't she brave our Agha's anger?'

'She is afraid,' Mother Hürü would reply. 'What else can she be but afraid, seeing that Bald Hamza has got five big villages full of scoundrels supporting him. And Hamza has got the Government behind him too, seven palaces full of them. What will the Government say to Hamza? More power to your elbow, they'll say. It was a shame it was the old man you killed, wasn't it? While he's soiling his hands, a fellow might as well kill the cleverest, the bravest, the youngest man in the village ... He should kill two hundred, five hundred of them. There are so many anyway! Afraid!

Of course she's afraid. What else can she be?'

The mocking, hopeless attitude of the villagers, and the sharp things they said about Memed pierced Hürü's heart like a poisoned dagger, and filled her with rage. These things were even harder to bear than her husband's death.

'Slim Memed's coming to save us! Imagine that!'

'Mounted on the Lord Ali's steed Düldül!'

'Coming to share out our Agha's land among the poor!'

Mother Hürü would listen to these jests for one day, for two days, and then she would explode. Her spotless blue dress fluttering in the wind, her snow-white hair falling from beneath her kerchief all over her copper-coloured, wrinkled face like a fluffy cloud, she would burst out:

'Yes, he will come! I'm waiting. He will come before I close these eyes, before I lie in the dark earth. And mounted on a chestnut horse too. I'm waiting. Do you think the good Lord who brought Joseph out of the well will forget us? Do you think there won't come a time when a new day dawns for us? He will come, Slim Memed! And how! With a whole band of young heroes, mounted on chestnut horses. He'll come! He did not fail to avenge his mother and Hatché, nor will he fail to avenge the blood of Durmush Ali. And he'll spit in the faces of those villagers, those slimy parasites. Faugh! I spit in your faces, too. And when he comes that Hamza of yours will be hunting for a hole to creep into . . . And your Government too . . . Oh, he'll come, as sure as he went away, he'll come . . .'

The villagers took no notice of her.

'As a man sows, so shall he reap,' they said. 'Durmush Ali got his deserts. As for us, we have sown and reaped another man's land for years. Now Hamza Agha, the owner of the land has come. Well, thanks be to God, our granaries are full, our cows have calved, our hives are full of honey, we have pairs of oxen and horses. Has anyone heard of a village without an agha? Like a head without a brain! It's a good thing Hamza Agha came, or we would soon have been scratching one another's eyes out. It's a good thing he came quickly and took the reins into his hands.'

The peasants thought that things would go on like that. Yokes of oxen, horses, hives full of honey . . . First of all a posse of police came to the village. Then another . . . A Sergeant was in charge of them, a white-haired severe-looking man. For two or three days he prowled about the village without talking to anyone. Hamza Agha had a sheep killed for him every day, and gave him crackling, kebabs, raki and mushrooms . . . The Sergeant was pleased with life.

One day he summoned all the peasants. Lame Ali was the first to be interrogated.

'You assassinated Abdi Agha,' he said, 'and took possession of all his property. You commandeered his land, his wheat, his barley, his goods and chattels, his house, his villages, you seized everything he had. The five villages on the Plain of Thistles are all guilty of theft and murder. Now tell me, Lame Ali, my good man, is what I have said true?'

Lame Ali took two steps forward, and said,

'It's true.'

Then the Sergeant turned to the villagers.

'What do you say?'

'It's true,' they said.

'In that case you will return what you have taken. Under our Turkish Republican Government the era when property could be seized is over. To kill a man, a great landowner like Abdi Bey and then to seize his property is a capital offence. If I don't send you and your children and adherents to the gallows it's entirely due to Hamza Bey's kindness. He says you committed a crime through ignorance and does not want to punish you. But first of all you have to bring all your animals, big and small, within two days and put them in front of this gate.'

A few people tried to raise objections.

'We didn't kill Abdi Agha. Slim Memed killed him,' they said. The police immediately rounded them up, took them into a back room and began to beat them. Hamza Agha went after them.

'Don't do that,' he said. 'They are ignorant, stupid people. They don't know the law or anything. They don't know that the law will condemn them in the place of Slim Memed who has decamped. Leave them, they can't grasp it.'

He turned to the villagers, and said,

'After he had killed the Agha, Slim Memed came to this village,

244

didn't he, and brought you good news, didn't he? Did you do everything he told you to? Yes, you did. Since that was the case, in the Government's view you assumed responsibility for Slim Memed's crime. But I came to your help. I said to the Government, "They are not guilty; I'll take back the property that they stole from Abdi Agha. If you hang all my peasants, who will work on my land?" I said. The Government acknowledged that I was right.'

The peasants dispersed. They were bewildered. First Hamza told them they were in the right, then he put them in the wrong. Hamza's henchmen had rounded up all the animals in the village within two days. They took them to Hamza's house. All the cows in the village, in fact all the animals in five villages became Hamza's property. And the next thing the village was full of dealers buying up the horses, oxen, cows, sheep and goats. Hamza was selling the property taken from five villages at one fell swoop before the peasants' very eyes.

Then Hamza's henchmen, taking the peasants unawares, carried away the stores that they had not been able to hide. Hamza's granaries and cellars were overflowing. And now dealers turned up from the town with strings of pack mules.

The villagers did not understand that they were being plundered; they accepted cheerfully whatever Hamza or the Sergeant did. Hamza had left them oxen to plough the land and seed to sow. But as soon as the ploughing was finished he took the oxen away.

'After my big brother died you didn't give a single grain of the produce to his children but took everything for yourselves. So for five years I shall not give you a single grain. Let justice prevail.'

'He's right,' said the villagers, 'let justice prevail ... we acted very badly towards our dead Agha.'

Then winter came and with it heavy snowfalls. All the food in the houses was used up. The villagers crowded in front of Hamza Agha's door and said humbly,

'We did wrong, please don't take it out on us. Do what you like, for you are completely right. As long as you don't let us go hungry this winter, do whatever you like.'

Hamza took money from those that had some, and lent it to

245

those who had none, if he liked them. If he did not like them, he chased them away from his door.

All winter long there were peasants at his door, hands folded, heads bent, begging. To see them in this state delighted Hamza. What fun to have them begging there throughout the whole winter!

*

Towards March deaths began to occur in the village. The children and old people died one by one. The villagers had grown so thin they were just skin and bone, and they were so weak they could not even walk. The village had never gone through such a winter. The Sergeant built himself a house in the town with the money he had received from Hamza Agha. As the shortage of food became more acute, the villagers grew more and more cowed; they withdrew into corners and did not talk. Although the Taurus villagers are some of the most talkative people in the world, nobody opened his mouth.

The nearby villagers, hearing about their misfortunes, made an effort to help them, but they hardly seemed aware of it. There was not a smiling face anywhere. People were resentful of each other, of the land, the forest, the trees, the clouds, the birds and beasts, everything.

Every year the coming of spring would only just save them from dying of hunger. They could forage for green plants then, and forget the hard times they had lived through. This year too they were saved by the coming of spring. But only just! It was a thousand times more welcome than any other year ... No one knew just when their resentment came to an end, and when they began to talk again. They talked so much nobody listened. They talked and talked to everyone they met. They did not get tired of talking. They spent whole nights talking instead of sleeping.

At one stage all conversation turned on Memed and what did they not say about him!

'That crooked Memed!'

'Mounted on a white horse, too!'

'Like a little fly on that beautiful horse, the misbegotten wretch!'

246

'Light a fire, you villagers! I killed your Agha. The land is yours!'

'What conceit!'

'Ah, what stupid ignorant people we are! We deserve what we've got. Following a slip of a boy!'

'A slip of a boy, snotty-nosed Memed!'

'So you celebrate when our Agha's killed?'

'And what a celebration!'

'Well then you pay for it. As a man sows, so shall he reap.'

'When did our Agha do us anything but good?'

'Who came to any harm when he was alive?'

'Then this fellow came out . . .'

'This so-called Slim Memed!'

'Poor Ibrahim's son.'

'He killed our beloved.'

'The light of our eyes.'

'The beauty of the world.'

'Our Agha.'

'Abdi Agha.'

'Curse Slim Memed, curse his hearth!'

'A murderer with blood on his hands . . .'

'May he be struck blind . . .'

'May he be racked with fever . . .'

'A pox on him . . .'

'How could you kill our Agha? The one who fed us and clothed us . . .'

'You orphaned the five villages of Dikenli . . .'

'Have you no conscience, no pity? Have you no humanity?'

'You are like a dark night.'

'Like a dead rat.'

'Like a naked bloody sword.'

'Smiting and hacking us to pieces.'

'You are like the cold face of death.'

'Like the earthquake.'

'You are like the hunger of hungry children.'

'Why did you kill our Agha?'

'He was like a gentle breeze at dawn.'

'Like warm bread.'

'Like our feasts and our celebrations.'

'Like the pure water of bubbling springs . . .'

'Like the pure race of our Prophet Mohammed, blessed be his name.'

'Alas, Abdi Agha!'

'The best of aghas, the bravest of the brave!'

'May light flow on his grave . . .'

'How could that worthless wretch dare lay a hand on you?'

Suddenly, after so many years, laments were composed and songs sung in honour of Abdi Agha, and he began to haunt the villagers' dreams.

'I saw him in a dream last night. Our Agha was smiling. "I have forgiven Memed for killing me," he said. "But it's you I'm grieving for. In my grave I weep for your misfortunes, my good people. But you too are to blame for my death." That was what he said, and he vanished in a flash of light.'

Everyone had a dream to relate about Abdi Agha. Then someone saw him mounted on a horse and shrouded in a white unstitched robe, flying over the village. On moonlight nights, on dark nights, at midnight or towards dawn, Abdi Agha could be seen flying on his horse from Alidagh to the village. Sometimes he came and sat astride his horse on a mound in front of his house, then when the first light came the white horse would vanish in the direction of Alidagh.

Almost everyone in the village saw Abdi Agha mounted on the white horse. Only Mother Hürü, 'Beetroot' Hösük, little Hüssein, and Mustafa stubbornly insisted that they could not see what the whole village had seen.

'Our Agha is cross and offended with them, and will not show them his face,' people said. 'If Hürü goes and sacrifices a cock on the Agha's tomb, in order to bring him peace, perhaps then he will forgive her and show himself to her. Otherwise the saintly man cannot save Hürü.'

By and by the dreams, Abdi on his white horse, and Memed were all forgotten. The peasants were feeling the pinch more and more, and Hamza's tyranny was getting worse every day. The peasants of the Plain of Thistles were mere pawns in his hands. Work, he said, and they worked. Lie down, get up, sit down, sleep, he

248

ordered, and they did exactly as he said. They buried themselves increasingly in their sullen gloom, and rubbed along in a strange mood, unheeding, unfeeling, neither laughing nor crying, neither angry nor glad. There was nothing for them to hope for. They were in a kind of vacuum of not hoping.

One night the news that Memed had arrived flew from one end of the village to the other. But no one paid any heed, there was not the slightest quiver of excitement. Only their voices said he had come and their ears heard it, such was their lethargy and dejection.

For a time they appeared to take heart. Within them, something that resembled gladness and hope alternately gleamed and faded. Then for a moment this inner gladness grew stronger. They began to laugh wholeheartedly. The village rang with laughter for a time. There had not been such a lot of noise for years. Everyone laughed, talked, swore, wept, clapped and cheered.

In the afternoon an extraordinary wave of anger came over them. Sticks, guns, old swords and axes were brought out. They attacked Hürü's house. Not finding Memed there, they pulled down her fence, broke her door and smashed the only window of her house. Memed's old house was empty. In no time at all they demolished its walls and turned the whole house, its trees and all, into a heap of ruins.

They could not control their anger and began to fight among themselves with stones and cudgels. Arms, legs and heads were broken. It was a fight with no quarter given. Everyone fought whoever he happened to come across. Friends, acquaintances, mother and daughter, father and son, they were all at loggerheads.

The police and Hamza Agha stayed out of the way, watching in alarm what the infuriated peasants were doing, and not daring to go anywhere near them.

The fight went on until midnight. Everything in the village was damaged or shattered and everyone was bruised or injured.

No one knew how it was that the fight came to an end at midnight.

When the peasants went to bed that night, they slept a peaceful dreamless sleep, such as they had not slept for years.

249

34

IN the afternoon Black Ibrahim's band and the police surrounded the mill. 'Give yourself up, Memed,' they shouted. Memed replied with a shot. They laughed at Memed. This time he was really caught; there was absolutely no means of escape. A little later on all the police in the district, all the brigands, and all the peasants, armed with mattocks, shovels and rifles, would come and surround the mill. Memed thought and thought, but could not find any means of escape. There was a hail of bullets on all sides of the mill. Every now and then Black Ibrahim shouted in his hoarse voice, 'Don't waste your fire, Slim Memed, you can't get out of the mill alive.'

Memed did not reply. Crouching beside the window he fired back at the places from which he saw smoke coming. The mill was roofed with packed earth. If they thought of piercing a hole at the top and firing down, then he was lost.

He shuttled between the back window, the side window and the door. Five or ten shots from the front window, some more from the back window, and others from the door . . . How long could he keep up that battle? For a moment he lost hope. Then, resigned, he laughed to himself. 'There is no escape,' he said several times. 'For me there is no escape . . .'

Earless Ismail had retired into a sheltered corner and was squatting there calmly and quietly as if he knew nothing of what was going on. His knees were pulled up to his chest, his two arms were round his knees, and his head was resting on them. He did not blink an eyelid.

Black Ibrahim flew into a temper.

'Let's throw some hand-grenades into that mill, and let that greenhorn die buried under the stones,' he said. 'Is that how brigandage is carried on? Does a brigand worthy of the name get himself shut up in a cage and ask to be killed?'

Memed heard what he said. He at once stopped firing and for

some reason the others stopped too.

Memed spotted Black Ibrahim behind a rock. He too was on the alert, trying to guess what Memed was getting ready for. He was a dark-complexioned man with hollow cheeks and a toothless mouth much sunken. He was quite old now. Memed knew him from a long time ago, when he had been the most renowned brigand in the Taurus, a law unto himself. Then after an amnesty he had come down to the plain and given up brigandage. Now, he gained a livelihood by hunting down brigands who were hostile to the aghas.

When Memed saw Ibrahim his heart gave a leap. There must be some mistake, he thought. He looked again. Ibrahim, a handgrenade in his hand, was looking suspiciously in all directions. Memed said to himself, this man does not think much of me. Otherwise such an experienced outlaw would not fight with so little concealment. Perhaps it isn't Black Ibrahim. Then he looked again and saw from his drooping moustache it was he. At that time there were very few men with drooping moustaches.

Memed raised his gun, and at the same time the others began to fire at the mill. As Black Ibrahim turned from left to right and prepared to fire, Memed pulled the trigger. Black Ibrahim leapt into the air as if propelled by a spring, and fell. Then Memed fired a few more bullets. Black Ibrahim, with a dreadful cry which rang out from earth and sky, tore at the earth and rocks with his hands and began to bite the plants and trees; a few moments later he collapsed at the foot of a rock. For a moment there was silence. Memed saw some brigands and policemen running away. Could he escape now? No, he couldn't. The most cowardly brigand or policeman could shoot him as he was escaping. Darkness would soon be falling, but on the other hand Captain Faruk and Sergeant Asim coming from Kesme village would be sure to reach the mill before nightfall.

Memed could not help glancing from time to time at Black Ibrahim's body lying curled up at the foot of the rock. In a little while he himself would be lying in a heap, at the foot of the blackened cobwebbed wall of the mill, and everything would be over. Suddenly the words, 'Abdi went, Hamza came, Abdi went, Hamza came,' rushed into his mind. He began to say them to himself over and over again. He wanted to understand what they meant. Would it always be like that? Was everything useless? Was there no way out? For a while he remained deep in thought, his hands lying idle. How strange it was that when he stopped firing, the men outside also stopped firing. He stole a look at Black Ibrahim's body. It was in shadow. His head had fallen on to his chest, sideways, and the drooping moustaches were drooping still further. Memed had a feeling that there was a mocking smile on his lips. He had been sweating a great deal, and his sweat was gradually cooling. He began to feel chilly and shivered. He caught sight of Earless Ismail, sitting motionless in the dark corner like an owl, his eyes rolling in their sockets. He wanted to laugh at Earless Ismail. Suddenly he remembered that he was surrounded in this mill, that he would probably soon be killed, and a spasm of fear passed over his cold body. He did not want to die. 'Abdi went, Hamza came,' he murmured to himself, and as he walked to the window a terrible clamour came from outside; it was made up of the whinnying of horses, the whine of bullets and the rolling of thunder. The sound of rushing water beneath the mill grew louder. Memed fired at a dark figure outside which was trying to take cover behind a rock. The figure leapt into the air like a cannon-ball and gave a deafening cry. Darkness was falling. It was thundering and lightning. It grew quite dark. Memed heard an order given in Sergeant Asim's voice:

'Throw two grenades at the door.'

Soon afterwards, the wall near the door collapsed with a crash. Memed immediately started firing in that direction but the windows and the opening over the mill-wheel were left unprotected.

Sergeant Asim shouted at him: 'You are an intelligent man, Memed. The Captain does not want to kill you. There are hundreds of people surrounding the mill. You have no means of escape. Give yourself up! The Captain will spare your life. He knows everything. We shall destroy the mill with grenades.'

Now darkness had fallen. The rain began to pour in torrents. The horses – how many horses there were in the vicinity Memed could not make out – kept on whinnying. An uninterrupted hail of bullets pelted down on the ruined door.

Memed heard Sergeant Asim's voice:

'Turn the water on to the mill.'

This was impossible. Memed realized that the Sergeant had shouted it in order to frighten him. If it were not dark he might have hit the Captain. If he could have taken the Captain prisoner, he would have asked him, 'Abdi went, Hamza came. What does that mean?' He was an important, three-star captain. Perhaps he would have known. His hands began to function like a machine. Just at that moment two more grenades were thrown at the side walls close to the ruined door. The roof collapsed together with the wall. At once he felt a hand on his shoulder, which made him jump. Earless Ismail said to him in a hoarse voice, 'Stop and listen to me a moment.' His face was just visible in the darkness. 'Bald Brigand left me his gun and a hundred and fifty rounds of ammunition three months ago. "I'll come back and get it in a week," he said, but he hasn't come. I'll go and get that gun from the storehouse. Don't surrender. You mustn't give yourself up, Memed,' he said. 'You're not going to surrender, and you're not going to die. Take cover over here,' he rasped. 'Imagine such a stupid fellow becoming a brigand! If those chaps on the other side hadn't been as stupid as you they would have smoked you out of this mill long before this.'

He took Memed by the arm, and drew him under an archway made out of a tree-trunk.

'Now let those dogs throw as many grenades as they want,' he said. Memed kept on firing blindly.

Sergeant Asim said or shouted something, but what with the pelting rain, the whinnying horses and the whistling bullets, it was impossible to hear anything.

Earless Ismail came back with a brand-new German carbine in his hand; he loaded it and fired two shots into the darkness.

'It's a nice piece of work, this gun of Bald Brigand's,' he said. He caught Memed's arm again: 'I'll keep these dogs busy until dawn. You get into the water down there. Don't be afraid, just let the current carry you along. Don't be afraid, I'll keep guard. I won't let anyone come near. Just let yourself go with the current. Go on . . . It's the only way. After you've gone I'll give myself up.'

Earless Ismail was firing steadily at the rain-soaked police.

Memed stood in the middle of the mill, thinking. Sometimes a wave of delight came over him and enveloped his whole body, making his spirits rise. Sometimes a sadness came over him, a sadness as acute as an ache or pain, and a lump came into his throat.

Earless Ismail yelled,

'What are you waiting for, you snivelling child? Is this a time to stop and think? Get on with you.'

Memed did not hear. He stood there in the midst of the tumult, like one bewitched.

'Don't stand there, man,' shouted Earless Ismail. 'Get going. Child, boy, Slim Memed, don't stand there like a statue, get going! Don't be afraid!' He was firing into the rain and darkness, and at the same time he went on imploring Memed:

'My dearest boy, my child, Memed, the rain has saved you. If it hadn't been for the rain this mill would have been down over our heads long ago. Please go. Earless Ismail beseeches you to go! Don't waste this heaven-sent opportunity, go!'

He fired and fired outside, then turned to Memed again,

'Go brother, go! The rain has saved you, go! I'll hold them until tomorrow morning, go! It's not your turn to die yet, go! I've thought about it carefully, and you mustn't get killed at this stage, go! The rain has saved you, go!' he entreated.

He ran to the window, and fired two or three rounds, then ran back again. He seized Memed by the arm and tried to drag him to the hole under the mill, but he could not make him budge.

'Damn the fellow,' he muttered. 'What a strong one he is! He won't go! The stupid ass, he won't go. He's just asking to be killed. Great God, did ever such an ass come into the world?'

At that moment a volley of bullets came in through the ruined door and hit the wall not far from their feet.

'There you are! Now will you go? They'll kill us both here. Go, my child, for pity's sake, I beg you on my knees not to get killed. The rain has saved you. Don't get killed, don't get killed, Memed, I kiss your hands, don't get killed, go now. Well, you jackass, you cuckold whose mother was kicked by a donkey, be off with you and don't get killed!'

The voice of Sergeant Asim was heard again. Memed did not hear it, and he did not take in what Earless Ismail was saying.

If Earless Ismail had not thrown himself down behind a stone near the ruined door he would have stopped a bullet. Outside the flashes from the rifles made little spurts of flame and lit up here and there the rocks, the rain, the trees, the water and the ruined mill. The rain was slackening.

'What can I do? How shall I send him off?' Earless Ismail thought to himself. 'The boy has suffered a lot, and I didn't make him welcome. I was rude to the boy. I was led astray by the peasants. And to tell the truth, I was stupid with hunger . . .'

An enormous flash of lightning split the sky. For a moment it was as light as day. Memed started, almost fell, and recovered himself. Suddenly he was soaked in sweat. He sweated to the ends of his hair. In an instant the sweat had cooled and dried, and he began to shiver. His teeth chattered.

'My child, Memed, I don't want them to kill you. Look, the rain is dwindling. Get going.'

Memed took two paces towards Earless Ismail and embraced him.

'Goodbye, Uncle Ismail, take care of yourself,' he said. His voice was sad, like a lament, 'I'll come back. I shall be well away from here in half an hour. Don't use too much ammunition. Stop firing soon. And hide the gun. It's a fine gun. Take care of yourself . . .'

He said no more, but went to the hole, with Ismail behind him, and slipped through into the water, taking care not to let the slightest sound escape him.

Earless Ismail resumed his firing into the darkness, joyfully. To be on the safe side he did not stop firing all night.

The rain lessened and, as gleams of daylight began to appear, Captain Faruk threw in all his armed men. Grenades and bullets rained on the mill. This lasted ten minutes. No sound or echo came from the mill. There was a long wait which tried their patience. Sergeant Asim shouted at the mill. There was no reply. Fearing some trick of Memed's, they attacked the mill again with all their strength, rained bullets and grenades on it, until the whole front wall had collapsed into a heap of stones. Sergeant Asim called out. Captain Faruk called out, but from inside there was no sound.

Sergeat Asim said,

'He's dead. I am very sorry about that young man, Captain.' Two big tears rolled down his cheeks. 'It is a great pity.'

'Were you so fond of him?' asked the Captain.

'I don't know.'

They waited impatiently for daybreak.

Dawn came. Sergeant Asim called. There was no reply. He got up, his legs trembling, swaying as he walked. One could see even from a distance that he took each step shrinkingly, in distress. He could not bear to see Memed's dead body. He had got fifteen years older since all sounds from the mill had ceased. Grief pierced him like a deadly poison. He stopped ten paces from the mill. He wanted to call out once more to Memed, but he could not open his mouth. He stayed there, unable to move. He knew that Memed was alone and that after he had stopped firing it was impossible for him to have escaped anywhere. If Memed had not died he would have replied. That meant that he had been hit. 'I hope to God he is only wounded,' said the Sergeant to himself.

Behind him the Captain called out,

'What's up, are you frightened, Sergeant? Are you afraid of Memed's corpse?'

Sergeant Asim looked round at him and then entered the mill. A smile of thankfulness spread over his face.

'He was hit, Captain, he is dead,' he called out. The Captain came running up. 'But the man who was hit is not Memed.'

Earless Ismail had crumpled to the ground on his knees. His hand was on his trigger. The stock of the gun was against his breast and the barrel was touching the ground. The bullet had gone through the left side of his chest and had come out at his back. There was very little blood. A little way in front of him there was a whole heap of empty cartridge-cases.

35

On the plain of Anavarza
Where noble horses frolic
They have stained his shirt with blood
Oh, do not hurt him, tribes, oh do not touch
The blind old woman's staff, her one and only.

EVER since killing the horse Adem had not had the heart to go
to the farm. What could he have said when he met Ali Safa Bey?
He missed his wife very much. On some nights he felt an over-
whelming longing and love within him; he wanted to go secretly
to the farm and see his wife, but could not bring himself to do so.
Without having killed the brown horse how could he go to the
village, how could he look his wife, his Agha or other people in the
face? How was it that a hunter who had never before missed his
mark could not shoot a horse in the middle of the plain of Anavarza! Wouldn't the whole world scoff at such a hunter, such an
Adem? Didn't he know that all the villages and towns were talking
about him, from Adana to Mersin and Tarsus, from Jeyhan to
Kozan and Kadirli, from Osmaniye to the Crossroads and Payas,
from the Gavur Mountains to Alidagh! Weren't they all saying
that Ali Safa Bey's chief hunter Adem could not shoot a horse,
poor thing? He knew only too well . . . People would be all eyes,
on the look-out for him. So that's the hunter who has been
running about a huge plain and who can't shoot a moving horse!
It's absurd! People don't understand that the horse is bewitched,
that it is bullet-proof. People don't realize that the bullet shot at
the brown horse just turned and went and buried itself in the
white horse you were riding. They only talk and laugh behind
your back. The important landowners, the beys, the Arif Saim
Beys, are all asking Ali Safa Bey about Adem, expecting a reply.
What answer could Ali Safa Bey give? The poor man would hum
and haw, and say nothing. What could he say? That our Adem

has gone and hasn't come back? Perhaps he would invent something. He was a man who was easily embarrassed, not good at lying or prevarication. I've given him a lot of trouble.

His annoyance with himself increased. Either the brown horse would be found, or Adem would go on roaming the Anavarza plain with a carbine on his shoulder.

The brown stallion had vanished. For days Adem had explored every possible place, but had not found the slightest trace of him anywhere. Adem would stand for hours, deep in thought, or he would rush hither and thither in the blazing sun. The earth must have opened and swallowed up the horse. Perhaps he had gone to Urfa, to his native place, thought Adem or was he hovering just in front of Adem in the shape of a bird? Or a snake, a beetle, a butterfly or a fox? Was it he, that swallow darting and flashing a few yards away, was it he? That huge, solitary eagle wheeling over the Anavarza crags, was it he?

One night he had woken up to find a gigantic animal licking his face. It was neither a boar, a wolf, a dog or a cow. It was white and larger than a large horse. Adem had snatched up his gun from where it lay by his head and had fled to the Anavarza crags. That strange beast had followed him for a while and then it had given up. Was it he?

A fire had broken out in the plain. When the fire started Adem was asleep. Suddenly in his dream he found that he was surrounded by the glow of a burning crop. He sprang up at once, and realized that he had narrowly escaped being burnt to death, for the flames were almost upon him, advancing from every side, encircling him. He rushed desperately about in the circle of flames. The fire was sweeping over the whole plain. Forgetting his own danger Adem lent an ear to the cries and shrieks of animals and insects. The face of the earth, covered by the flames, swelled, burned and groaned.

Suddenly the brown horse descended before him, like a cloud, like a shadow. The shadows in front of him multiplied, and hundreds of different shadows moved as the fire crept forward. They broadened, lengthened, and danced around the brown horse. And the brown horse, without moving from the spot, became broader, longer, bigger and thinner.

A wave of flames submerged Adem. If he had not thrown himself into the marshes, which lay only a short distance beyond him, he would have been burnt to ashes. In the marshes, together with the thousands of creatures which had taken refuge from the flames, he wandered about till morning, while the animals moaned, sang, cried, swam and leapt. When the sun came up he was up to his waist in marsh-water.

Even if Adem forgot everything else he would never in his life forget the night of the fire.

For days he had searched every nook and cranny of the Anavarza crags and the whole of Ahjasaz as well, mounds and hollows, reed-beds and bushes, marsh and woodland but he had not come across the brown stallion. Where could he be? If he had been in the plain, wouldn't one have come across him once at least? I'd better go, he thought. I'd better clear out. I'll forget about my wife, and Ali Safa Bey and being the chief hunter. I'd better throw in my hand and go to Yüregir to become an agha's groom. In the old days there was no one who understood horses or looked after horses better than I. Perhaps I can't be a groom, either . . . All because of this infernal horse . . .

Two big bay mares were ambling along the dusty track, each with its leggy wide-eyed foal. Their broad, fat rumps gleamed in the sun and the foals ran around them, jumping, turning and playing.

In this heat the brown stallion would have retired to some cool spot. He took good care of himself, that horse. He must be beside an ice-cold, pebbly sunny stream, or a spring. Adem thought of all the cool spots he knew, but could not be sure of any of them.

He must run away. He must go, leave everything, but . . . Everything, his wife, Ali Safa Bey, his homeland of Anavarza . . . But if I leave the plain, he thought, I can't live anywhere else. Suddenly he would set out bent on leaving everything. He would get on to the ferry-raft at Jeyhanbekirli and go over to the other side, but then he would turn back again to the Anavarza plain. Something guided his feet back, tugged at his very heart.

For a long time he did not realize what it was that prevented him from giving up. One day, when he was again standing in the heat of the day with drops of sweat running off him, thinking about the stallion's whereabouts, it suddenly occurred to him what it was. He could not give up the brown stallion. He was willing to leave everything but he could not leave the brown horse still unvanquished in the Anavarza plain. At first he could not understand this feeling. 'I'm clearing out, man,' he shouted. 'Is this horse my father, my limbs, my eyes? I'm clearing out, man.'

He got on to the ferry and pulled himself across the River Jeyhan, but he could not go further and came back. Every other day he would pull the ferry-raft across the River Jeyhan, and then come back.

It was very hot. Could the brown stallion be in the shade of the rocks, among the crags?

The rocks were burning hot. They shimmered in the heat. On every side there was a smell of sun-warmed thyme. The gullies, the stunted trees, the dried asphodels, the snails, all smelt of thyme. Everything was dry. There was not a single living creature or a green leaf among the purple, grey, blue, crimson and yellow crags. In the earth that had collected in the hollow of a rock, Adem saw a hoofprint. The trail led to a cavern some way ahead of him. This cheered him a little, though he had not much hope. At the same time he felt frightened, and his hands began to tremble. His feet, sore with scrambling over the rocks, would carry him no further. The rocks were so burning hot that you could not tread on them. Adem clenched his teeth. Sweat was running into his eyes, and they stung. He reached the cave. There were thistles, needle-sharp, growing among the rocks, and grey, poisonous rocksnakes glided away to right and left. At the entrance to the cavern he saw bird tracks on the brown earth, which was almost as fine as dust. Among the many tracks, big and small, were the foot-prints of jackals and foxes . . . And right in the middle were hoofprints. The stallion had lost its third shoe.

Treading on the prints Adem came to the mouth of the cave, beside which some mastic trees were growing. The interior of the cave was dark and it seemed to stretch a long way inside. It was full of bats, which were clinging to the rocks, or hanging from them.

A shadow moved in the darkness. From the depths of the cave came the faint neighing of a horse. The shape of the horse in the darkness became denser and clearer, then gradually vanished.

Adem sat down on a stone and loaded his rifle. It made a clicking noise. He fired five shots into the cave, and loaded the gun again. He flushed three rabbits out of the cave; they streaked down the slope and were lost to view. A snake came slithering over the tracks, lifted its head and looked around. Adem aimed at its head, and smashed it to pieces. All the Anavarza crags reverberated with the sound of the shot. As twilight came on, the air gradually grew cooler. The south-west wind had arisen, wafting the scents of warm thyme, dry grass, scorched earth and rock in all directions.

The brown stallion came out of the cave like a pale cloud. He loomed up at the mouth of the cave and passed over Adem before he could pull the trigger. The horse's figure grew smaller in the distance, and disappeared from sight. Adem fired five shots after him down hill. The sounds of the shots echoed, rebounding from crag to crag. Adem listened to the echoes for a moment. The wind increased the sound, and made the rocks ring out like empty jars.

The fear in Adem's heart grew less intense. He had been without food for a long time, and now he must go to Sefer's house. But he was terribly ashamed. Was it right for him to go at nights and wake tired people up out of their sleep, to get a meal for him?

'Ah,' he said, 'brown horse, I shall go away without settling accounts with you. I shall go away, brown horse, I shall go. You've ruined me in the eyes of the whole world, friends and enemies. Whether you're a djinn, a fairy, a man or a horse, you've destroyed me. You win.'

Only if he shouted could he get rid of the incurable fear within him. And then only for a moment ... After that the fear of the horse would return, and coil itself up in his heart. A fear that took away the use of his hands, and paralysed him.

'I shall go away, do you hear?' he said, and took a step downwards from the crags; he stopped, and then exclaimed, 'No, I won't go, do you hear? I'll kill you.' He shouted to the rocks and then listened to the rumbling sound of his voice reverberating.

'Do you hear? I shall go away, and leave the Anavarza crags to you. You can have Anavarza and Ahjasaz. You can have the whole lot. You have driven me out of hearth and home. I've lost my livelihood, my friends and my enemies, thanks to you. I've lost my birds and my honey-bees. I shall go away, go away, do you hear? ... I could not punish you as you deserved. You've won, you've vanquished. You've got the better of me, though nobody ever did before ...'

He admitted defeat, and turned to the south, where the plain, bathed in light, dazzled and pained his eyes.

Then suddenly he turned back, joyfully, challengingly, and shouted out in a loud voice. The echoes grew louder and resounded among the crags, putting new heart into him: 'I shan't go, do you hear?'

He listened to his voice rebounding from rock to rock, and again cried out: 'I'm not going, do you hear me?'

He went on with this game until he had no voice left. Then he still went on muttering to himself in an undertone:

'I'm not going. Either you'll kill me, or I'll kill you. One or the other. One or the other ... If you'd not been a fairy or a djinn, or an invisible being, if you had been an animal, or a human being ... One or other of us. One or other of us ...'

*

His shadow stretched towards the west. It was a thin, crooked, tattered shadow. The morning mist was rising; it was vanishing as the sun got stronger. By mid-morning the burnt, black plain of Anavarza was reflecting its glare towards the Anavarza crags which sparkled dazzlingly. The sun was shining through a haze and wisps of mist floated over the crags.

The grass is dry everywhere, said Adem to himself. There is only one place where fresh green grass is to be found and that's the Grassy Glade in the middle of Ahjasaz. Would the stallion be there? When the thought of the Grassy Glade came to him he was delighted. By now he had a name for every possible place where the horse might be found in Anavarza or Ahjasaz.

He stepped through the warm marsh water. The bottom was sandy. The water came up to his knees, and stung his legs like boiling water. Water buffaloes were lying in the hot water, immobile. He waded on and came to a place where the earth, dry on top, and bedecked with mauve flowers, made a crackling sound

262

like hoar-frost when he trod on it. As his feet broke the dry crust, they sank into slimy mud. The dry earth with its carpet of mauve flowers stretched as far as a dark sedge-brake. It was a dangerous place. The water round the roots of the sedge was green, coated with weeds, and on it floated a host of birds' feathers of different colours, long and short, big and small. Adem was always afraid of this water, for there were deep holes in it that could suck a man down. So, when Adem waded through this water, he always grasped the roots of the trees. With great difficulty he managed to get through the sedge by mid-day and came to one of the Ahjasaz marshwoods, which he called Sky's End. He did not know whether he had named it thus, or whether it had been known as Sky's End from olden times. It was true that when you looked up you could not see the sky. The marshwood teemed with big tortoises, snakes, foxes, wild pig and many kinds of birds. There was a nest on every branch and every creeper, and a big bee-hive by every nest. In the afternoon he emerged from the marshwood. Before him was a large plane-tree, with a huge stork's nest at the top, and all its branches bedecked with nests, big and small. The nestlings craned their necks and from the dozens of yellow beaks came an ear-splitting noise. Adem leant his back against the plane-tree and rested awhile. He had not yet touched the huge loaf he had bought at a nomad village and which he was carrying in his food package. There were fig-trees in the marshes. He would find one and eat its big golden honeyed fruit with his bread. The chicks in the nests squawked so loudly that Adem was deafened. Smiling he looked up into the branches, where hundreds of yellow beaks opened wide were creating such a hubbub.

'Curse you, what a row. You're upsetting the sky and the earth,' said Adem.

He had seen this plane-tree several times but had not thought of giving it a name. So now he named it 'Birdland'. This is a breeding-place for birds, he said to himself, so this is 'Birdland'. The young birds sprouted like corn, with their big golden beaks. Their ridiculous open mouths made him chuckle delightedly to himself.

Then he went on to the Dark Hollow. It was a pond like a well, all covered with black weed. For a moment he saw the big black shape of the stallion in the black water. The water was dark, the horse was dark ... They mingled together. Adem, shuddering, fired some shots into the middle of the water. It was so thick and full of mud that the bullets did not send up any spray.

After the Dark Hollow, he suddenly came out into the Grassy Glade. It was green all over with fresh, untrodden grass. There were no flowers, bees, butterflies or birds on the grass. It was a pure unblemished expanse of delicate green. He was very tired, and sat down at one end of the glade. The sun could not be seen, but from the beams that came from behind Anavarza it was clear that it was still in the sky. Part of the glade was in the sun, part was in the shade. The shady part gradually lengthened and broadened. Not a single bird flew over it.

'He's not here either,' said Adem with a sigh. 'And yet wouldn't a horse that is like a horse come to this grassy clearing? But birds don't come, or bees ... No living creature comes here.'

He got up, and began to wander round and round. At the edge of the grassy patch flowed a bubbling brook, with clear water and a sandy bed. The shining water came up to his ankles as he waded through it. But there was no trace of any animal, neither horse, nor bird, nor tortoise. Adem turned back, and looked at his own footprints by the water's edge. Then he walked from one end of the glade to the other. A scent of water-mint came to his nostrils, but he could not find the plant. He sat down on the other bank of the stream for a while. Then he said to himself, I must go to the Tailless Willow-trees before the sun sets, perhaps the brown stallion is there. A cool spring welled out beneath the Tailless Willow-tree ... Adem was soaked with sweat; the sour smell of sweat enveloped him and although he was used to it, he could smell it.

The horse would be by the willow-tree. It could not be otherwise. There, under the tree close to the big wild roses, he would be standing with his right hind leg drawn up under his belly, looking all around with his big eyes. If he wasn't by the tree, he would be at Bald Mistik. If he wasn't there, he would be at Kurdish Maiden; if he wasn't there he would be at the Spindle Flower. If he wasn't at any of those places, he must have gone to heaven. You might seek him for a whole lifetime and you wouldn't find him. 'If it takes me my whole lifetime, I'll find you! Do you hear, brown horse? I'll seek you till my eyes are dim, till my white beard is down to my knees, till my joints are rickety and I take my last breath! Do you think you've got all the courage and persistence, and I'm just a doormat? I'm just as brave as you are.'

He reached the willow-tree before sunset, but there was no horse or shadow of a horse. He sat down, tired out, by the water, and ate a few scraps of cheese and a big piece of the loaf. A cloud of mosquitoes fell upon him and whined about his head. He was asleep before he had swallowed the last mouthful. When he awoke, the sun was upon him, and he was bathed in sweat. The thick, steamy, sticky heat clung to him.

He rubbed his eyes and at once set off towards Bald Mistik. Bald Mistik always used to fix a dry leaf to his collar. On the slope of a mound in the middle of the marshes, there was a tree like Bald Mistik with dry leaves at the top and green branches down below. That was why he had likened this place to Bald Mistik. The place he called Kurdish Maiden was full of gay flowers of many different colours and sizes. He had once seen a Kurdish maiden a long time ago, dressed in embroidered garments like this place.

'I'll find him today,' he said.

He went to Bald Mistik and to Kurdish Maiden, he went to the Crazy Tree, he went three times to Billygoat Bluebell, but he saw neither hair nor hide of the horse. He saw a greyish-green bird, a big long-legged bird as tall as a man at Billygoat Bluebell. He did not know why he had given it that name. It had simply occurred to him once. When he got near the bird, it did not fly away; he put his hand on its neck and it did not move. One of its wings drooped and when he looked at the wound he saw that it was festering. He took some salt out of his pack and sprinkled it on the wound. The bird, in terror, leapt out of his hand and escaped. In spite of having only one wing, it hopped away very fast.

'I'll find that horse today at Kurd's Camp.'

His spirits rose, and he began to walk jauntily towards faraway Kurd's Camp. There, there, the brown stallion would be there. He took his carbine off his shoulder, and made sure it was loaded. He felt for his knife; it was in its place. Today he would get the brown horse's head and return to his wife. He was angry and joyful in turns. He longed more and more for his wife, and was consumed with burning desire.

'There,' he muttered, 'if he weren't there, I wouldn't have this feeling. He's there!'

As he came to Kurd's Camp he closed his eyes. Then he opened them again but he did not look ahead. He kept them on the ground. It was very hot. The heat grew heavier and mistier. He came to Kurd's Camp and stopped in the middle of it, took his gun in his right hand, and looked up. He turned round and round but there was nothing to be seen not even a shadow, in the sunlit haze. He sank down to the ground:

'I must go away, to the land of Yüregir,' he said quietly. 'There's no way of finding that infidel.'

As he said 'infidel' he suddenly felt afraid. As if he had sworn at something sacred. Then he grew calmer. 'Infidel, infidel', he repeated to himself, gnashing his teeth. 'You've wrecked my life. You've made me unable to face people, unable to look at anyone. I had lived in grinding poverty and just as I'd found a living, you took it away. And my home too, and my lovely wife.'

A lump came into his throat. If he could have burst into tears it would have relieved him. He stayed there without moving in the hot field, sweating, the sweat running off his back, his face, and down his legs like water.

He suddenly jumped for joy. 'He must be at Gülfatma!'

When he had been doing his military service in the mountains near Bolu, he had come across a beautiful flower as tall as a man, and had been very much struck by it. He had never seen such a big flower even in Ahjasaz. When he asked the peasants its name, they said 'Gülfatma'. The plant bore a mass of bell-like flowers. In the place to which he had given the name Gülfatma he had seen some similar flowers, even bigger ones, which had bell-like clusters too.

The flowers at Gülfatma were taller than Adem, and he disappeared into them. Twilight descended upon him. It was like the time when dawn is coming. On the one hand the night was getting brighter, on the other the darkness was spreading. Adem feared this strange darkness more than anything else, he dreaded it. It was at this moment that he heard the beat of a horse's hooves and saw the stallion gliding away through the flowers. He passed out of sight in a moment, fading like smoke, and before Adem could take aim, he had vanished altogether.

'He will come again today,' said Adem. 'He likes places he is used to. He loves Gülfatma. Adores it.'

The heat pressed on his shoulders like a heavy stone. He could not breathe, but kept on walking.

The huge flowers of Gülfatma, their outlines blurred in the misty heat, looked even more beautiful.

36

MEMED, half covered in mud, was waiting at Kurdish Kerem's door. The sun was only half visible behind the Gavur Mountains, but the heat bit into one like a knife. Dappled shadows fell between the houses. He turned away and moved along the road that ran through the middle of the village, up to his ankles in dust. He came to Selver Gelin's door, and stayed there a moment before turning away again. The houses could only dimly be seen. How had he found Vayvay in this state, in the darkness? How had he come, without being caught by the police or seen by anyone? He did not know. When he let himself down into the water from the mill, and the current swept him away, had his legs carried him along without his knowledge and brought him here? Was it instinct that had brought him here? Or Yellow Ümmet? He vaguely remembered Yellow Ümmet.

He stopped for a moment at Seyfali's door. He looked at everything with a vacant stare, as if seeing nothing. Then he came to the big plane-tree. The marshy mud was oozing from his body. Even the stock of his gun was coated with mud. The early morning shadows retreated, and the angry sun, like a heap of embers, bore down on the withered plants, the dusty track and the houses of Vayvay which stood as if scorched up.

With his rifle, field-glasses, dagger, cartridge-belts, and the
tasselled red fez, Memed looked like an overgrown child playing
at brigands. After stopping for a moment under the big tree, he
walked on again. He continued to wander round the village in a
daze.

The first to see him was the boy Ibrahim. Then Hüsam saw
him, and Hüsam said to Ferhat Hodja,

'There's an armed man who looks like a child wandering round
the village. Who can it be?'

Ferhat Hodja was standing at his door, in a gloomy mood. The
loss of the harvest had been a crippling blow for him. He did not
know what to do. He glanced outside and saw a small, mud-caked
man, armed to the teeth, staggering along, bent in two. He rushed
off to Seyfali.

'Seyfali, come outside quickly,' he said, 'come out, there's
something very strange . . . Look at that man!'

Hüsam, who had accompanied Ferhat Hodja, said,

'Yes, he's been wandering about the village like that for quite
some time. He goes up to a door, waits a little and then walks on
again. Just like that.'

Seyfali twisted his long neck and watched the man swaying on
the dusty road as though walking in his sleep.

'That's odd; that's strange,' he said. 'The man's fully armed.
What can it be?'

Then the other villagers heard, and in a moment they had
assembled under the tree. Holding their breath, they watched with
fear and curiosity the man who was going round the village like a
sleepwalker. The man walked backwards and forwards, stopped
and walked on, talked to himself and passed close to the crowd
several times. He saw no one and heard nothing. At this juncture
Old Osman saw the crowd, and came up to the tree, leaning on his
stick. Pushing up his right eyebrow with his hand, he gazed in the
direction in which the villagers were looking. 'Heaven pity us!' he
said. 'Is it a dream, is it a dream that I see? Am I imagining things,
am I dreaming?'

His hands and legs trembled. His stick fell from his hand. Then
he pushed up his right eyebrow again, and shaded his eye with his
hand. 'Heaven have pity on me, look there, is that man armed?'

'Yes,' they cried out, excitedly.

Old Osman, limping and gasping, ran towards Memed and embraced him.

'My child,' he said, 'welcome. You've come back to us in our need. I knew you would come. I knew you would not leave us alone in these difficult times. He's burnt them,' he groaned, 'burnt our harvests, all we had to eat, the whole plain of Anavarza! What a state we are in!'

At this point Ferhat Hodja reached his side. Old Osman clutched at Ferhat's hand. But he still kept his other arm around Memed:

'Look,' he said. 'This is my hawk. He's come! Didn't I tell you so? Didn't I tell you he wouldn't abandon us in the dark days of our trouble?'

People crowded around them; women, girls, old men, children. Memed, numbed, looked at the crowd with a vacant stare, with no expression on his face. There was not a quiver passing over it.

The crowd were quiet. Nobody made a sound.

Ferhat Hodja said,

'Osman, there's something wrong with him. Look at the boy, covered with mud, and his clothes in tatters.'

Up to then Old Osman had not noticed what a state Memed was in. He uttered a cry.

'My hawk, my boy, what's happened to you?' he asked. 'How did you get into this state? My hero, my hawk . . . Ferhat, forgive me, look carefully, make sure my hawk is not wounded . . .'

Ferhat Hodja took Memed's other arm, and they dragged him to Old Osman's house.

Only then did the crowd burst into speech. They began to talk about the incident. No one mentioned Slim Memed's name. They referred to 'the hawk' or 'him'. They talked, but not for long. They had been very disappointed with their first sight of Memed. They looked and looked at him, and said to themselves, 'Is this Slim Memed? Can this small, miserable, bent, helpless child be Slim Memed?'

The crowd moved on to Osman's house, silent once more. After standing for some time, they sat down all around the brushwood fence, and leant against it, silently. The children did not talk, and the babies did not even cry.

Inside, Ferhat Hodja undressed Memed with his own hands, and gave his mud-caked trousers to Mother Kamer, saying, 'Wash them at once.' He examined his body carefully. There was a bullet wound in the calf of his right leg, but it was not deep and there were no other wounds, only a few scratches.

They kept on asking Memed questions, but got no reply, and then Ferhat noticed that his teeth were locked together.

'Osman Agha,' he said, 'the boy has been in some terrible trouble, for his teeth are clenched. He would not have got into this state, into this paroxysm of terror, simply through a clash with the police. Something worse than that has happened to him. Look, he doesn't see or hear anything.'

Mother Kamer, as if washing a child, washed his hands and face and feet with warm water and soap. Then they made up a bed and Ferhat put him to bed with his own hands. As soon as his head touched the pillow he was asleep.

It was noon, and in the heat of the day not a sound came from the crowd. The sun was burning. The dusty ground in Old Osman's courtyard was as hot to the touch as the ashes from an oven. Suddenly Mad Muslu got up. He was very tall and brown-skinned. With his long legs he looked like a greyhound.

'Well, what about it?' he shouted, waving his long arms. 'You stupid things! The hawk is a small bird but he does not give up his prey. This one has fought an army in the mountains, he has routed a huge army, and that's where he has come from. Why do you let yourselves be cowed? Why have you lost hope? He has come. Isn't that enough? He has come to our help. The hawk is small too, but eagles cannot fight him. Damn you spineless people.'

The crowd was roused, and everyone now began to talk. From outside Osman's house a great clamour arose. Everyone talked to everyone else, and their hope and gladness gradually began to grow stronger. In a little while, the women first of all, and then the men and children began to laugh wholeheartedly. An air of gaiety spread through the village. The suffocating dark cloud which had lain over it was lifted.

'He's asleep,' they said. 'He has had great burdens to bear and now he's asleep. He fought with an army in the mountains, he

270

defeated the army, and was slightly wounded in the leg. Nobody knows what terrible misfortunes he has lived through. That is why he is in that state. He was like a sleepwalker, and now he is asleep.'

They slowly dispersed. The village reawakened to life. They were like an eagle that is slowly, stealthily putting out its claws. That day the finest food was cooked in every house. Jokes were bandied about from one house to another. Jokes mixed with bawdy oaths rang through the air. Towards evening, hearing of the event, Aptal Ashir brought out his drum, and came to the village with his son who played the fife. People began to dance the halay in a long row, and when night came the *sinsin* fire dance. In the sticky heat of a summer night, around a fire as big as a threshing-floor, they sweated and danced; it was the first time they danced the sinsin in the summer. In the busy summer months there was no time for festivals and even if there was, the sinsin could not be danced on summer evenings. The other villages – Narlikishla, Yalnizdut, Öksüzlü, Akmashat, Shihmemetli, and Dedefakili learnt of Memed's arrival. That very day they took their horses and carts and came to Vayvay, to join in the celebration. Those who stayed at home celebrated in their villages.

After the gaiety of the festival was over, the villagers, from seven to seventy, became anxious. So did all the other villagers who knew that Memed was at Vayvay.

'Why didn't he come at night?' they said, 'when nobody could have seen him? What kind of bravery is that! To enter a village in broad daylight! Better not to be so brave.'

'What if an agha heard about it?'

'Or one of their henchmen?'

'What if a policeman saw him?'

'Such recklessness, is it possible?'

'In broad daylight! To enter a village like that! . . .'

'Swinging his arms!'

'Let him be as brave as he can be, does a brigand go into a village in broad daylight?'

'Even if his father's house is there, does a brigand enter a village in such a way?'

'Even if he's bullet-proof, does a brigand wander about the Chukurova plain like that?'

'Even if he's the hawk . . .'

'Even if he's the hawk, does he go looking for trouble with the Government like that?'

Their talk contained an element of boasting. The more worried and frightened they were by Memed's having entered the village in broad daylight, the more pleased they were and the more they boasted about him.

'He's small in stature, but that doesn't matter,' they said. 'He's got a heart in him as stout as a blacksmith's anvil.'

'When you're Slim Memed, that's how you enter a village!' declared Selver Gelin.

All the villagers glared at her. Selver Gelin realized that she had broken the unspoken rule.

'I mean he does, our hawk does.'

She saw by their looks that they had not forgiven her. 'A curse on me for being a silly old woman,' she said apologetically. 'Please excuse me, I'll never mention that name again. He, our hawk, enters Chukurova in broad daylight, and absolutely nobody touches a hair of his head . . . He's our hawk.'

Suddenly Muslu appeared. He had been going from house to house, asking,

'Where has he gone? Where's Zeynel? Come on, tell me, where is he? Didn't he see him come? Wasn't he under the tree with us when we were looking at him? Wasn't he with us when Old Osman embraced him? Wasn't he looking on with his neck stretched out as though he was going to eat us?'

As soon as Zeynel had set eyes on Memed, he had scurried off to Ali Safa Bey, his heart beating fast. He was so excited that he fell over his own feet. Yet a vague feeling like regret seemed to churn him up inside. Slim Memed was a strange man. He seemed to be tired of life, and not to be of this world. They had killed his mother and his Hatché, and had forced him to take to the mountains. According to rumour Sergeant Asim protected him, and if this had not been so, they would have killed him long ago.

'They would have killed him long ago. A little handful of a man. You could hold him and squeeze him. And he would be dead.'

He went into the courtyard of the mansion, and stayed there hesitating. He began to condemn himself, to despise himself.

Because of Memed a tiny ray of hope was born in him too. A feeling resembling gladness began to take the place of regret.

'Great Allah, get me out of this dilemma,' muttered Zeynel. 'What's up with me? Shan't I be able to tell him?'

What was there about that boy? Had he magic or divine powers? Such a thing had never happened to Zeynel before. Did I like him? he thought. Like that little bastard? Of course not. Well, what's the matter with me then? Is it pity for that dwarfish bandit whose hands are steeped in blood? No, it was not pity. Yet, when he was mentioned a certain happiness and confidence came over Zeynel, and a little ray of hope burned fitfully. Allah, Allah, what on earth was that? What was it?

While Zeynel was wondering whether to go home again or to go upstairs and see Ali Safa Bey, Ali Safa's voice came from above, within the mansion.

'Is that Zeynel?' he said cheerfully. 'What are you standing there for? You're taking a long time to think about it! Come on upstairs.'

Zeynel looked up and smiled at Ali Safa Bey with an uncertain expression on his face. Ali Safa Bey had never seen Zeynel look like that, and it made him shudder. His hand went to his revolver with the mother-of-pearl inlaid handle.

'What's up, Zeynel?' he asked, when he met him at the head of the stairs.

I must tell him, Zeynel thought fleetingly. They would surround the village and take Memed captive, and the curse of Slim Memed would be lifted. Then he said silently to himself but as if shouting, 'No, it can't be, no, no, no!'

Zeynel sat down on the divan opposite the Bey. He smiled and talked and tried to pull himself together.

'After the grain was burnt, the villagers were broken in spirit. They were finished,' he said. 'I looked one morning, and there they were, packing up to go. They were going to burn their houses behind them, that's what they were saying. I too picked up my things, and put the bundles ready by the door. Then Ferhat Hodja appeared from somewhere. He coaxed and cajoled them. He brought them round, and towards noon the people took their bundles inside and unpacked them again. That hodja's a pest.

Even Old Osman was sitting on his bales outside his door, his head bowed, reciting his prayers, and saying it was fate. He was waiting for some relatives to come for him with a cart from Narlikishla. That man's a wizard. He makes everyone do what he wants.'

Ali Safa Bey went red with fury while Zeynel was speaking and became as tense as a bow. He jumped to his feet, and yelled.

'I – I – ' stamping his feet, he began to stride furiously up and down. The floorboards shook under his tread as if in an earthquake. 'I, I'll get even with him, that so-called priest! That man who came from God knows where! I . . . I'll make those peasants sorry for what they've done. I'll make them sorry they were ever born. Listen to me, Zeynel, if they don't get out of that village before winter, I'll bring down such a disaster on their heads as was never known on the face of the earth before. Those peasants have been occupying my land for too long – that land I bought, for which I gave my most valuable things, which I acquired at the cost of my horse. I won't allow it. There's no right, or law or justice left in this world. And the Government and the Governor are very weak . . . If they can't even protect a citizen's rights, let them give up governing! Who's forcing them to go on?'

He gnashed his teeth; his face was distorted, his jaw twitched, and his bleary eyes blinked rapidly. He tapped his boots with his whip.

'They don't know me. They have no idea of what I can do to them. And as for this Government, if the Government doesn't defend my rights . . . I, I, I know very well how to defend my rights myself. I won't let them trample even on my shadow, d'you hear? My shadow! That village . . . that village . . . they'll see, and pretty soon too . . .'

He talked, he raved, he paced to and fro. He cursed Old Osman and Ferhat Hodja. He repeated a dozen times how he was going to drive the peasants out of the village in a day or two. When he finally sat down, he was pale with exhaustion.

'I'll make them sweat blood. I'll make them suffer,' he repeated. 'I'll make them sweat blood, blood, blood . . . I'll put a spoke in their wheel . . . a spoke in their wheel . . . They'll pay dearly for the bad turn they've done me. They'll pay dearly, dearly!'

He took a cigarette out of his pocket, and fixed it carefully into an amber holder. Zeynel at once picked up a glowing coal from the fire with a small pair of tongs and the Bey, puffing hard, lit his cigarette.

'Well, Zeynel,' he said, 'my friend, my lion, you haven't been able to cope with those stupid people – have you? And yet if they had listened to you and had evacuated the village, they would have had houses and land in another village by now. Well, what's the news? Last night we heard the sound of drums coming from Vayvay. Is it because their harvest was burnt that they're holding a festival, those insolent scoundrels? What was it?'

'We have some hill-folk in our village,' explained Zeynel, 'and their son or somebody had come home from the army, or anyway so I heard, and they were holding a celebration in his honour. It was nothing,' he said, making it sound unimportant and not dwelling on it.

'I . . . I . . . ' said Ali Safa Bey again, 'anyway I'll show them! Come back in four or five days, Zeynel. We're going to make an end of this business. I can't go on struggling with these uncouth scoundrels for a whole lifetime.'

'Very well, Bey.'

'It'll be a relief to you and to me.'

'So it will, Bey.'

'Keep your eyes and ears open at Vayvay these days. I think something's going on there. After the grain was burnt they should have decamped. But they held out. It's not only Ferhat Hodja . . . There are other things. The peasant's a cowardly creature, he wouldn't hold out so firmly. Find out what it is. Look and listen. If I had taken my present precautions two or three years ago, if I had been able to take them . . . True, the Government in those days was not as it is now, its control was tighter, it tied us hand and foot, it treated those animals as gentlemen and puffed them up, so that only the late Kalayji, the brigand, fought them. Why, a single Kalayji would have been enough to turn out half the village then! It's an amazing thing that all the measures I'm taking don't seem to affect them at all! Their horses are stolen, their village raided, their grain-harvest burnt, the police beat them to death, and yet they don't turn a hair! Look and listen, Zeynel

. . . What's the secret of these people's resistance? Those cowards, those scared rabbits?'

'Very well, Bey.'

'I investigated thoroughly, but I didn't find out anything about who is inciting them.'

'I'll find out, Bey.'

From within came a smell of roast game, tarhana soup and fried onion.

'Shall we have a drink, Zeynel?'

'Very well, Bey.'

Zeynel was still burning in a hell of uncertainty. Should he tell or not? What if someone else came and told the Bey? How would he explain his silence? Bey, he would say, the villagers were suspicious of me. Everything that happened to this village was concealed from me. They also concealed Slim Memed. What was I to do?

37

The three of them, Mad Muslu, Yellow Süleyman and Ahmet sat under a tree at the top of a gully in the thorn-forest and talked in low voices. Muslu had been a sergeant in the army. He was twenty-eight years old. He had broad shoulders and long, thin legs. He looked like a greyhound. His eyes were the long slanting eyes of a greyhound. He wore velveteen trousers and corrugated leather boots. Before the horses were stolen, he had possessed a fine, half-thoroughbred chestnut Arab horse. He was the only child of well-to-do parents. Mounted on his Arab horse, he would gallop over the Anavarza plain. He had not married, and was the only bachelor of his age in the village. A harsh, headstrong man, he had earned himself a reputation for daredevilry in the Anavarza plain. He had never intervened in Ali Safa Bey's affairs up to the present. Whatever Ali Safa Bey did, all his oppression of Vayvay village had been let pass with scarcely a murmur of disapproval. When the chestnut horse was stolen, he was angry and cursed for some days, but then he forgot it. Muslu had no hope. Anyway Ali Safa Bey would turn the villagers of Vayvay out of their homes. It was useless to struggle. For this reason he did not get involved, but followed events from a distance, not missing anything.

Yellow Süleyman and Ahmet were twenty or twenty-one years old. They too had held themselves aloof from the Ali Safa struggle. They agreed with Muslu. Behind Ali Safa Bey there was a powerful Government. All the police were under his orders. Then, too, he maintained a squad of armed thugs at his house. Also he had behind him a village like Chikchiklar, a village that made a living through stealing and banditry. Ali Safa Bey had relations at Chikchiklar. How could they cope with all these people? Sooner or later they would have to leave the village anyway. This neutral attitude of the three men lasted until the day Memed came to the village. As soon as he saw him, Muslu felt ashamed of himself, and for the first time, in Old Osman's yard he condemned himself for his defeatism.

'Brother,' he said to Süleyman, 'we have our own fortress now, something to lean upon. He has come. Let him stay where he is. His turn will come.'

'Let him wait,' Ahmet said.

'His turn will come,' Süleyman said.

'First we must take care of his safety,' Muslu continued. 'The aghas and the Government must not hear that he is in our village.'

'How can they not hear?' said Ahmet. 'He came to our village in broad daylight.'

'It was well done,' said Muslu. 'Can anyone get a word out of a villager, whether a child or an aged man, even if they torture them?'

'No, they can't,' said Süleyman.

'Even if they massacred the whole village one by one, no one would say that he is in our village.'

'Except one,' said Muslu.

'Except Zeynel,' said Ahmet.

'The three of us are here now,' said Muslu. 'First we shall save him. We need him.'

'We need him badly,' said Ahmet.

'He's as brave as a lion!' said Süleyman.

'Yes,' smiled Muslu. 'So we must save him. Do you think Zeynel's told Ali Safa Bey?'

'It's his job to tell.'

'Perhaps he hasn't yet told him, but he will.'

'Perhaps he hasn't found Ali Safa Bey, but he will.'

'If he'd told him, the police would have surrounded the village, already.'

'Ali Safa Bey had gone to the town.'

'He'll come back.'

'Before the police come, before they find him . . .' said Muslu.

'Before they find him,' echoed Süleyman.

'. . . We must find Zeynel.'

'If he hasn't told him . . . ?'

'He may not tell him today, or tomorrow. But one day . . .'

'He will tell.'

'We must find Zeynel.'

Because Muslu had a sharp temper and did not talk much, because when he did he spoke plainly, and told people bluntly to their faces what he thought of them, they called him mad. Mad Muslu with his long thin legs was like a greyhound. His face too was long like a greyhound's. He ran very fast like a greyhound.

Their minds were made up. Taking out a dagger they put their hands on it and swore an oath. Then they got up and went to the place where Chikchiklar valley meets the plain. They would wait there for Zeynel to pass. He had to pass that way, whatever happened. Either going to Ali Safa Bey or coming back, he would necessarily have to go along the path round the end of the valley.

There was a broad reed-bed at this place, a huge expanse. Every reed was very tall. It was like a forest.

They entered the reed-bed at about noon, and hid in a hollow a few yards above the path.

*

Seyfali came to see Ferhat Hodja.

'Zeynel is not in the village,' he said. 'Zeynel's gone.'

'That's bad news,' sighed Ferhat. 'The hawk is not in a fit state yet. The poor boy is ill. As if he'd been struck by a thunderbolt. He hasn't got strength enough in his finger to pull the trigger. How can he fight the police?'

'How shall we hide him?' asked Seyfali.

'He's chosen a bad time,' said Ferhat. 'This moment is not the moment to come down to Chukurova. But the poor boy was exhausted and ill. He still can't eat or drink. How shall we hide him, do you think?'

'Yes, how shall we hide him?'

Old Osman heard this. Seyran too ... Everyone heard that Zeynel had vanished. Everyone knew where he had gone to. They were filled with alarm.

'Where shall we hide him?'

'Where?'

'The police will come . . .'

'Alas, my hawk, alas!'

'Alas, my unlucky one, alas!'

'We couldn't even gaze upon your face to our heart's content.'

'Who knows how he speaks?'

'We didn't hear his sweet voice even once.'

'Dark days for us . . .'

'A little bird came and took shelter in a thicket.'

'How shall we shelter him from the claws of those birds of prey?'

'Where shall we hide him?'

'Where?'

'Where won't they find him?'

'Where?'

A whole village, like a single individual, thought, worried, fretted, expecting the police at any moment. They tried to find a place of refuge for him but they could not. They alternately despaired, then hoped again, were discouraged, then took heart.

'Where are we to hide him, where?'

'Where?'

'Wait, you cursed creatures, wait,' was all Old Osman said.

'The police can't know which house he's in . . .'

'If they search this one we'll smuggle him into another.'

'They can break our bones . . .'

'Or grind us to powder . . .'

'No one will reveal his hiding-place.'

'The whole village will be dumb.'

'Horses and people, animals and birds . . .'

'There are no horses.'

'Birds and insects.'

'Wait a minute, neighbours, wait, damn you . . .'

'Let's hide him in Ahjasaz.'

'Let's take him to Anavarza Castle.'

'To Hadjilar, behind Anavarza Castle.'

'To the land of the Lek Kurds behind Anavarza Castle.'

'The Lek Kurds were like eagles.'

'You hear of them in the old songs.'

'How shall we hide him?'

'Where?'

'There was a brigand, Kurdish Reshit. He would go up into the Anavarza crags, and no one could find him.'

'The whole land about here used to be a forest, where an army could get lost.'

'What shall we do?'

'Once in a thousand times we were lucky and found him . . .'

'Wait a minute, damn you, wait! From every hill a sun will rise. Just wait, be patient a little while.'

They collected in scattered groups and talked about Zeynel. The women assailed Zeynel's wife with a string of questions. Will he tell Ali Safa Bey about him, or won't he?

And the hawk sleeps, curled up in the bed near the hearth. He sleeps without stirring, his lips slightly parted.

They come and go from one house to another. Even children are sad, anxious, alarmed. Everybody is on edge, everyone is like a cat on hot bricks.

All that night the villagers did not sleep a wink but waited tensely for the police to come or for shots to ring out. But no one came or went. In the morning they got up tired but happy.

They waited the whole day, and the whole night. They tried to find out where Zeynel was, but he had disappeared. Since the police had not come, where was Zeynel?

'We must find a hiding-place for the hawk.'

In all of the Chukurova and the Anavarza plain, all over that smooth expanse there was not one hiding-place they could be sure of. They could not trust him to their brother or father or mother, not even to their own eyes.

*

Mad Muslu with his long thin legs, his long thin face and slanting eyes, looked like a greyhound sniffing the ground. Five people passed along the path on horseback, seven on foot. A shepherd led his flock through the reed-bed. But Zeynel did not come. The day declined and the shadows lengthened. They went to sleep, leaving one of their number on guard, and when they woke up Zeynel had still not come. Then the sound of footsteps passing along the path made them jump up.

'Stop, traveller,' they cried, and placed themselves in the middle of the path. The traveller stopped.

'Hallo, Zeynel,' said Muslu.

'Hallo!' said Zeynel.

'We were waiting for you, Zeynel. You're late.'

'What?' said Zeynel.

'You're late.'

Zeynel collapsed on the ground.

Süleyman and Ahmet took him by the arms and pulled him up. Zeynel was swaying on his feet, and walked with difficulty.

'Don't be afraid, Zeynel,' said Muslu. 'What happens to one has to be endured. Everyone sows as he reaps. Don't be afraid. It's useless to be afraid.'

Towards noon they reached Ahjasaz and entered a thick, gloomy wood of alders. There was not a glimpse of the sky through the trees.

'Are you tired, Zeynel? Sit down,' said Muslu and, rolling a cigarette, he put it in his mouth. Zeynel's lips were trembling. He sat down on the ground.

'Don't kill me,' he said. 'I know a lot. After this I can be useful to you. I know you brought me here to kill me. But please don't kill me.'

'We brought you here to kill you,' said Muslu.

The trees, the sky, the marsh, the flowers, Muslu and the others were all blurred together. A huge orange butterfly alighted on the branch of a bramble, and folding its wings began to rub its big

281

blue head and protruding eyes with its legs. Zeynel could see nothing but the orange butterfly, rubbing its eyes, and its slim legs. The butterfly did not fly away, but stayed there quietly. Then the butterfly was blotted out and everything became blurred and confused. On a pink bramble-flower an insect alighted, a long, steel-green, bee-like fly, that gleamed blue and more steely as the minutes went by.

'Don't kill me.'

Muslu took out his revolver and fired two shots at Zeynel's head. Zeynel rolled over. Süleyman and Ahmet each fired a shot too.

The orange butterfly flew away at the sound of the gun and alighted on a mullein flower, then it flew off again. It flitted from flower to flower. Then it rose and flew right up over the trees and into the sky.

'That's finished him off,' said Muslu.

'He asked for it,' said Ahmet.

'Well, we must be going,' said Süleyman.

At one end of the marshes, just beyond the place where the muddy water bubbled, they dug a deep hole and threw Zeynel into it just as he was. Then they heaped the earth on top of him.

'Even we shan't be able to find Zeynel by next summer,' said Muslu. 'The bubbling water will have covered him.'

They were very tired. When they returned to the village they could hardly stand on their feet.

Muslu was like a long, thin greyhound.

*

Süleyman woke Muslu.

'There's a strong west wind blowing. Hurry up, we're late, Muslu,' he said.

'Where's Ahmet?'

'Here, waiting under the chardak,' said Süleyman.

Muslu dressed at once and they set out.

Ali Safa Bey's harvests had not yet been threshed. Only the day before a harvesting machine had begun to work in one of the fields.

'You'll set light to the upper fields, Süleyman,' said Muslu.

'Fire the grain-stacks first and then the standing corn. And you, Ahmet, you'll go down towards Mistikölen and set fire to the stacks and unreaped corn there . . . I'll burn the reaping machine.'

Towards midnight the fire broke out on Ali Safa Bey's farm. The strong south-west wind which had sprung up in the evening, was still blowing. The flames spread from the heaps of grain to the fields. Towards morning all Ali Safa Bey's fields were in flames. There was a lake of fire spreading all over the plain.

At Vayvay and the nearby villages, they jumped out of bed, saying, 'Ali Safa Bey's harvests are on fire.' Some climbed on to the trellises, others on to the roofs, and others up a tree, and watched the burning fields until daybreak.

Old Osman could not contain his excitement. He went in and out, loaded his pistol, thrust it into his belt, took it out again.

'There you are, Ferhat Hodja,' he said. 'You're a man of God, and you tell the truth. As a man sows, so must he reap. There you are. Ferhat Hodja, my hawk came and look what's happened. And who knows what else may happen while my hawk is sleeping here! Who knows! It is sufficient if his mere shadow is present over the plain of Chukurova. He could sleep there, snuffling a little, till kingdom come. Just his shadow is enough. As a man sows, so shall he reap. It's enough if the people know that he is treading on the plain of Chukurova. It's enough. He'll pierce the mountain and open a road through it. The more frightened the peasants are, the braver they become. It's enough if they find something to put their backs against, even if it's only rye-stalks. As a man sows, so shall he reap.'

As the morning wore on, another piece of news spread through the village. Last night as Ali Safa's crops were burning, his mansion had been attacked and all the horses from his stable stolen. It was a fact. Ali Safa Bey had not expected this. He was mad with rage, tearing at his hair. 'I, I, I . . .' he spluttered. 'Wife, what have I, I, I, ever shown these people, these ungrateful wretches, but kindness?'

His wife was in tears.

'What have we ever done but kind actions,' she kept repeating. 'What have we done . . . What have we done?' And she cursed the villagers.

'I won't let them get away with this. Those Vayvay peasants, those madmen . . . As I'm my father's son, I won't let them get away with this!'

38

Ali safa bey simply could not believe his eyes and ears. 'How was it they set fire to my harvests, and stole my horses? How, how, how was it? Who put them up to this?'

'Who can have put them up to it?' said his wife, trying to help him. 'Who can have put them up to it? There's someone giving them confidence, someone supporting them from behind the scenes . . .'

'I think and think, but can't imagine who is behind them. At one moment they are utterly demoralized, ready to pack up and leave the village, and the next they pick themselves up again and come to life. They stand out against me, and very obstinately too! They set fire to my crops. They raided my mansion and might have killed me. These scoundrels, these ungrateful wretches, who forget all my benefits and return evil for good. I shouldn't be surprised if one day they rise up and kill me without compunction.'

'They would kill you, those infidels, those wicked men. If it hadn't been for you, Arif Saim Bey would have treated them all like those Akmezar peasants. If only he'd done so, if only you hadn't prevented it. Ah, good deeds! See what you get in return!'

'Zeynel hasn't come either. What's happened to the man? Zeynel doesn't leave me alone on days like this, he brings me news. What's happened to him? I'm worried. Who, who, who did this to me? Who incited those scoundrels? Who put them up to stealing my horses and burning my grain-harvest? That godless, religion-less man they call Ferhat Hodja isn't strong enough. Old Osman is senile and talks nothing but a load of rubbish. Who, who, who?'

'There's someone,' said his wife, bending her head and becoming very grave. 'There's someone. Someone has a grudge against

284

us. If only we had never come to this plain! Nobody knows what we've put up with, how we have stuck it out in spite of fever, heat and mosquitoes. They have a grudge against us. They talk of Ali Safa Bey's farm, and nothing else, nothing else. They forget the days when you took the name of Typhoon, when you shielded them from the French among the Taurus peaks, when you drove the enemy into the sea, when with a band of forty people armed with flint-lock guns, you took a whole battalion prisoner in one of the high passes. They forget those days, they forget them . . . They think that the couple of acres you own is too much for you, after you have shed your blood to save our great fatherland . . . Yes, saved it at the risk of your own life . . . They, the people who bear a grudge against us, fled to the mountains instead of defending the honour of the fatherland against the French; they concealed themselves in holes, or lay in thickets, every one of them . . . A day or so ago, in the town, the ironmonger's daughter asked me pointedly if you'd gone to the farm again. "Yes he has," I said. "To the farm . . ." Then I really let fly. "My girl," I said, "when your father was in Adana under the French flag, doing a belly-dance for the French commandant, waggling his hips in front of him, my Ali Safa Bey, my great Typhoon Bey, was firing at the French soldiers. Firing and being wounded. Do you think two dunums of land is too much for a hero of the Independence, a Typhoon Bey? My girl . . ." She didn't say a word, and slunk off like a bitch, with her tail between her fat legs. Did I do right?'

Ali Safa Bey was lost in thought. He did not hear her.

The woman said again several times,

'Did I do right? Typhoon Bey, did I do right?'

The Bey, coming back to earth said quickly,

'Yes, you did right, wife; you did quite right.'

'Everyone is hostile to us. The fact that we have a farm seems to stick in the gullet of everyone in Chukurova. It's really your own fault. I told you enough times: write to Mustafa Kemal Pasha and tell him all that has happened in detail. Let him have them hanged, those deserters, traitors, enemies of our Independence. I told you enough times: write to him, I said, and tell him, Pasha, people who couldn't do anything to your Typhoon in the days of the War of Independence have now started to be aggressive. Aah, you are kind, so kind, so gentle and good-hearted that you don't want even mountain wolves, or crawling ants or poisonous snakes to be hurt.'

She began to cry. Then she uncovered her plump pink and white legs up to the groin, and showed them to her husband:

'Look at the state I'm in. Just look: look at these legs, at my pink skin. Doesn't it tear your heart? The mosquitoes have devoured me ...'

Meliha Hanim's legs were covered with mosquito-bites, and much inflamed. The mosquitoes had really devoured her.

Ali Safa Bey went up to his wife and kissed her hair.

'Don't cry, Meliha,' he said, 'I'll solve this problem. I routed the French in this district, and I'll cause the same havoc to our enemies, and a thousand times more. This plain is ours by right, and these lands shall be mine.'

Meliha wiped her big almond eyes:

'How easily Arif Saim Bey got the people out of the Circassian village and away from his farm! He did well. We are stuck with those miserable wretches in Vayvay who don't understand a thing. Our fatherland would have gained a farm which would have been a model for the whole world.'

'Don't cry, Meliha,' said Ali Safa Bey. 'I'm an old fighter. I like difficulties. The Turkish Republic doesn't support me as they support Arif Saim Bey. I won't stoop to getting the Government to intervene on my behalf ... If I could only find out who it is, who's inciting these villagers. ... There's someone behind this business who has a lot of influence, who's trusted and believed in by those villagers. But who? Who, who, who is that man, Meliha?'

'Everyone,' said Meliha. 'No one has any sympathy with us. No one realizes how difficult it is for us. Was I meant to be like this? Did my father give me all this education to be eaten by mosquitoes in the plain of Anavarza, to have to put up with the sight of these miserable peasants from morning till night and to have to talk to them? Look at the state I'm in, did he bring me up for that?'

She again uncovered her legs and showed them to her husband.

'Don't cry, Meliha, don't cry. I'm going to deal with those people.'

He began to walk up and down the room again. Meliha knew his moods and when he began to walk about, she kept silent. Tirelessly and with admiring eyes she watched her husband moving to and fro, and only spoke when he asked her a question.

His striped brown breeches came over the top of his dusty yellow boots. He tapped the boots with his whip, making a sound like a little drum. It had become a habit over the years to do his thinking while walking to and fro making this sound.

It was being said that Memed had again been seen in the Taurus. A few days before, Zeynel had heard a young girl in the village singing a song which had been made up about Memed. By the way, what had become of Zeynel? He must have a search made.

'Murtaza!'

A voice came from below:

'Yes, sir.'

'Come upstairs.'

Murtaza, whose face was puckered under the weight of several cartridge-belts, for he had never before carried so much ammunition, came upstairs.

'What is it, sir?'

'Murtaza, my boy, Zeynel hasn't been here for days. What's happened to him? I hope there's nothing wrong. He's never stayed away so long. I hope they haven't done anything to the poor fellow. Go to Vayvay and have a look round, and find out what's up. Perhaps he's ill.'

'Shall I go armed, or leave my rifle here?'

'Leave it here.'

Murtaza went off.

Whenever Slim Memed appears in the Taurus these peasants here come to life, they go mad. Could he have been the cause of that night's rioting? Could it have been Slim Memed who stole the horses?

Ali Safa Bey's face, dark as if blackened with soot, alternately brightened and grew sombre.

Could one man up in the mountains inspire them to such resistance that they committed these vile crimes? One simply could not tell with these men, these scoundrels ... They were scared at the fall of a leaf, and yet if it rained cannon-balls they were not afraid . . . Arif Saim Bey must be supporting that Slim Memed. If not, they would have killed him long ago. The police kept on capturing him and letting him go.

He was very annoyed about Arif Saim Bey. If Arif Saim Bey wanted to, he could seize all the land in Chukurova, and no one could stand out against him and say, 'Bey, what are you doing?' It suited him to have the mountains full of brigands, and disorder reigning everywhere. Wolves like Arif Saim Bey thrived on cloudy weather, would even create the bad weather if it suited them . . . He envied Arif Saim Bey very much.

He turned and went up to his wife. Bending down, he kissed her on the brow.

'Don't upset yourself, Meliha,' he said. 'I'll cope with this. Now I'm off to see our relations at Chikchiklar. If they are men they had better show what they're made of. If they don't repay me in these dark days, when will they repay me for what I've done for them?'

Meliha smiled, and dimples appeared in her plump face:

'When else . . . ?' She smiled brightly. 'I beg you, Typhoon Bey, take a lot of men with you. Those scoundrels are capable of anything. People who stoop to burning our grain harvest, stealing our horses and taking the bread out of our mouths, those people who won't vacate our property will do all kinds of vile and wicked things to us. Please, Typhoon Bey, do take care . . .'

Ali Safa Bey nodded, and ran down the stairs. He did not have to wait in the courtyard, for they had brought out his horse and were holding it ready. He mounted, and three men also mounted their horses at the same time.

The people at Chikchiklar met him outside the village. Ali Safa Bey's father, Hadji Kahya, the most important man in the village, had been a poor landowner. It was with the greatest difficulty that he had got together enough money to educate his son. As for Ali Safa he had done a lot to help Chikchiklar in their dealings with the Government. If anyone there committed a crime or even a murder he got him out of the hands of the law. He was very popular there. The people were proud of him and never refused him anything.

Before he had even greeted them,

'We were so sorry, Bey,' they said. 'But God is great. And we're not here to just fold our arms and watch . . .'

Ali Safa said,

'Thank you, bless you. I'm pleased with you all. You sent Musa the Warden to me; and he gladdened my heart. The fact that he came to see me on the morning after the fire was a great consolation to me. Now the matter is getting more serious. But having you behind me, like a rock . . .'

The people of Chikchiklar said,

'With God's help.'

Chikchiklar, a village situated in a valley in the foothills of the Taurus, occupied itself solely with stealing and brigandage. Even the women were horse-thieves. The children began to use a rifle at the age of seven.

'Don't worry, Bey,' they said.

'The place where your horse has trodden shall be yours.'

'May Allah never take you away from us.'

'Our lives and property are yours, Agha.'

'The stone that strikes your foot shatters our hearts.'

Ali Safa Bey, full of pride, smiled from ear to ear and rubbed his hands, saying nothing but 'Thank you, bless you.'

'What's up with you, Ali?' burst out an old man. 'Did you think we would just sit back and watch while the people of Vayvay hit at you? Why are you so upset? I'd sacrifice this whole village for your toe-nails. Get back to your house and don't worry. This year the Vayvay villagers will leave your land and go away. If they don't, we'll do so and never show ourselves among men again. D'you hear, young Agha? Go about your business. Leave the Vayvay people to us.'

Ali Safa Bey's eyes watered and a lump came into his throat.

'Thank you, Uncle Hadji Veli,' he said. 'You've made me happy.'

'Be happy, don't be uneasy,' said Hadji Veli.

They at once killed a goat in Ali Safa Bey's honour. They lit a big fire and roasted the meat in the embers. They brought out raki too. Ali Safa Bey ate his midday meal in the village. After the meal he summoned Dursun Durmush to him.

'Dursun Durmush, my son,' he said. 'Today's the day. What will you do to Vayvay?'

'Whatever you say.'

'They have nothing left. Their horses have gone, their harvest has been burnt. But their bulls, oxen and cows are left. And their ducks, geese and hens ... Dursun Durmush, no living creature, in the way of animals, must be left in Vayvay. You will kill them all forthwith and put them in a row around the village.'

'At your orders, Agha.'

The question of Slim Memed worried Ali Safa Bey, but in order not to appear to give it too much importance he could not ask anyone anything. He waited for the peasants to broach the subject, but nobody mentioned Slim Memed. At last he found himself obliged to ask about Slim Memed himself.

'You remember,' he said off-handedly, 'that brigand who appeared in the mountains once. A boy, what on earth was his name? I mean the man who killed our Abdi Agha.'

'Slim Memed,' they said.

'I heard that he has again been seen in the mountains.'

'He's a lion,' said Hadji Veli. 'He killed Black Ibrahim some time ago. He did battle with an army of policemen for three days and three nights, and in the end he escaped. He's a brave man, that Memed. And then . . .'

All heads turned angrily towards Hadji Veli. He at once realized the mistake he had made.

'And then . . .' he went on, trying to cover it up, 'and then he sent a telegram to Mustafa Kemal Pasha saying, "Don't send those poor things against me, if you are a brave man come and fight me yourself".'

Ali Safa Bey regretted having asked. Among the villagers there was a deep affection and respect for this young brigand. Where did it come from? It was puzzling. Why, even Hadji Veli was ready to make a legend of him. He was a danger to everybody, this Slim Memed. Whether he encouraged Vayvay to rebel or not, he was a very dangerous man and must be removed.

A lot of crazy ideas about Memed came to him, and made him shudder. Was that boy one of the heroes of the people? But what had he done except kill the poor old agha of a small village? What was the real reason for their making so much of this boy? Why when he mentioned Slim Memed, had everyone fallen silent – his relations, his closest friends, and even the peasants? If Hadji Veli, that garrulous old man, had not spoken, no one would have spoken. Had he magic or divine powers?

'Am I afraid?' he asked himself, and rose to his feet.

'I must go to town,' he said.

They brought his horse and he mounted.

'Am I afraid? I stole their horses and they stole mine. I burnt down their harvests and they burnt mine . . . I'll have their cattle killed and they . . . I'll have them killed and perhaps Ferhat Hodja too . . . and they'll kill me? . . . Is it likely?'

He shivered. For the first time he felt death deep inside him, close to his heart. Would these peasants kill him? Would they dare? Was it possible?

He began to laugh at himself. 'I'm afraid,' he said. 'The burning of the grain-harvests has made me jumpy. They can burn harvests, I know. But there is nobody at Vayvay capable of stealing horses.'

The thought of Slim Memed obsessed him. Were all these troubles due to Slim Memed? Good heavens, no. Today he's seen in the mountains, tomorrow he disappears, ten years are wiped out . . . He is a strange kind of brigand. Perhaps he came to kill Hamza. Once he has killed him, he'll disappear again. The peasants will again burn the Plain of Thistles in his honour, and again fires will burn on the mountain top. How strange! Perhaps these peasants are fire-worshippers. Hamza is done for! Well, he too treated the people with great cruelty. The Agha's revenge and all that, but after all we're not in the Middle Ages! Such severity leads to such results. Let's see you get out of this, Hamza!

The thought that Slim Memed had come to the Taurus to kill Hamza pleased him. Slim Memed would kill Hamza, and disappear again. The peasants would again light fires after he had gone. There was nothing to be afraid of. No, and yet . . .

Turning these things over in his mind, he entered the town. He left his horse at his house, and taking one of his men with him, he went down to the market.

39

'HE's an extraordinary man,' said the Captain. 'And courageous too.'

Hamza, his eyes as round as saucers, said,

'Isn't he ever going to be caught?'

'It's impossible for a brigand not to be caught, but the question is when?'

Sergeant Asim joined in,

'You never know where and how he's going to strike! He's like a fish in water . . . He slips out of your hand.'

'Where has he gone now, do you think, Sergeant?'

'I can't say. He disappears, and nobody can be certain where he's going to appear again . . . Today he'll be in Chukurova, you think, and then before you know where you are, tomorrow the fellow is in Alidagh. Today he's in Alidagh and the day after he's in Chukurova! The man is unpredictable. He can walk like the wind for three days and nights, without rest, without sleep, without food. If he wants, he will show himself, if he doesn't, he won't. He's a strange fellow.'

Sergeant Asim was boasting a little about Memed. As he talked his eyes gleamed and his voice became livelier and warmer.

'You mean he'll never be caught?'

'He'll be caught,' declared the Captain, 'but only after wearing us down. How should he not be caught? Even Chakircali Efe was caught, who held the Ottoman army at bay for fourteen years in the Izmir region. Of course, he will be caught.'

Hamza was getting more and more upset and worried, but he tried not to show the fear that was gradually increasing within him. He pestered the Captain and the Sergeant with questions. In the end he understood that it would not be easy to cope with Slim Memed.

With relish Sergeant Asim launched into a story:

'One day we came across him below Andirin. Three people

were walking through a green rice-paddy, flat as a tray. It was morning. We began firing. Then we saw smoke rising from the rice-field. A little later when the smoke cleared, there was no one there; they had disappeared. That day more than a thousand peasants and a posse of policemen combed the rice-fields and there was nothing. The following day he was seen together with his band at Yellow Garden. I made enquiries, and it was true. How could a man cover so much ground in one night? That's what I could never understand. I don't say he won't be captured, but he'll give us a run for our money. I've come into conflict with lots of brigands, but I've never seen a man who was so quick with his hands and feet. I saw him once. He's a tiny little man. For some reason he has the support of the peasants. I've been hunting brigands for years, and I've never seen one who was so loved. It will be difficult to get Slim Memed out of the hands of the people.'

'Our villagers are bitter enemies of his,' said Hamza. 'They hate him. If he falls into their hands they'll have no mercy on him. They still say, "How we loved our Agha." They're always weeping for Abdi Agha. They're right. Abdi Agha was an angel, a saint. Recently the peasants have seen him mounted on a white horse, shimmering with light, and flying over the village. I waited fifteen nights until morning and I didn't see him. He was angry and did not show himself to me . . .'

Sergeant Asim was amused at what Hamza said. So was Captain Faruk.

Hamza's voice trembled with the fear he had been hiding for days, and suddenly he blurted out tearfully,

'But he'll kill me. I know it. He heard that I'm here and he turned back. He turned back to kill me. I'm sure of it! If only I'd stayed in Chukurova. I only came here to look after my dead brother's family, to watch over their interests. But it'll cost me my life. He'll kill me.'

He looked insistently at Sergeant Asim and the Captain, waiting for a word from them that would give him some help, or advice, or a ray of hope.

The faces of Sergeant Asim and the Captain wore no smile now and their expression was absolutely blank. From the very day when they heard that Memed had come back from the mountains, they had said to each other that he had come to kill Hamza.

'There's nothing to be done,' Sergeant Asim had said. 'Memed will kill him. Memed won't be captured until Hamza is killed.'

In the clash with the police, Memed had said pleadingly, 'I have a job to do, Sergeant,' and everyone had realized what that job was going to be. Memed would certainly carry out his task.

'He'll kill me, won't he, Sergeant? Nobody can prevent him. You, Arif Saim Bey, Mustafa Kemal Pasha, or great Allah; nobody can prevent him, can they?'

The Sergeant did not answer.

'Can they, Captain?'

The Captain looked at him vacantly as if he had not heard.

'He'll kill me, he'll kill me, Captain. You can't bring yourself to say it, can you?'

They were sitting beside the hearth in which big logs were burning, and they gazed into the flickering flames, not uttering a word.

'Ah, ah, ah,' cried Hamza. He got up and walked down into the ravine. It was a starless night.

'Oh, God, give this stone life. Breathe life into the corpse. Give life to the iron that is red-hot in the fire. Give leaves to the dry tree, sight to the blind eyes. Give light . . .'

He regretted everything bitterly. That Pitirakoghlu! Ah the dirty old scoundrel! It was all his fault if his life was in danger.

'Before I die, I'll kill that Pitirakoghlu,' he yelled into the darkness.

When he thought of death his fury against Pitirakoghlu grew stronger and stronger.

'You racketeer, why did you ever think of me? There I was settled quietly in Chukurova and making a living for myself as best I could. You've killed me for the sake of two dunums of land. You've killed me. What can I do? What can I do now? And that, Captain, after eating my bread and salt, after gorging himself on my lambs and butter and honey. He just stands in front of me now and laughs at my plight. You scoundrel Pitirakoghlu, d'you think I'll die without first wringing your thin, bird-like neck, and strangling the lies in your throat. It's because of you ... Everything is because of you!'

A little brook ran bubbling in front of him. Without noticing he stepped into the water, and again without noticing he crossed to the other side. The darkness was impenetrable.

'This night is interminable,' he said. 'Even the darkness won't let go of me. It'll never end ...'

He wandered on, not knowing or caring where he was going, lost in the darkness, full of trouble and anguish. In the end he found himself at the door of Lame Ali's house. There was still a light in the house, which meant that Lame Ali had not yet gone to sleep.

'That poor fellow goes in fear of his life, too,' he thought. 'I have brought misfortune upon him.'

He looked through a crack in the door. Ali was sitting in a corner, with his knees drawn up and his chin resting on them.

'Ali, my friend, Ali,' he said. Ali at once jumped up and opened the door.

'He'll kill us,' was the first thing Hamza said, 'He'll kill us. He's come back to the mountains on purpose to kill us!'

'He'll kill us,' said Ali, bowing his head, with the look of a man already dead and lost.

'He's come on purpose to kill me.'

'To kill us,' said Ali.

'If only I hadn't come back from Chukurova. I've brought trouble on you too, Ali ... On you too ... It was all Pitirakoghlu's fault. If only ...'

'Someone else would have been agha at the Plain of Thistles. Another one would have died,' said Ali.

'Another one ...' said Hamza.

'How did he give them the slip? They had him surrounded in the ravine, but he escaped. It was worse at Earless Ismail's mill, and still he escaped. He was only one man against a whole posse of police ...'

'Like a fish,' said Hamza. 'He slips through your fingers. He's like a bird; today he's here, and a little later he's in Chukurova. Like Swift Musa ... Faster than he.'

'Swift Musa says that man is faster than he is. "I've followed every trail," he says. "Birds, timid gazelles, yellow ants, centipedes. I've followed the trail of every living creature, but I couldn't follow this man's trail, or run him to earth," he says. There's something mysterious about this man.'

'What am I to do, Ali? Think of something. Think of something to save my life.'

'He'll kill us,' said Ali. 'Ah, he'll kill us. What can we do?'

'Let's escape somewhere. To some place where people don't know us.'

'He'll find us, he'll find us,' groaned Ali. 'If we crawl into a snake's hole, or take refuge under a bird's wing, he'll still find us. He'll kill both of us. He'll torture us and kill us. He'll destroy our homes and make our children orphans . . .'

'Can't the police kill him, or the aghas of Chukurova or Arif Saim Bey?'

'Nobody can kill him. He's bullet-proof. The only place where bullets can harm him is his eyes, they say. One day he was caught in a downpour on a mountain. Long Jabbar and Sergeant Rejep were with him too. They took shelter under a big tree. Thunderbolts struck the tree again and again, and it was enveloped in smoke. They ran off and took shelter under a rock near by. Lightning flashed about the tree, and it seemed to grow larger until it was enveloped in a ball of fire, so dazzling that no one could bear to look in that direction. Suddenly they saw Memed leap from the rock to the tree, just as a huge flash of lightning zigzagged over the tree. A moment later he was back with something in his hand which was about the size of a button, and which gave out a blinding light. Memed said, "This is the thunderstone. I have caught a thunderbolt." And he put it in his amulet. "Sergeant Rejep, fire a bullet at me," he said. Sergeant Rejep would not. "Sergeant, if you don't fire at me, I'll fire at you," he said, with an oath. The Sergeant saw that Memed would kill him, so what could he do? Memed stood there as a target, and kept on saying, "Come on, Sergeant." So, against his will, the Sergeant took aim, and saying to himself, "I don't want to kill that madman," he fired at his leg, shutting his eyes . . . when he opened them again, what did he see? There was Memed laughing at him. "I didn't hit him," he said, and fired again and again. He saw that when the bullets touched Memed's body they just bounced off and fell to the ground, leaving only a mark like a flea-bite. Memed said, "Sergeant, I caught the thunderbolt. And whoever carries this about him is proof against bullets." He hung the amulet round the Sergeant's neck and began to fire at him ... The bullets didn't touch the Sergeant either; they just scattered all around him.'

'It must be true,' said Hamza. 'Because if not, how could he possibly escape when he was encircled by so many policemen? It's true. He'll kill us. Isn't there any way to escape from this man, Ali? Suppose we begged and pleaded with him, suppose we fell at his feet ...'

'He'll kill us.'

'Is there no way of escape?'

'Yes,' said Ali. 'There's a slight hope. A ray of hope as big as a needle's eye.'

'What's that?' said Hamza, reviving a little.

'It's Mother Hürü. If Mother Hürü went to Memed and asked him to forgive Hamza, perhaps he would spare you. Maybe Mother Hürü will speak to Memed on your behalf, but not on mine ... She'd die rather than open her mouth on my behalf.'

'Then let's go to her straightaway. Let her get him to spare me. The rest is easy. I'll offer Memed one of my villages, and get him to forgive you too. Come on, come on, quickly, let's go,' said Hamza.

At Mother Hürü's house, they knocked gently on the door.

'Just a minute, my child,' called Hürü, 'just a minute my valiant one, I'm coming. I'm just lighting a torch. I heard, I heard you'd put those infidels to flight. The wounded ones groaned at my door for three days. They're all saying that bullets can't touch you. Why didn't you tell Hürü, so that I could have slept sound, slept peacefully. I couldn't sleep a wink, while you were roving about in the mountains ... Why didn't you tell your Mother?'

She opened the door, but no sooner had she opened it than she cried out 'Who's that?' and shut it again, the pine-torch in her hand falling to the ground. As she picked it up again, she yelled, 'Who are you?'

Lame Ali said into Hamza's ear,

'You do the talking; don't mention me.'

'It's Hamza, Hamza Agha,' said Hamza.

'You scoundrel,' said Hürü, 'what right have you got to call yourself an agha? Call yourself a dog first, for you're not a man; after you've been a dog, you might become an agha! What do you want at this hour of the night?'

'I want to talk to you a little, Mother.'

'I have nothing to talk to you about. You, my husband's murderer! You tyrant, with your hands steeped in blood . . . Get away from my door.'

'I have something to tell you. It's urgent.'

'Get away from my door! I don't want to see your dirty face. The children are dying of starvation and it's your fault. I don't want to see your accursed face.'

'Please forgive me, Mother.'

'Get away from my door, you dog. It's you who left the villagers without a morsel of bread!'

'I beseech you, open the door.'

'Be off with you, Bald Hamza. I won't open the door. There are ten thousand, thirteen thousand, sixteen thousand, a thousand thousand people in the great Taurus Mountains for whom we have become a laughing-stock, and it's all your fault.'

'Look, Mother, I have something to tell you, I have some news for you. When you hear it you'll be glad, you'll be crazy with happiness. You'll be absolutely crazy.'

'Get away from my door, Bald Hamza. You shall never cross this threshold with your blood-stained feet and your shameless body. Take yourself off, get away from here. Keep your news to yourself. Even if you brought me to life again, even if you promised me the whole world, I wouldn't want your news. I wouldn't look at your face, you filthy wretch, if you killed me . . .'

Hamza begged and pleaded. Mother Hürü kept on saying, 'Go away!' and would not say anything else. Hamza and Lame Ali stayed there by Mother Hürü's wall till morning.

As soon as the first light came up over the village, she opened the door, and recognizing Lame Ali, who was with Bald Hamza, she cried out,

'So you're frightened to death, are you? You're terrified of Memed, are you?'

Hamza jumped up and seized her hands in his:

'Mother, it's not my fault. Tell Memed not to kill me. I'll buy you three dresses, ten dresses. As many as you like. I'll buy you some gold ear-rings too. I'll buy you ten gold pieces too, for your head-dress.'

Mother Hürü snatched away her hands with loathing.

'Go about your business, Bald One,' she said. 'Get out of my way! So I'm to be a bride, am I? I'm to dress up in the things you bring me, like a bride, am I? So I'm to dance by Durmush Ali's tomb, am I?'

She turned to Ali, and laughed shrilly,

'You're frightened to death, aren't you? You're frightened to death. Memed's got nothing to do with me. I can't see him. Even if I did, I couldn't make him listen to me. Lame Ali knows that if Memed had listened to me, Ali wouldn't be here now, he'd be rotting away in his grave. Get off, and go about your business, children, be off with you. I have nothing for you. I'm not going to give you any help. Not the very least . . .'

She locked her door and went into the village, leaving Ali and Hamza there, rooted to the spot.

After that morning, Mother Hürü roamed about the village in a whirl of anger. She looked at everyone in the village with hatred. Everyone who met Mother Hürü bowed his head and could not look her in the face.

All the people in the five villages of the Plain of Thistles heard how Hamza and Lame Ali had gone to Mother Hürü's door and stayed pleading with her all night. The news spread gradually all over the Taurus, passed on in frightened whispers.

Mother Hürü had not opened her door to them and had said,

'Get away from this door, you dogs. If Slim Memed doesn't kill you, I will. I'll strangle you with my bare hands. I was waiting for this day to come, you scoundrels. This happy day. Do you understand? Creatures like the tiger of the Red Rock, the Ahjasaz dragon, the snakes of Snake Castle, the vampires of The Forty Springs, they can all cross my thereshold – but not you! If Memed doesn't kill you very soon, I claim the right to kill you myself. Myself, do you understand?'

The peasants repeated Mother Hürü's words, merely exaggerating what she had said, but not putting any interpretation on them, either good or bad. From the tone of their voices, and the expression on their faces, no conclusion could be drawn. Or rather, they did not know what attitude to adopt in the face of what was happening.

40

BLACK IBRAHIM's body too was thrown over a bare-backed horse and brought to the town. It was buried in the graveyard there.

The town where the plain ended stood at the foot of the mountains, in the entrance to a valley. To the west there was a bare hill below which flowed the clear waters of Savrun brook. A bridge over the brook, made of white limestone, looked like a pretty toy bridge stuck on a green and blue background. The quarter which the Armenians had occupied had begun to fall into decay after they left. It was now occupied by Kurds who had migrated from Eastern Anatolia and who took no interest in the happenings of the town. From the earth-roofed Armenian houses there now came a constant clamour of Kurdish cries. Every evening without fail the Kurds fell upon each other with sticks and stones; arms were broken, heads were split open, and their shouting filled the whole town. The townspeople had got used to these fights.

Big olive trees and fig trees stood parched in the heat and dust of the old Armenian quarter and there were pomegranate groves where long black snakes in the mating season would turn as fiery red as iron in a forge.

When the pomegranate flowers were in bloom the whole quarter looked gay. Swarms of bees, butterflies and red snakes rioted all over the garden until the trees shed their flowers.

Every afternoon, like a grey cloud over the town, a swelling, spreading, suffocating dust-cloud formed. The inside of houses and shops, people's clothes, and the white streets paved with big pebbles were covered with a thick layer of dust. When seen from

300

a distance, the town, with its red roofs, its pomegranate trees in bloom, its olive, fig and plane-trees, its panes of glass in the windows, its bridge and pennyroyal meadows, appeared wrapped in an unbroken whiteness.

The people, their noses and mouths full of dust, continually talked and slandered one another. Officials, aghas and beys would sit in Nazifoghlu's restaurant, drinking hard and letting their tongues go. The less well-to-do people, tradesmen or craftsmen would sit in Tevfik's café drinking tea. There were also the peasants walking idly round the market-place.

Everybody knew everything about everybody else. Nothing could ever be kept a secret in that town. By now probably thousands of people had discussed the struggle between Arif Saim Bey and Idris. They also followed every detail of the struggle between Ali Safa Bey and Vayvay, and awaited the outcome of the two battles with great excitement. One day Arif Saim Bey had driven his wife's brother into the thornbush and whipped him to death, together with some Circassians who refused to give up their land. No one knew the reason why he had killed his brother-in-law. Some people said he had felt sorry for the Circassians and had tried to stop Arif Saim Bey who had turned upon him and let him have it. Other people said there was a woman in the case. They invented all sorts of reasons. But there was only one thing certain and that was that the young man had lost his life among the thorn-bushes under the lash of Arif Saim Bey's whip.

What would Ali Safa Bey do to the Vayvay villagers after this? What method of intimidation would he use now? Some said one thing, some said another. And they discussed very animatedly what he would do, and how the villagers would react.

Everyone was amazed at the way in which the peasants had behaved recently, and none of the townspeople ventured on any interpretation of these events for several days. The burning of Ali Safa Bey's grain, and the theft of the horses were new kinds of behaviour. The peasants had neither strength nor traditions to encourage them to take such action. What on earth had happened?

That Slim Memed had returned to the mountains recently was a strange business too. From what had been seen of brigands before this, they would take themselves off after they had got what they wanted, and having once disappeared would never come back to the mountains again. Years later a few of them might come back, but they would have lost all their prestige, and even the toughest of them would get himself shot in four or five days, or at the most a fortnight. But this Slim Memed had descended on the mountains like an angry eagle. He had killed an experienced brigand like Black Ibrahim in the first skirmish, he had wounded a troop of police, and had again vanished into thin air.

Except for Ali Safa Bey, everyone was sure it was Memed who had revitalized the people of Vayvay and inspired them to resist. A lot of rumours were going round about Memed, but neither in Chukurova nor in the mountains had anyone but Sergeant Asim seen him. As for Sergeant Asim, he was Memed's man. He would not have touched him. Who knows, perhaps it wasn't Memed in the mountains, but someone else who was engaged in brigandage under the name of Memed. Yet who but Memed could fight like that, could drive a troop of police in front of him from the Taurus to Chukurova?

The police, having fled in disorder from the mountains, crowded into the town exhausted. 'What a time we've had!' they said in heartfelt tones.

'What we've had to put up with on account of that Slim Memed!'

Slim Memed had not attacked the police with five or ten men only . . . Hundreds sprang from every nook and cranny and fought alongside him. And he had a ball of lightning hung round his neck . . .

Ali Safa Bey shuttled backwards and forwards from Tevfik's café to Nazifoghlu's restaurant, from there to the police station, from there to the district governor's office, to the lawyer Politician Ahmet, from Politician Ahmet to the post office; and all the time the fear within him grew stronger and stronger. He simply could not find a reason for the peasants' revolt. He could not put his finger on anything, or find a really convincing reason. Slim Memed? That was most unlikely . . . But someone was interfering and it might well be Arif Saim Bey. Without Arif Saim Bey behind them, the peasants would have been incapable of doing all these things. 'Our peasants,' he said, 'would not have taken part in any movement without having some powerful backing. They don't trust

302

anybody. Least of all themselves . . . They wouldn't rely on a man like Slim Memed and burn my harvests, steal my horses and kill my followers. Friends, we must take great care. In my opinion the Government has begun to follow a new policy and the first move in the game is at my expense. Friends, let's take care, Arif Saim Bey is planning this business. Now I understand why he wanted to own a farm in Chukurova . . . What need has that sort of man for a farm or any other property? . . . The whole of Turkey is theirs, isn't it? Now it's clear why the men of the Republic want to be landlords . . . Now it's clear. The reason for seizing the olive groves of Mudanya, the reason for founding farms by the Aegean . . . Now it's clear. The Revolution is not yet over. The Republican leaders have dispersed throughout Anatolia on various pretexts. They are investigating. Then they'll come out with their final blow and make a master of the peasant. The Revolution is growing and spreading. This business has been contrived by Arif Saim Bey. Even Slim Memed is his creation.'

Those who were listening did not argue with him. They remained silent. Ali Safa Bey might be right. The Republic was intending to introduce certain innovations, that was plain. A wind of change and reform was blowing from Ankara.

In a few days' time Ali Safa Bey had convinced himself, and the men of property in the district, that Arif Saim Bey was the prime mover in all this business. But why was Arif Saim Bey doing it? Was there an order from above, or was he doing it on his own responsibility? They could not decide on this, but whispered one to the other, and stayed up all night talking, by the light of feeble oil-lamps.

Just about this time Arif Saim Bey arrived in the town. The townspeople, frightened, made themselves scarce. The men of property were terrified, and only dared to come into his presence in an attitude of humble respect. Arif Saim Bey was not slow to perceive the air of depression and fear in the town.

'Slim Memed?' he said with a laugh. 'He's only a poor child. What makes people so scared, so terrified of him? Our Republic is very powerful. With a flick of its fingers it can annihilate not one Slim Memed, but thousands of Slim Memeds. Don't take any notice, my good men.'

303

Among those present was a certain Murtaza Agha.

'Flies are not dirty, but they upset one's stomach,' he said. 'This Slim Memed is of no importance, but he puts the donkey in mind of the water-melon rind. He incites the peasants and sets them against us. He stirs the peasants up to rebellion, against the aghas, the beys and our protectors, the Government. It was from him that the peasants learnt to steal the aghas' horses, to burn their harvests and to kill their men. If you are honestly organizing a real farm, well . . . it's us today and you tomorrow . . .'

'And what d'you think I'm organizing?' Arif Saim Bey interrupted him in thunderous tones.

'That is to say . . . I mean . . . perhaps it's a means of investigating, a screen for other activities . . .'

'What? Are you mad? I've poured money into that place. Do you think I'm playing at farming?'

'Well, I meant to say . . . Forgive me, sir, you mistook me . . . I did not mean . . .'

'Murtaza Agha can never express himself properly,' said the others.

'God forbid!' said Ali Safa Bey. 'Your farm will be the most modern one in the world. Throughout the centuries this noble service of yours will be praised as much as your heroism in the War of Independence.'

Glancing pityingly at big Murtaza Agha, who had withdrawn to a corner, Arif Saim Bey said,

'I thank you, Ali Safa Bey. I thank you for those kind and generous words. So what did you mean, Murtaza Agha?'

Murtaza Agha jumped up, came to the Bey and kissed his shoulder.

'With all due respect,' he said. 'Saving your presence . . . I meant to say just what Ali Safa said . . . That is to say we know . . . that is to say he told us . . . I mean . . .'

Again he became tongue-tied and crimson with embarrassment.

The others were amused at the state Murtaza Agha had got into.

In order to calm him down, Arif Saim Bey said,

'Don't upset yourself, Murtaza Bey, I understood what you meant.'

'I'm very glad you did,' said Murtaza. 'It would have been

terrible if you hadn't. I should have been distressed, annihilated. If you had misunderstood me, it would have killed me, and ruined my home and family. I salute you, Bey. I kiss your hands.'

He went and sat down quietly in his place. He made a vow never to speak to irascible statesmen again. 'When you say one thing they hear another,' he said to himself. 'If only that bastard Ali Safa Bey had not been there; how he twisted my words!'

Arif Saim Bey left the elders of the town in some consternation. As soon as he had gone, their anxieties and fears went on growing. Why had Arif Saim Bey come to the town? There must have been a reason, that's for sure!

Hamza Agha too was in a pitiful condition. He had come down from the mountains and roved around the town, trying to find some corner to hide in, some place of refuge to save his life. He went backwards and forwards between the lawyer, the scribe Fethi Bey, and Mad Fahri, and every day he sent telegrams to Ankara, and spent money lavishly in the market. With Lame Ali at his heels, he spent his day at the post office, pouring out his woes to every corner.

'He'll kill me, that infidel. It was because of me he came out of his hiding-place, and went back to the mountains. What am I to do? Give me your advice, my good friends. What am I to do? What did I do, what did I do to my villagers? They were leaderless and I came to be their leader. I didn't harm a hair of their heads. They loved me, they simply loved me; you should see how much they loved me. And then he, that jealous man, heard this; he heard that the villagers loved me like a father, like a friend, like their children, so he came out of the hole where he had been hiding. He doesn't like the peasants. He's their bitter enemy. My goodness, he's against our aghas. Even against the Government! I know, he says, what I'm going to do to the Government! He hates the peasants, he doesn't want them to be happy and that's why he will kill me. Because I treat the peasants well. Now that I'm the Agha, the peasants live off the fat of the land. It is because of his hostility towards the peasants that he will kill me . . .'

Lame Ali, standing behind him, tearfully echoed his words.

'He will kill him,' he said, 'that infidel will kill our Agha. And me too . . .'

One day the *Vali** of the Province came to the town. He called a meeting of the men of property and Government officials at Hadji Halil Agha's house, and made a speech. He spoke about the telegrams that had been sent to Ankara. Such a thing must definitely not happen again. Ankara was very angry about these telegrams.

'I'll bombard this town,' shouted the Vali. 'I'll send you all into exile. A long way away. This Slim Memed, this upstart . . . I want you to hand him over to me. You will capture him. If the aghas did not protect them, none of these brigands could live in the mountains. Do you understand?'

Again Murtaza Agha rose to his feet and spoke up,

'We understand, but these brigands live in the mountains without our protection. We do not protect Slim Memed. As God is my witness, we do not. Up to now we thought the same. We thought that without our protection brigands could not survive in the mountains. Your Honour, come and see; we are amazed; he is living, he is surviving, very much so! Spoiling the reputation of the town. He's living. He'll kill all of us,' he said. Then he became tongue-tied and broke out into a sweat.

'What is your name?' asked the Vali.

'Murtaza Agha.'

'You're a frank, manly fellow. Tell me then of a way to capture this Slim Memed.'

'Your Honour, whether he's caught or not, that son of a bitch, the harm's been done. The wolf has now had a taste of blood. And the donkey's been put in mind of the water-melon rind. After this, we can expect no good from these peasants, neither we, nor the Government. And all on account of this Slim Memed.'

'I like people to be as frank as you,' said the Vali.

'I believe in doing one's duty,' boasted Murtaza. 'I am always frank and open, like a spindle . . .'

'Come and sit down beside me.'

Murtaza went and took up a position on the divan near him, his hands on his knees.

'Your Honour,' he said, 'I'd like to tell you one more story, and then I'll go off to my work.'

* A *Vali* is a provincial governor.

'Tell it then,' said the Vali. 'I shall be glad to hear it.'

'It's about Slim Memed. I hope it will be acceptable and not offend anyone. A snake must be crushed while it is small. Slim Memed has grown big. Perhaps the brigand who has recently sprung up in the mountains is not the original Slim Memed. We'll never be able to kill Slim Memed now. Slim Memed won't die. Just a minute, let me explain. Do you know the snake, the big snake? Do you know how it can be killed?'

'No,' said the Vali.

'If you crush its head with a stone, you can kill it. That's one way! Then if you strangle the snake, that's a second way. You can shoot it, that's a third! There are all sorts of ways in which the snake may die ... Through sickness, through being eaten by a stork, this way or that way. But do you know how else it can die?'

The Vali was enjoying this chat with Murtaza.

'How else?'

'How else can it die, you ask. Well listen, Your Honour. If a snake is wounded just a tiny wound, no bigger than the point of a needle ... If a person or an animal gets a tiny scratch, what happens? Nothing happens, you don't think about it, it gets better at once. And yet if a snake is wounded, however tiny the wound, it dies. How can it die, you will say, and if you never saw it, you can't know about it. I do. When a snake is wounded, even if it is only a tiny scratch, the yellow ants swarm over the wound. In one day they eat the snake and finish it off. Do you understand now, Your Honour?'

The Vali looked him in the eye thoughtfully.

'Yes,' he said, 'Finish your story.'

'Well, Slim Memed is the tiny wound that has been inflicted on the snake.'

'Yes.'

'You see, Your Honour, Slim Memed killed Abdi Agha, he distributed his land among the peasants, and inflicted this wound. Now the yellow ants are attacking the body. Whether Slim Memed lives or dies, neither we nor the Government can turn back the clock. We cannot avoid trouble for ourselves. The peasants are like yellow ants, stupid and blundering ... But nevertheless, if a tiny wound is caused somewhere, they consume the whole. So on

307

account of this Slim Memed they will consume us, first one by one, and then the lot. Both you and us, Your Honour. I am a peasant and I know the peasants through and through, sir. You are clever, very clever people, and highly educated. In my whole life, as they well know, I was never afraid of anything, and yet I'm terrified of this Slim Memed. Alive or dead . . .'

'You're exaggerating, Murtaza Bey.'

'All right, if you like to think so, Your Honour. I count myself dead already. The yellow ants have begun to crawl over my body.'

'You're exaggerating.'

Murtaza Agha began to shout and gesticulate:

'By God, by God, all that has happened to Ali Safa Bey is due to Slim Memed. It's the work of the yellow ants . . . Whatever Ali Safa Bey says, whatever he thinks, it's the work of the yellow ants.'

'Murtaza Agha, you seem to be in mortal fear,' said Ali Safa Bey. 'You're exaggerating, you're imagining this poor boy to be much more important than he is.'

'Listen to me,' said Murtaza. He was soaked with sweat and the veins of his neck had swelled. 'Listen to me. Very soon all the farms will be burnt, all the aghas will be killed, all our possessions will have been looted, you'll see. Take it from me. Yes, yellow ants . . .'

They talked together and laughed together till evening, and came to an agreement. The Vali would have no telegrams about brigands sent from the town to Ankara, nor any petition or letters. The aghas assured him that such a thing would not happen again.

'And don't make out that poor boy to be any more significant than he is,' said the Vali. 'This country has experience of many great brigands. In the Taurus we have had Gizik Duran, Black Snake, Yozjuyu, Jotdelek, and Kurdish Reshit. Very soon Slim Memed's corpse will be dragged through the streets of this town.'

He got into his motor-car and left the town in a cloud of dust.

That very evening the District Governor summoned Hamza Agha:

'You will at once go to your village, and you will not come to the town again in the near future. You're ruining the morale of this town. What do you think you're doing, sending telegrams to Ankara every day, pestering our superiors! No more telegrams of any kind must be sent to Ankara.'

Hamza was quite worn out.

'But he'll kill me. Your Honour, he'll kill me. Ah, where am I to go? He'll kill me.'

The Governor nodded, sharing Hamza's distress.

'He'll kill you,' he said. 'I know. He came out of hiding on purpose to kill you. I know, but what can I do? Our Government is still very weak. I know but . . . The Vali promised to catch him, but I don't think he will, my dear sir, my dear friend Hamza Bey . . . You must resign yourself, return to your village, and wait. Maybe by some miracle . . .'

'Oh, he'll kill me . . .'

That day Hamza mounted his horse, and with Lame Ali behind him, set out for the mountains.

It was afternoon. The town was enveloped in a cloud of dust, and yellowish dust swirled towards the mountains.

The bees were clustering on the red, dusty pomegranate flowers. On an ancient pomegranate tree there was the body of a big butterfly, and thousands of yellow ants were making their way towards it . . .

It was very hot.

41

'OLD OSMAN salutes the hawk.'

With his pipe in his mouth and his right hand on his revolver, Old Osman roamed around the village like a youth, saying a few words to everyone he met, and patting them on the head.

'Old Osman salutes Memed,' he said, 'he salutes the prowling wolf, salutes the hawk. He salutes the one who gives life to the withered tree, who makes it bring forth leaves. Old Osman salutes Memed.'

The village joined in Old Osman's rejoicing:

'Vayvay salutes Memed. All the Anavarza plain and the villages of Chukurova salute Memed!'

The fact that Vayvay had paid Ali Safa Bey back in his own coin, by burning his harvests and stealing his horses, had given new life to the whole of the Anavarza plain. Before long even Muslu would believe that Memed had done everything. Stories, tales, legends and songs about Memed again began to circulate.

'Heaven knows why,' said Old Osman and Ferhat Hodja. 'These peasants are absolutely incomprehensible! Our hawk is on everybody's lips from morning till night, but neither the Government nor a single agha or bey hears about it. Is it possible?'

Ferhat Hodja and Old Osman could not believe that these talkative villagers could keep a secret so well. The villagers themselves hardly believed it of one another. If the police had arrested any peasant and flayed him or gouged out his eyes, they would not have got a single word out of him.

'People are strange,' said Old Osman. 'Sometimes you can't trust them to look after a fly, but at other times you put your life in their hands and they guard it with their own.'

There was another thing that made the peasants delirious with joy. Every night just at midnight Ali Safa Bey's farmhouse was fired upon, just as Vayvay village had been.

Sefché the Warden said,

'He'll run away. Ali Safa will leave his farm and flee from the plain of Anavarza.'

The police and Ali Safa Bey's men stayed on guard every night, yet on the stroke of midnight shots were fired at the farmhouse. It was not clear in the darkness where they came from and the men who fired the bullets disappeared as if the ground had swallowed them up. Ali Safa Bey was petrified with terror. He went three times to Arif Saim Bey and told him what was happening. Arif Saim Bey listened and merely smiled.

'The peasants are in a state of rebellion,' said Ali Safa Bey. 'Open rebellion. They are preparing a counter-revolutionary movement.'

Arif Saim Bey again smiled.

'The peasants cannot rise in rebellion. Turkish peasants are incapable of it,' he answered. 'They can't rebel. They have no such tradition.'

Ali Safa Bey wanted to cry out, 'And what about my burnt harvests, my stolen horses, and my farmhouse being raided every night? If it is not the Turkish peasants doing these things, is it you, Arif Saim Bey? The peasants are drawing strength from some important source. They are leaning against some very stout bulwark. Otherwise I'm absolutely certain that they wouldn't have dared to do a single one of the things they have done. You may be providing them with that strength, Arif Saim Bey. Or maybe it is the Pasha. Or maybe it is the agents of the Secret Police.' But he did not dare say this.

He was greatly alarmed. His face, which was as dark as if smeared with soot, was covered with beads of sweat. He was in a continual state of worry, and sweated continually. He had sent several men to the villages, telling them to find out the truth of the matter and report back to him. But none of them had been able to bring back any rational explanation.

'The Forty Holy Men came down from their mountain, set fire to Ali Safa Bey's harvests, mounted their horses and rode away. Seven of them remained behind, and at midnight every night they throw stones at Ali Safa Bey's farmhouse, and then vanish into the blue.'

Ali Safa Bey was mad with anger.

'Rubbish!' he shouted. 'Soon, very soon, I shall discover who is firing at my house, who stole my horses, who burnt my harvest; I shall find it out very soon and make it public. I shall prove who is inciting the peasants to rebel, and then I shall go to Ankara. They'll see. If holy men shooting up my house isn't a counter-revolutionary movement, what is? I shall ask in Ankara, yes, I shall. Did we save the fatherland for this? We thought we had driven invisible people who raid houses into the sea, together with the enemy. I shall ask, I shall ask them all about it.'

What was it that had happened to him? He went to Kozan, Osmaniye, Jeyhan, and Payas, talking his misfortunes over with other aghas and asking them why it was. Nobody could say anything reassuring. Only one agha, Kurdish Ali, an old Turcoman chief who had a farm at Jeyhanbekirli said something clearly to him.

'Ali Safa, my son,' he said. 'You oppressed the peasants a lot. Put a kitten in a room, torment it continually and in the end the kitten will scratch out your eye. And whereas a kitten is a kitten, a man is not a kitten. The more frightened he is, the braver he is. Don't look for any other reason, there you have it.'

Ali Safa Bey did not believe this either. Because he knew the peasants like the palm of his hand. The tighter your hold on them, the more they cringe. He did not tell Kurdish Ali this. Without powerful support behind them, Turkish peasants would not have rebelled in this fashion.

As time passed without his finding a reason for the peasants' resistance, he got more and more angry. He would mount his horse and ride from one village to the other. Seated stiffly on his horse in the middle of the village, he would harangue the peasants.

'I shall make them sweat blood in Vayvay village! Blood!' and spurring on his horse, he rode at full speed over the Anavarza plain in a whirl of anger.

'Even among those animals there's some concord, those peasants who raid my house every night and who've risen in rebellion, but among ourselves there's no unity at all. None of the landowners or the Government asks, how are you getting on, Ali Safa Bey? They've thrown me to the wolves. Today it's me, tomorrow it will be them, won't it? They'll see! If I'm defeated, they'll see . . . All Chukurova will be plundered.'

He was continually racking his brains, cooking up something nasty to be done to the peasants. He went on inventing new and unheard-of means of intimidation.

The peasants were well aware of Ali Safa Bey's confusion, perplexity and helplessness.

'Old Osman's wonderful hawk . . . The apple of my eye, my brave hero, the admiration of the world, the light of Mohammed . . .'

People came to Old Osman's house from faraway villages by night or day, hoping to see him.

'No, he's not here,' said Old Osman. 'He is a hawk with strong wings. He came and perched for a moment in the Anavarza desert, and then flew away . . . A flat plain is no place for a hawk or a falcon! He has withdrawn to the crags. Congratulations to anyone who finds him. Hail to the mother who bore him, to the eye that saw him, to the path that he trod, to the spring from which he drank, to the sunbeams that fell upon him, to the rain that rained upon him, to the sun that rose and to the night that enveloped him . . .'

And the people, with drooping heads, and all their desires still pent up within them, returned to their villages.

Only one, Yellow Sefer, did not go away. 'I'm going to see him, I'm going to see the hawk,' he insisted; he had been sitting waiting on Old Osman's doorstep for three days.

Yellow Sefer was a young orphan from Narlikishla who worked here and there. He had cracked lips, grey eyelashes, and hair that stood on end like a hedgehog's spines; he appeared to be nineteen or twenty years old.

'I'm going to see him,' he said. 'I'm fed up with my life. If he'll accept me I'll join his band.'

Old Osman did all he could, but Sefer would not leave the doorstep.

'Don't drive me away, Osman Agha; I'm so tired of my life, it's such a dead-and-alive existence, that either I shall die once and for all, or I shall see him.'

'You won't see him,' shouted Old Osman. 'He's not here.'

One night Mad Muslu, spattered with mud, appeared at Old Osman's. They summoned Ferhat Hodja too. Ferhat threw his arms round Muslu and hugged him. He also embraced Süleyman and Ahmet.

'You have done well, my children,' he said . . . 'You are blessed and nearer God.'

He asked about Zeynel. They said nothing at all about Zeynel. Everyone in the village, even Zeynel's wife, was glad that he had disappeared from their midst.

'Zeynel would have told Ali Safa Bey and the Government that the hawk had come down to Chukurova,' said Old Osman. 'Not today, or tomorrow, but the day after tomorrow. He wouldn't have been able to keep the secret.'

Muslu said he wanted to see Memed.

'He's in a bad way, Muslu,' Ferhat Hodja told him. 'The sad state of his village completely overwhelmed him. He's not himself at all, his wits are still wandering. It would be better for you not to see him.'

'I simply must see him,' insisted Muslu. 'It's out of the question for me to go away without seeing him, I must see why he is in that state.'

'All right,' said Old Osman. 'Perhaps Muslu has something to ask him. Isn't it my hawk who gave his hand to Muslu, who drew Muslu like the thunderbolt on to Ali Safa Bey's head?'

They discussed things until morning. For this reason at midnight that night Ali Safa Bey's house was not raided.

Eventually Ferhat Hodja gave way.

'Come back again in five or six days and Mother Kamer and Seyran will take you to him,' he said. 'They're looking after the hawk, and treating his wound. Perhaps in five or six days his wound will be better and the boy will be more like his old self. But I'm very worried about the state he's in. I didn't like the look of him at all.'

'Nothing can happen to him,' said Muslu.

All the Anavarza villages were waiting as one man to see what Ali Safa Bey would do. He was not the man to take all this lying down. What reprisals would he take? Ferhat Hodja asked Muslu about this.

'Whatever Ali Safa Bey does as a reprisal, *he* will take ten times, a hundred times as much. Now we have him near us in our village,' he thundered.

The heat of summer lay heavy over the countryside, and mosquitoes filled the evening air with their buzzing. Most of the village children, and half of the grown-ups were suffering from fever. In the yellow heat, the peasants lay on the ground, which was as hot as burning coals, and from morning to night they shivered and shook. But even the fever did not affect them quite as it did every year. While they burnt, while they shivered, their newly-found pride never left them. News reached them every day from Ali Safa Bey's mansion. The news spread in a trice from Vayvay all over the Anavarza plain. They did not know where he had gone, or where he was staying, but they invariably received some news of him. At one moment you might hear that he had attacked the house of some tyrant on Kayranli mountain; then again you might hear that he had driven a whole posse of police in front of him from Hachin Mountains to Chukurova.

Meanwhile Idris Bey came to the village two or three times. After the fight at Anavarza he came down only at night to Chukurova, like a wolf.

'I simply must see the hawk,' he insisted.

Old Osman asked Ferhat about this.

'Impossible,' Ferhat objected. 'Certainly not; this man cannot see the hawk. He's completely unknown to us, and on top of that he's a bey himself.'

'If he were an evil man, an agha, a bey, or a Government man, would the villagers have trusted him? Would they have told Idris Bey that the hawk was in the plain? This man is a good, friendly soul. He should see him,' said Osman, disagreeing with Ferhat. 'He is a good man, a sincere man. Perhaps he has something to say to my hawk.'

But Ferhat Hodja was adamant: 'That man will not see Memed. Do you understand, Osman Agha? We have no proof of what he is. He must have learnt his whereabouts from some stupid villager.'

And to Idris Bey he said,

'We haven't seen him, and we don't know where he is. Surely he would not be mad enough to come down to the plain. He is roving about in the mountains.'

Idris Bey did not believe him, but he mounted his horse and rode away into the night.

*

Old Selver, whom they called Selver Gelin, the Bride, had a grandson in the village of Endel. He was everything to her and all winter long she would save and hoard for him. The largest pomegranates, the juiciest melons and water-melons, sweetmeats from Marash, dried mulberries, grapes, anything she could lay her hands on was for her grandson. She also possessed a large beehive which yielded an abundance of honey each year. Everyone raised bees, but Selver Gelin's bees were different, fatter, and more brightly coloured; her honey was lighter and clearer and smelt of heather.

She had cut the honey, drained the combs and filled up a large patterned firkin, and was waiting impatiently for the day when she would take it to her grandson. The firkin hung on the wall and she watched it with pleasurable anticipation. It was the same each year. She would never even taste the honey which was destined for him.

But this year something disturbed her. The firkin hung there on the wall and somehow her hand would not go to it. She could not make up her mind to take it down and go to her grandson.

Then one morning she went resolutely to the firkin and un-hooked it. In her chest she had stored mountain apples, pears, dried figs and raisins, mulberries and sweetmeats. She emptied everything into an embroidered sack and took it straight to Old Osman.

'Here Osman,' she said. 'I've thought and thought and I've decided not to take these to my grandson this year. I simply couldn't do it. You give them to our hawk. He's suffered so much, gone hungry and cold up on those wild mountains, poor thing. He's still young, but all dried up and stunted. If he's fed properly he'll grow yet. Take these to him and tell him it's all his as his mother's milk. Tell him Selver Gelin sends it, that she'd do anything for him, will you?'

Old Osman proudly stroked the brightly patterned firkin of honey.

'I will,' he answered. 'I'll tell him that my beautiful Selver Gelin sends you all this so that you should eat and get strong again. So that you should be like a mountain and that people should be afraid of you. The hawk's small too, a brave bird that won't give up its prey, but still, you try and get bigger, I'll say. Selver Gelin's a sensible woman, I'll say, and that's what she wants.'

'Yes, tell him just that,' said Selver gravely.

Old Osman stroked the firkin.

'What a beautiful design you have made, Selver,' he said. 'It's bright and shiny. You've put the whole world, you've put Paradise into this firkin. Congratulations.'

On the dark background of the firkin there was a large hand-painted blue gun. Near it there was a hand, slightly clenched.

'Osman salutes the hawk, his child, his lion, his hero, the light

316

of his eyes, the hope of the world,' he said. 'And the design drawn
by a beautiful hand . . .'

Selver the Bride was delighted that Old Osman had understood.
'Selver also salutes . . .' she said.

42

TOWARDS the upper end of the Ahjasaz marshes the pebbly bed
of Savrun widened; then the stream, trickling gently over the
pebbles, divided into two, leaving a sand-bordered island in the
middle. It descended towards the Ahjasaz marshland, and passing
under clumps of bushes mingled with the bubbling mud of the
marshes. All the plants were a brilliant green. The north side of
the island towards the marshes was screened by a curtain of
ancient willow-trees. To the south there were thick clumps of
alders, sedge and reeds. To the east, in the place where the island
began, there rose a small group of plane-trees. The stream had
gradually built a heap of pebbles at the foot of them. To the west
were marshes, as far as the eye could see . . . The thickets were a
paradise for birds. Every day of the year a different species of bird
thronged the trees in the thickets. There were hundreds of varieties,
both large and small. In the morning before daybreak, when it was
just beginning to get light, thousands of birds suddenly began to
sing. The birds perched in the thicket like a cloud, and rose into
the sky like a storm-cloud.

This island belonged to Seyfali. From his grandfather and
father onwards his family had cultivated a melon-garden here.
The largest water-melons and the most honeyed melons in
Chukurova were grown in the silt of the island. There were also
peonies, perhaps the largest in the world, and sweet basil as big as
bushes. In the summer heat the scents would be perceived from
far away. Halil had been the caretaker of this melon-garden for
six years. A beardless man had come to see Seyfali one day. He
was tall, slightly bent forward, his head tucked in between his

317

shoulders; he had protruding eyes, no eyelashes and no eyebrows; his age was uncertain, and his face was puckered.

'I'm sick of this life, friend Seyfali Agha,' he had said. 'Let me be a caretaker in that melon-garden of yours. If you let me, you'll be doing a good deed. I know that the caretakers can only put up with three years there, and then they kick the bucket. The poisonous marsh fever accounts for the gardeners one by one.'

'Very well, my friend,' Seyfali had said, and had given the job that year to Beardless Halil.

Beardless Halil had not died, he had not even caught the marsh fever. To those who wondered about it, he said, 'I have obtained a magic talisman against the mosquitoes,' and he would show them the big, painted amulet hanging round his neck.

Beardless Halil came every spring for the planting of the garden, and every autumn, when the plants died down, he would leave. No one knew where he came from or where he went to.

On the third day after Memed's arrival in the village, Seyfali went down to the melon-garden.

'Halil, my friend,' he said. 'Can I entrust to you my life, my possessions, my honour and my good name? Can I entrust to you the treasure of a multitude of poor peasants?'

Halil at once guessed what was afoot, and began to laugh.

'There's no need for a long speech about it, he's my treasure too, and the light of my eyes,' he said. 'While I, sinful creature that I am, am still above ground, not a hair of his head shall be harmed by any trickery. I will make such a shelter for him that no man will see or find it.'

They said no more. That night Memed slept peacefully in the cool of a spacious trellised hut that had been contrived in the branches of two willow-trees. Beardless Halil had interwoven reeds, making something that looked like a mosquito screen. He had made air-holes in the reed mosquito-screen in such a way that it was cool inside and the mosquitoes could not get in. And although a whole cloud of mosquitoes was buzzing outside, not a single one penetrated inside the reed screen. This was the reason why Halil had never caught the fever in six years.

There was a moon and Halil could not sleep that night. He listened all the time to Memed's breathing and pondered deeply on the hazards that this fragile little man had faced. Here he was now, wounded, tired, oblivious of everything . . .

In this refuge Beardless Halil did what he could to help Kamer, Seyran, Ferhat and Osman to treat Memed's wound. The plants, flowers and aromatic gums that Mother Kamer needed for salves, he found for her in the reed-bed, on the Anavarza crags, or in the mountains. Without Halil, Kamer's and Seyran's salves could not have begun to cure Memed's wound before a fortnight had passed. As his wound began to heal, Memed became more and more reserved; he did not talk to anyone, or even look at them. If Halil, Mother Kamer or Seyran asked him anything, he did not hear, did not see, did not answer. He ate the food they set before him tremendously fast, without seeming to see it or to notice the flavour. After eating his meal, he would go and lie down in a cleft roofed with sweet-smelling myrtle branches, which Halil had made for him like a tunnel. When he emerged from this shelter, he staggered dazedly about the garden or waded in Savrun brook, stumbling over the stones or the dry stalks of the melons.

To those who asked what was the matter with him – Seyran, Mother Kamer, Old Osman, and Ferhat Hodja, Beardless Halil said,

'He is possessed by an evil spirit. I have seen lots of men who were possessed and they were exactly like this one. Exactly . . . In our village there was a man called Freckled Mustafa, and one night . . .'

And then he would relate, in great detail, the story of Freckled Mustafa, and of how the djinn had cast a spell on him. The djinns were having a celebration, and while they were feasting Mustafa pissed on top of them – how should he know – and so the djinn sent him out of his wits. Halil swore that Memed, when in the mountains or in some cave, had pissed on top of the djinn. No hodja or doctor could cure him. Only the djinn he had thus offended could make him better if they decided to be merciful.

Old Osman's eyes flashed, and with one hand on the handle of his revolver, and the other on Beardless Halil's neck, he shouted,

'See here, Beardless. I swear by my mother and my wife I'll kill you. If you tell any man that he's possessed by the djinn, I'll have your blood.'

Beardless Halil said coolly,

'Would I ever do such a thing, Uncle Osman? Would I ever say it and destroy the people's enthusiasm? If the peasants heard that he is in this state, they would lose heart and run away. Of course it can't be told to anyone. Ohhoo, Uncle, you don't need to tell me that! Beardless Halil is too old a bird to be caught with chaff.'

One day Beardless Halil asked Seyran for a big cauldron, a cake of soap and a set of new underwear. The next day Seyran brought what had been asked for. The soap was pink and scented. It had been brought in her bundle all the way from Harmanja, and she had not had the heart to use it. Halil lit a fire there and then, and heated some water. He stripped Memed behind the roots of a clump of canes, and washed and rubbed him with the cake of soap like a child, then dried him and dressed him. Old Osman had had a new pair of dark-coloured shalvar-trousers made for him, and a shirt of striped Marash linen. He had also bought him a pair of shoes from Adana. In the new clothes that he was not yet used to, Memed looked handsome, yet a little smaller, a little more like a child. If it had not been for his curly beard which had grown long, you would not have been able to convince one man in a thousand that this child was Slim Memed.

'While I am about it,' said Halil, 'let me give him a good shave.'

He spent some time bringing his pocket-knife to a really sharp edge and then in the cool of the afternoon he gave Memed a beautiful shave, and painstakingly combed his tousled hair to one side. At one moment Memed looked at Halil, smiled at him, and pressed his hand. Halil rushed over to where Seyran was sitting under the plane-tree, and said, choking with emotion,

'Seyran, my sister, did you see what happened? He's come to life, he's come to life! Good heavens, he pressed my hand, and really smiled at me.'

'He smiled?' asked Seyran. 'Did he really smile?'

She got up, and they walked towards Memed.

Memed was on his feet. He looked at the two people coming towards him. Opening his eyes wide, as if he had never seen them before, he looked at them in surprise. He looked, and smiled.

Seyran took him by the hand and a flaming blush rose to her cheeks.

'Get better soon, my brother,' she said.

Memed looked at Seyran admiringly and smiled.

'Do you know Maid Seyran?' asked Halil. 'She and Mother Kamer together have healed your wound. I am Beardless Halil, the keeper of this melon-garden.'

Halil perceived that Memed was looking for something. He seemed to be slipping into a strange vacuum.

'What are you looking for, my friend?' asked Halil.

Memed continued to grope all around.

'Are you looking for your rifle? It's over there.'

He took him by the hand and led him under the hut in the tree. He raked to one side a heap of weeds growing underneath it. Then a hole was revealed under the heap. In the middle of the hole there was a rush mat done up in a roll. Halil bent down and opened it. The rifle, the bandoliers, the field-glasses, the revolver, were all there. Memed pressed Halil's hand again with all his strength.

He kept on smiling.

They sat down under the willow-tree and leant their backs against its trunk. Seyran could not take her eyes off Memed. Gentle, warm feelings bubbled up within her, feelings which she had completely forgotten. As she looked at Memed's face a faraway, forgotten warmth stole over her. Seyran lowered her eyes to the ground, and then suddenly found she had them on Memed's face again. A strange feeling had come over her. Every now and again she cast a glance at Halil to see if he had noticed anything. Halil was not paying attention. This reassured Seyran, and she forgot where she was and looked long and searchingly at Memed's face. She was aware that within her something had stirred, that a different emotion had bloomed, that she was being agitated by mixed feelings which resembled pity, love, motherliness and friendship.

Halil walked around the melon-garden several times, picked two bunches of amaranths and sweet basil and gave one to Seyran and one to Memed. Memed smelt the flowers, inhaling their scent deeply, as if he had never smelt flowers before.

The south-west wind had arisen, and below, on the dusty tracks near Anavarza Castle, it was driving long sand-devils before it. Seyran quickly got up.

'I'll light a fire,' she said, 'and make some hot soup.'

She began to collect firewood. Halil helped her, and they soon had the fire going. The fat sizzled in the pan, and the smell of onions filled the air.

Seyran rapidly spread a meal-cloth and brought the soup plates. 'Please begin,' she said.

Memed and Halil sat down cross-legged.

That day, for the first time, Memed drank his soup calmly and slowly, savouring every mouthful. He closed his eyes, as if to get the full flavour of the soup, and put each spoonful into his mouth in ecstasy. This did not escape Halil.

When the soup was finished Memed glanced around him several times, with the unbelieving wonder of a man who is slowly freeing himself from a spell, awakening from a long sleep, and emerging out of a vast dream world into a real world. His eyes fell on Seyran. For a moment they gazed at each other. Then Seyran dropped her eyes.

Memed began to speak:

'I congratulate you, my sister, I've never had such excellent soup,' he said. At the sound of his voice a thrill went over her whole body, such as one may feel only once in a lifetime. Her limbs felt weak. Memed's voice came from far away, from another world. From a strange enchantment.

The shades of evening began to fall. At one stage Memed's face vanished in the shadows. She got up, walked waveringly to a willow-tree where the firkin was hung up, and brought it back.

'Some honey?' she said. 'Selver sent it to you. It's good honey. She doesn't give it away to anybody. But she sent it for you.'

Rapidly washing Memed's plate, she poured some honey into it.

'Thank you, sister,' said Memed. 'How quickly you cured me of my wound!'

Seyran was overcome by shyness; she blushed and her voice shook,

'Mother Kamer's family are all healers. Mother Kamer comes from the high mountains, from Saritanishmanli. They know all about salves for bullet wounds. I too am from the mountains. Our people always get bullet wounds,' she said, and then was silent.

She regretted having spoken. Her hands and legs were shaking and she was terrified that Memed and Halil would notice. Fortunately the light was fading and darkness was coming on. Hordes of mosquitoes were whining in their ears and round their heads.

Seyran wanted to run away at once, and yet at the same time she wanted to stay on for ever. Up to now she had never stayed so late. She could hardly see Memed's face in the darkness. She rose to her feet. Memed and Halil got up too.

'It's late,' said Seyran. 'May Allah protect you.'

'So late at night . . . All alone . . .' Memed began.

Halil laughed.

'Oh, Memed, my friend,' he said. 'You don't know Maid Seyran. She could pass through an army in the night. She fears nothing and nobody . . .'

Seyran went away at a run. At Savrun brook she took off her shoes and waded through the water. She reached the other side in no time at all, put on her shoes again, and continued along the dusty track. She was still shivering, melting and trembling from an inner feeling that had been forgotten for years. At times she was in a state of joyous excitement, at other moments she gave herself up to a tranquil happiness.

43

SEYRAN did not sleep a wink that night. She was floating in a delicious, enchanted, gentle dream, and through her veins were running rapidly sweet-smelling, warm things like love, affection, compassion and friendship, purifying her blood, and comforting her for all the pain and grief she had suffered.

She got up before it was light. She stretched her whole body towards the rising sun: her hair, skin, nails, eyes and ears. She was in an infinite dream of happiness. The melon-garden, the bubbling, ankle-deep water in the pebbly brook, the willows, the butterflies alighting like a blue cloud over the green of the reed-beds, the plane-trees, the birds, Beardless Halil, everything, everything quivered around her in a blaze of delight.

As she stretched in a long shiver of excitement, her whole body was aflame. If you had touched her you would have burnt your hand.

The peaks of the mountains in the east were tipped with light. Up to now she had never noticed that the mountain peaks became white before sunrise. The gentle dawn wind was blowing, and mist was rising from the earth. Birds were chirping. Big butterflies, blue, yellow, purple and red, with wings that appeared wet, were fluttering about. Bees, grasshoppers and ants were waking up, emerging from their nests on to the damp earth, and awaiting the rising sun. The earth, the sky, trees, brooks, flowers, animals, birds and beetles felt the impatient thrill of awakening, the delight of the day that was about to dawn. Everything was beautiful, and everything was flying for joy. A little later the sun was up. Seyran had never seen such a sunrise. The sky cleared, in a gentle, hazy blue. It was a clean, shining, washed, brand-new sky. There was no cloud. There was not a single bird in flight.

Seyran walked towards the Savrun. She ran towards a pool between some willow-trees. She stripped mother-naked, and plunged into the pool. She swam, with her marvellously graceful long, slim body in the scattered brightness among the pebbles . . . She lay down happily. She was out of breath. But lest someone should see her she dressed at once She had never known such beautiful water, such a sunrise, such a sky. She had never been born for such a world. The whole world was bubbling with friendliness and contentment. Sparks of happiness rained upon the world.

The village also awoke. Plaiting her wet hair she turned homewards. The first to meet her was Ali Ahmet. He had been bent even when he was young; and now at seventy he was all crooked. He stopped and stared at Seyran's face.

'What's happened to you, my dear?' he asked. 'You're smiling, my child. You look like the angels. What's happened to you?'

Seyran put her arms round his shoulders.

'You crazy girl, now then, you crazy girl. What's happened to make you like this? How much more beautiful you have grown! Nobody's ever seen you like this. You've grown so beautiful,

Maid Seyran! Is your family descended from the angels?'

How handsome Ali Ahmet was too, with his hennaed whiskers, his twisted back, and his bleary eyes. Irritable Ali Ahmet, who was always beating the children from morning to night, what a good man he was!

Seyran entered her house, and opened her chest. A mingled scent of apples from the hills, dried basil, narcissus and pennyroyal wafted out. She took out a dress she loved which she had only worn once, when a girl, and put it on. It was a dress kept for a day of happiness and rejoicing. She put on a necklace made of coral, silver and gold, which she had forgotten about for years, she put new shoes on her feet, and wound a fine Lahore shawl round her waist as a sash. She put on gold ear-rings and gold bracelets and looked in the mirror. She looked and looked. She really had become more handsome. She went out into the village. Old Selver was the first to see her dressed like that.

'We-e-ell, my dear,' she said. 'How beautiful you look! And your face is smiling too! How much more beautiful you are when you smile, my dear.'

Her long-lashed eyes, her whole face was shining bright.

'We-e-ell, how beautiful you've grown.'

Seyran put her arms round her too and kissed her warmly. The kiss came from her heart. She was overflowing, exuberant. She wanted to kiss everyone she met, friends and enemies, trees, beetles, bees. She could have kissed the whole world. For years the exuberant, warm affection within her had been repressed and had found no outlet. Now it had burst its bounds and overflowed. Those who met her and grasped her hand felt a current of warm affection flowing from her hand to theirs, from her eyes to theirs. They felt it, and they felt comforted by her affection.

Seyran smiled, caressed and kissed them.

At one moment a slight worry creased her brow. In another she had wiped this shade of worry from her face. She walked to the other end of the village where the houses of her mother and brothers were. Her mother heard that she was coming and went out to welcome her. Her brothers and their wives, her cousins, children and women, all sorts of people poured out into the street to welcome Seyran. Seyran, smiling, went up to her mother and embraced her, then she took her hand and kissed it respectfully. Her mother wept, and kissed her daughter's hair and face.

'This means that you have forgiven us, Seyran, my dearest,' she said, half choking with her tears. 'If only your father had been alive to see this day. Your father was longing for you and asking for you with his dying breath. Now your father's bones can lie at peace in his grave. We treated you very badly, my dear. You have done a good deed by forgiving us.'

The mother's tears fell like rain.

Her brothers, and their children and relations embraced Seyran. Their great grief was now healed. What was the reason? What had happened to Seyran? Why was her sad face now full of smiles even as she shed a few tears? That was not the right moment to ask or to think about it. Whatever the reason was, Seyran, with whom they had pleaded for years, for whom they had left their homes and come to Chukurova, Seyran, who had never said a word to them, never smiled, never even looked at them, was now smiling spontaneously, and had come to see them in a happy mood. Her mother stood rooted to the spot, amazed and quite at a loss, unable to take her eyes off her beautiful daughter.

Not even this subdued Seyran's high spirits. The happiness she was pouring out on her mother, her brothers and their children was inexhaustible; it filled her to overflowing. Suddenly she ran out, saying with a smile,

'I'll come back again.'

It was after that that her mother and brothers began to think about the reason for this exuberance and unexpected reconciliation. They thought and thought, but did not know what to attribute it to.

'Don't think about it,' insisted the mother. 'Whatever it may be I love and respect her. Whatever Seyran may do, she has brightened my life at the end of my days. My beautiful, my darling child, Seyran.'

It gave fresh heart to her brothers, too. The state that Seyran had been in since she came to Chukurova had torn their hearts. The fact that she never looked them in the face, that she had never forgiven them for being the cause of her terrible misfortune, had distressed them all. It was because of this that their father had

326

silently died of grief. The brothers and relations who had come to Chukurova were cowed and kept to themselves solely on account of Seyran. A new era had dawned for them today. Seyran had smiled. Everyone was in better spirits because of Seyran.

Seyran ran straight to Mother Kamer's house.

'What's happened to you, my dear?' Kamer asked in alarm. 'The villagers are all talking about you. You dressed up in your best clothes and went to see your mother, they say, is that right? What's happened to you?'

Seyran, with her dimpled cheeks, living in a dream of contentment, in childlike gladness, looked even more beautiful as she smiled.

Kamer stroked her hair, and looked at her long and lovingly:

'Seyran, my dear, how beautiful you are! Much more than we'd ever thought. What is it?' she asked.

Seyran, with lowered eyes, did not reply. But a moment or two later she raised her head, her cheeks aflame.

'Mother Kamer . . .' she said, but could not go on. 'Mother Kamer . . .'

Kamer lost her patience.

'Well, go on, for heaven's sake. Are you learning my name by heart? Mother Kamer, Mother Kamer!'

Seyran again stared at the floor.

Then Kamer said gently and lovingly:

'Tell me, my dearest, what is on your mind. I think something pleasant has happened to you. Tell your Mother . . .'

Seyran raised her head again, and her big black eyes were shining. Her eyes shone with love.

'Mother,' she said, 'let's go there, come with me to the melon-garden.'

Mother Kamer laughed delightedly.

'So that's how it is! So what made you smile is . . . You crazy girl,' she exclaimed, hugging her. 'For pity's sake, nobody must hear about it or notice. You crazy, crazy, crazy girl.'

She went on saying, 'Crazy girl,' while she gently patted her on the back, and kissed her hair.

'If my crazy girl goes there now, at once, everybody will realize exactly how it is. The whole village is talking about you anyway.

"What's happened to Seyran, she's smiling," they are saying. We'll find some pretext or other, and go.'

'I can't wait, Mother . . . I can't keep still. Help me, Mother, nothing like this has ever happened to me before.'

Mother Kamer smiled.

'It's always like that,' she said. 'When this kind of business is in earnest, a person can't stay still in one place. It's always like that. It's like a fire inside you.'

She pressed Seyran's hand.

'Please Mother, let's go,' Seyran begged. 'You understand how I'm feeling. I'm desperate. From the first day I saw him.'

Old Osman came in, and when he saw Seyran, he said cheerfully,

'Kamer, what's up with this crazy girl of ours, she's been smiling. The whole village is talking about her. She smiled, and she went to see her mother and brothers. What's happened?'

Mother Kamer said sharply,

'Nothing's happened. A curse on those villagers. Have they nothing better to do than to gossip about a girl having smiled? Of course people aren't always exactly the same . . . Sometimes they smile and sometimes they weep. What is there to talk about in that? Is it a bad thing that the girl should have had a reconciliation with her mother and brothers? Is it a bad thing?'

'Now then, Kamer, don't flare up like that! Would you want me to shoot the whole village because they're talking about Seyran? They noticed a change in her, so they're wondering what the reason is. What is there to take offence at, or to fly into a rage about, Kamer? The villagers wouldn't think anything bad about Maid Seyran.'

'So they might have thought something bad about Seyran! What next, I'd like to know,' she scolded him.

'There's no talking to you now, Mother Kamer,' said Osman mildly. 'You're touchy today.'

'So I am,' said Kamer. 'What of it!'

Then she went to the door, dragging Seyran along with her.

'Osman, go and have your meal with your children this evening. I shall not be at home. Seyran and I are going down to the reed-bed,' she said and walked off.

They went behind the house, and quickly set off along the dusty track. The dust was ankle-deep. It filled their shoes and burnt their feet like hot ashes. The sun behind them scorched their backs and necks. The plants and flowers at the side of the track were white with dust, and looked withered. The mullein, its damp stems not burnt by the fire, had white, button-like snails clinging to it from top to bottom. Seyran hated snails, but now even they looked beautiful to her eyes.

Seyran went in front, at a pace that was almost a run, and Kamer, exerting all her strength, tried to keep up with her. She was out of breath, and dripping with sweat. At last she called out behind Seyran,

'Stop, girl, stop! I can't keep up with you, wait!'

Seyran turned round and saw that Mother Kamer was a long way behind. She was ashamed. Kamer, dragging her feet, took some time to catch up. She was choking, exhausted.

'I'm dead, my girl, I'm dying, with trying to keep up with you. Oh, my poor knees. A curse on old age.'

Maid Seyran was ashamed of her thoughtlessness, and hardly dared look at Mother Kamer.

Then Kamer, in order to ease matters, said, with a smile,

'My dear, why are you in such a hurry? We shall get to the melon-garden in any case. And before sunset . . .' she looked pleased.

A little later Seyran again forgot, and went on ahead. Kamer did not try to call her back. Seyran flew along in a cloud of dust, and was lost from view. When Kamer reached the melon-garden somewhat later, Seyran was too embarrassed to look at her.

'Mother,' said Beardless Halil, hastening towards her, 'what a good thing you came. I shot two francolin today. You can cook one for us with pilaff and take the other one to Uncle Osman, will you? They're nice fat birds . . .'

Memed too came running up and kissed Mother Kamer's hand. Kamer saw that his face was no longer pale. His eyes too had lost their dead look, and were shining a little.

'Welcome, Mother. I've been longing to see you. How is Uncle Osman? What's going on in the village?'

'Everything's all right,' said Kamer.

She watched Seyran out of the corner of her eye. Seyran was blushing, and panting a little. As for Memed, he did not even notice. This did not escape Mother Kamer. To herself she said, 'Oh my poor dear, my beautiful girl, so he doesn't even know! So that's the state your affairs are in. He doesn't even look at that flower-like face, at that swan-like neck, at those beautiful eyes; he doesn't even see those fine clothes. You're trembling like a leaf in front of him, and he doesn't even notice . . . Oh luckless Seyran, you're going to be hurt again. I had no idea it was like this . . . Now what are you going to do? Even Beardless Halil has noticed, but *he* hasn't noticed anything, my beauty, my poor darling.'

Seyran did not even think about whether he had noticed her or not. Spellbound, lost in admiration, she could not take her eyes off Memed. She did not talk, she did not hear, she only looked at him without seeing anything else around her.

They remained seated in the cool shade of the willows until evening. Mother Kamer grieved for Seyran, her heart ached for her. If Allah does not help a person, he cannot be helped. Before, it was her love for Aziz, an ill-fated love, that had not been fulfilled. And now her love for Memed . . . she would burn with this love and all in vain. Poor Seyran, how she looked at him! Madly in love, lost to the world. How was it that he couldn't see . . .

Memed suddenly looked up, and gazed at Mother Kamer.

'Mother,' he said, his voice shaking and charged with emotion, 'you have a lot of experience. I want to ask you something.'

All the things that had happened to him, his mother, Hatché, his child, Sergeant Rejep lying in the Ahjasaz marshes below, Jabbar, Lame Ali, Old Süleyman, Durmush Ali, Mother Hürü, Hamza, the state the village was in now, Earless Ismail – he enumerated these things one by one, pouring them out rapidly. At the end he said again,

'Mother, you have a long life and lots of experience, and you've got lots of courage. Tell me what to do. Abdi has gone and Hamza has come. Hamza will go and Bekir will come. Ali Safa Bey will go . . .'

'And Kenan will come,' said Kamer.

'Vayvay village too will be hostile to me, they will heap curses on me, and every Friday they will read prayers for the repose of Ali Safa's soul . . .'

Kamer reflected, and after a long time, she said at last,

'These things are too difficult for me to comprehend, Memed. Please forgive me.'

Memed turned to Seyran.

'Sister,' he said, 'what do you think about all this?'

He noticed for the first time how beautiful Seyran was. He noticed, too, how she was dressed. 'Can anyone be so beautiful?' he said to himself. 'Can anyone be so beautiful, so beautiful?'

Seyran trembled and did not speak. She blushed deeply, her hands were numb and her mouth was dry.

'What do you think, sister? Old Süleyman said that it was right to struggle and fight and resist tyranny. What do you think? If it never comes to an end, is it worthwhile struggling against oppression, and trying to overthrow it? What do you think, sister?'

Seyran had a lot to say, but she could not speak, she was tongue-tied. If she spoke her voice would betray her, and she was frightened of this. She lowered her eyes, merely saying gently,

'I don't know, brother, I don't know anything. You know better than any of us, than anybody else. You are Slim Memed.'

Mother Kamer got up, and lit a fire then and there. Halil brought a bag of *bulgur** and a tinned copper pan, shining clean, and put them by Kamer. Kamer admired the cleanliness of Halil's pan. Salt, fat and the fat francolin as big as a chicken . . . The fat sizzled over the pilaff. A soft westerly breeze was blowing, and wafted the smell far away in waves.

Seyran did not move from the place where she had sat down, and kept her eyes on Memed.

Memed gave a long sniff of appreciation when he smelt the stew. 'Congratulations on your cooking, Mother,' he said. 'Kind mothers know how to make nice savoury pilaffs.'

'Get up, child,' said Kamer sharply to Seyran. 'Why are you sitting there? Get up and spread the meal-cloth.'

Seyran at once jumped up, and, getting the meal-cloth from the hut she set it out on the grass a little way away. There was cold

* Wheat.

water in the pinewood jar. Halil had brought it a little earlier from a spring some distance away.

The four of them sat down cross-legged and ate the francolin and pilaff with relish. Judging by the way he ate, Memed had recovered completely. But if he had really recovered his senses, why did he not notice this beautiful girl who was so madly in love, Mother Kamer wondered. There was something wrong with the boy, something lacking, but what?

After they had finished the meal Mother Kamer proposed to wash the dishes, but Halil would not let her. He would wash them himself.

It would be sunset before long, and the twilight shadows were gathering. The sun was dropping down behind Anavarza, about to touch the plain. Seyran was still in a reverie, her eyes fixed on Memed. May God preserve everyone from such an ill-fated love. Mother Kamer was about to get up and go, but when she looked at Seyran, she relented. Let the poor girl look at her beloved's face a little longer, she thought.

At that moment the sun set, and darkness fell. Memed's face could only faintly be seen, but Seyran did not take her eyes away.

What will happen to her? thought Kamer. A brigand who is always risking death . . . However you look at it, there's no way out.

'Come on, my dear, get up, it's late,' said Kamer, suddenly getting up and beginning to walk away. 'Take care of yourselves, boys. If there's anything you want, we'll bring it tomorrow or the day after.'

Memed ran to the flower garden, made up two bunches and gave one to Kamer and the other to Seyran.

They set off. Seyran kept turning round and looking back. She would take a step, and then look back. Night fell, and the moon rose. Neither Memed nor the huge melon-garden could be seen, and yet Seyran kept on looking back. Her legs seemed to pull her back. This time it was Kamer who was going quickly, and when she saw that Seyran had fallen far behind, she waited for her to catch up. They were approaching the village, when Seyran called out from behind,

'Stop, Mother Kamer, stop. I'm frightened.'

Kamer stopped. Before Seyran had reached her, she asked,

'Why are you frightened?'

Seyran came up and clung to her arm.

'They will kill him,' she moaned. 'They'll kill him, Mother. Did you ever see or hear of a brigand coming to a good end? They even killed Gizik Duran. They'll kill him, Mother.'

Kamer said nothing. The girl kept on talking, but Kamer made no reply. At last she said,

'Say something cheerful, my dear. Say something cheerful to bring good fortune. Who do you think will kill him?'

'Everyone, everyone,' said Seyran. 'The aghas, the police, the Government. Everyone will kill him.'

Mother Kamer was thrown into confusion. She had not expected all this and yet she thought the same as Seyran. Had a brigand ever been known to live long? Especially a brigand like Slim Memed . . . The very stones, the birds and beasts about him would turn on him. The aghas and the beys . . .

'But bullets cannot touch him . . . He has the thunderbolt in an amulet round his neck. And the Lord Hizir protects him.'

These things that Kamer grasped like a lifebelt should have been effective, but Seyran did not listen, did not pay any attention at all . . .

'They'll kill him. They'll kill him,' she kept on saying.

'But he has captured the thunderbolt . . . Imagine, he has the thunderbolt.'

But Mother Kamer herself did not believe this.

'Bullets cannot hurt him anywhere but in his eyes.'

Seyran, clinging to her arm, dragged her to the village.

'Bullets do not pierce him. Only his eyes. His eyes must be protected . . .'

44

ALI SAFA BEY turned things over in his mind, and since there was
no hope of assistance from anywhere, he decided to seek his own
remedy. Neither the District Governor nor the Vali was willing
to remove the village of Vayvay, being afraid of what might
happen. The District Governor had gone back long ago on the
decision taken and the words spoken at Vayvay.

Ali Safa Bey said scornfully,

'Well, my friends, is this a Government? Just look at those men,
that District Governor, that Vali! Good heavens, man, I wouldn't
even take them on as labourers on my farm! Both the Pasha and
Arif Saim think they have established a Government and can now
take their ease, do they? Why even our Murtaza Agha could have
established a Government as good as that! Indeed, a more intelligent one.'

He summoned his trusted, trigger-happy young men from
Chikchiklar, and made plans night and day with them to give
Vayvay its finishing stroke. He had already taken steps for the
defence of his farmhouse. He had brought brand-new German
carbines, boxes and boxes of ammunition, revolvers, daggers,
field-glasses, red fezzes, soldiers' uniforms . . . He had piled sand-
bags against the doors and windows. The disappearance of Zeynel
and Adem had alarmed him greatly. Those people from Vayvay
had become so rebellious that they might have made away with
them. The news brought by Zekeriya seemed to confirm this.

'I've looked everywhere and asked everyone,' Zekeriya said,
'and there's no trace of Zeynel nor of Adem . . . It's rumoured that
the villagers strangled Zeynel, with the help of his wife too, and
buried him in Ahjasaz. As for Adem, it's said that Yobazoghlu
killed him.'

Ali Safa Bey was making ready. He had sent word to Vayvay
that they were to expect him today. He decided to put on the
yellow boots that Zekeriya had carefully brought to a high polish,

and the still new khaki officers's breeches left over from his days in the War of Independence. He put on a gold chain that he had not worn for years, and a big black hat. He curled his moustaches, hung his ivory-handled revolver over his left hip, and fastened a delicately ornamented cartridge-belt round his waist. He slipped some large gold rings on to his fingers. Peasants were always impressed by gold, weapons and soldiers. With his military breeches, his silver-chased riding-stick thrust into the leg of his yellow boot, his Independence medal, his revolver, his black hat, and his chain, he was dazzling and majestic when he looked at himself in the mirror. This get-up was imposing enough. The peasants would be impressed by it and would feel some respect for him. The peasants had never been the most intelligent part of the nation. Intelligence was something acquired. But peasants were always observant. If he had been sure that Arif Saim Bey would not hear about it, he would have gone to see the villagers dressed from top to toe in his officer's uniform. That Arif Saim had become a real nuisance to Chukurova, a real pest.

He made Dursun Durmush put on a military uniform too. Zekeriya's riding breeches were khaki-coloured and every one of the eighteen men who were to go with him to Vayvay wore some sign, however small, that called the army to mind. One of them had a soldier's star on his cap, another wore puttees, another had a sword-bayonet, another a bandolier, a jacket, an epaulette . . .

To replace the horses that had been stolen, his father's friend Yaghmur Bey had sent him fifteen handsome four- or five-year-old horses, and would not take a penny for them. The horses he had sent were really very handsome, good-sized animals.

Before they mounted, Ali Safa Bey gave his men their final instructions.

'While I am talking to the villagers, you will all stand behind me, your eyes fixed on one point ahead of you, your right hands on the muzzle of your rifles, and you will not move an inch,' he said.

They mounted and rode off. The peasants awaited them under a huge mulberry-tree, whose branches were stretched out like giant wings. They were all impatient, and visibly agitated.

Followed by his riders, Ali Safa Bey entered the village at full speed in a cloud of dust, and leapt off his horse under the tree before he had completely reined in.

'God be with you,' he cried.

The villagers, restraining themselves, and trying not to show their agitation, answered mildly, 'And with you also.' Then they invited Ali Safa Bey to sit down on the wooden bench nailed to the trunk of the tree, on which they had put a thick mattress, covered with a Turcoman carpet. Ali Safa Bey, smiling at the crowd who stood back and made way for him, advanced to the couch and sat down, crossing his legs. He undid the buttons of his jacket so that his ivory-handled revolver and silver-worked cartridge-belt would be seen. After greeting everyone individually he was silent. His men came up, in a single line, their stomachs pulled in and their chests thrown out, their eyes fixed in front of them, their right hands on the muzzle of their guns, and their left hands on their brightly polished cartridge-belts, and stood like statues, not moving a muscle.

For some time Ali Safa Bey sat with his head bent, thinking, then he looked up and let his blazing eyes range over the crowd, one by one. All the villagers he knew were present. Seyfali had thrust his hand into his breast and seemed to be shaking with fear. He was glad about that. Old Osman seemed indifferent, but his old weathered face was such a maze of wrinkles that it was impossible to read anything on it. Ferhat Hodja's head was bent to the right, and his two hands were folded across his belly. With eyes closed he seemed resigned to the will of Allah, and was waiting tranquilly.

But Sefché the Warden had something quite different about him today. He was oddly dressed; on that summer day he had put on thick, embroidered woollen stockings, and serge shalvar-trousers; he had tied two hand-worked holster-belts to his waist, and had thrust his pistols into them. His striped linen shirt was indigo-blue. On his head he wore a wide-brimmed hat made of white felt. The two-inch patch of hair that he wore long was plaited and the silver-white plait hung down his back to his waist. He paced to and fro muttering to himself behind the crowd. Selver the Bride was there also. She had put on her most dazzling head-kerchief, white as a cloud. On her right was Seyran, the beauty, all dressed in green, an expression of infinite felicity on her face.

336

What surprised and rather disturbed Ali Safa Bey was that Seyran's brothers and cousins were also among those who had come to the meeting. These hill folk were shrewd men, and literate. Up to now they had not taken part in any of the doings, the goings and comings of the village, but had lived apart from Vayvay, like guests, here today and gone tomorrow. If they had intervened earlier in the affairs of Vayvay, the situation would have been quite different, since Ali Safa Bey would have met with far greater opposition. Now the position was that they had evidently decided to intervene.

As Ali Safa Bey looked at the villagers in silence, an ungovernable fury came over him. At any other time Ali Safa would have tried to combat his rage, and would have been able to control it. But now he let himself go. If he spoke in an angry voice, he would have more effect on the villagers.

He cleared his throat and coughed. As one man, they all waited for him to finish coughing. Then he began:

'I wouldn't have set foot in this village, after so much harm had been done to me. I wouldn't even look at a single one of you, after you had made me the talk of all Chukurova. But I have a last warning to give you, that's why I've come. And after this I wash my hands of you. Don't say afterwards that Ali Safa Bey, that Typhoon Bey didn't warn you! Uncles, brothers, I can hardly bring myself to call you uncles or brothers, but anyway . . . You have done me a great deal of harm. You obstinately refused to leave the lands that I obtained by pouring out money and handing over my matchless stallion. Why? Is there no vacant land elsewhere? You chose to insist on this land, this mosquito-infested land, where every insect is like a ravenous wolf. There is so much fertile land, so much unoccupied land to build a village and a home on that a thousand more villages could be founded in Chukurova. You, breaking the law, infringing Government regulations, and trusting in your strength, have refused to leave my land. Tell me, why have you not left? Is this not my property, are the title-deeds not in my hands?'

He darted furious looks at the villagers. They were silent, listening attentively, and otherwise not making the slightest movement. Ali Safa thought to himself that the prospects were bad. There was something very ugly about this business.

'It isn't yours, my dear Ali Safa, sir,' said Sefché the Warden. 'This property is ours, this village is ours, these are our permanent homes ever since our great-great-grandfathers' time. Where did you come from? Before Typhoon Bey existed where were you, my boy?'

He said no more. Thrusting his pipe into his mouth, he began once more to walk to and fro.

Ali Safa Bey had not expected this. This sally on the part of Sefché the Warden inflamed his anger, and with his anger increased his fear.

'I've warned you,' he shouted. 'I gave Yobazoghlu my horse which had a hundred-and-fifty-year pedigree, and this land I took in exchange is mine, is it not? If I have no right to this land why has half the village left already? Why has Yobazoghlu left?'

Sefché, who had been walking up and down stopped dead. He straightened his bent back and stood very upright for a moment,

'The people who went away,' he cried out, 'were lily-livered. They went because they were scared. As for Yobazoghlu, you had him beaten within an inch of his life.'

'All right then, stay!' yelled Ali Safa. 'Stay and plant your stake on my land. Plant olive trees too while you're about it, and may you live to eat the fruit!'

'I'm staying,' said Sefché. His thick lips trembled and his mouth foamed like a camel's, as he walked up and down, up and down, muttering to himself.

Take this, Old Osman! And you, long-necked Seyfali! And you too, black-eyed Ferhat Hodja! Could any of you stand up and talk to Ali Safa like that, like a lion? Good heavens, here am I with one foot in the grave . . . Yet I'm the one to challenge him. I'll show you Ali Safa, my boy, you so-called hero Typhoon Bey.

I'll show you . . . I will indeed plant olive-trees. And plane-trees too . . . And sweet-smelling oranges and bright-coloured cherries. 'I will plant men and bring up people.'

'Bring up whatever you like,' Ali Safa Bey said, waving his hand as if brushing away a fly. 'What's it to do with me? I came here out of kindness. You burnt my harvest, and I said nothing. Is it the act of a decent man, of a Moslem, to burn someone's harvests? You have stolen my horses, and you come and fire on my house every night. Isn't all this against the laws of the Turkish Republic, the laws of Islam, the laws of humanity? I have been patient, I suffered in silence. I restrained myself. I put up with all these evil deeds and did not take reprisals. You thought I was afraid. But it was out of common decency, and in order not to harm my friends. You didn't understand this. Not in the least. You continue to break the law, to oppose the state and the nation. What you're doing is plainly a Sheik Said rebellion. If I had informed the Government, every single one of you would now be swinging at the end of a rope.' He pointed two fingers downwards and made a sign like swinging legs. 'Like that! So, gentlemen, come to your senses. Gentlemen!'

His voice rang out into the distance. The heat shimmered, but it was cool in the shade of the big mulberry-tree. Yet Ali Safa was bathed in sweat.

'And then, gentlemen . . . ' He measured the effect of his voice, 'And then, gentlemen, what did you do then?'

He glared around, his eyes darting over all the villagers in turn. The veins in his neck had swelled to finger thickness.

'You committed murder, all of you! You killed my men. Ye-e-e-s, you killed Zeynel and Adem and the whole of Chukurova knows it. The Vali of Adana, the Central Government in Ankara, and Arif Saim Bey, who co-operates with me, all know it. Our friend and brother Arif Saim Bey . . . And he is hopping mad about it. What harm did Adem do you? What harm did Zeynel do you that you should kill the poor wretches? Besides, Zeynel was a man from your own village. Besides, he has left five children. Gentlemen, gentlemen, do you think I shall leave the murder of my men unavenged? If there is any law or right or justice in this country, their blood will not be unavenged.'

Suddenly he jumped up, and waving his arms madly, began to stamp his feet.

'No, no! It won't be unavenged! Not while I'm alive! You are relying on those who are supporting you, whoever they may be, but I rely on mighty Allah!'

He turned and pointed to his men who were still standing there rigidly.

'I've got these people too,' he said, his voice lower and he made

339

a sign almost like a wink. 'So don't go about trusting anybody and doing unlawful things. No power will save you from the arm of the law.'

His voice was low now, dry, rough, decisive.

'Now this is my last word to you. Ten days' grace is what I'm giving you. You will evacuate this village within ten days. If you don't it'll be a struggle to the death. I will marshal all my resources against you. I shall eject you from my land by force. If you're thinking of killing me, then kill me. Blood will be shed, families will be extinguished, then let that be. Houses will be destroyed, and hodjas will have their beards set on fire, and if they lose their lives too, then let them lose them. Houses will be raided at night; your wives and children will be carried off to the mountains, all right, let them be abducted. The village will be burnt down, let it burn. I shall not blink an eyelid. If fire or water or death or dragons or the Government attack me, I shall not blink an eyelid.'

He turned round, and pointed to his men, who were standing there like statues.

'Look, these men also, if they are attacked and death comes to them, they will not blink an eyelid.'

'With the help of God,' cried Dursun Durmush.

'Yes, gentlemen, if you don't leave my land and go away within ten days things will happen that you've never dreamed of. This village will become another Karbala, d'you hear me? You've heard of Karbala, where our Prophet's grandchildren were martyred. You know how Karbala was cut off from water? How the people died of thirst? Well, that's exactly how this village will be. Another Karbala.'

The villagers remained silent and impassive. Sefché continued to walk up and down, with his empty pipe in his toothless mouth. Ali Safa Bey was amused to see him. Why was that little old man swaggering about like that? His neck was as thin as a reed, and he looked like a sickly child of ten. He must be over a hundred years old.

'So there you are, gentlemen. I've come here today to tell you all these things and to warn you of the storm, the earthquake and the flood that threaten you. Either you get out of my village within ten days or you must be prepared for a fight, whoever is behind you. And this time it will be a fight to the death.'

He looked at Sefché as if expecting a reply, but Sefché did not raise his head. Ali Safa Bey sat down again on the couch, and loosened his bright red tie, which was held by a gold pin with a large pearl in it; he also wiped the sweat off his neck and face with a white handkerchief, which became soaked through.

Sefché the Warden was watching him from under his eyebrows; he's beaten, he said to himself. Cringing like a dog. Apprehensive, so he is pleading. This is a different way of pleading. And if he also knew that *he* is here, in our village, that son of a bitch would be so terrified he'd shit himself, shit himself . . .

He stood still and stared hard at Ali Safa. If I went up to him now, he thought, if I went up to that dog and said, 'Ali Safa, man, Slim Memed is in Chukurova, and what's more in this very village,' why he'd shit himself well and truly!

He began to walk up and down again, muttering to himself: 'I shall tell him, I shall let Ali Safa hear that he has come down to Chukurova like a grey hawk. Let that scoundrel die of fright. Let him hunt for a hole to hide in all over this huge Chukurova plain!' He looked at Ali Safa Bey and laughed out loud. Ali Safa stared. Now what was the matter with the old man, he must be going mad . . .

The villagers also stared at old Sefché. Then Seyfali the Headman, his hands clasped in front of him, his head bent respectfully, went up to Ali Safa Bey.

'Bey,' he said, 'it is midday. When we heard you were coming we killed a sheep . . . please come and eat with us.'

Ali Safa Bey got up and strode to his horse, followed by surprised looks. A youth was holding the horse, and steadied the stirrup. Ali Safa Bey leapt on the horse.

'I won't eat your food!' he thundered, and followed by his men he galloped furiously out of the village, in a cloud of dust.

Old Osman looked thoughtfully after them.

'There's no decency left in that man,' he said. 'People eat a meal even with an infidel – even with an age-old enemy.'

The villagers echoed his words:

'No decency . . . left,' they said.

Maid Seyran drifted through the crowd like a breeze of loveliness and happiness. In an instant she had left the village and was on the path that led to the melon-garden.

45

FROM below, along the track which ran beneath Anavarza Castle, a long caravan was approaching, raising a trail of dust. A wave of hope came over the villagers, Old Osman and Ferhat Hodja. Could it be those who had left the village? They waited expectantly till mid-morning. At that time a rider galloped into the village. It was a youth called Grasshopper Süllü. He was riding bareback, and the horse had no bridle or saddle-cloth.

'We could not bear to be exiled from our homes,' he began. 'As soon as we heard that he had come to the village we pulled down our huts, packed up our belongings and set out for Vayvay. Let us sink or swim together, we said. If our fellow-villagers die, we will die with them. If they starve, we'll starve too. Let our houses and harvests be burnt with theirs.'

Towards midday the head of the caravan reached the village. The returning villagers were much abashed; they could hardly look anyone in the face, and were very silent. Whereas the villagers welcomed them with great enthusiasm.

Each of them brought his bale and opened it up in front of his own house. Everyone helped and they were all settled in by late afternoon. They spread rugs under the big mulberry-tree and ate their evening meal there all together. Each family made one kind of dish and took it to the mulberry-tree.

'We have suffered a lot,' they said.

'May God never force anyone into exile.'

'Exile is worse than death.'

'Even if it were a paradise, it wouldn't do.'

'I don't want a paradise, give me the home of my fathers.'

'We have suffered a lot. How we've suffered.'

'We would have come back earlier. Why didn't we come? How could we look you in the face, we felt so ashamed!'

'But in the end we couldn't stand it any longer . . .'

'Forgive us what we did.'

'A curse on anyone who deserts his village.'

'To hell with anyone who abandons his home.'

'It's because they frightened us.'

'We were deceived.'

'Fear of the Government.'

'So we said, "let's go back to our village, and if we die, let's die with our own people".'

They sat and talked under the mulberry-tree till midnight.

Old Osman and Ferhat Hodja were astounded at the arrival of the villagers. They had begged and implored them to come, that time; why hadn't they been able to bring them back?

'This is a miracle worked by the hawk,' said Old Osman. 'And a great miracle it is.'

Ferhat Hodja gave a meaning smile, but whatever Osman and the others said, he did not oppose them and nodded agreement. The new arrivals had horses, too.

They could not sleep that night, and many of the villagers stayed up with them. They kept asking about him untiringly. They would hear the same story repeated by half a dozen people, and still they listened avidly.

'What's he like?'

'His eyes, his hands, his feet?'

'What is his hair like? And his eyebrows and eyelashes?'

'What is his voice like, how does he speak?'

'How does he hold himself?'

The villagers could not say how he held himself, or how he spoke, or anything else about him. They got over the difficulty by saying, 'He's brave, like a hawk, like a bird of prey, proof against bullets, he has a lightning flower. In an amulet . . .' Nobody had the heart to say, 'If you see him, you'll find he's no bigger than a child, with a small face, all eyes. His hands are small, too.' They could not say this. In any case, Memed's hands were not small. And his shoulders were not narrow. But everything about Memed looked small to them. Nor could they say anything about his voice or his way of speaking. Indeed, they had never heard him speak. Only Mother Kamer kept on saying, 'He's special,' and she smiled broadly, and confidently, glancing secretly at Seyran by her side.

In a few days the village had returned to normal again. Just as if half its inhabitants had never migrated and lived for years on the barren lands of Saricham. Just as if nobody had ever left. But those who came back were slightly disappointed. They had thought to encounter Memed, armed to the teeth, with curling whiskers, and immensely tall. Yet no one had ever seen his face, and no one knew where he was.

A few days later Yobazoghlu returned to the village, with his wife and children. As his house had been burnt down, he put down his bale under the big mulberry-tree. A stable was at once emptied and Yobazoghlu was settled in there. Yobazoghlu and his family were in direst poverty. The villagers helped them promptly, and met their needs as far as lay in their power.

'I wouldn't abandon my home again and go elsewhere, not for the police or the aghas, not even if the Angel of Death himself came,' said Yobazoghlu. 'Let them kill me. I will stretch out my neck to the sword and say, do what you like; strike, strike, let my blood be shed on my father's land.'

Ali Safa Bey heard the news. At first he did not believe it, and laughed it off. Then he sent his most trusted men, Zekeriya and Dursun Durmush, to Vayvay. They confirmed what had happened. Ali Safa Bey flew into a rage and foamed at the mouth. For a whole morning he paced up and down his mansion.

'I, I, I, I . . .' he said, 'if I do anything, I'll do it to them. So they're challenging me? Defying me? I, I . . . I, I . . . they'll see, those filthy beasts . . . filthy beasts . . . filthy beasts . . . I, I . . .'

He tired himself out. His body felt weak, and there were tears in his eyes.

'God almighty, what have I done? I only strove to build up a good farm for the nation. Whereas those people don't need this land in the least. I would have found them some land a thousand times better than this. What did I do to them that they should create these difficulties for years? They are usurping my rights. My farm has been incomplete for years on their account. Like a donkey's tail it never gets longer or shorter . . . Instead of going into business in Ankara or Istanbul, taking my ease, I made desperate efforts, for the country, for my fatherland. They don't understand, they don't understand kindness, these peasants won't understand anything. Here I am dragging out this miserable

344

existence with Meliha. The poor woman, I brought her here and imprisoned her in this hell. Her body is covered with abscesses.'

He had a vision of his wife's plump body covered with sores.

'It's cruel,' he groaned. 'The torture those peasants have put me through. The insults . . . It's inhuman. I can't go on carrying this heavy burden, ah, my friends, my comrades-in-arms, my dear brothers! I cannot carry this burden. Since the world began there was never a creature who had to endure what I have endured, who has been treated as I have been . . .'

'These things happened to us because of your mildness, your kindness and your humanity . . .'

He looked up and saw his wife sitting on the divan near him, her face bathed in tears.

She again opened her skirts up to her belly:

'Was it for this that my father sent me to high schools and had me educated in Istanbul? Was it for this, my dearest? Very soon my flesh will become rotten and disintegrate.' Apart from mosquito bites, there were discoloured patches on her legs . . . 'Was it for this? To endure cruelty and torture at the hands of those Vayvay fiends? Don't they realize what we have had to put up with, what we have suffered? I hope to God that this land will be their graveyard, for all of them, the children, the women, all the lot!'

Ali Safa Bey was deeply grieved about his wife's condition. His heart bled for her.

'It will be!' he cried out. 'I'll make this land into their graveyard, their graveyard . . . I, I, I will indeed! If I do anything I'll do it to them . . . For every tear you shed, one of them shall be cut off . . . I swear by all that I hold sacred, by the nation and the fatherland, that they shall be made to pay for this vile cruelty. A thousand times over!'

He stroked his wife's hair, and said in caressing, affectionate tones,

'Forgive me, Meliha. I brought you to this primitive place. I left you at the mercy of nature and of men, and imprisoned you here. Please forgive me. But you can see that I've been quite successful. The land I've got into my possession is not chicken-feed, it's worth millions. To tell the truth, I'm rather pleased. For a thing to be of real value it should not come too easily. Life is a struggle. If it weren't, it wouldn't be worth living, Meliha, my dear. The struggle for land is the most sacred struggle of all. To gain a farm or to gain a fatherland is the same. There's no difference. Don't cry, Meliha, we're still young. We have a long life ahead of us still.'

He bent down and lifting up her hair kissed the nape of her neck, which smelt of sour sweat.

'Meliha, my beloved, the whole of the Chukurova is not worth your little finger-nail! But it's no use, life is like that . . . We are obliged to keep on struggling.'

He walked to the head of the stairs, feeling better now, and called to Zekeriya and Dursun Durmush:

'Get a few men and come here. Reliable men. We are going to the town.'

They rode off. Everyone in the town had heard of the villagers' return to Vayvay.

'Poor Ali Safa Bey,' they said. 'Friendless, alone, without support. The peasants have come back and invaded his property. Those Vayvay villagers! He went without food to feed them. He denied himself everything to ensure their welfare. If anyone was ill, he at once got the doctor and the hodja to his bedside. All Ali Safa Bey's profits, all his possessions were given to the Vayvay villagers. To those who said "Don't do that, Ali Safa Bey, don't spoil these villagers," he said: "No-o-o, they are my friends, the apple of my eye, and respected fellow-citizens." He nurtured a viper in his bosom. He fed the crow that pecked out his eyes. Poor Ali Safa . . . The villagers raided his farm one night. They rained bullets upon it, caught two of his men, hanged them from a tree, and flayed them alive. Then they cut them up and threw the pieces into Ali Safa Bey's house.'

A great many stories were told with great earnestness about the fate of Adem and Zeynel . . . The townswomen beat their breasts.

'Alas poor Meliha, poor woman,' they said. 'She will have a lot more misfortunes on account of that stupid Ali Safa.'

'How can anyone ever trust those peasants? Those ungrateful brutes.'

A mood of pity came over the town. Everyone had tears in their eyes. They looked at the ragged peasants in the market with

346

loathing and terror.

Ali Safa Bey told the police commandant, Captain Faruk, what had happened, making it sound as tragic as he possibly could. When the Captain heard about those frightful atrocities, he looked extremely upset. It was only in the evening when he had drunk a glass or two at Nazifoghlu's eating-house that he managed to shake off the painful effect that the recital of events had had on him, and recover his normal spirits. The Public Prosecutor and the judges were even more upset than Captain Faruk. Only the District Governor clapped his hands with delight and said, 'That's good; that's fine; it's most satisfactory. Let dog eat dog. In the days of our great Sultan such atrocities never occurred, my dear sir, did they?'

Ali Safa Bey made Politician Ahmet, Fethi Bey and Mad Fahri send one telegram after another to Adana and Ankara. The peasants were rioting, they were burning farms, destroying homes and shedding blood. They were watering the earth of Chukurova not with water but with blood! Let the Vali say what he liked. It was all true, after all, wasn't it?

That very day a posse of police was sent to Vayvay. The police arrested Yobazoghlu for the murder of Adem, and Ferhat Hodja for the murder of Zeynel. Ali Safa Bey had discussed everything in an open and friendly manner with the Public Prosecutor, and they had considered these two as the most suitable people to be accused of murder. Hassan had no relations or supporters in Chukurova, and it had never been known where Ferhat had come from.

'Safa Bey,' said the Prosecutor, 'that hodja is a mysterious man. So if we hint that he is a spy, the accusation will stick. Even Vayvay people will believe it. Come on, get to work. Find some sound evidence of his spying. I can get Ferhat Hodja condemned to death. Ferhat is a good choice. Don't forget he is a Moslem hodja and in Ankara everyone shrinks from them these days . . . Safa Bey, we've hit the mark!'

Ali Safa shook the Public Prosecutor warmly by the hand:

'Very, very appropriate, my dear sir. One's a hodja and the other's a Kizilbash . . . This'll break the villagers' backs. Leave the *mise-en-scène* to me.'

347

The Vayvay villagers accompanied Ferhat and Yobazoghlu, who were handcuffed, on their way out of the village.

'Come back soon, come back soon,' they encouraged them.

'May great Allah assist you.'

Yobazoghlu stopped outside the village.

'I came back knowingly,' he said. 'Knowing that this would happen. But please believe that it is wrong to kill a man; no one will believe me, but you at least must believe that I didn't kill Adem. I entrust my children to all of you.'

At first Ferhat Hodja did not want to speak. Then, smiling bitterly, he turned to the villagers, with tears in his eyes.

'You know who I am,' he said in a choking voice. 'I don't need to tell you. I shall not return to the village. They will hang me. Bid me Godspeed, my brothers.'

His black flaming eyes and his black beard that looked green in the sun, flashed like lightning. Ferhat was praying in a low murmur, with the same bitter smile on his face.

They reached the town on the next day at mid-morning. Ferhat's handsome eyes were swollen and bloodshot. His face, too, was bruised. There was dried blood on his chin, and his clothes, which were in tatters, were stained with blood. He had lost his shoes, and blood was oozing from his feet and legs on to the ash-grey dust of the road. Yobazoghlu was even worse. One could not bear to look at him. He was a heap of bleeding rags.

As they neared the town they put a thick, black horsehair rope round the neck of each one. In the town a big crowd awaited them, holding melon-rinds, dirt, mud, sticks, stones, rotten eggs, rotten tomatoes and buckets of mouldy yoghourt. As soon as their heads appeared from the ravine below, they were met with shouts. Rinds, mud, rotten eggs, stones, rained on them. And the foulest curses and oaths imaginable . . .

Ferhat Hodja in front, and Yobazoghlu behind, their heads drooping, saw and heard nothing. First they were taken to the market-place, surrounded by the shouting, cursing, stone-throwing multitude. Here the town-crier, Crooked Ahmet, made a long speech about criminals and humanity and blood. A tear-jerking speech. Then the stones, dirt, mud and the rain of curses began again.

348

With the ropes round their necks, and hundreds of people behind them, Ferhat and Yobazoghlu were hounded round the whole town. Crooked Ahmet stopped twice in each district and repeated his terrible speech.

When they were taken to the gaol neither of them could stand on their feet. They sank down, half-fainting, at the foot of the wall.

That night Ali Safa Bey invited the local officials of the judiciary and the Government to drink raki at Nazifoghlu's restaurant. At the banquet he said what good, friendly, loyal people Zeynel and Adem had been. He recounted their virtues and merits. They had not deserved such a vile, base, monstrous death.

Ali Safa Bey spoke in such a fine, sincere way that everyone was deeply touched that night.

46

I T was still some time before sunrise, but the day was already light. There was dew on the leaves of the blue-flowering water-mint that grew along the muddy curves of bubbling Savrun brook. Honey-bees and other bees, with their wings folded over their backs, were drowsing among the flowers. Every now and then the bees quivered as if shaken by a slight tremor.

Below and all around the hut in the melon-garden there were water-melon rinds. A smell of rotten water-melon permeated the whole garden and its surroundings.

Memed had woken early and was walking around the melon-garden, thinking. The things that have happened to me, he said to himself, and he could see it all in his mind's eye, how he had started, where he had got to. And now the mighty Government, the Chukurova aghas, were all intent upon finding him, despatching whole platoons of police against him. What if he had been a real brigand? What would they not have done then? he thought.

Old Osman had happened to come to the melon-garden a few

days before, in a state of great good humour:

'My hawk,' he had said, 'we've come out on top. We've broken Ali Safa's back. When the peasants who had been frightened and run away heard your name, and that you were here, a fire of bravery was lit in their hearts, and they hastened back to the village, even Yobazoghlu. So long as you stay here with us, the peasants will move mountains and Ali Safa will get his deserts sooner or later. Mad Muslu's son is doing good work and everybody thinks that it comes from you. And it's true, without you to give us courage, we should have given in to Safa like weak women.'

Then suddenly Old Osman changed. There was a shadow of fear and hopelessness in his eyes.

'My hawk,' he said, 'you ought to know, but please don't have any doubts, that the whole of Anavarza plain knows that you are in Chukurova. Nobody knows where, of course. Also, no agha or government will ever learn anything from the peasants. You needn't worry.'

Memed realized how much they were expecting of him. What did they think he was? He was simply a man who had been in the mountains for a few years, who had been forced into this, who had had the most incredible things happen to him, who had been driven from one village to another, from one mountain to another, and, finding no hole into which he could crawl, had come to take refuge here.

Memed was making great efforts to understand the events that had taken place around him; he racked his brains from morning till night, and from night till morning. Some things he understood because of his experiences. But there were others that he could not begin to understand. Old Osman, for instance, straining and striving, but in vain. Ali Safa Bey was sure to drive them out of the village in the end. He had the Government behind him, the aghas on his side, and a troop of armed men at his beck and call. And Old Osman, what had he? Only him, Slim Memed! Just one man. Didn't Osman know that if the police got wind of this, and surrounded the Ahjasaz marshes, with a posse of policemen as beaters, they would get Slim Memed like a partridge?

'I shall not surrender, and they will kill me,' he smiled to himself.

Suppose they kill Ali Safa, won't another, more evil Ali Safa emerge against them? Much, much worse. He had heard every detail of what Hamza had done to the people of Deyirmenoluk. I tried to help, to do some good, yet I brought greater oppression upon them. However much they curse and abuse me, even if they kill me, they will be justified.

I shall never get out of Chukurova plain alive. I must await death calmly in this melon-garden. It's as though I had a writ of execution tied around my neck. If it were only that when Abdi goes, Hamza takes his place, it would be easy. But when one Abdi goes, a thousand Hamzas come. Every struggle is useless. All Old Osman's and Vayvay's straining and striving is in vain. They'd better leave here soon and go and settle in another place . . . But won't there be another Ali Safa to oppress them wherever they go? Before autumn comes the police will catch me here. The Vayvay villagers themselves will inform against me. My blood will be shed on the rotting soil of the Ahjasaz marsh . . . I can only wait and drowse away my life here, with Beardless Halil, half asleep and half dead . . .

This business of Abdi going and Hamza coming he had discussed over and over again with Beardless Halil. They had racked their brains but found no solution.

Beardless Halil was an active, vigorous man. And bold too. Tell him to march on Ali Safa's house and he would do so at once. Memed admired him. As for Halil, he did not understand Memed's depression, his exhaustion, his strange resignation. How can Slim Memed be like that, he wondered. Who knows, perhaps that's how Slim Memeds are really.

The day before, when they heard that the police had taken Ferhat Hodja and Yobazoghlu away, Halil caught a look on Memed's face and his opinion of him changed. Memed's face, his eyes, hands, voice, everything, had suddenly altered. Even the shape of his body was different now. Beardless Halil said to himself that this might well be the Memed people had spoken about, and he was pleased.

It was Seyran who told them. She related everything, down to the smallest detail. The heavy chains round their wrists, the insults of the townspeople. Memed was silent. Halil suddenly saw that his face was quite different, sharp as a knife. Sparks flashed once or twice in his eyes, and then a steely glint came into them and stayed there.

Seyran suddenly stopped talking and looked at Memed as if she were seeing him for the first time. There was deep silence all around. It was hot. Everything was burning, melting, oozing in the dazzling heat.

Yellow lights flashed through Memed's head. Yellow lights that sparkled and scattered, blinding him, lights that tossed and whirled. The world turned yellow, plunged in a flowing, cascading, sparkling, yellow storm.

Memed staggered to the spring, and put his head into the ice-cold water. Then he began to walk rapidly about the melon-garden, not looking where he was going. Now everything had been swept away. Plants, trees, the Anavarza crags, water, earth, the bushes of Ahjasaz, the mountains in the distance, everything had vanished, and Memed himself remained, like the personification of anger. Halil and Seyran could not take their eyes off him. Suddenly he stopped short in the middle of the melon-garden. Very upright, like a sharp sword thrust into the ground.

Halil came over to him: 'Memed, my brother,' he said, 'don't stay standing here. It's very hot. You'll get sunstroke.'

He led him to the shade of the tree-house, where myriads of insects swarmed about the melon-rinds: red wasps, bumble-bees, honey-bees, blue hornets and black bees, their translucent wings scintillating under the blazing sun.

Memed looked at Seyran, and perceived her. His face changed again into a warm, friendly, gentle, pleasant face. He smiled, and seating himself under the tree-house, said,

'Poor Ferhat Hodja. What a lion of a man! I have never seen a hodja like him. You know what Old Süleyman said once, Halil?'

'Haven't the faintest idea,' said Halil.

'Old Süleyman said to me, "If Abdi goes and Hamza comes in his place . . ." that's what he said. "Nothing in the world is useless, nothing is in vain," he said. "It is right to struggle. It is right to give battle. To struggle is not in vain, it is right," he said.'

He smiled a little, then became sombre.

He must leave here and go. His presence brought nothing but

harm to these poor people. Ferhat Hodja had been arrested. Perhaps they would even hang the poor man for nothing. Ali Safa would never stop. He would fall upon them tooth and nail. There would be a life-and-death struggle. And the result? Nothing! Vayvay village would be crushed, that was all . . .

But where, where could he go? The mountains, the villages, the people, even the thickets rejected him.

He sighed deeply.

Old Osman had told him many things. He was a shrewd man and knew that they would be defeated by Ali Safa Bey. He also knew that if Ali Safa went Kenan Safa would come in his place, to prey upon them a thousand times worse . . . But still he did not shrink from the struggle at all costs, even death. Old people usually cling to life, but Old Osman treated it with contempt. If it had not been for him, not a fly, let alone a man, would have remained in the village. Everyone would have surrendered to Ali Safa long ago.

Thousands of gazelles used to come in February from the south, from the desert, to Chukurova and the Anavarza plain. They would rove about the plain in flocks, and swift eagles would follow them everywhere with pointed wings. The eagles would perch on their backs, thrust their beaks into the gazelle's eyes, pluck them out and eat them.

'Blind gazelles are a heart-rending sight,' Old Osman used to say. 'In my youth there were hundreds of them on the Anavarza plain, blind, helpless, wandering hither and thither. No one had the heart to hunt these blind gazelles. They gradually died out.'

He liked to think about the gazelles. They were akin to him. 'I'm a blind gazelle, that came to the Anavarza plain. I'm a helpless gazelle in an eagle's talons.'

It was getting light on the Anavarza plain. A thick mist lay over the ground, waist-high. Trees sat on top of the mist as if they had no trunks.

In the half-light, a dark figure glided out of the shadows and stood on a hillock that lay on the nearer side of the willows. During the past week Memed had got to know this shape, which came and planted itself there every night.

It was a dark brown Arab stallion.

All through the night the brown stallion would gallop over the plain below Narlikishla; he would stretch, and neigh, and at the faintest flicker of light he would turn like a top. Then before the east began to pale he would come to the melon-garden, and quietly, making no noise, would ascend the hillock in front of the willows, and would stand there without moving. Memed would leave the little palace that Halil had made against the mosquitoes, and would watch the stallion coming from far away every night at the same hour.

As the morning light increased the brown stallion would slowly take shape and when the sun rose he was resplendent, a sight that made Memed's heart beat fast and held him spellbound.

His eyes on the horse, Memed held his breath and again watched as the stallion materialized out of the darkness and then stood there clearly in all his beauty. It was many years since Memed's heart had beat so at the sight of something beautiful.

The horse's long body had become very slim. His tapering ears were pricked up. His long, thick tail, which hung down to his fetlocks, switched imperceptibly. His long mane lay to the right. His smooth, clean coat shone as if it had been polished, and changed with the light, now silvery and now jet black. As no flies had alighted on him, there was no twitching of his taut skin.

A little later, as the sun grew warmer, the brown horse would move; he would swing his head forcefully from right to left, and suddenly stretch out to perhaps twice his normal length. Then, passing like a cloud over the melon-garden, he would glide on towards Ahjasaz. His coat would slowly turn to silver, becoming lighter and lighter until he would fade away into the air, the bushes, the water and the trees.

Memed had not yet told Halil about this horse that he saw every morning. He would be so absorbed in the horse that he would forget everything. When he remembered it would be too late and the horse would have taken flight, vanishing in an instant into the reeds of Ahjasaz.

This time he ran to the trellised hut and called out in a voice hoarse with excitement,

'Halil, Halil, wake up.'

Halil at once jumped up and rubbed his eyes. Thus awakened out of his sleep, pouting, he looked like a child about to cry. He began to pull on his trousers.

'Come, Halil,' said Memed, and catching him by the arm, he dragged him along. 'Let's wait here.'

Halil, blinking, asked sleepily,

'What's up?'

Memed pointed to the horse.

'There's a horse, there . . .' he said.

They waited. Now Halil was fully awake.

'I know that horse,' he said. 'I know him very well.'

Then he was silent, not opening his lips again. Side by side they began to watch the horse. They both knew what would happen.

The sun began to appear above the horizon and the brown horse became visible in all his beauty. As though about to take wing he raised his forefeet two or three times into the air, rearing, and then from under the willows he glided through Ahjasaz, and flowed silently into the marshes and out of sight.

'I know that horse,' said Halil. 'I know him . . .'

He began to relate the saga of the horse to Memed.

'Let's catch that horse, Halil,' said Memed. 'I too know him – I was in the village on the day when Yobazoghlu's house was burnt down. At Vayvay . . . if we could catch him . . .'

Beardless Halil interrupted him: 'Nobody, absolutely nobody can catch that horse. Nobody can even get near him. He's a strange horse. Suddenly he disappears and for days you can't see him. Then when you least expect him, he looms up before you. Nobody knows where he goes, what he does . . .'

'Ah, if only we could catch him,' muttered Memed to himself.

'Get that idea out of your head,' said Halil. And he continued telling the saga of the horse.

47

MEMED had not long fallen asleep when he was roused by the shrill whinny of a horse, followed by the sound of three shots. The horse went on whinnying as if mad with terror. Memed clambered down from the tree-hut, and without stopping to put on his clothes, grabbed his rifle and made swiftly for the stream. He crossed over to the opposite side and concealed himself behind a mound. Halil followed him in his shirt and drawers; this annoyed Memed.

'Come here,' he whispered. Halil came and crouched down at his side. Two more shots sounded in the distance, and the horse's frenzied whinnying swelled and woke the echoes in the night.

Memed took aim and fired five shots. It was a strange sensation to fire at the flame of an unknown rifle in the middle of the night.

A few moments later they saw the elongated shape of a horse galloping past madly, only a few feet in front of them. In an instant it had vanished and only the thudding of its hooves could be heard growing more and more distant until it faded out altogether.

They put their ears to the ground. What was the reason for those shots? Had the police found Memed's hiding-place? If they had done so who had informed on him? Only Mother Kamer, Old Osman, Ferhat Hodja and Seyran knew about it. And also long-necked Seyfali . . . None of them, even under pain of death, would have betrayed him. Perhaps they had tortured Ferhat Hodja in prison and he had spoken.

What about Halil? Memed turned and looked searchingly into Halil's face in the moonlight. Would Halil have informed against him?

'Who do you think told them about our hiding-place, Halil?'

'I can't imagine,' said Halil. 'Nobody knows you're here, and those who know would rather die than tell.'

'What about Seyfali?'

'Don't let yourself be deceived by his long goose neck. Seyfali is a very brave man.'

'If we're surrounded here, there's no way of escape, Halil. This isn't like the mountains. There you can hide under every rock, in every clump of bushes, but in this plain everything betrays you. One can't trust Chukurova. Come on, get up and let's go into the marshes. Or if you wish, wait for me here.'

'I'll come with you,' said Halil. 'Ah, if only I had my gun.'

'Go and fetch my revolver from under the hut and come back quickly.'

Halil ran to the hut, and came back at once with the revolver in his hand.

'Look,' said Memed, bending down. 'Look there . . . Someone's coming.'

Halil looked and said, 'He's got a rifle, but he isn't a policeman.'

The man was coming their way.

'I'm going into that clump of reeds; you stay and meet that man. I'm curious. Who on earth can it be?'

He waded through the Savrun, made his way into a clump of reeds, and sat down.

Suddenly from further down came the thud of horses' hooves once more. When the unknown man heard this he stopped, and then at once took cover behind a hillock. Then the rattle and click of a gun was heard.

The thudding of the horse's hooves was drawing nearer. Three spurts of flame flashed from behind the hillock, and the sound of shots tore through the darkness. Immediately afterwards the horse whinnied at the top of his voice. A few minutes later the sound of his hooves had died away.

The man's figure was two hundred paces away. Halil saw him rise to his feet. He rose, too, and the man saw him. He took a few steps towards Halil, then for some reason he stopped, turned back and made off in the direction from which he had come.

Memed emerged from the clump of reeds, and ran to join Halil. The unknown man had disappeared into a gully.

The moon was setting over the Anavarza crags. In the distance the moonlit rocky outcrop of Anavarza looked like a big, gleaming silver ship, fully-rigged. It seemed to sail slowly onwards in the haze, while the Ahjasaz marsh below, with its bushes, its clumps of reeds and its rushes, was like a dark, misty, billowing sea. Soon it would be submerged in darkness and only a vague shadow would be left, floating in the night.

'Was there any rider on the horse?' asked Memed. 'I couldn't see one.'

'I didn't see one, either,' said Halil.

'Can it be our horse?'

'Yes, it's ours,' said Halil firmly.

The night was warm, suffocating. The call of some strange bird came at intervals. It was an eerie call that made one's hair stand on end. The night was full of tiny sounds, and hummed with the whine of mosquitoes. Clouds of them buzzed around Memed and Halil.

'I'm mystified,' said Memed. 'Chukurova is an odd place. In the middle of the night a man comes across a plain and fires at a horse. It's absurd. On top of that he misses the mark. It's absurd.'

'It's our horse,' repeated Halil firmly.

They hastened back to their trellised hut, and got inside their mosquito-proof shelter. The moon had set. Hosts of stars appeared, and began to twinkle brightly. The whole sky was carpeted with them, clustering thickly with not a needle's breadth between them. There were no shooting stars; it was a still, windless night.

A tinkling sound came from the Savrun. Then the beat of hooves was heard again, gradually coming nearer.

Memed left the protection of the mosquito-net and came down out of the hut.

'Brother Halil,' he said. 'I'm very curious. Do you think there is anyone riding our horse?'

'I'm coming too,' said Halil, and jumped down out of the hut. They returned to their former hiding-place, and concealed themselves behind the mound.

The thud of hooves grew louder. The horse was before them now, but suddenly he saw them and reared up startled, a long, long shape stretching up to the sky again and again. Then he faded into the darkness and the sound of his hooves died away.

'It's ours,' said Memed.

'Ours,' said Halil.

'Someone wants to kill the horse.'

'Ali Safa Bey,' said Halil.

'Maybe,' said Memed.

They climbed back into the hut, inside the mosquito-trellis. All night long, they heard the horse's hooves, now faint and far, now nearer and louder.

The morning-star appeared. The night grew cooler. The morning-star was very brilliant, four or five times as big as any other star. At times it shone like a sun, at times its light would be dimmer, now yellowish, now dazzling white. It whirled and blazed, sparkled brightly, then glittered frostily.

They came down out of the hut, and going to the willow-trees, hid behind a clump of reeds. The horse was approaching with long strides, as if on tiptoe. He came and stopped in the same place as before.

In the spreading light of day, the horse could clearly be seen. He had been sweating, and there were flecks of foam on his neck and flank. His brown body was black with sweat and gleamed wetly in the first rays of light. He was tired, and his head drooped as if he were dozing.

'Shall I go to him?' asked Halil. 'Perhaps he'll come to me. Animals aren't scared of me, not even the most timid ones, not even jackals and foxes.'

Memed did not reply.

Halil got up, took off his shoes, and began to glide forward towards the horse. He made a chirruping noise, and the horse did not change its stance. Halil's hopes rose as he drew nearer. Memed followed his every movement eagerly. Now Halil was only three paces away. He was just about to leap forward and catch him, when the stallion pricked up his ears, turned to him and looked at him like a human being. Suddenly he raised his head, and reared. Memed saw him take one long, long leap that took him out of the melon-garden in an instant. Over the melon-garden, in the empty air, only a long dark shadow stayed swaying for a time before the eyes of Memed and Halil.

48

'MOTHER KAMER, Mother Kamer,' said Seyran. 'What's wrong with me? I'm burning. My head's dizzy, and I can't stand still. I'm frightened, Mother.'

Mother Kamer smiled confidently and understandingly. But there was grief in her face. Ah, my ill-starred girl, you beautiful creature, you have started out on a difficult road once more. Your fears are not groundless. That Memed is after all a brigand, a man who is here today and gone tomorrow . . . Once more the flame and the fire will be shut up in your heart, my beauty, she thought to herself. She could not tell Seyran what she was thinking. First Aziz, then Memed . . . Beauty never brings luck. Beautiful girls are ill-fated from birth. For years every man in the village had been in love with her, but she would not look at any of them; she said that no man should take Aziz's place . . . And in the end she had gone and lost her heart to a brigand. A hopeless, doomed passion. And Memed not even aware of it! For days the girl had been madly in love, contriving to see him every day and seizing every opportunity to sit until evening gazing into his face. Doesn't a man understand, especially a clever man like Memed? Of course he understood, but knowing that no good could come of this love perhaps he pretended not to notice, in order not to distress the girl further . . .

'Don't upset yourself, my dear,' said Mother Kamer to her. 'Every man who sees your face falls in love with you. It's impossible for them not to. Is there a single man in this big village who hasn't fallen in love with you? Young and old, ill and well, aren't they all mad about you? The birds in the sky, the insects and snakes on the ground, they're all in love with you. Memed has had so much on his mind. His brain is addled, the poor thing.'

'He doesn't look at me, Mother, he doesn't look into my face. He doesn't seem to know of my existence. It's as if I weren't there. When he does look at me, he does nothing but ask me, "Abdi went and Hamza came, isn't there a way out of this?" He doesn't think about anything else. He can't get it out of his head. Perhaps he is always thinking of Hatché. Was Hatché more beautiful than I am?'

She roved up and down endlessly, and only by taking herself out of the village and looking in the direction of the melon-garden could she find a little calm. If he gets to know of it, and tells me he doesn't love me, I shall kill myself, she told herself in an access of desperate courage. His face, and his childlike man's body were always before her eyes.

When the longing to see him gripped her whole body up to the roots of her hair, she would come to Mother Kamer.

'Mother Kamer,' she would plead. 'I'm dying, please find something for me to take to him.'

Kamer would laugh at her: 'Crazy girl, you've taken so many things to the melon-garden that there's nothing left in the house . . .'

But she would always find something for her to take.

'Crazy girl, my beauty, my unlucky, ill-fated girl, what will become of you in the end?'

Seyran never thought about what would become of her, she only thought about Memed; that something should not happen to him, that he should not be hurt, she was ready to die. Let her die of love, of grief, of fear that some misfortune would come upon him . . .

Seyran came to Kamer again one morning; she had not slept a wink that night:

'Mother Kamer, I can't keep still. Find something for me to take to him.'

They searched, they racked their brains, but they could not find anything. Whatever there had been in the village, whatever there had been in the house, had all been taken to the melon-garden . . . Milk, butter, honey, stockings, shirts, *tasbihs**. Seyran could only go to the melon-garden with the excuse of taking something there . . .

'Go this time without taking anything. It'll be better. If you go without taking anything he'll realize better why you go to the

* a Muslim rosary.

361

garden every day. Go empty-handed for a few days, and he'll think to himself, why does this girl come every day?'

Seyran could not do this. It would have been dreadful for her to go there empty-handed, without an excuse. The very idea hurt her pride. It would be like standing naked in front of Memed.

They searched and searched all over the house, but could find nothing. At last Kamer cried out:

'I have it!' She went to a carved walnut chest, and quickly opened it, rummaged inside and produced an amber cigarette-holder. 'Here,' she said. 'That's enough for today. God will take care of tomorrow. We'll find something else. This cigarette-holder was offered to your Uncle Osman by the nomad chief Kerimoghlu when we were newly married.'

Seyran threw her arms round Mother Kamer's neck and kissed her.

'Forgive me, Mother Kamer, dear, kind, golden-hearted Mother,' she said, and then before finishing the sentence, her face fell. 'But he doesn't smoke!' she said, and prepared to hand the cigarette-holder back to Kamer.

'Crazy girl,' she said, 'how are we supposed to know that? You take it to him.'

Seyran complied, and set out at once. She went on her way, in the heat and dust, half-running, half-walking, panting for breath, perspiring, but bent on reaching the melon-garden as soon as possible.

On the second day they roasted a chicken. On the third Seyran took cream.

Then she became too embarrassed to go to Mother Kamer again. As soon as evening came on, at the twilight hour, Seyran would quietly steal out of her house and go to the melon-garden; she would gaze at the tree-hut where Memed was sleeping, and wait there until dawn. Hordes of mosquitoes pestered her, and her arms ached with waving them away. Their stings even penetrated through her clothes to her skin.

One night Seyran summoned up all her courage, and slid under the hut; she listened all night to Memed's breathing and was comforted.

An armed man was roaming in the vicinity of the melon-garden all night. He was a short man, with a silent tread. From time to time he came up to the trellised hut and listened, then he hastened away towards Narlikishla. Seyran could say nothing of this to Memed. For one thing, on account of this armed man she thought of herself as Memed's protectress. 'Let him sleep, my hero, my lion, and I will watch over him,' she said to herself.

The armed man came one night and sat down on the bank of the Savrun, not far from the hut, and stretched his legs over the edge. He was a short man, but that was all that Seyran could make out in the darkness.

She got up and advanced on the man; he at once jumped up, turned his back, and prepared for flight.

'Stop,' said Seyran. 'Who are you?'

When the man heard a woman's voice he stopped and waited. Seyran waded through the stream, walked up to the man and asked harshly,

'Who are you? What are you doing here every night?'

'I'm Adem,' said the man. 'Ali Safa Bey's chief hunter. We lost a horse and the Bey told me . . . the Bey told me . . . not to come back without catching the horse, I don't know how many months ago it was.'

Seyran got a little nearer him.

'Sister,' he went on, 'do you know that horse isn't a horse at all. No, he isn't. That horse is a djinn . . . That horse is a good spirit, a fairy, one of the invisibles . . . You look and he's there; you look again, and he's vanished.'

Seyran, recovering from her amazement, interrupted:

'But didn't they kill you? They said you'd been killed and that's why they put Yobazoghlu in prison.'

'I don't know,' said Adem. 'I don't know anything. That horse is a djinn or a fairy . . .'

He turned, and began to run as fast as he could towards the gully. Hearing their voices, Memed had woken up, and jumped down from the hut.

'Who's that?' he called out.

Seyran, trembling, at once lay down. At the sound of Memed's voice her limbs would not obey her.

Memed and Halil called, and searched the garden thoroughly,

but found no one.

Seyran did not leave her hiding-place until the light was beginning to touch the peaks and the morning star had risen. She stayed there, her limbs all a-tremble. The hot earth warmed still further her passionate, flame-like body.

49

THEY were awakened from a deep sleep by the noise of rifle fire. The village was surrounded; the sound of the firing came from every side. The villagers were not expecting it, thinking that this kind of thing was over and done with. They were sleeping peacefully. The firing was coming nearer and soon it was heard within the village.

An uninterrupted burst of fire raked the village for a while, then suddenly the screams of women filled the night. Horses whinnied, dogs howled, cocks crowed, women shrieked, and children cried. The noise of firing ceased, and the sound of horses' hooves receded into the distance.

The peasants poured out of their houses. Three girls, from among those who had recently returned to the village, had been dragged away by their hair and abducted. The girls' mothers and the other village women gathered under the big mulberry-tree, beating their breasts and tearing their hair. They rained curses upon Ali Safa.

The raiders had also driven off all the cattle and had stolen the horses belonging to the newly-arrived villagers.

That day the villagers wandered about the village, their arms hanging limply by their sides, not doing anything, not even talking.

On the second night, the raiders came again, and after a burst of firing set light to three huts.

The next morning Ali Safa Bey sent Durmush to the village.

'Have you had enough?' said Dursun Durmush to Seyfali. 'The Bey says if you haven't had enough, if you still won't leave the village, we still have plenty of ideas up our sleeves.'

Dursun Durmush put one hand on his hip, leaned back like Safa Bey, and began to talk like him.

'One village, five villages, the whole of Adana Province cannot get the better of us. Understand this, villagers, fellow-countrymen and brothers, if you don't go away within a week, if you persist, this village will be wiped out together with all its men, children, birds, swallows, every living thing. One night we shall surround the village. It'll be a windy night and we shall set fire to the village. No living thing will be able to get out. Anyone who tries to get out we shall shoot and throw into the fire. Have you no sense of right and wrong, you scoundrels? Why don't you leave this land, which isn't yours, and go?'

He leapt on his horse and rode away.

Shortly after this a wave of distress swept over the village. The kidnapped girls had been left outside the village, exhausted, naked, with bloodstained breasts and bruised bodies. Trying to cover themselves up with their hands, they were dragging themselves along to the village. Sheets were wrapped round them and they were taken to the nearest houses. The girls had been violated by countless men, and the three of them were ill.

Police came from the police-station. The villagers told them that nothing had happened and that they had no complaint to make.

Sefché the Warden was consumed with remorse. 'Why didn't I tell him Memed was here,' he raged. He waited for night to fall. After his son, daughters and grandchildren were asleep he quietly slipped out of bed – he did not need to dress, since he had gone to bed with his clothes on – and set out. How far was the farm from the village? Would he get there by morning?

He was still only half-way there when the sun came up, and it was high in the sky when he stumbled into the house on Ali Safa Bey's farm. Ali Safa Bey was at home. When he saw Sefché the Warden he knew that something was up.

Sefché the Warden said,

'I'm tired, I'm dead, I'm hungry, I'm exhausted, Ali Efendi, my son. I have something to discuss with you. But just let me pull myself together.'

It was very hot. Sefché the Warden did not recover until evening.

They offered him an ice-cold drink of *ayran*, a vegetable stew and pilaff cooked with francolin.

After Sefché had finished eating, he said,

'Our conversation must be confidential,' he said. 'Nobody from our village must hear that I have come here. Otherwise they would kill me. Those monsters would tear me limb from limb. I've seen some brutes in my time, but never any as ruthless as in our village of Vayvay. May God give them teeth but no claws. Or let him give them claws but not teeth as well.'

Ali Safa Bey took him by the hand, raised him up and led him into the other room. It was very hot.

'Now you can speak, Agha,' said Ali Safa. 'I'm listening.'

'You don't know me, Ali Efendi,' began Sefché. 'Your father was my closest friend. For a time we were both wardens. I at Vayvay, he at Chikchiklar . . . Warden was the same as Headman now. You are young, too young to remember the era of wardens. That period was the time when the Ottomans conquered the world. Well, you are in great danger at present. That is what I came to tell you.'

Ali Safa Bey said in agitation,

'Tell me, Uncle.'

'They are going to kill you.'

'Who?'

'And very soon.'

'Who?'

'Slim Memed,' said Sefché calmly. 'Slim Memed will kill you, Ali Efendi.'

'Where is Slim Memed, when, what's happened, who, how many people?' cried Ali Safa Bey in great alarm. What he had feared was coming to him.

'I've thought about it a lot. I've thought about it for two months. I mustn't tell him, I said, but I couldn't bear it. I didn't want you to die. That's why I've come to your house today and am giving you this bad news.'

'I knew there was someone!' said Ali Safa Bey. 'If there hadn't been someone behind them the villagers would not have stood out against me. Now it's clear. I understand.'

'Quite clear . . .'

366

'Where are they now, and what are they doing?'

'Wait, Ali Efendi, be patient! It was one night. Maybe two, maybe three months ago. They said Slim Memed had come to the village. I went to the mulberry tree and what did I see? There was an assembly. A fire had been lit and carpets and *kilims** spread under the mulberry tree. Seyfali had slaughtered three sheep. They were talking. The one they called Slim Memed was a thin man, as long as a pole. God had certainly given him stature. He was like a poplar-tree. "Why have you come," asked Seyfali. "You're welcome and it's a great pleasure to have you, but is there anything you require?" asked Seyfali. Long-necked Seyfali. He said, "I've come to kill Ali Safa. I heard that he was oppressing the peasants, and I've come down from the mountains to Chukurova to kill him," he said.'

'So he said that, did he?'

'He said that, and a lot of other things too. "Let them not call me Memed any more, if I don't destroy their mansions," he said. "I killed Abdi," he said. "Abdi was nothing but if you kill Ali Safa your fame will spread through the world, over the mountains, as far as Ankara." He laughed. "Now," he said, "that dog Ali doesn't know a thing. He doesn't know he's going to die, that the Angel of Death has descended from the mountains," he said.'

'Let him say it . . .' said Ali Safa. 'I, I, I, I, I . . . How many men has he?'

'A lot . . . They're all armed, and all wearing silver-worked cartridge-belts. He has a lot of men. His eyes were like steel. He swore all the time. "Don't be afraid, you peasants," he said. "While I'm alive, you needn't be afraid. While I'm alive, you needn't bow down to any lord or sultan. I'll overcome them all." His hands were enormous, just like the talons of a bird of prey. "If I'm not able to kill an Ali Safa, why did I become Slim Memed, why did I take to the mountains," he said, "Why did I become the mountain hawk?" The people who know him have given him a nickname. They don't call him Slim Memed; they all call him the hawk.'

'Where is he now, in the village?'

'How cunning he is, how cunning! Do you think he would ever

* Rugs.

stay in the village? Even in our village he only stayed that one night. "I shall not stay in Chukurova, that's for sure," he said. "Let me finish off this business, let me drink Ali Safa's blood quickly and quench my thirst in this summer heat and I shall withdraw to my mountains. But I won't leave Chukurova until I've killed him.'

'Where can he be now, have you heard any rumours?' His voice shook audibly.

'Yes,' said Sefché. Oh dear, he said to himself, what a pity! If I had spoken to him that day he came to the village, and told him that Slim Memed had come down to Chukurova ... This contemptible wretch would have been too frightened to bring all this trouble upon us. Ali Safa Bey's dark face was gradually turning green, and this delighted Sefché inwardly.

'Firstly, he may be on Hemite Mountain now, under the Holy Tree there ... Two, he may be up in Anavarza Castle. Three, he may have crossed over to Karatepe. You shouldn't look for him in the plain. He's a very cunning brigand, that long, thin fellow.'

Ali Safa Bey racked his brains. His eyes burned. His whole body shook as if with a fever, and his soot-black face flushed crimson. Then a cold sweat ran down his back.

'That bloodthirsty monster will kill you,' said Sefché the Warden. 'Take care. He also said, "there's a very important man behind me. What does Ali Efendi know about who's behind me," he said. "If his identity was revealed to that filthy cur Ali" – that's how he said it – excuse the expression – "that filthy cur Ali", he said, "his lips would be cracked with terror, and he would abandon not only your village lands, but all his possessions in Chukurova. He would flee to the other side of the Mediterranean Sea. But don't tell him! These curs are very easily frightened, these scoundrels are like rabbits, they are cowardly. Please don't frighten him away. Tell him everything but that," he said.'

Ali Safa's eyes were starting out of his head.

'Did he say who?' he shouted. 'Who is it?'

'He didn't say. He's cunning, that fellow! Naturally he wouldn't say. But I heard that it is a very important man, who lives in Ankara.'

'I know,' said Ali Safa Bey, jumping up. 'I know.'

Then he stood in front of Sefché the Warden, took the old man's hand, kissed it and pressed it to his forehead.

'You, my father's friend, have saved my life,' he said. 'I guessed it all, except that I never expected Slim Memed to come down to Chukurova to kill me.'

'You have been unjust,' said Sefché taking his hand and stroking it. 'You have been very unjust to the people, Ali Efendi. Injustice is never a good thing.'

Ali Safa Bey drew away his hand; wondering what the end of the sermon was going to be, he waited, petrified.

'You did wrong to imprison Yobazoghlu and Ferhat Hodja. One is a man of God, the other is only a poor devil. They did not kill Zeynel and Adem. Slim Memed's band killed them. It is his bands that raid your house every night. You did wrong to have those village girls abducted and violated ... Do not do that again, Ali Efendi. They are going to kill you. Hide yourself away tonight. If they don't come tonight, they'll swoop down on your mansion tomorrow night. I heard that Slim Memed is coming with a hundred men to raid your house. Set Ferhat Hodja free. And give us back our horses and cattle.'

'I won't!' yelled Ali Safa. 'Either I drive the Vayvay villagers off my land or I'll die in the attempt.'

Then, opening the door of the room, he shouted downstairs, 'Bring out the horses!'

He turned back to Sefché the Warden, who was standing, and embraced him.

'Take care of yourself,' he said, and hastened away. Down below the horses were ready. Eight men jumped on their horses and took the road to the town.

*

The news that Slim Memed had been seen in Anavarza at the head of thirty men spread in a moment to the whole town, and from the town to the whole of Chukurova in a few days. When the news got back to Ali Safa, it had changed and was quite different. Memed had not thirty men, but a hundred and eighty-four. Not only had he been seen on Anavarza, but he had set up his headquarters there, and was issuing a challenge to all the aghas and beys and to the Government, saying: 'While I am alive I will not let the poor be despoiled by the Government and the bloodthirsty aghas and beys; if necessary I shall do away with them all. Down with the aghas!'

The men of property began to be frightened. These worthless peasants, this tribe of monsters certainly only awaited a spark. This was the eternal fear that lay hidden deep down in the hearts of the men of property.

Songs came to their ears that began with 'Slim Memed says'. When the people put something into a popular song, it was very dangerous. I will not leave Chukurova until I have torn down the mansions . . . Slim Memed says, In the mountains the police hunt after the valiant brave . . . Night and day he haunts the aghas. How the beys fear the eagle in the high mountains!

These songs made Ali Safa more frightened than ever.

The Vayvay villagers were delighted. We salute you, Slim Memed, the hawk, the eagle of the heights, we salute you. We would give our lives, our property and our families for you, they said.

Their daughters' honour had been violated, their cattle driven away, their horses stolen, their houses burnt down, and their men put in prison, but it did not matter. Slim Memed had come to the Anavarza crags and had issued a challenge . . . He had sworn to take Ali Safa's life. That was enough for them, come what may.

The most beautiful and most unforgettable songs composed about Slim Memed came from Vayvay village. No one knew who made them up.

Old Osman said, 'Allah, Allah, how many Slim Memeds are there in this world? As far as I know, Slim Memed is hiding in the melon-garden, with Beardless Halil. Is our boy a *dervish** by day, and a gunman by night?'

One morning they heard that the police had surrounded Slim Memed on the crags of Anavarza. Sky and earth teemed with police, who were spraying Memed with bullets. On that day, it was said, Slim Memed fought single-handed against all those policemen. He had no men with him. Memed had sent them away

* A Muslim friar, who has taken vows of poverty and austerity.

so that they should not run into trouble. That day Slim Memed drove the police single-handed three times from the crags to the River Jeyhan.

The battle raged up on Anavarza, and all the while good, hopeful, encouraging news came to the villagers. The people of Vayvay did not sleep all that night and sat up for news from Anavarza. Memed held out against the police alone all night long. He gave them a tough time of it. Memed never killed a man if he were not an agha. Why, if he had wished, he could have killed all those policemen . . .

As the news came in, Old Osman and Seyran conveyed it to Slim Memed in the melon-garden. He, too, did not sleep that night, but awaited the result of Slim Memed's battle against hundreds of policemen on Anavarza.

By morning the police had taken possession of the whole of Anavarza. The rifles were silent. The resisters had either been hit, or they had escaped. The police searched every hole, every cave among the crags of Anavarza Castle, and found no living thing, not even a snake or a lizard. Finally inside Taurus Castle, they found two youths clinging shivering to each other. It was they who had done battle with the police. The youths had replied to the policemen's fire on the first day; then they had run away and sought refuge here. Bullets had rained above them, beside them and around them for a day and a half without ceasing. Their four horses which had been tied up below had all been hit, and were lying there dead. The tall, fair-haired youth did the talking, but the dark one was still shivering, his teeth chattering.

'Captain,' said the fair one, 'we joined Yaghmur Agha's band two months ago. Yaghmur Agha sent us to a master-thief, to give us training. We stole these horses from Endel village, and then on our way back we saw the police a good way off, so we hid among the crags. We swear never to do any horse-stealing again. We take our oath.'

'Who gave you those guns?'

'Yaghmur Agha.'

Captain Faruk gave the youth a sound box on the ears.

'If you mention Yaghmur Agha's name again I'll kill you,' he said.

Captain Faruk was raging. How was it he could not capture Slim Memed, how did he miss him every time? If this man could slip between their fingers on those crags that were like an island in the middle of the Chukurova plain, then he would never be captured . . .

The Captain rode hither and thither in the summer heat and dust, searching the plain of Chukurova. Suddenly he would get news from Mount Hemite and rush off there; then a message came from Karatepe or from Kazmaja, or from the mountains of Nurhak, or from Payas on the shores of the Mediterranean, and he would be off again at a gallop. All his efforts served only to create more legends about Memed . . .

After every skirmish, a white hawk soared from the rocks to the sky, a pure white hawk, shining like light . . . It flew very fast, too fast for bullets to hit it, or the eye to see.

While the Captain was searching for Memed, he caught eighteen horse-thieves, and six petty brigands, but all the while Memed's legend grew apace. Captain Faruk lost all control and began to thrash any peasant he met. For two days and nights he stayed in the village of Anavarza at the foot of the rocky hill and had all the peasants thrashed, young and old. When he and his policemen left the village not a single peasant could walk; they were all lying groaning on their backs. If they had known Memed's hiding-place, they would undoubtedly have spoken. They did not know it, but the Captain did not believe them. All these rebels, these vile wretches knew where he was, every one of them! It's just that they had made a god of him. Every day a new story sprang up to show him to be a creature more than human. The story about the protecting hawk that hovered over Memed, or the one about the thunderstone amulet made him roar with laughter. He did not believe any of them, and yet, when he thought he was clashing with Memed, his eyes would seek a white hawk in the sky above.

'Where is Slim Memed?'

'I haven't seen him, I don't know, I've never heard of him.'

'Never heard of him?'

'No, never!'

'Make him lie down!'

They would throw the man to the ground. His legs were left bleeding, his face bore the mark of boots . . . and his body the traces of bayonet-thrusts.

'I've never heard of him. I don't know.'

The village of Tozlu, the nomads of Mejidiye, the Turcomans of Öksüzlü, the villagers of Narlikishla, Dedefakili . . . Not one of them had seen Slim Memed or heard his name.

In the end it was Vayvay's turn. Captain Faruk stayed there for a whole week. Everyone was given more than one beating. He even thrashed women and children. Old Osman passed blood for a week afterwards. They were afraid he would die. He was delirious for a week before he came to himself. The Captain personally tore out Seyfali's finger-nails.

There was only one man in the village they did not beat, and that was Sefché the Warden, and they did not even make a pretence of bruising him. The villagers did not understand this at all.

'Either you tell us where Slim Memed is, or I'll have you all beaten to death.'

'We haven't seen Slim Memed, we don't know him, we've never heard of him.'

The villagers sobbed and cried, protested and shouted, but not a word more would they say.

'Slim Memed, my hawk.'

50

THIS morning, like every other morning at daybreak, Halil took a handful of fresh fodder and tiptoed towards the horse. He held out the fodder well in front of him, and kept his eyes on the horse. The stallion did not budge. As if oblivious to all around him he stood there, with his right hindleg drawn up to his belly. His ears were drooping, his mane as smooth as if it had been combed, and part of his tail lay over his rump. Today, more than other days, it looked as if he might surrender. Memed, holding his breath, watched Halil first stop, and then walk on towards the horse. Halil, calling, 'Hey, hey, hey', swung the fodder in his hand gently towards the horse. He took a step, then stopped, and waited for the animal to come towards the green food. The stallion did not even look.

Halil went nearer and nearer. Then changing the fodder over to his left hand, he stopped one pace away from the horse, stretched out his hand and touched him on the neck. He began to stroke the long, smooth, shining brown neck. The stallion turned his head. Halil, trying to get the horse to like him, gave a huge ingratiating grin that stretched from ear to ear. But all of a sudden the stallion stiffened and pricked up his ears. At the same moment Halil got hold of him by the mane. The stallion reared. Halil clasped him round the neck with his two arms. The stallion tossed his head violently, but could not shake Halil off. Then he began to turn in his own length, as fast as he could, like a spinning-top. Halil's legs and body flew into the air. Then, unable to withstand the horse's strength and quickness any longer, he let go, flew through the air and fell prostrate. He felt a pain in the calf of his leg. After turning a few times more, the horse stopped and glanced at Halil, who was trying to pick himself up off the ground; then he trotted across the melon-garden, his feet sinking into the soft earth, and went and stood among the fresh, green, clean-looking rushes. The rushes hid his belly and rump, and only his long, straight neck and bristling tail were visible. In the morning light, his back steamed a little.

Beardless Halil went over to Memed, exhausted and breathless:

'It was touch and go today. He was just about to give in, but something caught his eye and frightened him. Did you see his nose, Memed?' he said, 'how his nostrils were distended, how he breathed like a bellows?'

'He'll give in,' smiled Memed. 'He's gradually getting used to you, he wasn't like that at the beginning. Perhaps you'll be able to catch him tomorrow.'

'I'll catch him,' said Halil, doggedly, stroking his beardless chin. 'I'll catch him tomorrow. You see, he didn't go far away today, he's standing there, saying, "Come and catch me, Halil." Nothing doing! If he is to be caught, let him come of his own

374

accord. All animals like me, they're really fond of me . . . All of them. Not even a snake will touch me.'

'Not even mosquitoes,' said Memed smiling.

'Not even mosquitoes bite me,' said Halil very seriously. 'You see I understand every single creature.'

'You understand their language too, don't you?' said Memed. 'Like King Solomon.'

'Just like King Solomon,' repeated Halil, 'Everyone has some particular skill. Animals love me. That is my skill.'

Talking to himself, he went to the hut, took a cartridge-belt that was hanging on a post off its nail, and after fastening it carefully to the slim trunk of a willow took an Elbistan knife out of his pocket, and looked at it admiringly: 'Pure steel,' he said. He spat on the cartridge-belt, opened the knife and began to sharpen it.

For a week now Halil had spent his days first struggling with the horse, and then sharpening the knife until evening.

'Today I'll shave off your beard,' he said to Memed. 'It's so sharp now that you won't feel it. I found some nicely scented soap too. And you can rub on some lotion that our sister Seyran brought.'

Memed's beard had grown long and scratchy. He was not un-used to that, but these days he did not want to wear a beard. That cursed Beardless Halil would never finish sharpening his knife, it seemed . . . At any rate it would take him a year to sharpen it.

Halfway through the morning Halil said, 'All right. It's ready, razor-sharp now.'

He got Memed to sit down on the ladder of the trellis, and tied a towel round his neck; the water was tepid anyway. He soaped his face and made a lather. He took the knife between two fingers, just like a master-barber, and after lifting it up and looking at it he began. He removed a part of Memed's long beard, without touch-ing his face.

'Bravo, brother Halil,' said Memed. 'You've done good work on that knife. I don't even feel it. Your hand is very light too.'

Closing his eyes he submitted himself to Halil's sharp knife.

Halil had soon finished. He washed and dried Memed's face and applied plenty of the lotion that Seyran had brought.

'Well, that's over, my friend,' he said.

'Bravo, Halil,' said Memed. 'That was fine. I didn't feel a thing.'

He walked away. Then as if he had remembered something, he turned back again.

'Did you see that man today?' he asked.

'Yes, I did,' said Halil. 'He went by about midnight, a long way away. Going up towards the hills.'

Memed waited. Halil knew why.

'Sister Seyran did not come last night,' he said quickly. 'There's a lot going on in the village these days.'

Since the horse had begun to frequent the melon-garden, Adem had taken to roaming around the outskirts all night long. He knew that the horse came to the melon-garden every day before the sun was up, and stood there under the trees, but he still could not bring himself to enter the place. He had a deadly fear of it. Adem had never come across such a fine marksman as the man in the melon-garden. The man had fired at the flame of his gun, and almost hit him in spite of the distance. He had only escaped by the skin of his teeth. From that day to this he had been trying to find out who the man was. Beardless Halil he had known for years, but the other one was a stranger, and though his body was no bigger than a child's, it must be he who had fired and not Beardless Halil.

Then Adem heard of Slim Memed's presence in Chukurova. Could the deadly marksman be Slim Memed? If it was, and if Adem went and told Ali Safa Bey about his hiding-place, if the police surrounded the garden one night, and captured Memed, then Adem would be released from pursuing that djinn, that fairy, that foul horse; he would once again win respect, and return to the loving arms of his longed-for wife, and to the peace of the farm. But if the man turned out not to be Slim Memed and the police wasted their time ambushing the melon-garden and went away empty-handed, there would be the devil to pay. There was a woman, too, who came to the garden every night, and roamed around it. That melon-garden was a strange place, a frightening place. And the horse went and took refuge there.

For days Adem had been in a dilemma; he wandered in the vicinity of the garden all night, but did not dare to go any nearer it.

Memed went to the Savrun and sat down with his back against

376

the foot of an old willow-tree. The brook was clear and bright, sparkling over the white pebbles, only ankle-deep. The tops of big pebbles that lay half out of the water were dry. Right in front of Memed the water was deeper, and at the bottom were not pebbles, but thick sand of different colours; little fish shone brightly, darting up from the bottom one after the other.

First a leaf floated by on the surface of the water. Then the dead bodies of some big red wasps . . . Then an orange-coloured butterfly, as big as a bird, its wings spread over the surface of the water. It was not dead, or so it seemed to Memed. Its shadow, thrown on to the bed of the stream, flowed along with it over the white pebbles.

The sun blazed down, and a heavy, blinding heat scorched the plain like a furnace, melting everything in its path. In a little while that running water would evaporate and vanish, the pebbles would split and crumble, and the bed of the stream would be webbed with cracks . . . This brook, so beautiful, so bright, flowed down from those mountains only faintly visible in the distance. Running and bubbling between rocks, fir-trees, hornbeams, huge cedars, now smooth, now turbulent, it foamed and frothed, it spread its pebbles in flat places and rushed into deep valleys . . .

Memed knew the Savrun well. In his youth he had followed it from one end to the other. As he looked at the water, he allowed himself to dream, and for the first time in days he forgot the nagging problem of Abdi went and Hamza came.

Seyran loved him! From the first day he had felt it. Then he had been assailed by doubts. But now he was sure of it. That proud passionate girl was madly in love with him; and could not help showing it. That she should come to the melon-garden at night and wander round, delighted and thrilled Memed. When he thought of Seyran his blood ran wildly in his veins.

He could not sleep since the night when he saw Seyran coming back to the melon-garden for his sake, desperately in love with him; his eyes sought her figure on the shadowy paths, and when he saw her he was enraptured, in ecstasy. But he was afraid for her. She had been through so much suffering and he did not want anything to happen to her on these nights.

To come to her one night . . . To hold her hand . . . He desired this madly, but could not bring himself to do so. The feeling of being loved made him a different man. Now he thought of nothing but Seyran. Her violet eyes, soft as velvet . . . Such affectionate, charming, loving, friendly, kind, pure eyes had never before been seen in this world. Her face, her dimples, her lips, her unbelievably lovely complexion . . . Her tall, swinging gait . . . as if she walked without touching the ground.

In his eyes Seyran became taller and more beautiful than ever. He stayed awake each night, listening for her step; he could hardly contain himself, so enraptured was he with the tenderness of such infinite love; he climbed down from the hut, intending to go and clasp her hand, but he could not, he crouched at the foot of the tree, caught up in a whirlwind of love, and secretly trembling. Memed could not imagine how to touch Seyran, how to hold the hand of such a beauty; the very thought of it made him dizzy. Yet he grieved for her too. One day he would be killed. Even if they did not kill him, he could not stay here indefinitely. He was consumed by a fever of revolt that shook his brain, heart, limbs, hair, his whole body. That steely glint of old came into his eyes, while through his brain there shot a golden yellow, sunlit flash.

He saw the sky over Anavarza and a white cloud that remained motionless . . . How blue was the sky, how dazzling white the cloud . . . Bending over, he dipped his hand in the water, and felt it slipping through his fingers. How bright the water was, it was not water that flowed but light! Beardless Halil was working in the melon-garden, digging up roots, and filling in holes. What a good, friendly, sincere man Halil was.

Captain Faruk, the battle on Anavarza . . . the white hawk wheeling over the battle, the Captain hastening from rock to rock in Chukurova, from peak to peak . . . The villagers being beaten and passing blood . . . on his account. Old Osman too . . . How could anyone beat such an old old man . . . Memed did not want to think about these things. Some days he felt that the grief in his heart would well up through his skin and overflow. He was weary in spirit, and writhed with frustration. Not caring whether or not Halil could hear, he would shout:

'Kill me, kill me, kill me and save me, Oh God! Either show me a way out, or kill me. I can't bear this hell you've thrown me into. I shall burst.'

He was cut to the heart when he heard how Old Osman had been beaten: 'If only they had killed me instead of beating that old man. They should have killed me,' he groaned all night, rolling on the ground.

Suddenly in the night he would leap madly to his feet, seize his gun, run out of the melon-garden and go towards Anavarza; then all at once the thought that Abdi went and Hamza came would pierce him, his limbs would fail him, and helplessly he would sit down on the earth and stay there motionless consumed by his own fire. On nights when he ran away like that, Halil would follow him and find him in a hollow or in some clump of trees, crouching unconscious of his surroundings. He would take him by the arm and bring him back to the melon-garden.

He rubbed his shaven chin, just like Beardless Halil. His shadow fell over the stream and lay on the bed. A crowd of fish passed over it. The flying shadows of the fish, emerging from his shadow, scattered over the bright pebbles. The air smelt of chaste-trees. It was the first time since he came down to Chukurova that he had noticed the scent of anything. He breathed it in with delight. A slight breeze brought a smell of bog-myrtle which mingled with the other. His childhood passed before his eyes. All around Earless Ismail's mill there was a lot of fragrant heather. His mother used to make brooms out of it – Memed had not yet heard that Earless Ismail had been killed. He brought to mind Ismail's hostile reception and how he had behaved afterwards and wondered over the incomprehensibility of man. It made him happy to think of the old miller.

Then the air smelt of burdock. It was a true Chukurova smell. In the heat the whole of Chukurova smelt of the pungent smell of burdock . . . That burning earth . . .

He got up, turned towards the village, and looked at the gently winding path, but nobody was coming along it. If he were to set out now along that path, and go to Seyran's house, and say, 'Seyran I've come,' what would happen? What would Seyran do? Her cheeks would flame, and she would not look at him. She would lower her beautiful eyes. Her tall, fine body . . .

He sat down and stared at the water again. Seyran was in front

379

of him. He could not see anything but Seyran's face. Her face wore different expressions: she was crying, laughing, shouting, angry, gentle, harsh. Her violet eyes were upon him shining with love. Spell-bound, he could think of nothing else, lost in a gentle enchantment. He forgot the beatings, Old Osman, Lame Ali, the tyranny of Ali Safa, the police, Abdi and Hamza, death and separation, he forgot it all.

On the opposite bank, among the weeds, long, red-legged storks strutted about.

All day long he kept getting up and looking towards the village; then he would sit down by the stream again, gazing at the bright pebbles, and watching the things that floated by. The evening passed slowly. Seyran did not come in the evenings. She often came after midnight, and would curl up and sleep in her usual place.

Memed did not speak to Halil at all that day. Beardless Halil understood Memed's mood.

He went to bed but could not sleep. He got up again, and wandered round the melon-garden. He kept turning to look towards the dark village path. The moon, hanging over Anavarza, had not yet set, but it would descend behind the rocks quite soon. He came out of the melon-garden and began to wander around like Adem. Some nights at this hour the stallion would gallop madly from the east, from below Anavarza. Then towards dawn, after circling the garden a few times, he would stand in the deeper water under the plane-tree and have a long drink, and afterwards he would come to the mound beside the nearer trees and stand stiffly on it.

Adem was out and about again that night. But he saw Memed long before the other noticed him and he took to his heels. In the distance, by the fading light of the moon, he appeared to Memed's eyes to be a very tall man.

Just then the moon set. Memed went to the place where he had been during the day and sat down. He dipped his feet into the water, which had got cooler. The west wind that had begun to blow in late afternoon was still blowing gently and fitfully.

Memed was startled by the sound of a footfall, but he did not move, for fear of alarming Seyran. She came along quietly, waded through the stream and went to lie down in her usual place. The starlight was brighter than the dim moon had been a while before, but Memed could only just make out Seyran's form. When he heard her step his limbs and body had grown weak, and his heart thudded madly. Several times he almost dared to get up and go to her, but his heart beat so fast and he trembled so much that he was obliged to sit down again. Eventually he managed to get up. She saw someone coming, and without getting up she slipped behind the bole of the tree, and crawled back towards the stream.

Memed tried to say something but his voice faded away. At once Seyran recognized him. She halted and Memed hastened towards her, with beating heart. He took her hand; it was burning, like red-hot iron. He drew her towards him, and she yielded herself to him gently, as if swooning. He held her in his arms and kissed her neck. His lips were burning.

In an instant they were oblivious of everything, of the night, the trees, the horse that came and stood near them . . . They did not notice when they undressed, or when their two bodies were clasped together as in a flame. They did not hear the mosquitoes buzzing in clouds around them, nor did they feel the thistles prick their naked bodies, nor did they smell the pungent smell of the burdock. They experienced not merely the delight of love-making, but the union of two bodies filled with longing meeting at last in a fiery enchantment.

They went into the water and out again several times. Their bodies joined in a flame as if they would never be parted. In this union there was a rich enjoyment like earth, like light, like growing life. It was as if they were alone in the world, the first man and the first woman uniting in love, fulfilling an agonizing longing.

As the mountain peaks began to pale, Memed came back to reality. Seyran was still lying panting, on her back at the edge of the stream, the water lapping round her feet. If Memed had not pulled her up she would have stayed there panting with desire, until the sun was high in the sky.

They plunged into the stream. Away from each other, looking at each other timidly, they washed, then ran to pick up their clothes and dressed hurriedly. Then side by side not looking at each other they walked downstream by the water's edge. Memed went and picked a ripe water-melon; they cut it open and ate it. The water-melon was cool. The dawn breeze was blowing. From the coolness, and from being satiated, they shivered a little.

It was getting lighter, and looking into each other's eyes, they suddenly began to chuckle. They looked at each other and smiled in admiration and surprise, spell-bound.

They saw the stallion. He was standing in his accustomed place. His right hindleg was drawn up to his belly. His ears were drooping. Seyran went up close to the horse as if they had been friends for a thousand years; she stroked his neck and then, taking hold of his mane, led him forward. The stallion came like a lamb.

Memed called to the hut,

'Halil, Halil!'

Halil was half asleep. He could not believe his eyes. 'Am I dreaming?' he said to himself.

'Halil, Halil, look!'

Halil rubbed his eyes and looked again: 'Allah, Allah!'

Seyran led the stallion forward and left him close to the hut. He stood quite still. She went on stroking his neck, flank and forehead. She laid her cheek against the horse's head, and they stayed like that for a while.

Memed thought to himself, this friendship must have been founded nights ago. They had been close together at night; to let her embrace him like that, the horse must have got used to the smell of her. Or how could a woman and a horse make friends like that, on the spur of the moment? But Seyran was a different kind of being.

Halil soon brought a thick halter and put it round the horse's neck. Then he took the end of the rope and tied it to a nearby tree.

51

'IT's him, I'll swear to it!' Adem muttered as he hastened to Ali Safa Bey's farm. 'It's him!'

He was saved. He was saved from killing the stallion, saved from blame for the white horse's death. The Bey would never know how to reward him, what to do to thank him! Who else would have found such a man's hiding-place and brought the news to the Bey?

'It's him, I'll swear to it! It's him!'

In a very little while, before daybreak, the police with the Captain at their head, our men with Ali Safa leading them, and as many villagers . . . will surround the melon-garden. He won't even have time to use his gun . . . 'I surrender, I surrender,' he'll call out . . .

But what if it wasn't Slim Memed?

He stopped dead. Would such a renowned brigand have come to live for months with Halil in a melon-garden? Would a man who had sworn to kill the Bey stay so long in such a place without doing a thing?

'It isn't him, it isn't him . . .'

He broke out into a sweat. The sour smell of sweat pervaded the night. He turned back slowly, swaying a little.

The Bey hated to be taken in. If a person lied to him, he would pull out his finger-nails. What had that night-wandering woman with the beautiful voice said to him? She had said, 'You were killed, Adem.' Who killed me? If it was anyone, it was that brown horse that killed me. He took my life. He's a djinn, a fairy! He's enchanted! Bey, I swear to you he's really enchanted. He can't be shot. No one can hit him. Never. If any human being should dare to touch him, his hand would be paralysed and his eyes would go blind. That horse has a pedigree of a century and a half. Surely it says on the pedigree that he belongs to a race of fairies, of good spirits . . . You were mistaken, Bey. You were quite wrong to send me after that horse. He's not a horse at all.

He longed for his wife, with her big breasts, her moist, thick red lips. When he thought of her he forgot his sufferings and exhaustion; he felt a wave of passion rush over him. He could not get her hard, moist loins out of his mind, and his hands tingled.

'It's him, I'll swear to it! It's him!'

He turned back and began to hurry towards the farm.

All night long he walked first towards the farm, then back

towards the reed-beds. He was still there in the middle of the plain when the sun came up. For three days and three nights, until his food gave out and the water in his gourd was used up, he went on like that, making first for the farm, then for the reed-bed, again to the farm, and back to the reed-bed, tortured in a purgatory of indecision, until one night he found himself at the bottom of the Bey's stairs.

He sat down on a step, waiting for morning and for the Bey to wake up.

At daybreak the guards called out, 'Who are you?' and marched on him. Adem at once jumped up. 'It's me,' he said, 'is the Bey awake?'

Just then Ali Safa saw him. He ran down the stairs like a fury. Adem could only gasp, 'Bey, my Bey, my Lord . . . I . . .'

'Dursun Durmush,' hissed Ali Safa Bey between his teeth. 'Come here, my boy.' Dursun Durmush came at once.

'Here I am, sir,' he said, standing to attention.

'Come, come,' he said and walked upstairs. He stopped on the landing and pointed to Adem standing down below, blinking, the legs of his shalvar-trousers hanging in ribbons, his hands, face, legs and feet filthy and bleeding, scarcely human, like a creature from another world.

'Dursun Durmush my son,' he said, 'wasn't that man killed? Aren't there some men in prison on his account, for whom the death penalty has been requested? What shall we do with him now?'

'What can we do, Bey?'

They stared at Adem with loathing. Then Ali Safa Bey said calmly and indifferently, 'Dursun, my boy, we needn't think about it any further. Doesn't everyone know this man was murdered? And it wasn't us, was it?'

'That's right, sir.'

'In that case take him to Ahjasaz quickly, before anyone sees him. Take a spade and go alone. You must do this job by yourself. Bury him so that nobody will find him. But mark the spot. It may be needed.'

'At your orders, sir.'

'Excuse me, my boy, for sending you on such small jobs, but

if it were known that he is alive, my reputation in the district would go down to zero. Why in the world did this wretched creature have to appear now and spoil my arrangements? Is that thing a man?' he muttered. 'He disappears for months, then one day without warning . . . I loathe such creatures! I loathe them. I – I – I – I! Ah, my son, how long will I have to put up with this lot of stupid beasts?'

Dursun went downstairs, took Adem's gun and cartridges, and gave them to one of the men standing by.

'Follow me,' he ordered Adem harshly.

'Dursun, my brother,' said Adem. 'I want to see the Bey. I've brought him good news.'

'To hell with your good news, come on!' shouted Dursun. 'You good-for-nothing nuisance.'

'I want to see the Bey.'

'Shut up!' shouted Dursun. 'Do you think the Bey wants to see you? Fall in in front of me.'

Adem obeyed. 'All right,' he said. 'Let's go and you'll see for yourself. You'll see that bullets can't touch that horse. I know where he is. When we get there I can find him straight away. But I didn't come for that . . . You know Slim Memed? Well, I saw him! And a girl too . . . Try firing at the brown horse yourself and see if you can hit him! Nobody can hit him, he comes from the race of fairies, of good spirits . . . But that isn't what I wanted to tell you. That Slim Memed, I saw him. I'll show you the horse first, and then I'll show you Memed's hiding-place. How thankful the Bey will be when he hears this, won't he, Brother Dursun?'

Dursun Durmush did not even listen to him. That man's seemingly senseless whining only served to whip up his resentment. Because of this piece of filth, he Dursun Durmush would be forced to stain his hands with blood. Ah, but they deserved to be killed people like that!

Adem, walking in front of Dursun's horse, stopped and smiled:

'Won't he, Brother Dursun? If we show the Bey his hiding-place, won't the Bey be pleased? And with you too?'

'Very pleased! Go on,' yelled Dursun.

They reached Ahjasaz as the sun was setting.

'Brother Dursun,' said Adem, 'the horse will come in a little while; it will come galloping past us. Let's wait. You have a try, too, perhaps you will hit it. But I haven't much hope of that. Then we'll go to the melon-garden. It's better if you see him, too, with your own eyes. Slim Meme . . .'

He did not finish the word. A bullet had pierced his chest.

'Brother Dursun, don't kill me. Why? I haven't seen my wife . . .'

He swayed and fell down. Dursun put three more bullets into his writhing body. Adem's left leg twitched for a time, and then became still.

He lay there on his face, his arms and legs outflung. A pool of blood was forming under his chin.

52

THE July heat is terrible in the plain of Chukurova. Flames leap out of earth and sky. The earth is cracked, the plants wither, and the whole world turns a scorched-looking brown. Snails cling to the burnt, dry stalks. The bright colours of wing-cases fade and shine with a whitish gleam. Bees, flies and an odd butterfly or two left over from early summer grow bigger and tougher. Even the birds do not fly so easily in the July heat, and at noon not a single one can be seen in the sky. They say that this heat can overcome a bird in the air and make it fall to the ground in a swoon.

The mountains and hills melt away in a hot, bright haze. From the greyish sky millions of almost invisible tenuous threads hang down to the ground. The Taurus Mountains, crouching all around the wide plain, Mount Hemite, the Nurhak range, the Gavur Mountains, Snake Castle, Dumlukale, Anavarza Castle, and hundreds of hills and mounds, both large and small, can only faintly be discerned in the distance, as if from behind a veil.

From morning till late afternoon the whole plain is aflame and very few living creatures are to be seen. People sweat all the time and their sweat dries instantly.

The earth, the rocks, the stones steam as if melting. Only the running water does not steam. In the still, torpid heat the streams just lie there as though they were not flowing at all.

It was the first time that Memed had experienced such heat, and at times he thought he was going to suffocate. Beardless Halil was used to it, and took no notice. 'Brother Memed, you'll get used to it without any trouble, without any trouble at all,' he said.

It was only in the late afternoon that the plain of Anavarza revived, when, in the distance, over the Mediterranean, masses of white clouds rose into the sky, and with the rising clouds the cooling south-west wind began to blow, in fitful gusts at first, then suddenly unleashed in all its strength, whipping up sand-devils that raced along the tracks and through the passes. Rising high as poplars, getting bigger and smaller, longer and shorter, they whirled across the plain and all at once earth and sky were shrouded in a huge cloud of dust. You could not see anything for dust, not even the end of your nose. But sometimes the south-west wind blew so gently that it did not raise a speck of dust, like the wind that blows after rain . . .

Sometimes the heat was so intense that the bees were parched in their hives, the nestlings in their nests, the tortoises in their shells, the flowers in bud, the ants in their ant-hills. The scorched earth had a smell of its own, a tang that was dry, bitter, acrid and peculiar. The pungent smell of dry, bitter burdocks and of dry crackling heather dominated all other smells. As water bubbles in a cauldron, the marshes of Anavarza bubbled night and day, so hot you could not put your finger in, and from its depths, like a huge giant stirring, came a low rumbling sound that startled people who were new to the region, and made their hair stand on end, especially at night.

If Memed had not had someone like Halil by his side who knew this district well, he could not have adapted himself so easily to life in Anavarza, in the Ahjasaz marshes.

That morning, rising early as usual, Memed went to the stream to wash. Suddenly he could not believe his eyes. Was he dreaming? There was no sign of water anywhere. He knelt down and touched the sand and pebbles of the stream-bed. Perhaps I've come to the wrong place, he thought. He hurried from one side to another, up and down, looking at all the familiar spots, the places where he used to bathe, but he was not mistaken. The water had drained away. But where could a big flowing stream drain away to? Who knows, maybe this is one of the mysteries of Chukurova, he thought. Then it occurred to him to wake up Halil and ask him.

'Halil, Halil,' he called out, 'the stream's dried up, Halil.'

Halil woke up. 'What's happened?' he asked.

'The stream's dried up,' said Memed.

Halil ran up to the stream and stared at the empty bed.

'Does it always dry up like that?' asked Memed.

'Sometimes,' said Beardless Halil thoughtfully. 'When they are sowing rice. But I have never seen it drained completely like this.'

They sat down at the edge of the stream, their legs hanging over the low bank, and did not speak.

The sun rose slowly, like a heap of embers. It dried up the dews at once and began to scorch the land. Even the moist bed of the Savrun was dried up by noon that day and the earth of its banks cracked open like small spiders' webs.

In the afternoon Seyran arrived, in great distress, crimson with the heat, her hair, eyelashes, brows, and limbs covered with dust, and only her teeth shining white. She had been running, and was out of breath.

'They've cut it off,' she said. 'What are we going to do now? Ali Safa Bey has cut off our water. We put up with everything else, but what are we going to do now?'

Memed did not understand. How could such a large stream be cut off? Seyran explained. Years ago a man from Marash had come to the plain. His name was Mustafa Pishmanoghlu. He opened irrigation canals from the Savrun and made dams, so that they could flood the plain and plant rice. But he had never cut off the water completely. However little, after passing through the rice-fields, and even if it turned yellow, there was still enough of a flow to turn a mill.

'Yesterday,' said Seyran, 'three men galloped into the village. Dursun Durmush was at the head of them. He assembled the villagers. "I have news from the Bey", he said. "Safa Bey sends his greetings, and tells you to leave his land, and get out of his village. If they don't, he says, if they continue to put their trust in that snotty-nosed boy, Slim Memed, what I couldn't teach them by means of hunger and dishonour I'll teach them by means of thirst. I shall cut off Vayvay's water supply and turn the village into another Karbala. And all the other villages around will suffer the same because of Vayvay. I'm not responsible for that. Let those other villages which are left without water settle their accounts with the people of Vayvay. If they remove Vayvay from my land, the water is at their disposal. The Bey says you had better not be stubborn; you can put up with a lot of things but not with thirst. You had better not give the children marsh water to drink, either. They'll all die like flies. Don't say I didn't warn you!" That is what Dursun Durmush said; then he mounted and rode away.'

Seyran avoided Memed's eyes guiltily.

The affair became clear some days later. Ali Safa had gone to Pishmanoghlu and said, 'Mustafa Bey, if you can cut off all the water of the Savrun, and make the Vayvay villagers get off my land, I'll let you have my land free of rent for three years, so that you can grow your rice.'

Pishmanoghlu accepted with pleasure. He at once strengthened the walls of the dams and not a drop of water flowed down out of them.

Ali Safa Bey was gloating.

'I, I, I, I . . . When I want to, this is what I can do. Let them trust in those imaginary Slim Memeds if they will,' he boasted.

For Captain Faruk had searched the plain from end to end, and had not found a trace of Slim Memed. He was convinced that the peasants had created an imaginary Slim Memed. He had even sent an official report to the Ministry to that effect. Ali Safa Bey believed the Captain, but still he took no risks. He left the administration of the farm in the hands of Dursun Durmush for the present, until such time as the Slim Memed enigma should be solved, and himself withdrew to his town house. Whether it was imaginary or not, there was some calamity threatening his life, and this calamity haunted him.

The idea of cutting off the water seemed to him the best means of intimidation he had yet found to use against the villagers. He was very proud of himself. And in the month of July too! Let them put up with this if they could! . . .

For the first, second and third day they drank water from the pools that were left. A week later the pools had dried up. They tapped new springs, and forming queues waited by the springs from evening till morning, from morning till evening. Before long the springs had dried up too. The holes they had made in the bed of the stream or in the banks, did not yield a single drop of water. They dug wells but less than a fathom deep they would come upon a layer of pebbly sand, and however many wells they dug they found that after getting a pail or two of water, the sides of the well caved in. The villagers' hands were bleeding and torn. At Vayvay eight children were buried in a single day.

A hot, yellow dust settled permanently on the villages. It penetrated into the houses, into every nook and cranny, and even got under people's skin.

At Lower Chiyanli a man killed his closest friend, and all on account of a drop of water.

Memed woke up in the morning, went to the bed of the stream, and walked upstream for hours, until he came to a place below the town, and then he turned back. The bed of the stream got more cracked day by day, and the cracks got wider. In some places the mud had crumbled into warm dust that was just like ash. In others greenish evil-smelling pools had formed and the dead bodies of fish and tortoises were lying on the cracked earth . . .

In a greenish, dirty pool that smelt of rotted fish, a wretched tortoise struggling to save itself from dying of thirst, had thrust its head out of the muddy water and was looking about hopelessly. The mud was drying on its head.

Memed grieved over the death of this stream as he would have grieved at the death of a loved one. A dead thing it was now, evil-smelling, crisscrossed by millions of cracks. He did not want to think about the situation of the villagers, and tried to put it out of his mind, only sighing:

'I brought misfortune on their heads,' he said. 'Great misfortune.'

The villagers of Lower Chiyanli, Kumbet and Amberinarki met together, and tried to find a solution, but they could not . . .

If Ali Safa Bey in his fear of Memed had not withdrawn to the town, perhaps the villagers of Vayvay, in a moment of desperation, goaded by thirst in the noonday heat, might have been driven to flee. From the other villages, from Chiyanli, Dedefakili, Narli-kishla, not a single person came forward to remonstrate with them. They did not say, 'Friends, why don't you leave that village and save yourselves, and we shall be delivered too.' They did not say, 'Look at your children, dying of thirst . . .'

With one man from each village they went several times to see the District Governor, and explained to him the trouble they were in, and how their children were dying.

The Governor affected to be deeply concerned each time, but actually rubbed his hands in glee: 'I am most distressed, I do hope things will soon be better, I am most distressed. But what can we do? Mustafa Pishmanoghlu must plant his rice. It's part of the nation's wealth, we cannot let it dry up.'

'Well, what are we to do?'

At this the Governor began to shout, 'Well, find some solution! Do you expect me to carry water for you? Am I the Governor or a water-carrier?'

'It was on purpose to get us out; Ali Safa Bey did it on purpose to occupy our land. They've turned the stream in another direction where there are no rice-fields at all. Whole villages have been flooded on that side . . . the people are living on mud . . .'

'It's not my business,' said the Governor. 'It's not my business, my good sirs. I never interfere with Ali Safa Bey's affairs. Go and settle things with him, then come to me. His house is right over there. And what's more, are you the defending lawyers of the villages that have been covered with mud? If they have any complaint let them come to us. How much longer have we got? August, September . . . Put up with it, my good fellows. Putting up with it will make the body more resistant. To drink less water is good for health, you know. I am very sorry, I am very sorry to hear about your water shortage. It is very hot, very hot in this country of yours; one is bathed in sweat in a few moments, my friends. Even my bones seem to turn to sweat. It's very hot, very hot.'

They sent telegrams to Ankara and Adana, but no reply came, and as far as they knew, they had no effect.

Memed and Halil did not suffer so much from the lack of water. Halil had found a spring in the marshes, and they always had a supply of cool fresh water.

Whenever Seyran had a chance she came to Memed, and they again made love ardently and passionately at nights in the dry bed of the Savrun.

The villagers had turned against Memed a little. Despondent, helpless, they would let a word of blame for him escape their lips now and again, and this wounded Seyran to the quick. She could not bear that anyone should find fault with Memed, and she did her best to keep all this from him. As for Old Osman, he would fly into a rage and make the speaker feel sorry he had ever been born. But still you can't stop people's mouths . . .

'Well, what good did it do us, that Slim Memed should come down to Chukurova . . . ?'

'Ali Safa has ruined us.'

'We heard his name, so we came back to the village.'

'A curse on his name.'

'We lost our horses.'

'We lost our property.'

'We lost our honour.'

'We lost our lives.'

'We heard his name, so we didn't leave the village.'

'A curse on his name.'

As the lack of water made itself more felt, as sickness spread, people blamed Old Osman and Slim Memed more and more.

'Poor Ferhat Hodja, that man of God, there he lies rotting in jail, and all because of them . . .'

'He should never have listened to them.'

'They will hang the poor man . . .'

All this talk must not reach Memed's ears; Memed must not hear about the villagers' critical mood. It was difficult for Seyran. Memed perceived something, and brooded over it, becoming restless and anxious. This was evident from the way he plied her with questions. Perhaps his uneasiness was due to some words that had escaped Mother Kamer last time.

'Well, Memed, my boy, here you've been all this time doing nothing!' she had said. 'Aren't you ever bored? You have water, cool water too, haven't you? We in the village are burnt up. We would give our lives for a drop of water.'

Perhaps Kamer had not spoken with any unkind intention, but Memed had sensed a red-hot stone underneath and her words lodged in his heart like a bullet. She, too, bitterly regretted having said them, but what's done can't be undone. From that time on Mother Kamer had not gone to the melon-garden again.

'I brought disaster to the people. I brought them thirst. I brought them hunger. I brought them evil. I trampled their honour underfoot. I deprived them of hope, I deprived them of trust. It is all my fault, alas!'

53

IDRIS BEY roved through Chukurova at night like a hungry wolf, putting to flight any number of policemen who attacked him. This plain had seen few men as brave as he. The police had come to know his courage and recklessness, and contempt for his own life, so they kept out of his way. When they heard that Idris Bey was in a certain place, they went the other way, and pretended to look for him somewhere else. Everyone knew his story and felt a great respect for him on that account.

Idris Bey looked everywhere for help. There was not a single agha or bey or influential person in Chukurova that he had not appealed to. He even went as far as Antep, to the Kurdish Bey Hurshit, with his many herds of sheep. 'I know him, I know Arif Saim,' Hurshit Bey said. 'I was in the war with him, but he's grown so full of his own importance now, that it's difficult to explain things to him.'

Nevertheless he mounted his horse and travelled from Antep to see Arif Saim Bey and appeal to him on behalf of Idris Bey.

Arif Saim Bey gave him the same reply as he had given the others, and turned him away empty-handed.

Idris Bey also sent Ali Agha the Kurd three times to see Arif

Saim Bey. He was a respected Turcoman Bey, who still wore the ancient, three-kirtled costume of his fathers. and preserved his nomadic way of life, wintering in the Chukurova and migrating to the high pasture of the Taurus in the summer. The proud Turcoman Bey's request was turned down, but he went back again and again, unable to refuse Idris Bey's plea.

Then the learned Kurdoghlu from Kozan, whose family was related to the Osmanlis and Kayihanlis, went. He, too, came back without success. Then the impoverished Payaslioghlu, of noble descent, who lived alone in a huge mansion. Ramazanoghlu from Adana, Yaghmur the horse-thief, Tevfik Agha, of the Karamuftu family, long-whiskered Ahmet Efendi from Chokak, and sharp-witted old Mustafa Bolat. They all went. None of them refused Idris Bey's request, although they knew it was a useless errand. They all got the same reply from Arif Saim Bey:

'So he says it'll end badly, eh? Well, let's wait and see.'

Arif Saim Bey was very sorry about Idris Bey, his heart bled for him, but what could he do? This man was one of the race of honest, sincere, brave men which was dying out at present. It was an honour to have such a man as his enemy. Arif Saim Bey was truly proud of this.

'It's a pity, such a pity, he is the only man in the world that I could have made a friend of.'

Idris Bey had tried everyone and now he had lost all hope. One evening he came to Old Osman's house, and without dismounting from his horse, called out,

'Osman Agha, Osman Agha!'

Old Osman recognized his Circassian accent, and went outside. He knew what he had come for. 'Come on, let's go,' he said. Pulling Idris Bey's horse to the steps of the hut, he mounted pillion, from the steps. 'Ride on,' he said.

When they reached the melon-garden Memed had not yet gone to sleep. They dismounted. Memed and Idris Bey embraced each other in the darkness.

'Light a fire and let's see one another's face.'

They collected some dry haulms and lighting a big fire sat down at some distance from it.

Idris Bey began to speak at once. Pretending not to look at

394

Memed he examined him continually from beneath his eyebrows Not a movement of this copper-faced, handsome man escaped Memed, either. He looked like a man you could trust. Idris Bey too found Memed to be exactly as they had told him. But his face was rather innocent and childlike. His hands and legs looked like those of a naughty child. The hands of a child who had broken his toys and run away . . . Nothing about Memed surprised Idris Bey.

'Brother Memed,' he said. 'I want to co-operate with you. I came to propose this to you. Take me under your orders. For you are a very famous, very brave, sincere, honourable man. It will be an honour for me to fight our enemies under your command.'

He spoke at length. He mingled with his speech words that Memed had never heard; he praised Memed, he liked him.

Memed was silent, and made no reply. It was towards midnight, when he could withstand his prolonged insistence no longer, that he explained at length, in detail, the question of 'Abdi went and Hamza came.'

'So you see,' he said finally. 'Hatché's blood, my mother's death, my turning brigand up on the mountains, all came to this: Abdi went and Hamza came.'

'Kill Hamza too,' said Idris Bey.

Memed smiled at Idris Bey's naiveté. 'Then another Hamza will come. There are lots of Hamzas in the district. Can one exterminate them all?'

'I don't know,' said Idris Bey. 'I would first of all remove Hamza, and I would think about the next Hamza when he comes.'

Old Osman, Halil and the other Circassians listened to them without interrupting. They thought that Memed was right. If you kill one, another thousand come in his place. If you kill them wholesale, then another lot will spring up.

'This is what ties my hands, what tortures me,' said Memed. 'Not only have my efforts been useless, but they have made things worse than ever; it's this that has overwhelmed me, that has driven sleep from my eyes. My villagers have gone out of the frying pan into the fire. It is all because of me that they've been so cruelly treated, that they've starved and died. It is because of me that lovely young girls have been violated. This is what ties my hands.'

Idris Bey could not make head or tail of all this. 'I'm leaving now,' he said, getting up. 'I'll come back in two days. I have something most important to do. I have no time now. When I come back we'll go up into the mountains, and there you can explain all this to me again. Then I shall understand, and I shall be able to salve your wounds.'

Memed did not reply. Idris Bey leapt on his horse.

'Goodbye,' he said. 'In two days . . .'

'God be with you,' said Memed, and gazed after him with a strange expression on his face.

Old Osman did not look at Memed. He had not called him his hawk. His eyes looked hurt and his face, more wrinkled than ever, like a mass of cobwebs, was set in a mask of bitter sorrow.

'Memed, my son,' he said next morning, as he was leaving the melon-garden, 'that Safa has beaten us, finished us, and we were not even able to do anything to him.' He turned and walked away without looking back. He tottered along in the heat, like a ruined tree that is fast decaying, or like a sad melody.

A lump came into Memed's throat.

On the following day Idris Bey reached Arif Saim Bey's mansion before daybreak. The armed guards saw him, but they could not prevent him. Idris Bey rode his horse into the yard and stopped twenty paces from the house.

'Arif Saim Bey, Arif Saim Bey,' he called out. 'This is Idris. This is Idris. I have come.'

Arif Saim Bey, jumping out of bed, went to the window, and looked out through a gap in the curtains. Idris Bey, with his three men behind him sat erect on his horse; with his silver-chased equipment, his golden hair escaping from under his black *kalpak**, his flashing blue eyes like the eyes of a bird of prey, he sat like a statue of dignity and courage.

'Arif Saim Bey, Arif Saim Bey, this is Idris. I've come.'

Arif Saim Bey opened the window.

'Do come up, Idris Bey,' he said in his softest, warmest, friendliest voice. 'Do come up, I'll get dressed at once.'

'I'm not coming, Arif Saim Bey. You will honour me by coming down. And by bringing your revolver . . . You are a soldier. I've

* Sheepskin hat.

come to fight you, to settle accounts. Take your revolver and come down.'

Arif Saim Bey shut the window, and withdrew.

Idris Bey stayed sitting impatiently on his horse, waiting for Arif Saim Bey to appear at the door of the house. He waited and waited, getting more impatient. The sun licked the plain with its first rays, then rose to the height of a poplar, and still Idris Bey waited. In the end he could bear it no longer:

'Arif Saim Bey, Arif Saim Bey . . .'

He did not finish the sentence; a bullet from behind pierced the nape of his neck, and came out through his throat. Slowly Idris Bey slipped from his horse to the ground, lifeless. His kalpak fell to one side, a little way away from his head, and his golden hair was shaken loose over the dusty ground. His blood spread in a widening pool near his shoulders, till it reached his hair, soiling it.

His comrades dismounted, took off their kalpaks, and holding them in their right hands against their breast, stayed silent for a time in the presence of the Bey and paid their last respects. Then, gently, as though afraid of hurting it, they lifted the body on to the horse, and left silently. Arif Saim gazed after them,

'What a pity,' he said. 'What a great pity! We could have been friends.'

It was Lame Ali who brought the news of Idris Bey's death to Memed. His distress was great, but just as great was his pleasure at Lame Ali's presence.

54

EARLY one morning before sunrise, a crowd marched eastwards coming from the plain north of Anavarza. No one knew what they were about or where they were going. Then from the villages on the upper reaches of the Savrun, from Chiyanli, Narlikishla and Dedefakili, more peasants came and joined the crowd. Like bees emerging from their hives people poured out of their villages, men and women, young and old, sick and maimed, they all joined the crowd. Their destination was clear now. A long, broad cloud of dust stretched on towards the town, getting gradually larger and broader. Halil had climbed to the top of a tree and was reporting to Memed below what was going on. A little later he descended the tree in haste.

'Hide,' he said to Memed. 'A whole crowd from our village is coming this way.'

The whole village of Vayvay had set out on the road. The women in front, the children behind, and behind them the men. They entered the melon-garden and picked up a water-melon or two each, tucked them under their arms and passed silently on to join the main crowd further on. Halil too mingled with them.

Half the crowd were plastered with mud from head to foot. Pishmanoghlu had opened some of the irrigation channels and had sent the water down to the plain, flooding a number of villages. When asked, 'Why on earth did you do that, Pishmanoghlu?' he had only laughed. 'Well, I can't drink all that water,' he had said. 'I had to empty it somewhere.' Pishmanoghlu was a pot-bellied jolly individual. 'Let those scoundrels have their fill of water on a summer day like this! What would they have done if they'd been in the place of those without water? The people down below would give their lives for a drop of water, but these scoundrels scorn the good fortune that has come to them!'

He went from one market to another, from one shop to another, talking like this and making the people laugh. Ali Safa Bey, the Governor and Captain Faruk were the ones who laughed most at his jokes.

The crowd in the long, broad cloud of dust, which kept growing larger and broader, stopped for a moment when they reached a domed shrine that stood below the town. There was a slight hubbub, and the noise they made reached the town. Up to now the crowd had not said a word as they came along; they had been quite silent. It was only then that the townspeople realized that a big, angry crowd of peasants was marching on the town. At first, startled, they looked at one another, unbelievingly. There was a moment's silence. Suddenly from the archway below the dome there burst an amazing, endless multitude of people. Shutters were noisily lowered, and all the townspeople took refuge in their houses, closing and bolting their doors firmly. Captain Faruk did not know what to do. The District Governor, the other officials and the aghas took refuge at the police headquarters.

Eventually the Captain gave an order to the police:

'Fix your bayonets,' he said harshly.

Most of the aghas were shaking with fear. Was it an uprising? All of them were as pale as death. The Governor, slumped in a heap on the floor against the wall, his tasbih in his hand, was muttering prayers and blowing to right and left to exorcize the evil spirits.

The crowd, seeing the fine white stone bridge at the foot of the hill on the outskirts of the town, began to run. The dam by means of which Pishmanoghlu had cut off the waters of the Savrun was down below the bridge. The crowd came and stopped by the dam, then more came, and more. There was not a sound. More and more came and fixing their eyes on the large sheets of water held back by the dam, waited silently.

Suddenly without warning the crowd slowly stepped down into the water. And in an instant chaos broke out. Nothing could be seen in the water but people. When the crowd thinned out again, where the wall of the dam had been there was not the smallest thing, not a stone or a board or a piece of brushwood. The waters were rushing down the hill. With the roar of the water came a burst of rejoicing from the crowd. Their voices rang out so loud that the town shook. As the water cascaded downhill the peasants streamed after it. Intoxicated with victory, they drank and laughed and joked and made so much noise that nobody understood what anyone else was saying.

The roaring water poured downhill at the same speed for some miles and then slowed down. The dried-up river bed was criss-crossed with thousands of cracks as big as a man's leg. The water ran into these cracks and filled them up before flowing on. The crowd gazed anxiously at this cursed water which seemed not to move at all. They watched it all night long, but by morning the water had only progressed a thousand or one thousand five hundred paces.

When the townspeople realized what was going on, they came outside, relieved. They, too, went to watch the water which filled the cracks and stubbornly refused to flow on. Like the villagers they waited, gazing at the water.

The Governor had been so terrified that when he heard the news he was very angry.

'They must all be arrested,' he shouted. As this was just what Ali Safa Bey wanted, he spurred on the Governor. But Captain Faruk would not consent to this. Those people had been deprived of water, and so they had come and damaged one man's dam. What of it?

In Ali Safa Bey's opinion this was rebellion. There had been an uprising among the peasants and they had marched on the town.

'If this action goes unpunished, if these people are not severely punished, eventually there will be more serious incidents. This is a rebellion. All the peasants who participated must be placed under arrest,' he insisted.

The Public Prosecutor stood there without taking part in the conversation. Ali Safa Bey drew him aside and whispering something into his ear pressed a fat envelope into his hand.

'I am going to apply to the court for a warrant to arrest them all,' said the Prosecutor a few moments later. 'It will soon be issued.'

He took the judge by the arm, and they went out together.

It was the afternoon of the second day. The south-west wind was blowing and everything was smothered with dust. A posse of police, with Captain Faruk at their head, advanced upon the peasants who were waiting by the bed of the stream, watching the water filling the cracks, and fired into the air. The peasants shrank back. The police did not find it necessary to fire again. They herded the peasants together and filled the courtyard of the police headquarters. It was not big enough, so they filled the mosque, and the courtyard of the mosque. That was not enough, so they took them to the Red Mosque . . . They filled the primary school and also a ruined old Armenian building. All the empty yards in the town were now full to overflowing with peasants . . . with one or two policemen guarding each. They were tortured by hunger and thirst in the heat of the day. But no one who saw them there, hungry and thirsty, could get near to give them a drop of water or a crust of bread.

Meanwhile Ali Safa Bey sent one message after another to the people of Vayvay.

'If you leave my village and go away, I will get you a free pardon, but if not your leaders will be hanged for having raised the flag of revolt against the Government, and the rest of you will be condemned to fifteen or twenty years' imprisonment.'

The peasants held out a few days longer. But their hunger and thirst reached such a pitch that the crying of thirsty children and the moaning of the women rang out through the town all night long. The townspeople, unable to stand those cries, came out towards morning and gave the prisoners bread and water.

Old Osman would not go and see Ali Safa. 'I'll die before I go and look at that fellow's dirty face again,' he said.

Long-necked Seyfali, still not fully recovered from his wounds, Osman's son Hüsam, and Veli went to Safa Bey's house. The Public Prosecutor and the District Governor were there. They were drinking heavily. With bowed heads the visitors sat down on the edge of a corner couch and waited.

'You have done a lot of harm to Ali Safa Bey,' said the Prosecutor. 'You have persecuted him cruelly.'

'God forbid,' said Seyfali and got up. His head touched the ceiling.

'Be quiet!' said the Prosecutor. 'Sit down. Last night again five of your youths set fire to Ali Safa Bey's farm.'

Ali Safa Bey joined in: 'Mad Muslu and another one called Süleyman. Five altogether,' he said. 'What do you want of me, my friends, what have I done to you?'

Seyfali got up. 'Set us free. We will leave Vayvay, the centuries-old land of our forefathers. What can we do, it's fate,' he said, as if chanting a lament. 'The land of our fathers.'

'When?' asked Ali Safa Bey, agitatedly.

'At once,' replied Seyfali in the same mournful tones. 'As soon as they release us. We'll pack up and go.'

'Well, be off with you then,' said the Prosecutor. 'You'll be free tomorrow morning.'

They withdrew and early next morning they were released.

The people of Vayvay returned to the village, in a choked silence. They walked along by the Savrun river. The water had reached only as far as Amberinarki. Below that village it was still trickling into the cracks.

55

THE yellow gleam in his head widened and grew bigger. It came in thin rays from afar, unwinding, whirling, tossing, flashing. It scattered, then again it flared up deep down.

It was very hot. Memed looked at the dry bed of the stream where a thin trickle was silently filling in the cracks. So Vayvay village is emigrating he thought. The steely glint came into his eyes again, a spark stayed in his pupils. Old Osman, Seyran, long-necked Seyfali, bright-eyed Ferhat Hodja, stubborn Yobazoghlu, Mother Kamer, Selver the Bride . . . all of them, all would have to leave Vayvay. Maybe they had already left, maybe the village was quite empty now. Seyran had not come for two days, either. When she last came a tragic intensity shone out of her violet eyes. She had not said a single word of reproach to Memed but she looked so hurt that it made his blood run cold. Discouragement and defeat had set their seal on her brow. Sooner or later they would wear her down.

Lame Ali was sitting there, his lame leg drawn up under him. He was making a strange pipe out of a willow branch. Beardless Halil had gone to the bank of the stream, and was watching the water fill the cracks.

Ali raised his head and looked at Memed, and as soon as he did so he saw the flash in his eyes. An expression that was midway between joy and pain, laughter and tears passed over his face. Memed got up and going over to Ali, stood close to him. He placed his hand on his shoulder, and held it there, for a time. Then he went to the hut. He took off the shalvar-trousers and shirt he was wearing and laid them aside. Then he put on his own clothes. In the twinkling of an eye, he had fixed on his revolver, dagger and field-glasses, and strapped his cartridge-belts around him. He slung his carbine on his shoulder, and wrapped himself in his patterned Marash cloak. He turned his fez over and over in his hand and then thrust it into the pocket of the cloak. His stockings, came up to the knee. His shoes had shrunk a little and felt tight but they would stretch again. Now he was wearing the same clothes as when he had come to Chukurova.

He went over to Lame Ali. The gleam in his eyes grew brighter and stronger. The stream of golden light in his head flowed on without ceasing, it filled the cracks and glowed.

'Hamza's done for,' said Lame Ali. 'Even if he survives, however long he lives, that fear that's got into his blood will poison all his life. At the flutter of a bird's wing, at the buzzing of a bee, he would start up shouting madly: "Memed's coming" and would rush out of his house. In the end he could not trust houses or huts or the village. He took to the mountains and hid in a different cave or cleft every day, huddling in the darkest corner, not eating or drinking or sleeping. Then suddenly he would rush outside and clutch at me shrieking, "He's coming, Ali, save me, he's coming." We wandered all over Alidagh for days, never stopping for long in any cleft or cave. I can't describe the morning when we heard from a shepherd that you had gone down into Chukurova. He was so delighted, so delighted I can't describe it. I really pitied Hamza.'

'You pitied Hamza?' asked Memed.

'My goodness, yes, I pitied him,' said Lame Ali. 'He kept on saying, "He won't get out of Chukurova alive, Chukurova is a death-trap for brigands. Even if he escapes, he will only be half alive, and he'll fall into my hands, but I won't do anything to Slim Memed. I'll spare his life. And I'll make him a present of two of my villages. And he'll spare my life too," he said. That night he fell asleep as soon as he laid his head on the pillow, and slept for three days. But as soon as he awoke he called me: "Come quickly Ali", he said. "Be quick. Take my horse and go down to Chukurova, and help Ali Safa Bey and the Captain. If you're not there, nobody'll be able to track him down in the huge plain of Chukurova ... Slim Memed, that devil ..." I mounted the horse and came to Chukurova. I went to Ali Safa Bey's house. I said, Hamza sends his greetings to the Agha, and kisses his hands. The Bey took a fancy to me, and would not let me leave him for days; he treated me royally. He asked me all about the art of tracking. In the end I said to him, Bey, my lord, I came here with a duty to perform, I must go and follow the trail of that good-for-nothing Memed and I will have that renegade captured for you. I can't rest so long as he's alive, I said. So I've come here, and let me tell you, my friend, that I followed the trail of that scoundrel Slim Memed and I've found him!'

Ali had never seen Memed look so bitter, nor his face so hard, just like a rock. He had never seen the steely glint shine as clearly in his eyes.

It was mid-afternoon. In the distance, to the south, the white clouds massed above the Mediterranean Sea, and rose into the sky. A little later a strong gust of the south-west wind came, and the air became a little cooler. Then it dropped again. For a time it blew fitfully. Then the cumulus clouds swelled and mounted into the sky, and as they did so they grew brighter and bigger. The wind burst out in full force, whipping up sand-devils on the roads, and sweeping them on north, towards the Taurus Mountains.

Memed grasped Lame Ali's hand, and looked him in the face, silently.

'All right,' said Ali, as if talking to himself.

'I'll just look in at Vayvay . . .' said Memed.

'In that case I'll wait for you outside the town,' said Ali. 'Now, listen to me carefully, you know the dry gully outside the town.'

'Yes.'

'On the right-hand side of the path, as you go down into the gully, there is an old, old mastic tree. At the foot of it there is a single tomb. You can see that tree even on a pitch-black night. I'll wait for you under the tree.'

Memed leapt on to the barebacked horse. He pulled on the halter that Halil had spent days in plaiting. Beardless Halil, lost in thought, was looking at the waters still filling the cracks.

'Farewell, Halil,' cried Memed, and he rode out of the melon-garden into a cloud of dust. A little later he pulled up the horse in the middle of Vayvay village, underneath the big mulberry-tree.

Old Osman had fallen ill, and taken to his bed. They had made his bed, not in his house, but on a couch under the big mulberry-tree. Mother Kamer and Seyran were watching by his bedside. They had also laid Seyfali on another couch near the foot of Old Osman's. The mother of Mad Muslu, who had been arrested a few days ago, and Seyran's mother were also there. Not a soul besides these had stayed behind. The others had gone off into the blue without so much as looking back.

Seyfali had insisted, 'I'm not going, I'm not going. I'll die on my forefather's land. I am afraid to die anywhere else,' he said, weeping. Even his wife and children, knowing him to be so ill, had gone away.

But the hill-folk, that is to say, Seyran's brothers and cousins, had not left their homes. Ferhat Hodja's wife had taken refuge with them.

Memed dismounted and walked to Old Osman's bedside. When Osman saw him he slowly raised his head from the pillow and looked at him, then he let his head fall back and closed his eyes.

His face was pale, and more wrinkled than ever. His eyes could hardly be seen for wrinkles. Memed took his hand between his own two hands. Old Osman opened his eyes with difficulty, and looked at Memed. Memed saw in his eyes that he was hurt beyond forgiveness.

'How are you, Uncle? I hope you'll be better soon,' he said brokenly.

Osman did not reply. Memed waited and waited but Osman did not utter a sound.

Again he said, 'How are you, I said, Uncle Osman,' and when Osman did not reply Mother Kamer intervened.

'Osman, Osman,' she said. 'Look, Memed has come to take leave of you; the child is going. He asks you how you are.'

Old Osman opened his eyes and fixed them on Memed's face. He looked at him for a long while, then he said in an almost in-audible voice: 'I've grown old, my slim one, I've grown old. I'm tired, Memed, I'm tired. I'm defeated, my son, I'm defeated.'

He closed his eyes. Memed realized that the old man was deeply wounded. He had not even called him my hawk.

Memed went to Seyfali's bedside, and greeted him. Seyfali's

long neck had got even longer. His face was swollen and bruised.

Memed glanced round the empty deserted village. His eyes came to rest on Seyran. Then he went up to Old Osman again, took his hand again between his own two, stroked it and kissed it. In a hoarse voice, he said,

'Please forgive me, Uncle Osman.'

Old Osman's lips quivered. Memed went up to Mother Kamer, took her hand and kissed it. Mother Kamer embraced him and kissed him. Memed went up to everyone present and took leave of them one by one, and finally came and stood close to Seyran. He could not raise his eyes and look at her. He took her hand and pressed it tenderly. Then, still not raising his eyes, as if fearful of hurting her, he embraced her, leapt on his horse and rode swiftly out of the village in a cloud of dust. Seyran could not bid him goodbye and good luck. She could not even look after him. Unable to cry, unable to laugh, she just stood there beside the big mulberry-tree, in the heat of the sun.

When he reached the mastic tree on the outskirts of the town, the sun had set long before. Ali saw his moving figure coming in the distance, and stepped out on to the road.

'Ali,' said Memed.

'It's me,' said Ali.

Memed reined in his horse.

'We'll go and see if he's at home,' Ali said. 'If he isn't you will go up and await him. You'll say, "Dursun Durmush sent me from the farm." Don't forget, Dursun Durmush.'

'I won't forget,' said Memed.

'They won't be suspicious of you. A lot of armed men like you come to them every night.'

They passed along the unlighted, gloomy streets, and came to a large, arched gate in the high wall of a courtyard. Ali got off his horse and opened the wooden door, which creaked as he did so. Memed rode the horse inside and dismounted.

Ali, holding the horse's head, pointed to some steps a little way in front. Memed ran up the steps, and knocked at the door. From within came a woman's voice.

'Who's that?' she asked.

'It's me,' said Memed coolly. 'I've come from the farm. Dursun

Durmush Agha sent me. Is the Bey at home?'

The woman called inside to the Bey.

'There's a man here, from the farm. Dursun sent him.'

Memed heard the Bey say, 'Bring him in', and for the first time he lost his coolness and his heart began to beat fast. The Bey was in bed, a newspaper in his hand. Memed entered and closed the door softly behind him. The Bey raised his head from the newspaper,

'What is it?' he asked, unconcerned.

'My name is Slim Memed,' rapped out Memed, in a deep, challenging voice. 'Do you recognize me?'

The newspaper fell from Ali Safa Bey's hand, and he stopped short, half-sitting up. His face turned deadly pale. His lips quivered. He opened and closed his mouth several times, but no sound came out.

Memed raised his carbine and fired three times. The rush of the bullets put out the lamp in the room. At that moment all hell broke loose in the mansion. Memed slowly descended the stairs, he took the horse that Ali was holding, mounted and galloped at full speed out of the town. After he had been riding for some time he pulled up, and listened. Apart from a muffled hum, there was no other sound from the town. No shots, nor any other sound . . . He urged the horse on again.

It was daybreak when he reached the village of Deyirmenoluk. He rode straight up to Abdi Agha's house, and stopped at the door.

'Hamza Agha, Hamza Agha!' he called out. When Hamza heard his voice, he hurried outside. Memed pulled out his revolver, and said to him quietly:

'Fall in in front of me.'

Hamza stood blinking at the man on the horse; then, recognizing him, he broke into a run. 'They're killing me, they're killing me!' he yelled. 'Slim Memed is killing me, killing me, killing me!'

He ran through the village, knocking at every door, but none was opened to him. Memed trailed him on the horse from a little way away. Hamza, in a whirl of clamour, desperation and death, stumbled up to every door in the village:

'They're killing me! Forgive me! They're killing me,' he pleaded.

He even went to his own house door, pleading, but it was shut fast and did not open.

Sweating even to the roots of his hair, unseeing, fluttering aimlessly like a chicken with its head cut off, he ran hither and thither, knocking at the same door again and again, then suddenly summoning up all his strength he began to run towards the outskirts of the village.

Memed, remaining icily calm, followed behind him on horseback, keeping the same distance between them, hurrying when he hurried, and slowing down when he slowed down. In this way Memed gradually drove him back into the village square.

'Stop here,' he shouted.

There was no one about. Not a living thing was in sight. No cats, no dogs, no living thing. There was not even a bird to be seen in the sky.

Hamza shouted, in a last despairing effort: 'Help! They're killing me, they're killing me!'

He stopped where he was, swaying from side to side, and trembling like a leaf.

His teeth were chattering. 'Don't kill me, sir,' he implored. 'I'll give you all these five villages. For God's sake.'

Those were the last words he spoke. Memed emptied his revolver into his head. Hamza did not die immediately, but began to claw at the ground with his finger-nails. He turned round and round, tearing at the earth.

Memed slowly took the rifle from his shoulder and aimed it; he fired one round of ammunition. Hamza fell on his face where he was. Memed circled the body on his horse, and emptied his gun into the huddled dark figure. He rode the horse furiously backwards and forwards, round and round, firing round after round of ammunition into the corpse. Looking at him, it was as if Memed was performing some strange, traditional ritual with the horse.

At last Memed was tired, and reined in the horse beside the body in the middle of the square. He was sweating, and the sweat dripped off his black locks on to the horse's neck. It had also spread from his back to the outside of his cloak. The brown horse too was in a lather, which darkened him to coal-black. The peasants timidly poked their heads out of their doors and windows and then drew them in again. They saw him sitting on his horse, stiff as a ramrod, and firm as a rock.

The brown horse was panting like a bellows, but he remained as stiff and motionless as his rider.

The sun rose to the height of a poplar, bathing in light Memed with his black locks and his sweating face, and the long-bodied, big-eyed, foam-flecked horse. The shadows shortened. There was not a sound anywhere. If a fly had flown past you would have heard the noise of its wings. The village seemed deserted, enveloped in an eerie echoing silence. There stood the brown horse. There sat Memed on its back, and there below lay the dark, huddled body. Apart from them, the world was empty. Not a bird sang, not a bee hummed. In the distance, swelling and breathing smoothly, was the blue Plain of Thistles. It lay outspread in bright sunlight and the rays of light fell on the rump of the brown horse, which looked more and more handsome . . .

Memed sat his horse, and his eyes, like the eyes of a sparrow-hawk, roved over the spaces between the houses. Vainly he sought a movement or a sound in the empty open places. It seemed that one door, five doors, ten doors, all the doors in the village were about to open and now, or in a little while, people would pour out into the square. Why Memed expected this he did not know, but he was expecting it.

He waited a long time. The village looked even more desolate, more empty. Memed strained to hear the slightest sound.

Suddenly, he heard footfalls in the distance. Turning his head he saw Mother Hürü coming downhill, all dressed up, her white kerchief bound round her head, wearing ear-rings and a coral necklace, and with a many-coloured Tripoli sash carefully wound round her waist. He guided the horse towards her. In a few moments they were face to face. Memed's face brightened, he smiled, they looked at each other. Then turning their heads, they looked at the body lying huddled on the ground. Mother Hürü smiled too. Then their looks passed over the village, and again came back to the corpse. A pool of blood had gathered in a stony hollow beside the body. A greenish fly glinted over the blood like a flash of lightning.

Again they looked each other in the eye. Memed guided the horse two paces nearer to Mother Hürü.

'Mother, Mother,' he said. 'Mother Hürü, give up your claims on me. Farewell.'

That was all. Mother Hürü did not say anything. He pulled on the horse's halter, turned its head towards Alidagh, and rode off. The brown horse flashed out of the village like lightning. He streaked towards Alidagh like a black arrow, and in a moment he had disappeared and was lost from view.

For two days Hamza's body stayed huddled up in the place where he fell, beside the stony hollow. The villagers did not come out of their houses. Only the very curious ones stuck their heads out of their windows or doors, and looking as far as they could at the body in the middle of the square they pulled them in again. On the third morning 'Beetroot' Hösuk emerged from his house with a rope in his hand, came to the square, and tied the rope to the leg of the corpse. He dragged the corpse a long way from the village, and tipped it into the gully below Earless Ismail's watermill. 'You've got your deserts, you scoundrel,' he said, and laughed. 'You bald infidel! Go now and be food for the bald vultures!'

For a time after this nobody did anything. They did not work. They did not talk. Fearfully, they wandered about the village completely idle . . .

Then one day they came quietly and opened the door of Bald Hamza's storeroom. Hamza's wives, not daring to say anything, watched from a distance while the villagers entered the storeroom. It was full to the brim with fat, honey, molasses, boxes and boxes of raisins, almonds, walnuts, figs, dried mulberries, pears, apples and pumpkins. They shared it all out without giving rise to any complaints. They even set aside a share for Hamza's wives, saying, 'Take it, it's your share.'

Later on, a long while after sharing out the stores, they came in a group to Hamza's house and asked his wives for money. One of the women brought a sack filled to the brim, and gave it to them. They sat down and shared it out equitably. They gave one share to Hamza's wives. Then each of them went and took from Hamza's house what he had not sold; horses, donkeys, goats, oxen and cows. Then they opened granaries which had been full for years with wheat, barley and millet, and shared it out amicably. They gave one share to Hamza's wives.

They did all this very quietly, rather fearfully, and without making a fuss, as if they were a little ashamed of it.

The autumn came, and there was no movement from anyone. The cold winds blew, the shadows became longer and paler, the thistle-fields dried up, and made a crackling noise, but still there was no movement from anyone. Before long ploughing-time would have come and gone, and again the peasants, their hands behind their backs, looking hard at one another, would have been walking gloomily around the village, if the *Abdal** with his dawn drum had not come to their help.

It was one morning before the sun was up. The villagers heard a drum beating the dawn rhythm. It boomed out slow and confident. They knew at once that the drummer was Bayram the Abdal, and that it was his son Jümek, who accompanied him with the fife. For in the whole of the Taurus there was not a single abdal who could measure up to Bayram for playing the drum at weddings and festivals. As he beat his drum the Abdal lay back, rose again, leaped in the air, turning and dancing and uttering wild shouts. He danced through the village like a whirlwind of joy, in a state of exaltation such as he had never known before.

By mid-morning the villagers began to drift into the square one by one. They were washed and scrubbed and dressed in their best holiday clothes. The old women had tied milk-white kerchiefs over their heads, and the young girls gaily-coloured silk scarves. They were decked out in crimson, green and purple. Mother Hürü was like a flower today and even stood out among such a crowd. They filled the village square, so tightly packed that you could not have found room for a needle between them. Soon the crowd had joined in the Abdal's dance. They swayed and swirled in a wave of delight. Then, still dancing they made for the thistle-fields.

The Abdal's drum resounded all over the Plain of Thistles and drums began to beat in the other villages too. All the five villages set out for the thistle-fields, and assembled where the fields came

* An *Abdal* is a member of a semi-nomadic tribe in Anatolia and Central Asia who make their living by playing music at weddings etc.

to an end to the east, on the slopes of Alidagh. The youths took out their sickles and cut the thistles, and the girls collected the cut thistles and piled them in big heaps. The Abdal leapt on to one of the heaps with his drum, and embarked on a dance such as the villagers had never seen before. It was an old-time dance, in which he stretched and bent, turned and twisted, with sinuous movements of the hands and arms. As he danced, the peasants, at a sign from him, set fire to the heap beneath him. And for a time the Abdal danced in the middle of the fire, in harmony with the billowing flames. Then he jumped down, very straight, and mingled with the crowd.

The flames spread from the thistle heaps and in an instant, the whole, dry, thistle-covered plain was on fire. A north-east wind was blowing. It took the flames and scattering them, carried them to the south. Crackling sounds rose from the thistle-fields, and cries filled the night, as the flames raced over the plain. Towards morning the whole plain glowed as though flooded with fire.

Nothing more was heard of Slim Memed. There was no sign or trace of him any more.

From that day to this, the villagers of the Plain of Thistles come to the thistle-fields before the start of the ploughing season, and burn the thistles in a great celebration. For three days and three nights the flames rush over the plain like a river of fire. The plain glows in a tempest of fire, and cries come from the burning thistles. And with this fire, a ball of light explodes on the summit of Alidagh. For three nights the mountain peak is dazzlingly bright, as light as day.